D1174140

On Mark Twain

On Mark Twain

The Best from *American Literature*

Edited by Louis J. Budd and Edwin H. Cady

Duke University Press   Durham 1987

© 1987 Duke University Press
All rights reserved
Printed in the United States of America
on acid-free paper ∞
Library of Congress Cataloging in Publication Data
appear on the last printed page of this book.

Contents

Series Introduction

From Vol. 1, no. 1, in March 1929 to the latest issue, the front cover of *American Literature* has proclaimed that it is published "with the Cooperation of the American Literature Section [earlier Group] of the Modern Language Association." Though not easy to explain simply, the facts behind that statement have deeply influenced the conduct and contents of the journal for five decades and more. The journal has never been the "official" or "authorized" organ of any professional organization. Neither, however, has it been an independent expression of the tastes or ideas of Jay B. Hubbell, Clarence Gohdes, or Arlin Turner, for example. Historically, it was first in its field, designedly so. But its character has been unique, too.

Part of the tradition of the journal says that Hubbell in founding it intended a journal that should "hold the mirror up to the profession"—reflecting steadily its current interests and (ideally) at least sampling the best work being done by historians, critics, and bibliographers of American literature during any given year. Such remains the intent of the editors based at Duke University; such also through the decades has been the intent of the Board of Editors elected by the vote of members of the professional association—"Group" or "Section."

The operative point lies in the provisions of the constitutional "Agreements" between the now "Section" and the journal. One of these provides that the journal shall publish no article not approved by two readers from the elected Board. Another provides that the Chairman of the Board or, if one has been appointed and is acting in the editorial capacity at Duke, the Managing Editor need publish no article not judged worthy of the journal. Historically, again, the members of the successive Boards and the Duke editor have seen eye-to-eye. The Board has tended to approve fewer than one out of every ten submissions. The tradition of the journal dictates that it keep a slim back-log. With however much revision, therefore, the journal publishes practically everything the Board approves.

Founder Hubbell set an example from the start by achieving the almost total participation of the profession in the first five numbers of *American Literature*. Cairns, Murdock, Pattee, and Rusk were involved in Vol. 1, no. 1, along with Boynton, Killis Campbell, Foerster, George Philip Krapp, Leisy, Mabbott, Parrington, Bliss Perry, Louise Pound, Quinn, Spiller, Frederick Jackson Turner, and Stanley Williams on the editorial side. Spiller, Tremaine McDowell, Gohdes, and George B. Stewart contributed essays. Canby, George McLean Harper, Gregory Paine, and Howard Mumford Jones appeared as reviewers. Harry Hayden Clark and Allan Gilbert entered in Vol. 1, no. 2. Frederic I. Carpenter, Napier Wilt, Merle Curti, and Grant C. Knight in Vol. 1, no. 3; Clarence Faust, Granville Hicks, and Robert Morss Lovett in Vol. 1, no. 4; Walter Fuller Taylor, Orians, and Paul Shorey in Vol. 2, no. 1.

Who, among the founders of the profession, was missing? On the other hand, if the reader belongs to the profession and does not know those present, she or he probably does not know enough. With very few notable exceptions, the movers and shakers of the profession have since the beginning joined in cooperating to create and sustain the journal.

The foregoing facts lend a special distinction to the best articles in *American Literature*. They represent the many, often tumultuous winds of doctrine which have blown from the beginnings through the years of the decade next to last in this century. Those articles often became the firm footings upon which present structures of understanding rest. Looking backward, one finds that the argonauts were doughty. Though we know a great deal more than they, they are a great deal of what we know. Typically, the old best authors wrote well—better than most of us. Conceptually, even ideologically, we still wrestle with ideas they created. And every now and again one finds of course that certain of the latest work has reinvented the wheel one time more. Every now and again one finds a sunburst idea which present scholarship has forgotten. Then it appears that we have receded into mist or darkness by comparison.

Historical change, not always for the better, also shows itself in methods (and their implied theories) of how to present evidence, structure an argument, craft a scholarly article. The old masters were far from agreed—much to the contrary—about these matters.

But they are worth knowing in their own variety as well as in their instructive differences from us.

On the other hand, the majority of *American Literature*'s authors of the best remain among us, working, teaching, writing. One testimony to the quality of their masterliness is the frequency with which the journal gets requests from the makers of textbooks or collections of commentary to reprint from its pages. Now the opportunity presents itself to select without concern for permissions fees what seems the best about a number of authors and topics from the whole sweep of *American Literature*.

The fundamental reason for this series, in other words, lies in the intrinsic, enduring value of articles that have appeared in *American Literature* since 1929. The compilers, with humility, have accepted the challenge of choosing the best from well over a thousand articles and notes. By "best" is meant original yet sound, interesting, and useful for the study and teaching of an author, intellectual movement, motif, or genre.

The articles chosen for each volume of this series are given simply in the order of their first publication, thus speaking for themselves and entirely making their own points rather than serving the compilers' view of literary or philosophical or historical patterns. Happily, a chronological order has the virtues of displaying both the development of insight into a particular author, text, or motif and the shifts of scholarly and critical emphasis since 1929. But comparisons or trend-watching or a genetic approach should not blur the individual excellence of the articles reprinted. Each has opened a fresh line of inquiry, established a major perspective on a familiar problem, or settled a question that had bedeviled the experts. The compilers aim neither to demonstrate nor undermine any orthodoxy, still less to justify a preference for research over explication, for instance. In the original and still current subtitle, *American Literature* honors literary history and criticism equally—along with bibliography. To the compilers this series does demonstrate that any worthwhile author or text or problem can generate a variety of challenging perspectives. Collectively, the articles in its volumes have helped to raise contemporary standards of scholarship and criticism.

This series is planned to serve as a live resource, not as a homage to once vibrant but petrifying achievements in the past. For several sound reasons, its volumes prove to be weighted toward the more recent articles, but none of those reasons includes a presumed superiority of insight or of guiding doctrine among the most recent generations. Some of the older articles could benefit now from a minor revision, but the compilers have decided to reprint all of them exactly as they first appeared. In their time they met fully the standards of first-class research and judgment. Today's scholar and critic, their fortunate heir, should hope that rising generations will esteem his or her work so highly.

Many of the articles published in *American Literature* have actually come (and continue to come) from younger, even new members of the profession. Because many of those authors climb on to prominence in the field, the fact is worth emphasizing. Brief notes on the contributors in the volumes of their series may help readers to discover other biographical or cultural patterns.

Edwin H. Cady
Louis J. Budd

On Mark Twain

Science in the Thought of Mark Twain
Hyatt Howe Waggoner

MARK TWAIN lived the last fifteen years of his life a bitter pessimist and a philosophical mechanist. He came to despair of the possibilities of human life. He came to think of man as a machine buffeted by an indifferent, if not hostile, mechanical universe. Such an outlook was not unique in his generation. The cold drafts of the new scientific doctrines were chilling the hearts of many men who had known the snugness of a God-centered, benevolent world. So at once this question arises: Can Mark Twain's experience be likened to the typical experience of many thinking men in his generation?

Critics seem to differ on the question whether or not Mark Twain's experience was in any way comparable to that, for instance, of Henry Adams. Professor Percy H. Boynton says that it was:

Science overthrew the Christian mythology for him [Mark Twain], reduced the world to a "little floating mote," reduced mankind to a biological genus, reduced him to a philosophy of pessimism. . . . With his religious belief, never strong, unsettled by the theories of a mechanistic philosophy, and his fears as to humankind reinforced by the brute facts, Mark Twain came to the crisis in which he had no creed to appeal to and could rely only on a pattern of behavior. . . . [Mark Twain's thinking] was at the same time all his own and quite in the current of nineteenth-century thought.[1]

Professor Stanley Williams agrees:

As the implications of the Darwinian theory filtered through our thought, skepticism crept into the conversation and writings of eminent Americans. . . . Throughout his life he [Mark Twain] retained a consciousness of the goodness of life, an innate belief in the antiquated, benevolent universe, and, for this reason, the impact of subversive thought upon him was terrific, devastating. . . . His adolescence had been influenced by the new

[1] Percy H. Boynton, *Literature and American Life* (Boston, 1936), pp. 635, 644, 642.

Puritanism, that is, an orderly universe ruled by a benevolent God, but he was shocked by the logic of Lyell or Darwin.[2]

But Miss Brashear has advanced the thesis that Mark Twain's philosophy can be traced back to literary sources, to his early reading in the literature of the eighteenth century. She feels that the distinctive features of his thought come from Thomas Paine, or, possibly, from Hobbes, Locke, Hume, and Mandeville.

Mark Twain's philosophy of life, one is forced to conclude, must have had its foundation in the more rigid eighteenth-century trends of thinking. . . . From the first part of *The Age of Reason* Mark Twain as a young man might have got his initial glimpse of the mechanical theory of human life, which he finally formulated into a philosophical system. Part I explains the principles of Newtonian deism as based on the phenomena of planetary motion. . . . As has been said, Mark Twain's thought was not much touched by nineteenth-century speculative philosophy. It remained within the limits of the narrower experiences of the preceding age. In its main lines it seems to follow the doctrines of Hobbes (1588-1679), one of the precursors of English deism, and of Locke, Hume, and Newton.[3]

And Ludwig Lewisohn feels that Mark Twain's pessimism was the result of purely personal experience, and that his philosophy was puerile and entirely without a foundation in knowledge:

He was Tom Sawyer and Huck Finn and the Connecticut Yankee and when youth and romance and boundless optimism went out of his life, he reacted very much as they would have done, as thousands of simple-hearted Americans in agnostic and atheistic societies and clubs do all over the land and consider themselves bold thinkers. . . . Mark Twain had no suspicion, apparently, of the existence of either anthropology or psychology, or any knowledge of the growth and function of *mores* and their connection with the totality of human development. . . . He sat down to develop out of his own head, like an adolescent, like a child, a theory to fit the facts as he seemed to see them, and the only influence discernible in his theory is that of Robert Ingersoll![4]

To determine which of these attitudes is the more nearly correct, we have to know just what Mark Twain knew of science, what

[2] Stanley T. Williams, *American Literature* (Philadelphia, 1933), pp. 122, 124, 125.
[3] Minnie M. Brashear, *Mark Twain: Son of Missouri* (Chapel Hill, N. C., 1934), pp. 242, 247, 248.
[4] Ludwig Lewisohn, *Expression in America* (New York, 1932), pp. 227, 226, 225.

books he read, and how true it is to say, as Mr. Lewisohn says elsewhere in his criticism, that the doctrines in *What Is Man?* were "puerile" when they were written. Such knowledge should be of interest not only to students of Mark Twain, but to those interested in the history of ideas in the period; for, if he really reacted to science as Professor Williams thinks he did, his experience can stand in our minds for the experience of a generation.

A study of the *Notebook,* the *Letters,* the *Autobiography,* the official *Biography,*[5] and several unpublished sketches, discloses a knowledge of science that, while not profound or in any sense rigorously accurate, was nevertheless inspired by enthusiastic interest, and was, for the average layman of the day, comparatively comprehensive.[6] Mark Twain was well acquainted with the theory of organic evolution, and had accepted it, probably, even before his first reading of Darwin.[7] He had a philosophically sound, if not scientifically detailed, knowledge of the main outline of anthropology. This knowledge was, in fact, one of the principal bulwarks of his deterministic philosophy.

He had a very keen interest in, and some knowledge of, geology,[8] with its evidence for evolution and its time-scale that dwarfs all human history and makes the individual human life so insignificant an event as to be invisible to the observer accustomed to the majestic pulses of geologic time. Already in 1880, before his pessimism had taken definite philosophical shape, a letter to his friend

[5] A. B. Paine (ed.), *Mark Twain's Notebook* (New York, 1935); A. B. Paine (ed.), *Mark Twain's Letters* (New York, 1917); *Mark Twain's Autobiography* (New York, 1924); A. B. Paine, *Mark Twain, A Biography* (New York, 1912). Hereinafter these works will be referred to simply as the *Autobiography,* the *Letters,* the *Notebook,* and the *Biography.*

[6] For Mark Twain's references to science, see the later footnotes to this paper. He once made a record of his likes and dislikes thus: "I like history, biography, travels, curious facts and strange happenings, and science. I detest novels, poetry, and theology." See the *Biography,* p. 512.

[7] His connection with Macfarlane makes it seem probable that he accepted some form of evolutionary theory before reading Darwin. For the Macfarlane episode see *Autobiography,* I, 146, 147. For other evidence of his attitude toward evolutionary theory see the letter from A. B. Paine included in this paper; see also *Letters,* pp. 769, 770, 804; *Biography,* pp. 397, 708; *Notebook,* pp. 242, 264; *Autobiography,* II, 7ff. Negatively, there is at least no record of there having been any question in his mind about the truth of the theory as compared with the dogmas of revealed religion with which it came into conflict. That this was not the case with most men is shown especially well in a book on which Mark Twain spent one whole summer: A. D. White, *History of the Warfare of Science with Theology* (New York, 1896).

[8] See scattered casual references: *Letters,* pp. 383, 827; *Biography,* pp. 436, 1162; W. D. Howells, *My Mark Twain* (New York, 1910), p. 98.

Joseph Twichell was filled with his sad sense of geologic time and the comparative insignificance of even the greatest of human affairs. This time-scale, he felt, was the real one, the time-scale of the universe; our own years and lifetimes and centuries are but the pitiably meaningless measurements of microbes in the body of the universe.[9] But his grasp of geologic history was more than merely poetic and imaginative; it attempted also to be practical. As early as 1870 he and J. T. Goodman of *Enterprise* days were spending all their leisure time one happy summer sorting and classifying fossils they found in an abandoned quarry at Quarry Farm, Elmira. Nor did the interest in geology abate with the years. Near the end of his life, Mark Twain invited the geologist R. D. Salisbury from the University of Chicago to come to the new home at Stormfield to explain and classify the geological formations there.

He had a keen and lasting interest in astronomy, and an imaginative grasp of its implications, although his memory for its distances and speeds was somewhat inaccurate.[10] In 1870 in a statement of his religious convictions, set down after his revolt from family prayers, he gave figures for the distance to the nearest fixed star, and tried to conceive of the immensity of the universe. From that date on there occur notations of astronomical facts and speculations. He arrived at an unshakable belief in absolute determinism;[11]

[9] See especially "If I Could Be There" and "3000 Years Among the Microbes," selections included in the *Biography*, pp. 1158-1161; 1663-1670.

[10] See especially *Letters*, p. 17; *Biography*, pp. 1509, 1518, 1542; the letter from Mrs. Gabrilowitsch included in this paper. Note the percentage, out of the total list of scientific books he is known to have read, of books on astronomy. As in his history game for memorizing dates and visualizing their relations to each other and to the present, so in astronomy he liked to make concrete the unimaginable figures, by converting them into familiar terms of experience.

[11] The doctrine of determinism, as used to denote the belief of Mark Twain, means something essentially different from what we mean today by the "predictability" of events. Quantum physics, with the theory of "indeterminacy," and wave mechanics, have combined to make the Victorian concept of strict causal relation seem theoretically mistaken, if practically useful. Predictability is still taken for granted as the basis for science and thought in all but quantum physics; but predictability on the basis of confidence in the law of averages, and predictability on the basis of an assumed inviolable mechanical relationship are, metaphysically speaking, quite distinct. For a statement of Mark Twain's position, see Ernst Haeckel's *The Riddle of the Universe* (New York, 1900), *passim*, or T. H. Huxley's *The Advance of Science in the Last Half Century* (New York, 1898), pp. 32, 33, *passim*. For the contemporary position see A. S. Eddington, *The Nature of the Physical World* (New York, 1931), pp. 200-229, or his *New Pathways in Science* (New York, 1935), pp. 23 ff.; and Sir James Jeans, *The Mysterious Universe* (New York, 1933), pp. 24, 28, 30, 33, 46, 145; and Hermann Weyl, *The Open World* (New Haven, 1932), p. 55.

and his belief was scientifically grounded. If it was not inspired by science, it found, at any rate, ample support therein, especially in the emphasis on heredity and environment postulated by Darwin's theory of evolution.[12] Mark Twain's idea, "We are but a compost heap of decayed heredities,"[13] shows where he put his emphasis in his analysis of human life. Such a statement as this, too, while it shows little of the scientific background that undoubtedly existed in his mind, does reveal a coherent theory based on a monistic concept of nature quite in accord, for instance, with that of Ernst Haeckel:

When the first living atom found itself afloat in the great Laurentian sea the first act of that first atom led to the *second* act of that first atom, and so on down through the succeeding ages of all life, until, if the steps could be traced, it could be shown that the first act of that first atom has led inevitably to the act of my standing here in my dressing gown at this instant talking to you.[14]

That was the reigning scientific theory of his day carried to its logical conclusion.

As for psychology, there is no evidence that he had any real knowledge of the subject. But that is not strange, for psychology in his day could hardly be termed a science. It consisted of many conflicting opinions of many men, and even the modicum of agreement on first principles that has perhaps been reached today was yet to come. But several entries in the *Notebook* suffice to make doubtful the assertion that he had no suspicion even of its existence. He speculated on the theory of dual, or multiple personalities, existing independently within one individual, the possibility of attaching meaning to dreams; and he dabbled in theories of telepathy.[15]

There is little definite evidence, in anything that Mark Twain ever wrote, of the source of all this mixed knowledge and speculation. He was neither a systematic student of science, nor a persistent and profound thinker; and he had nothing of the scholar's love of documentation and reference. It was possible, however, from the preliminary study, to say definitely that he had read carefully

[12] For the emphasis on heredity and environment, see Mark Twain's essay *What Is Man?* For determinism see *Letters*, pp. 719 ff.; *Biography*, p. 397; *Notebook*, p. 312; *Autobiography*, II, 9.

[13] *Notebook*, p. 312.   [14] *Biography*, p. 397.

[15] *Notebook*, pp. 248-252; *Autobiography*, II, 222.

Lecky's *History of European Morals*,[16] J. H. Moore's *The Universal Kinship*,[17] Bayne's *Pith of Astronomy*,[18] A. D. White's *History of the Warfare of Science with Theology*,[19] Darwin's *Descent of Man*,[20] something of Sir Oliver Lodge's,[21] and some books on ants by Sir John Lubbock.[22] Despite the presence of the names of Darwin and Moore and Bayne, the list might seem insufficient to account for his knowledge of facts and theories. Two letters, however, the first from his official biographer, the second from his daughter, go far to make up the deficiency:

Mark Twain [says Mr. Paine] read all those books you mention, and many others—everything, in fact, that came to his hand. Darwin influenced him in the beginning, and all of them, perhaps, a little; but he was too original in his thought to be influenced much or long by anybody. He read Wallace and Crooks and Kelvin in a desultory way, as he read all the others. The only book he kept by him was not a scientific work: it was Suetonius' *Lives of the Caesars*. He loved the drama and wonder of science, but the pageant of history more.[23]

Mrs. Gabrilowitsch adds:

In addition to the books you have listed as having been read by my father, I am only able to mention a few more on which he spent a good deal of time. They were:

"The Pith of Astronomy"	Bayne
"Evolution and Ethics"	Huxley
'The Wonders of Life"	Haeckel
"The Heavens"	Guillemin
"Side Lights of Astronomy"	Simon Newcomb
"The Cycle of Life According to Modern Science"	Saleeby

[16] Lecky's book was published in 1877. Mark Twain read and reread this book for many years, making notations in the margin as he studied it (*Biography*, pp. 511, 1539). His thorough acquaintance with Lecky, one of the first scientific historians of morals, makes it seem improbable that he "had no knowledge of the growth and function of *mores*." His ideas on the subject, different as they may be from contemporary theories, should not be confused with ignorance.

[17] Published 1906. An exposition of scientific monism, based on cosmic and organic evolution, devoted to showing our physical, psychical, and ethical relationship with the universe. See *Letters*, II, 804.

[18] Published 1896. A popular handbook of facts and figures. See *Biography*, p. 1542.

[19] Published 1896. See *Biography*, pp. 1506, 1539.

[20] Published 1871. See *Biography*, p. 1540.

[21] Mark Twain quotes from Lodge in "3000 Years Among the Microbes."

[22] See *Notebook*, p. 283.

[23] Mr. A. B. Paine, in a letter to H. H. Waggoner. Quoted by permission of Mr. Paine.

"Curiosities of the Sky"	Serviss
"Aspects of the Earth"	S[h]aler
"Sound"	Tyndall

He had periods of being especially absorbed in the accounts of astronomical discoveries, and would pore over the vast figures noted, by the hour. His memory stood him in good stead, too—in these studies. The rapidity of the passage of light and yet the time required for it to reach us from the other planets was one of the topics he never tired of discussing. He was never attracted to subjects which demanded a knowledge of deeper mathematics, for his natural inclination was always stronger toward more poetic and mystic subjects; although I remember his saying that mathematics did not lack poetry either.[24]

We do not know when Mark Twain read these books; and so no accurate check on the connection of the ideas found in them with the very general ideas and attitudes outlined in his writings is possible. But by an examination of the dates of publication,[25] and a comparison of these with what he was thinking at definite periods of his life,[26] we can reach at least a negative conclusion: the list of eighteen names seems still to be incomplete, for it is insufficient to account for certain passages that appear in the *Notebook* and *Letters* and *Biography* as early as 1870. He had some very definite knowledge of geology, for instance, long before he could have read N. S. Shaler's *Aspects of the Earth,* the only geological book on the list.[27]

The ideas which he found in these books can best be briefly indicated by listing, first, the main assumptions in the scientific metaphysics of the day, and secondly, the chief scientific advances of

[24] From a letter from Mrs. Clara Clemens Gabrilowitsch to H. H. Waggoner. Quoted by permission of Mrs. Gabrilowitsch. The books referred to as having been "listed" (like those to which Mr. Paine refers) are those mentioned above the letters in this text, with the exception that Bayne's *Pith of Astronomy* was omitted, having been overlooked in the preliminary study.

[25] The publication dates of the books in Mrs. Gabrilowitsch's letter, reading from top to bottom beginning with Huxley, are: 1894, 1904, 1871, 1906, 1904, 1889, 1867.

[26] Entries in the *Notebook* in 1895 make it appear that his philosophy was complete by that time, substantially as we find it in *What Is Man?,* written in 1898. Miss Brashear says that we must look for the real source of his philosophy before 1874, but it seems to me that 1885 would probably be nearer to the truth.

[27] It is possible, perhaps, that he may have picked up his geological knowledge from his acquaintances of his mining days in Nevada; the fact that it was an old friend of those days with whom he sorted fossils, may point to that conclusion. It seems probable to me, however, that he had read Lyell before this time, though there is no conclusive evidence for the opinion, beyond his connection with the learned Macfarlane, and the fact that his reading of Darwin might have led him to Lyell.

the age. According to Huxley, the first principles underlying scientific monism were three in number and quite simple:[28] (1) matter, which was thought of as a "substratum" behind the appearance
of the phenomenal world, and which was said to exhibit the proper-
ties of extension, impenetrability, and mobility, and the principal
quality of inertia; (2) energy, capable of moving this inert substance; and (3) the law of mechanical causality. Whitehead's list
of the chief scientific advances of the period may be simplified,
for our purposes, to three main ideas which might have influenced
the thinking of the average man acquainted with science in a more
or less superficial way:[29] (1) the re-emphasis on the idea of atom-
icity, due to the work of Dalton, Lavoisier, and others; (2) the
principle of the conservation of energy; and (3) the theory of organic and cosmic evolution. These advances in scientific thought
were linked to the first principles in a dual relationship: they were
both the result and the confirmation of the metaphysics on which
they were based. If their philosophic basis is kept in mind, these
ideas lead to certain interesting implications.

In the first place, the stress on the *atomic* nature of matter seems
to give supreme place in the search for truth to the scientific method
of *analysis;* emphasis on analysis of the realities of experience into
their simpler or more primitive component parts leads the layman
to the "nothing but" philosophy. The principle of the conservation
of energy leads to the belief in the essentially *quantitative* nature of
reality. And the theory of evolution as developed by Darwin and
Wallace and expounded by Huxley and Haeckel stresses *natural
law,* the indifference of the impersonal universe to our personal desires and hopes, and the fact that we are "nothing but" animals more
or less developed. These are some of the implications that might
be drawn from nineteenth-century science.

As a matter of fact, they correspond closely with the doctrines
held by Mark Twain. They form a sort of background from which
most of the ideas in *What Is Man?* follow. In that much derided
essay, the following ideas are stressed: (1) man is a machine, both
his mind and his body;[30] (2) as a machine, he has no "free will"

---

[28] T. H. Huxley, *The Advance of Science in the Last Half Century* (New York, 1898),.
pp. 31-33.
[29] A. N. Whitehead, *Science and the Modern World* (New York, 1931), pp. 143-147.
[30] *What Is Man? and Other Essays* (New York, 1917), p. 5 and *passim.*

and no original or spontaneous thoughts—his life and what he is pleased to term his ideas, are both determined by the action of the environment on his inherited structure;[31] (3) where choice seems possible, it is an illusion, since it is always and necessarily made on the basis of self-gratification;[32] (4) the difference between the minds of men and animals is one only of degree of efficiency;[33] (5) the mind is a function of the physical organism;[34] (6) "thought" is automatic association of stimuli from the outside, and instinct is "petrified thought";[35] (7) the mind comes into the world like a blank tablet—what that mind will become depends solely on the stimuli to which its inherited patterns are subjected.[36]

In *What Is Man?* then, we find stress on the iron law of causality, dependence on the concept of evolution, and the use of the analytical method to prove that man is something much simpler than he seems. We find, that is, the common ideas of Victorian physical science applied rigorously to man and his body. But perhaps an even closer relationship with science may be found by examining two books: Darwin's *Descent of Man,* and Huxley's *Evolution and Ethics.*

In the *Descent of Man* Mark Twain found evidence for, if not the source of, his idea that there is no fundamental difference between men and animals, either in mind or in body.[37] Here he also found evidence for his ideas on the relation between instinct and thought, and the nature of intelligence.[38] But though he followed Darwin thus far, he differed violently on the question of the moral superiority of man. Mark Twain agreed, rather, with his old acquaintance of printing days, the philosophic Scotchman Macfarlane, who had anticipated, according to Mark Twain's recollections late in life, the theories set forth in the *Descent of Man* seventeen years or so before that book's publication, with the exception that he had held that man alone of all the animals is morally degraded.[39] The chief influence of the book, however, must have been in its general implications: its emphasis on the *natural order* of things,

[31] *Ibid.,* pp. 5, 43, 89-93, especially p. 6.　　[32] *Ibid.,* pp. 13-24, 54, 59.
[33] *Ibid.,* pp. 73, 76-89.　　[34] *Ibid.,* pp. 95-98.
[35] *Ibid., passim,* and for "petrified thought," especially p. 77.
[36] *Ibid., passim,* especially pp. 5, 6 ff.
[37] *Descent of Man* (New York, 1925). For physical similarity, *passim;* for mental, especially pp. 66 ff.
[38] *Ibid.,* pp. 68, 76.　　[39] *Autobiography,* I, 146, 147.

ruled by the law of cause and effect; and its evidence that man was "only an animal," thereby stripping him of most of his cherished dignity, and seriously damaging his assumption of superiority.

It is to Huxley, with his full development of the implications of Darwinism, that we must turn for the closest parallel between science and Mark Twain's ideas. Huxley stressed the fleeting, shifting, impermanence, not only of life, but even of the "eternal hills." Passage after passage in the *Notebook, Autobiography,* and *Letters* is merely a concrete translation of this general concept. Huxley emphasized at great length the amount of pain and suffering that is inevitable in the struggle for life. He stressed the reign of strict causality throughout the whole universe. He stressed the antithesis between natural processes and man's morals. He returned again and again to the struggle for existence, painting a picture of a nature that was "red in tooth and claw." All these doctrines are central in the thought of Mark Twain. Either Huxley or Mark Twain might have written this:

If the world is full of pain and sorrow; if grief and evil fall, like the rain, upon both the just and the unjust; it is because, like the rain, they are links in the endless chain of natural causation by which past, present, and future are indissolubly connected.[40]

Huxley wrote that. But Mark Twain frequently restated the proposition in more personal and emotional terms:

Idiots argue that nature is kind and fair to us, if we are loyal and obey her laws, and we are responsible for our pains and diseases because we violate the laws—and that all this is judged. Good God! Cholera comes out of Asia and cuts me down when I have taken every pains to have myself and my house in good sanitary conditions. Oh, in that case, my *neighbors* violated Nature's law—and Nature makes *me* responsible, takes it out on me—and that is called just! Very well, the caterpillar doesn't know what the laws are—how then are these people going to excuse nature for afflicting that helpless and ignorant creature? It would save those people a world of uncomfortable shuffling if they would recognize one plain fact—a fact which a man willing to see cannot be blind to, namely, that there is nothing kindly, nothing beneficent, nothing friendly in Nature toward any creature, except by capricious fits and starts; and that Nature's attitude toward all life is profoundly vicious, treacherous, and malignant.[41]

[40] T. H. Huxley, *Evolution and Ethics* (New York, 1894), p. 60.
[41] *Notebook,* p. 255.

Huxley would hardly have expressed himself in these explosive terms, but his idea of what Bertrand Russell has called "man in an alien universe" was in many respects similar.

Mark Twain's thought on the nature of the world and man may be summed up briefly:[42] the universe and man are of one piece, and both are mechanisms;[43] man is a pitiable creature, nothing but an aggregate of mechanisms, nothing but an animal; a single human being, all of human history even, is infinitely unimportant in the vastness of the impersonal universe. That these ideas are purely the result of scientific reading could not of course be argued. Mark Twain did not *depend* upon science for his conclusions about life, to the extent, for instance, that Theodore Dreiser does; but he *used* science to reinforce his thinking. It became for him an integral part of his experience, fitting in with and interpreting the "curious facts" he had learned about men and the world in his long lifetime, and serving as a starting point for speculation. Science seems to Dreiser to be denying the truth that he wants desperately to believe; it only confirmed the deep-rooted suspicions of Mark Twain.

It is quite possible to brand *What Is Man?* as absurd and puerile if one speaks from the standpoint of a learned student deeply versed in all the recent trends in psychology and physics, an idealist basing his thought on Freud and Eddington and Jeans. For it is quite true that the various doctrines contained in the essay are mutually inconsistent. But, then, it should not be forgotten that no one seems to have seen clearly the real inconsistency involved in holding at the

[42] It is quite true that Mark Twain never escaped the effect of his early training and environment. To the end of his life a small portion of his mind thought in terms of Heaven and Hell, while the rest of it was gathering and absorbing the facts of science. Leacock in his *Mark Twain* (New York, 1933), pp. 18, 19, 147-149, makes some interesting remarks on this curious inconsistency in the terms at least of Mark Twain's thinking. Edward Wagenknecht in his *Mark Twain: The Man and His Work* (New Haven, 1935) makes the point that Mark Twain never wholly outgrew his Calvinism: ". . . he could enlarge his God along the lines suggested and made necessary by the new astronomical speculations and discoveries, but he could not fundamentally alter his inherited conception of what we call the human side of God, of God in his relations with humanity. . . . And what is this "Gospel" but an inverted Calvinism?" (pp. 214, 216). Wagenknecht sums up the causes of Mark Twain's pessimism as follows, discounting all purely literary influences: (1) personal grief and misfortunes, (2) high idealism which asked too much of life, (3) the tendency to rage, violence, and exaggeration, (4) and finally, his philosophy of mechanistic determinism (pp. 225-230).

[43] Late in life, Mark Twain highly approved of the work of Jaques Loeb, the noted materialist-mechanist, and hotly defended Loeb's attempts at the creation of life in the laboratory, when those attempts were referred to slightingly in the newspapers. See *Biography*, p. 1161.

same time a complete evolutionary theory and materialistic mechanism in which there were only hard particles in motion, with no more creative guidance than the second law of thermodynamics, which now seems to many to be hardly adequate to account for the progressive evolution of highly organized forms out of the general flux. It was left to Whitehead and others in our day to point out the inconsistencies in Victorian science. Mark Twain was not alone in his position. His general doctrines can all be found in the pages of Haeckel and Huxley, and in the attitudes of Tyndall and Kelvin and other engineer-physicists of the day. Moreover, his *What Is Man?* might, with very little alteration, be taken for a statement of the general philosophical principles underlying the recent psychological fad, extreme behaviorism.[44] Thirty years after he had expressed those principles they still had some vogue and were accepted by many as the basis for advanced psychological thought. Finally, we are reminded of Mark Twain's position today, by Bertrand Russell's definition of mind as a "spot in space." If Mark Twain had been the only one ever to express such views, they might conceivably be labeled absurd; but standing, as they do in a general way, for the implications, and, in part, for the definite assertions of a whole movement in scientific history, they can hardly be so easily dismissed.

As for Miss Brashear's theory that Mark Twain's philosophy springs directly from the eighteenth century, and was untouched by the intellectual developments of his own times, it seems to me that the weight of evidence makes some other explanation more probable.[45] We know that he read the science of his own day, and that he interpreted it as best he could. It seems true, as Miss Brashear says, that he was not touched by the "speculative philosophy" of his day; but there was an increasingly wide divergence between speculative philosophy and physical science in the latter half of the nineteenth century. Like many other men of his day, he did not go to

[44] Mark Twain's position in *What Is Man?*, like Watsonian behaviorism, is based on the dogmas of kinetic-atomic physics; behaviorism takes for granted most of the positions Mark Twain insists upon. See Watson and McDougall, *The Battle of Behaviorism* (London, 1928), pp. 7-41, 72, 73; the connection between Locke's *tabula rasa* and behaviorism is suggested by Fletcher, *Psychology in Education* (New York, 1934), p. 20, and the comparison might as easily be made between Locke and Mark Twain. For Dr. Watson's most complete statement see *The Ways of Behaviorism* (New York, 1928).

[45] Wagenknecht suggests that Miss Brashear is treading on uncertain ground when she derives the essays in the *What Is Man?* volume from the eighteenth century.

the professional philosopher for his philosophy; he developed it directly, from what he considered "facts." Dreiser's interpretation (or misinterpretation) of Spencer is a case in point. He is, as Mark Twain was, untouched by Victorian "speculative philosophy," but his spirit has been crushed by its science.

The fact that Mark Twain adopted, as Miss Brashear notes, the "Newtonian universe," almost "ready made," does not point to eighteenth-century more than to nineteenth-century influence; for in the nineteenth century—indeed, until the recent "revolution" in physics—the Newtonian universe was the only universe science knew.

Furthermore, although it is quite true that Part I of Paine's *The Age of Reason* explains Newtonian deism, Newtonian deism is not so much a mechanical theory of human life as a mechanical theory of astronomy and the cosmos. There is no mention of man as a machine in *The Age of Reason;* rather, there is a long discussion of the regularity of the laws of astronomy, which seem to Paine to reveal the hand of God. There is a very great difference indeed between Newtonian deism and Mark Twain's "Gospel." Paine's speculations on astronomy brought him to the conclusion that, "As, therefore, the Creator made nothing in vain, so also must it be believed that he organized the structure of the universe in the most advantageous manner for the benefit of man."[46] The similarity between deism of this type and Mark Twain's philosophy lies only in the fact that both postulate a mechanical universe. But Newtonian mechanism reigned supreme in science, and in philosophies that followed science closely, not only in the seventeenth and eighteenth centuries, but in the nineteenth century as well. If Mark Twain's philosophy has points in common with those of Hobbes and Hume, that is not strange: Hobbes and Hume influenced the whole course of modern thought. The fact to be noted is that his philosophy also has much in common with the ideas of Darwin, Huxley, and Haeckel.

Mark Twain was no systematic student of science. But the facts of science stimulated his imagination; and the theories of science confirmed his pessimistic suspicions about life. We see how science and daily living worked together to form his philosophy, in his habit

---

[46] *The Age of Reason* (New York: Wiley Book Company, n.d.), p. 75.

of expressing his doctrines in semi-scientific terms, and then illustrating them with homely similes from experience. His pessimism
was partly, as Mr. Boynton has put it, the result of the conflict between the new science and the old theology, and partly, as Mr.
Lewisohn holds, the result of his personal experience of the sadness
of living. Mark Twain knew much of sorrow and death. And he
became convinced of the moral depravity of man from watching
men. He lost faith in conventional religion under the influence of
Thomas Paine, his scientific reading, and his own native skepticism.
He had nothing to put in the place of these lost values. Science
seemed to give the answer to his questioning. It seemed to justify
the position expressed in his letter to Howells in 1898: "I suspect
that to you there is still dignity in human life, and that man is not
a joke—a poor joke—the poorest that was ever contrived."

Mark Twain's Indebtedness to
John Phoenix
Gladys Carmen Bellamy

MARK TWAIN'S affinity with the tribe of humorists known as "literary comedians" may be demonstrated by going through his pages. In them the amusing verbal devices[1] which are the stock-in-trade of "literary comedy," are to be found "in abundance in his earlier works and scattered through his later ones."[2] It is the purpose of this article to exhibit the influence of the literary comedians upon Mark Twain, with special reference to the work of George Horatio Derby (1823-1861), better known as "John Phoenix," whose sketches began to appear in the newspapers and magazines of California about 1850 and were afterwards collected in two volumes, *Phoenixiana* (1855) and *Squibob Papers* (1859). There has been a conflict of critical opinion as to whether Mark Twain's work derived anything from that of Phoenix. In fact, a regular cycle may be discerned involving this question—the rise, decline, and fall of the idea that John Phoenix influenced Mark Twain.[3]

[1] Fred Lewis Pattee, *A History of American Literature since 1870* (New York, 1915), pp. 28-30. In describing the tricks of "literary comedy," Mr. Pattee enumerates: a solemn protestation of truthfulness, followed by an impossible story; grotesque exaggeration, used deliberately to excite laughter; an irreverence towards everything; the device of euphemistic statement; true "Yankee aphorisms"; and unexpected comparisons and *non sequiturs*.
To these devices may be added: anticlimax, understatement, puns, malapropisms, the incongruous catalogue, burlesques of all kinds, and—in the case of certain humorists—cacography. See Walter Blair, *Native American Humor, 1800-1900* (New York, 1937), pp. 119, 122-124.

[2] Blair, *op. cit.,* p. 148. Mr. Blair illustrates various devices of the literary comedians by presenting a series of comic sentences, taken from a single page of Mark Twain's *A Tramp Abroad*. Mr. Blair points out that these verbal devices, when used at all by the earlier humorists of the South and the Southwest, were employed "rather sparingly" (*ibid.,* p. 118).
Since Franklin J. Meine's edition of *Tall Tales of the Southwest* (New York, 1930) offered a new approach to Mark Twain through Augustus B. Longstreet, William T. Tappan, Sol Smith, Johnson J. Hooper, Joseph G. Baldwin, Joseph M. Field, George W. Harris, Thomas B. Thorpe, Hamilton C. Jones, and others, writers on Mark Twain during the last decade have generally emphasized his connections with these Southern and Southwestern humorists. See in particular Bernard DeVoto, *Mark Twain's America* (Boston, 1932), pp. 98, 152, 158, 253-258, 303; and Blair, *op. cit.,* pp. 153-161.

[3] Early writers on American humor linked the names of Phoenix and Twain, apparently as a matter of course. See in this connection E. P. Whipple, "American Literature

Mr. DeVoto is in pronounced disagreement with the view which considers Phoenix in such a light, and expresses himself accordingly:

... Geography and priority appear to compose the whole case for the professors. . . . It may be that his [Phoenix's] burlesque Fourth of July oration suggested the "Josh" letter to the *Enterprise*. . . . It may be— but permit me to doubt. . . . Phoenix did not invent burlesque for American humor, and all that he has in common with Mark Twain . . . is the writing of burlesque. Burlesque was a fashion and both drew on it freely. *Mark nowhere echoes the phrasing of John Phoenix and nowhere makes use of Phoenix's point of view.* . . . Both found grand opera, legal phraseology, and assemblies of women subjects to their taste—as scores before them had done . . . *the academic are here desired to produce evidence of influence.* . . .[4]

Subsequent writers on Mark Twain have presumably been so overwhelmed by Mr. DeVoto's dictum that they have made no further investigations; in general, they have either failed to take up the question of this particular influence,[5] or they have denied outright that such an influence exists.[6] Yet a recent writer points

---

in the First Century of the Republic," *Harper's Magazine*, LII, 514-533 (March, 1876), and H. C. Lukens, "American Literary Comedians," *Harper's Magazine*, LXXX, 783-797 (April, 1890). Whipple and Lukens point out that Phoenix and Twain belong in the same class of humorists, but go no further. In 1915 Professor Pattee remarked: "Mark Twain's earliest manner had much in it that smacks of 'Phoenix,'" and mentioned certain chapters of *Phoenixiana* which "might have been taken from *Roughing It*" (Pattee, *op. cit.*, p. 31). Yet Professor Pattee was cautious enough to add that such similarities may have come about naturally, from contact with the West.

In 1918, however, Professor Will D. Howe wrote of Derby, or Phoenix: "As a Western humorist . . . he influenced his admirer, Mark Twain," and again spoke of Twain as the "admirer and imitator of Derby and Browne . . ." ("Early Humorists," *Cambridge History of American Literature*, New York, 1918, II, 156-159). Some of the phrasing of the Howe article is used by Professor Hastings in his brief *Syllabus of American Literature* (1923) in a passage which is quoted—with scorn—by Mr. DeVoto (*op. cit.*, p. 219).

[4] *Op. cit.*, p. 165. Italics are mine.

[5] See, for instance, Blair, *op. cit.*, pp. 147, 160. But elsewhere Mr. Blair goes so far as to say that, while he himself agrees with Mr. DeVoto that "frontier humor is the greatest force in the shaping of his artistry," he feels that Mark's "alliances with other creators of American humor . . . also deserve emphasis" (*ibid.*, p. 162 n.).

[6] Ivan Benson, *Mark Twain's Western Years* (Stanford University Press, 1938). See a passage (pp. 155-156) in which Mr. Benson's very phraseology seems to echo that of Mr. DeVoto: "Twain had one thing in common with Ward . . . John Phoenix, Josh Billings, and . . . Nasby: he was, at the time, chiefly concerned with humorous writing. . . . That any of these writers had any rubber-stamp influence on Twain cannot be admitted when one makes a comparison of their works with the writings of Twain during his Western period." Compare with these lines Mr. DeVoto's statement: "The four humorists whose heir Mr. Hastings considers Mark Twain to have been, had in common with him the intention of producing laughter" (*op. cit.*, p. 219).

to Mark Twain's years in Nevada and on the Pacific coast as his formative period[7]—a period in which he was in daily contact with the "tricks" of the Western comic journalism, of which Phoenix is, perhaps, the chief exponent.

In his biography of John Phoenix, George R. Stewart writes: ". . . A number of parallels may be noted between wordings and incidents in the Phoenix's and Twain's writings. Although these are not very strong or convincing, they nevertheless show the possibility that Phoenix's work was one minor factor in shaping the development of Twain."[8] In this connection, Mr. Stewart points out that Phoenix's story of the "Eagle Bakery" was "thought by Mark Twain to be good enough for stealing" for use in his "Love's Bakery" sketch, although Mark Twain "merely adapted the story, not the action."[9] Mr. Stewart also remarks, "The ascent of the Riffelberg (in *A Tramp Abroad*) is suggestive of the *Official Report* in *Phoenixiana.*"[10]

Other comments dealing with the John Phoenix-Mark Twain question have been, usually, incidental remarks with no supporting evidence offered. In spite of long-continued comparisons of the two humorists, no one, it appears, has taken the trouble to investigate the connection between them through a close attention to details and a collation of specific passages from their works. Mr. DeVoto's point that "the academic" should "produce evidence of influence" was well taken.

After disposing of the idea that Phoenix had any influence whatever on Mark Twain, in a discussion of Twain's letters to the Sacramento *Union* Mr. DeVoto remarks: "He writes of astronomy, as Phoenix had, and calls Adah Menken 'the Great Bear.' "[11] But there is a stronger tie here than a mere writing on the same general subject of astronomy, "as Phoenix had." In Part II of Phoenix's "Lectures on Astronomy," written in San Francisco on October 10, 1854, the following lines occur: " 'The Great Bear' (which is spelled —Bear—and has no reference whatever to Powers' Greek Slave)

[7] Benson, *op. cit.*, p. 1.
[8] *John Phoenix, Esq., the Veritable Squibob: A Life of Captain George H. Derby, U. S. A.* (New York, 1937), p. 199.
[9] *Ibid.*, pp. 77-78; see also p. 235, n. 198: "The *Love's Bakery* sketch in the *Jumping Frog* volume . . . definitely echoes the *Eagle Bakery* story."
[10] *Ibid.*, p. 235 n. 198. [11] *Op. cit.*, p. 167

is one of the most remarkable constellations in the Heavens."[12] Ten years later, a sketch by Mark Twain, which appeared in the *Californian* on November 19, 1864, under the title "A Full and Reliable Account of the Extraordinary Meteoric Shower of Last Saturday Night," contains these lines: "About this time a magnificent spectacle dazzled my vision—the whole constellation of the Great Menken came flaming out of the heavens. . . . (N. B. I have used the term 'Great Menken' because I regard it as a more modest expression than the 'Great Bear.' . . .)"[13] In view of the fact that there are two other similarities to Phoenix's sketch in this same piece of Mark Twain's, there can be little doubt that Phoenix's reference to the Greek Slave, a nude, in connection with "the Great Bear," suggested Twain's reference to the same constellation as "the Great Menken"—with the implication that the terms are synonymous.[14] The second likeness consists in the fact that in burlesquing scientific papers, both Mark Twain and Phoenix have made use of the name of the same scientist—that of Professor Silliman.[15] There is, however, a third likeness in the same sketch, which is the most striking resemblance of all. Phoenix concludes his "Lectures on Astronomy" with the acknowledgment of "An Astronomical Poem" from a "young observer" with the request that he "introduce" it in his lecture: ". . . but the detestable attempt . . . to make 'slides' rhyme with 'Pleiades' . . . and the fearful pun in the thirty-seventh verse, on 'the Meteor by moonlight alone,' "[16] compel him to decline the introduction. In Mark Twain's "Acount of the Meteoric Shower," he relates the following incident: "On my way home, I met young John William Skae—the inimitable punster . . . and I knew from his distraught . . . air that he was building a joke. . . . Said I, 'Are you out looking for meteors, too?' . . . and says he: 'Well, sorter; I'm looking for my Susan—going to meteor by moonlight alone. . . .' "[17] It would seem that this, perhaps, is an "echo of the

---

[12] *Phoenixiana; or Sketches and Burlesques* (New York, 1856), p. 248.

[13] John Howell (ed.), *Sketches of the Sixties*, by Bret Harte and Mark Twain (San Francisco, 1927), p. 153.

[14] Mr. DeVoto has described Adah Menken's appearance in Virginia City, Nevada, in her famous "Mazeppa" act, with "her memorable body bare except for an apologetic shred of gauze" (*op. cit.*, p. 126). Mark Twain was a member of her audience.

[15] Mark Twain wrote his "Account of the Meteoric Shower" in the form of a letter to Professor Silliman, Jr., to be published in the *American Journal of Science*, "for the good of science" (*Sketches of the Sixties*, p. 151; cf. *Phoenixiana*, p. 251; also p. 142).

[16] *Phoenixiana*, p. 252.   [17] *Sketches of the Sixties*, pp. 156-157.

phrasing" of John Phoenix—one of those echoes whose existence Mr. DeVoto denies. And the fact that there are three parallels between a single sketch of Twain's and a single sketch by Phoenix would make mere coincidence seem very doubtful.[18] But evidence of parallels in other sketches must be presented:

In his "Legend of the Tehama House," Phoenix writes of General Brown, a large man of "stern and forbidding aspect . . . with a fierce and uncompromising moustache," who owned a "small . . . dog of the true bull-terrier breed," called "Fan." General Brown retired "with his dog under his arm, swearing he would not part with her for five hundred dollars."[19]

In "Blanketing the Admiral," Mark Twain describes the Admiral as having a face that glowed "through a weather-beaten mask . . . shaggy brows . . . a gnarled crag of a nose. . . . At his heels frisked the darling of his bachelor estate, his terrier 'Fan,' a creature no larger than a squirrel. The main part of his daily life was occupied in looking after 'Fan.'"[20]

The combination of the man with the forbidding aspect and the small extravagantly cherished terrier dog called "Fan," is the same in each sketch; one man is a "General," the other an "Admiral." Surely, there is more than coincidental likeness between the two sketches.

There are striking correspondences elsewhere. The first sketch in *Phoenixiana* is a burlesque on scientific pretensions in general and on scientific expeditions in particular. Phoenix relates, with much scientific unction, the story of a "Military Survey and Reconnoissance of the route from San Francisco to the Mission of Dolores."[21] This sketch should be compared with Mark Twain's "Some Learned Fables for Good Old Boys and Girls," in which he relates "How the Animals of the Wood Sent Out a Scientific Expedition."[22]

John Phoenix's Expedition

A footnote explains that Dolores Mission is 2½ miles from the City

Mark Twain's Expedition

The "most illustrious scientists" among the animals and insects of

---

[18] There is a fourth bit of evidence here in the line of associated ideas; there may be an indication that Mark had Phoenix in mind while he was writing this sketch, since in discussing the various problems with which scientific knowledge must cope, he raises the question "as to whether the extraordinary bird called the Phoenix ever existed or not . . ." (*ibid.*, p. 155).   [19] *Phoenixiana*, pp. 258-269.
[20] *Roughing It*, chap. lxii.   [21] *Phoenixiana*, pp. 13-31.
[22] *Sketches New and Old* (Hillcrest Ed.; New York, 1906), pp. 156-189.

Hall of San Francisco. The undertaking is handled as if Dolores Mission were in the wilds of a far, unexplored country. The expedition has many *savans*, each with notebook and pencil; it has also much scientific equipment, such as transit instruments, surveying chains, theodolites, a sidereal clock. Phoenix sets about arriving "at the length of the base line by subsequent triangulation." The result proves that a distance which before had been considered as around ten miles, is three hundred and twenty-four feet; but "there can, of course, be no disputing the elucidations of science, or facts demonstrated by mathematical process, however incredible they may appear *per se.*" There is much scientific lore, and scientific names are frequent. The company encamps for the night at the end of Kearney Street; the next morning, a group of "natives" gathers about their camp. These "natives" are of diminutive stature, and are in reality only dirty children, making mud pies. But to Phoenix and his party they are a new race, the zeal for discovery is so much in evidence. The *savans* are "constantly jotting down some object of interest," and one of them records the "natives." Phoenix continues:

"From the notes of Dr. Bigguns [the ethnologist], I transcribe the following description of this deeply interesting people:

the wood make bustling preparations for going forth into the unknown and unexplored world beyond the forest:

"Finally they set off . . . heavily laden with savans, scientific instruments . . . surveying chain . . ." chainbearers, etc. They discover a strange tree: "By triangulation, Lord Long-legs determined its altitude, Herr Spider measured its circumference at the base. . . ." They discover a railroad and call the hard rails "parallels of latitude." When the train rushes by, they decide that it is the "Vernal Equinox"; they know it to be midsummer, but the scientific explanations of Professor Snail are accepted, and due entry is made of the decision. The professors deluge the company with long scientific names meaning nothing. They all camp in a region of "vast caverns of stone," a deserted town, where they find some abandoned wax-works and decide that here is Man himself, "preserved in a fossil state." They make an "official report" of the wax figures, since much time is "given up to writing voluminous accounts" of marvels. Then Professor Woodlouse gets out their ancient records, to consult the description of Man there set down. The Professor reads aloud to the company:

" 'In ye time of our fathers Man still walked ye earth, as by tradition we know. It was a creature of exceeding great size . . . with a

"'Kearney Street native . . . height, two feet nine inches; hair, white; complexion, dirt color; eyes, blue; no front teeth; opal at extremity of nose; dress . . . of bluish bombazine . . . ornamented down the front with *crotchet* work of molasses candy . . .; occupation, erecting small pyramids of dirt and water; . . . religious belief, obscure. . . .' "

loose skin, sometimes of one color, sometimes of many, the which it was able to cast at will; . . . It had a sort of feathers on its head such as hath a rat, but longer. . . . When it was stirred with happiness, it leaked water from its eyes. . . . Two Mans being together, they uttered noises . . . like this: "Haw-haw-haw—dam good, dam good". . . .' "

Phoenix's explorers find a bottle of whiskey and bring it in as a specimen "of the products of the country." Twain's explorers find a bottle of whiskey, and many of them get drunk; the leaders pour the liquor out, but are careful to retain a bit for experiment and for preservation in the museum. "Slippery Bill," one of Phoenix's trusted chainmen, becomes intoxicated and dances for the amusement of the "natives." The Tumble-Bug is the clown of Mark Twain's piece; it is he who gets drunk first and comes to announce the finding of the whiskey, with many a hiccough.

The frontier humor dealt largely in smells; also in the physiological processes of both men and animals. But Phoenix and Twain strike a note of variation in shrouding the excrement of animals under pseudoscientific terms:

Phoenix finds that Kearney Street "is densely populated and smells of horses. Its surface is intersected with many pools of *sulphuretted protoxide of hydrogen.* . . ."

Mark Twain's expedition finds a "round, flattish mass," an "isoperimental protuberance . . . lamellibranchiate in its formation." The Tumble Bug pronounces it a "rich and noble property," and offers "to manufacture it into spheres of exceeding grace."[23]

Because of "the innumerable villages of pigs" on his line of march, Phoenix suggests that the name of the route be changed from the

[23] Before Mark Twain, Phoenix had turned his attention to the labors of the lowly tumblebug. See his "Patent Attachment for the Alleviation of Tumble Bugs," reproduced in Stewart, *John Phoenix,* p. 189. In Phoenix's drawing, the "emancipated bug" is standing on his head, gleefully kicking his heels in the air. Perhaps there is a suggestion here for Mark Twain's drunken, clowning Tumble-Bug.

"Central Route" to the "*Scentral* Route." In Mark's sketch, "that intolerable stinking scavenger, the Tumble-Bug," is reprimanded because he smells of the stable. Along Kearney Street, Phoenix finds "several specimens of a vegetable substance" which he classifies as "the *stalkus cabbagiensis*"; and the only mention of a vegetable in Twain's sketch is in his comparison of the neck of the whiskey bottle to "a section of a cabbage stalk divided transversely."

Phoenix feels that he and his party must be objects of general interest. He announces that "profiles" of himself and two of his officials have been "executed in black court plaster" and are on display at a business house, where they "may be seen for a short time."	Twain writes of his expedition: "How the members were banqueted and glorified, and talked about! Everywhere that one of them showed himself, straightway there was a crowd to gape and stare at him."

The general parallelism of these two pieces and the multiple coincidences of detail are surely beyond the possibilities of pure chance. The chief similarity seems to lie in the scientific descriptions of the "natives" of Kearney Street and of the "extinct species, Man," although there is a reversal in idea between the discovery of a "new" race and that of an old, extinct one. Finally, Mark Twain may have derived the whole fantastic idea on which he bases his sketch—that of having the "animals of the wood" set forth as surveyors and engineers—from this same Kearney Street foray; for in Phoenix's sketch the notes of Dr. Dunshunner, the chief geologist, comment on "The beautiful idea, originated by Col. Benton, that buffaloes and other wild animals are the pioneer engineers."

The delicacy of humor concealed in what has been called "the immemorial gesture of derision"—the thumb against the nose and the fingers spread apart—made it a favorite item on the frontier; it was "sure fire." It has been argued, with some justice, that "the world's humor has always dealt grossly with death";[24] nevertheless, the linking of this thumb-to-the-nose motif with the idea of death is decidedly not a commonplace, and here Mark Twain follows Phoenix in a striking innovation. Furthermore, both humorists use this novel combination in hoaxes; for Phoenix, as well as Twain, was an adept in the art of hoaxing the "too credulous reader." Compare this evidence from their pages:

[24] DeVoto, *op. cit.*, p. 153.

"The Death of Squibob"	"The Petrified Man"
. . . I had the mournful satisfaction of being with him in his last moments, and of closing one of his eyes. I say one of his eyes, for the other persisted in remaining partly open, and his . . . countenance, even in death, preserves that ineffable wink . . . which so eminently characterized him. . . . I found him evidently well aware of his approaching end, and calm and resigned. . . . He was . . . seized with an alarming paroxysm, during which his hands were extended in a right line from the tip of his nose, the fingers separated and "twiddling" in a convulsive manner.[25]	. . . The body was in a sitting posture . . .; the attitude was pensive, the right thumb resting against the side of the nose; the left thumb partially supported the chin, the forefinger pressing the inner corner of the left eye and drawing it partly open; the right eye was closed, and the fingers of the right hand spread apart [!]. . . . The verdict of the jury was that "deceased came to his death from protracted exposure". . . .[26]

Squibob is "calm and resigned"; Mark Twain's man is "pensive." Each has one eye "partly open," one eye closed in a wink; and the most noteworthy circumstance is that each meets the moment of death in the ancient attitude which means "sold."[27]

Squibob "passes away," and Phoenix leaves the room for a time; upon his return, he is surprised to find the deceased one sitting up in bed. Squibob speaks: ". . . By George! I quite forgot my last words—'This is the last of earth!—I still live!!—I WISH THE CONSTITUTION TO BE PRESERVED!!!—HERE'S LUCK!!!!' " Then lying down, and closing one eye he expired—this time "positively without reserve." And the "last words" of poor Squibob appear to have found echoes in at least two sketches by Mark Twain.[28]

[25] *Phoenixiana*, pp. 177-178.

[26] First published in the *Territorial Enterprise* of Oct. 5, 1862; reprinted in Benson, *op. cit.*, p. 175.

[27] Mr. DeVoto has suggested that Dan De Quille's "solar-armor" story probably produced the "Petrified Man" (*op. cit.*, p. 137). But item for item, Mark's sketch is much closer to that of Phoenix than to De Quille's, which describes a suit of India-rubber, plays upon extremes of heat and cold, and attaches an icicle eighteen inches long to its victim's nose.

[28] In "The Great French Duel," Mark Twain describes the painstaking care with which M. Gambetta makes his choice of "last words" before going out to fight a duel, only to forget them when he is actually on the field of honor (*A Tramp Abroad*, chap. viii). In his little sketch, "Last Words of Great Men," from all the famous "last words"

Readers familiar with Albert Bigelow Paine's biography of Twain will remember the account of the Whittier birthday dinner, an event of the night of December 17, 1877. On this occasion Mark Twain gave a speech in which he burlesqued Emerson, Longfellow, and Holmes, who were all present among the guests. This speech—"the amazing mistake, the bewildering blunder, the cruel catastrophe"— was not in the nature of a triumph for Mark Twain. The diners who sat there were petrified with horror at this sacrilege against the hallowed literary trinity. "It was a fatality," to quote William Dean Howells. "One of those sorrows into which a man walks with his eyes wide open, no one knows why."[29] Although it is still not possible to say "wherefore," it may now be possible to show "wherefrom." For John Phoenix had once published an enlightening critique on a certain poem of Emerson's. The correspondences are easily recognized in what appears below:

JOHN PHOENIX	MARK TWAIN'S SPEECH
The following lines published in the *Atlantic Monthly* by R. W. Emerson, Esq., have attracted much attention . . . from the fact that nobody can understand . . . what the man means:	". . . and pretty soon they [Emerson, Longfellow, and Holmes] got out a greasy old deck and went to playing euchre. . . . Mr. Emerson dealt, looked at his hand, shook his head, says—

BRAHMA

> If the red slayer think he slays
> Or if the slain think he is slain,
> They know not well the subtle ways
> I keep, and pass, and turn again.

The fact is, that Emerson has lately learned the game of Euchre, and being fascinated therewith, wished to express his feelings on

" 'I am the doubter and the doubt'
—and calmly bunched the hands and went to shuffling for a new layout. Says he:
" 'They reckon ill who leave me out;
They know not well the subtle ways I keep.
I pass and deal *again!'*
Hang'd if he didn't go ahead and do it, too! Oh, he was a cool one!

available Mark selects "I still live" (attributed to Daniel Webster), and follows it with "This is the last of earth" (attributed to John Quincy Adams). And he makes Queen Elizabeth say, "Oh, I would give my kingdom for one moment more—I have forgotten my last words." See *The Curious Republic of Gondour, and Other Whimsical Sketches* (New York, 1919), pp. 132-140. This sketch was first printed in the Buffalo *Express*, Sept. 11, 1869.

[29] Albert Bigelow Paine, *Mark Twain, a Biography: The Personal and Literary Life of Samuel Langhorne Clemens* (New York, 1912), II, 606.

the subject. . . . A little careful consideration of the terms used convinces one of this at once. This [*sic*] "the red slayer" refers to the Right Bower (probably the Jack of Hearts); "the slain" is undoubtedly the Left Bower, not guarded, and you perceive that Emerson probably euchered his adversary by "passing," keeping the Ace and some strong cards, and coming again after the Bowers were out. . . . This explanation is made to save Emerson's reputation in the matter. . . .[30]

. . . I see by Mr. Emerson's eye he judged he had 'em. He had already corralled two tricks. . . . So now he kind of lifts a little in his chair and . . . down he fetched a right bower. . . ."[31]

Such an oddity as this—the bizarre combination of the transcendental Emerson, the roistering game of euchre, and identical lines from the mystical poem, "Brahma"—is not likely to have been twice assembled, spontaneously, in two separate brains.

And there are various isolated passages in Phoenix which seem to recall correspondences in the work of Twain.[32] Consideration must be given to the well-known "mustard anecdote," which may have been a common story of the time; at any rate, it reached print in the pages of John Phoenix as early as 1855, and bears the stamp of the Phoenix brand of humor. According to Phoenix, Captain B. visited an army camp just as "O. B." was going in to dine at a small pine table on which a servant placed a large tin pan full of boiled rice, and a broken bottle half full of mustard.

[30] First appeared in the Mobile *Register*, Dec. 9, 1857; reprinted in Stewart, *op. cit.*, pp. 190-191. Professor Stewart calls this "explanation" Phoenix's "last sniping shot at the haziness of the romantics."

[31] Paine, *Mark Twain*, III, 1645-1646.

[32] For instance, a Californian of Phoenix's acquaintance beseeches the tollgatherers who wish to collect toll from him at the Mission Dolores, "Oh, don't bother me, gentlemen . . . *I'm an orphan boy!*" (*Phoenixiana*, p. 75). When Mark Twain grows weary of having the "Queen's Chair" pointed out to him in Gibraltar, he pleads with his officious guide: "Sir, I am a helpless orphan in a foreign land. . . . Don't—now *don't* inflict that . . . old legend on me any more today!" (*Innocents Abroad*, chap. vii).

In addition, Phoenix describes the farewell scene as a steamer leaves the dock. He knows none of the passengers, but hates to seem entirely without friends; he shouts "Good bye, Colonel," and "thirty-four respectable gentlemen" take off their hats (*Phoenixiana*, pp. 190-191). Mark Twain has written satirically on the American surplusage of "Colonels" and similar titles, in at least three passages (*Life on the Mississippi*, chap. xlvi, and *The Gilded Age*, chaps. i and v).

. . . The Captain looked despairingly around—there was nothing else. "Abe," said O. B. . . . "are you fond of boiled rice?" "Well, no," said Abe. . . . "I can't say that I am. . . ." "Ah," replied Lawrence coolly, *"well, just help yourself to the mustard!"*[33]

At a stage-station on the plains Mark Twain was trying to eat a meal of stale bread, condemned army bacon, and "Slumgullion," but he could not. And when he looked at "that melancholy vinegar-cruet," he tells us:

. . . I thought of the anecdote . . . of the traveler who sat down to a table which had nothing on it but a mackerel and a pot of mustard. He asked the landlord if this was all. The landlord said: "All! . . . I should think there was enough mackerel there for six." "But I don't like mackerel." "Oh—then help yourself to the mustard."[34]

Mark's anecdote is much nearer to the version of Phoenix than to Artemus Ward's "Bakin an Cabbidge" story.[35] In Mark's "last hoax" on the reader, a paragraph in "The Double-Barrelled Detective Story," there is found the following line: ". . . far in the empty sky, a solitary oesophagus slept upon motionless wing. . . ."[36] This idea may have been suggested by Phoenix, who quotes lines from Poe's "Al Aaraaf," and then comments: ". . . Observe that note: *'The Albatross is said to sleep on the wing.'* Who said so? I should like to know. Buffon didn't mention it; neither does Audubon. Coleridge, who made the habits of that rare bird a study, never found it out. . . ."[37] Phoenix believes that Poe's sole reason for deceiving the reading public by inventing this fanciful habit for the *albatross,* was that he was faced with the desperate alternative of using *hoss* to rhyme with *toss.* The whimsicality of Phoenix's thought throughout the albatross passage would have appealed immeasurably to Mark Twain. In another whimsical mood, Phoenix once remarked in the pages of the sophisticated *Knickerbocker,* the

[33] *Phoenixiana,* p. 211.

[34] *Roughing It,* chap. iv.

[35] Yet Mr. DeVoto calls Mark's anecdote a "reminiscence of Ward." Incidentally, it should be observed that Mr. DeVoto has misquoted Mark Twain in connection with the mustard story. Mark's meal was not mackerel and mustard, as Mr. DeVoto states (*op. cit.,* p. 220); Mark was only *remembering* the mustard anecdote.

[36] *Harper's Magazine,* CIV, 264 ff. (Jan., 1902). Collected in *The Man That Corrupted Hadleyburg and Other Stories and Essays* (New York, 1900).

[37] *Phoenixiana,* p. 76.

New Yorker of its day, that Longfellow's recently published *Hia-watha* was a poem "which it strikes me any one might have waited to read, six months at least, and probably longer, with satisfaction and advantage."[38] This pronouncement might have been cut from one piece with Mark Twain's terse comment on Jane Austen: "A very good library may be started just by leaving Jane Austen out of it." And both humorists developed a fellow feeling for King Herod.[39]

As to general similarity in subjects treated by Phoenix and Twain, the list is an extensive one;[40] and there are occasional verbal reminiscences of the earlier humorist scattered through Mark's lines.[41] Parallel uses of the various "devices" of verbal humor might be presented from the works of the two men; but the scope of this

[38] Later collected in the volume, *Squibob Papers*, p. 190; see Stewart, *op. cit.*, pp. 184, 233.

[39] Phoenix makes moan that the crying of his infant daughter robs him of his nightly rest, and adds, "I begin to adore the memory of Herod, and wish a similar character ruled Mobile . . ." (letter sent from Mobile to Derby's mother, March 15, 1859; see Stewart, *John Phoenix*, p. 192). This recalls Mark's fear that his eldest child might have destroyed a part of his *Mississippi* manuscript, and his anguished cry, "If so, O for the return of the lamented Herod!" See *Mark Twain's Letters* (New York, 1917), I, 241; a letter to Howells, dated Dec. 18, 1874. Since Phoenix's quip on Herod was presumably unpublished in his lifetime or in Twain's there is quite possibly no connection here; on the other hand, such a quip spreads far by word of mouth, and this one might have traveled up and down the river on which Mark Twain was a pilot in this year of 1859. In one passage, Mr. Stewart enters this attractive field of conjecture: ". . . we may recall that Derby frequently traveled between St. Louis and New Orleans by steamer in the late fifties; it would be interesting to know whether Sam Clemens was ever his pilot" (*op. cit.*, p. 199).

[40] Besides the treatment of astronomy, grand opera, legal phraseology, and assemblies of women which Mr. DeVoto has noted (*op. cit.*, pp. 165, 167), both humorists give whimsical discourses on fleas, dentistry, and "spiritual mediums"; and both burlesque dramatic reviews and newspaper correspondence addressed to themselves. Both, also, burlesque bad poetry: compare the poem in which Mr. Mudge laments the death of "Jeames," who was "accidently shot on the bank of the peacus river" (*Phoenixiana*, p. 131), with Mark Twain's plaintive ballad, "He Done His Level Best" (*Sketches New and Old*, pp. 84-85); in each case the poem is contributed by an admirer of the hero celebrated, with the request that it be printed in the paper. In addition, each humorist tells of his experiences as temporary newspaper editor in the absence of the regular editor; and each describes the lack of enthusiasm for his methods which the editor exhibits on returning (*Phoenixiana*, pp. 93-115; and Twain's "How I Edited an Agricultural Paper," *Sketches New and Old*, p. 307). However, it must be noted that such topics as burlesques of spiritualists, dramatic reviews, and bad poetry are widely used by other humorists than Derby.

[41] For example, Phoenix remarks of a man who has spoken slightingly of his literary efforts, "I pity that person, and forgive him." This comment, with variations, became a favorite with Mark Twain for use in like circumstances. And Phoenix's exclamation on taking a drink of bad liquor, "Turpentine and aqua fortis!" is echoed by Mark Twain's "Turpentine, *aqua fortis*, and brimstone!" on a similar occasion.

discussion permits the use of but one, as an illustration of technique
—that of euphemizing a painful truth.[42] One fact, however, should
be stressed: it is significant that Twain follows Phoenix in shunning
the device of cacography, except on rare occasions, in spite of the
fact that this device was inordinately popular among the funny men
of the period.[43]

An examination made with regard to dates will show that the
passages selected from Twain's work and presented here as suggesting influences from Phoenix, range from the "Petrified Man"
story of October 5, 1862, to the "solitary oesophagus" which "slept
upon motionless wing" in 1902—representing forty years of Mark
Twain's life as an author. That is a long time for an "influence" to
persist, however faintly. The records offer evidence that Mark
Twain had an opportunity to know of Phoenix in his youth; he
speaks directly of the California humorist in his middle life, and
again in the reminiscences of his later years.[44]

It is extremely doubtful whether Mark Twain had the slightest
sense of guilt in his relationship to John Phoenix. For years he believed himself to be the most original of men, and once denounced
plagiarism as "a crime I never have committed in my life."[45] Later,
however, he found out that he had stolen, quite unconsciously, the

[42] Phoenix relates that "Joe Bowers the elder," who was "engaged in business as a
malefactor," finally "ended his career of usefulness, by falling from a cart in which he
had been standing, addressing a numerous audience, and in which fall he unfortunately
broke his neck" (*Phoenixiana*, pp. 221-222). The same trick of literary comedy is
employed in the passage in which Twain speaks of a man who was hanged as having
"received painful injuries which terminated in his death." But, again, it must be stated
that such devices are generally used by other humorists than Derby.

[43] For example, Artemus Ward, Petroleum V. Nasby, Bill Arp, and Josh Billings.
In the periodicals of San Francisco, however, ". . . the trend was toward . . . a distinctive
thing that Bret Harte had and . . . that was the very character of Mark Twain. It had
flashed out in the Gold Rush with John Phoenix. . . . What the San Franciscans discovered was that their western humor need not be illiterate." See G. Ezra Dane (ed.),
Letters from the Sandwich Islands . . . by Mark Twain (Stanford University Press, 1938),
Introduction, p. vii.

[44] DeVoto has noted that the May 1, 1852, issue of the *Carpet Bag*, which contained
the earliest sketch by Mark Twain that has been discovered—"The Dandy Frightening
the Squatter"—contained also a drawing by John Phoenix. If Mark Twain read the
Carpet Bag around the time when his own sketch appeared in it, he must have known
something of the work of Phoenix; Mark was then seventeen years old. In *Roughing It*,
published when he was thirty-seven, Mark relates a humorous anecdote of a soldier stationed
at Fort Yuma, and remarks that the story has been "attributed to John Phoenix" (chap.
lvi). And in the *Autobiography* (I, 25-26), he tells a Phoenix story which was passed
on to him by General Grant, and speaks of Phoenix as "a West Point man."

[45] *Letters*, I, 182.

dedication of Oliver Wendell Holmes's *Songs in Many Keys*, and had used it as the dedication for his own *Innocents Abroad;*[46] thereupon, his opinions on plagiarism suffered a sea change. In 1875 he went so far as to write to Howells: "I would not wonder if I am the worst literary thief in the world, without knowing it."

George Horatio Derby died in 1861, at the age of thirty-eight, and "John Phoenix" ceased to exist. There is no intention here to display Mark Twain as rising from the ashes of the Phoenix in the fabulous way of the legend; but enough textual evidence has been presented to show that John Phoenix served Mark Twain well.[47] Certainly, Twain's connections with the Southern and Southwestern humorists should not be minimized;[48] but neither should an attempt be made to narrow his "influences" to that group alone. Mark Twain is a synthesis of American humor. Constance Rourke was near the truth when she said that his "scope was nation-wide, because of the quality of his imagination. . . ."[49] And Mr. DeVoto's statement is at least questionable when he writes of John Phoenix: "His work was somehow amusing . . . but he suggested nothing whatever to Mark Twain."[50]

[46] *Autobiography*, I, 238-242; see also *Letters*, I, 267; II, 732. Evidences of Mark Twain's photographic memory of what he read and his keen retentiveness of what he heard, are to be found elsewhere. The sensitive plates of his mind would have been especially receptive to humorous material, printed or oral, as the field in which he himself was a skilled practitioner.

[47] Mr. Stewart offers as "a good example of that process of folk-lore by which the great grow greater by assuming the exploits of the less," the fact that in 1935 in their book, *I Wish I'd Said That*, Jack Goodman and Albert Rice attribute to Mark Twain a story originated by Phoenix. (See Stewart, *John Phoenix*, p. 203; the story appears in *Phoenixiana*, pp. 113-115.)

[48] In 1915 Mr. Pattee (*op. cit.*, p. 28) ranked Phoenix above Longstreet, Harris, and Baldwin; but present-day critics place the humor of character and environment in which the Longstreet group excelled—"the comedy of background, custom, and character" (Blair, *op. cit.*, p. 62)—on a higher level than the humor of mere verbal devices of which Phoenix was a consummate master.

[49] *American Humor: A Study of the National Character* (New York, 1931), p. 219.

[50] *Op. cit.*, p. 166.

Mark Twain as Translator from the German
Dixon Wecter

MARK TWAIN'S use of German was more fluent than accurate. On the eve of his first trip to Germany, in the spring
of 1878, he began vigorously to learn that tongue, hired a German
nurse for his children, and soon was finding the language so comic
that he thought of having Captain Wakeman (Stormfield) in
Heaven ensnared in the Laokoon of German syntax.[1] Soon, it appears, he began to speak and write a German of sorts—or a piquant
blend of German and English—helped by his innate gift of the gab,
that Western relish for sonorous idiom that underlay his love of
declamation and profanity. The endless sentences and mouth-filling
compounds in German struck him as inexhaustibly funny. The
Teutonic language was a joke that never palled for this innocent
abroad. In 1878 he wrote polyglot letters from Heidelberg to
Bayard Taylor, full of Anglo-German atrocities.[2] In 1887, for a
German study class that met in the Clemens home in Hartford, he
wrote a three-act play called *Meisterschaft,* about the struggles of
beginning German.[3] Later, before the Vienna Press Club on November 1, 1897, Twain delivered his speech "Die Schrecken der
Deutschen Sprache," in comic German, asking the arbiters of the
language to ban parentheses and the introduction of more than
thirteen subjects to the sentence—averring, "Ich bin ja der treuste

---

[1] Albert Bigelow Paine, *Mark Twain: A Biography* (New York and London, 1912),
II, 616.
[2] J. R. Schultz, "New Letters of Mark Twain," *American Literature,* VIII, 47-51 (March,
1936).
[3] Given twice by the class with great success, and later published in the *Century* (Jan.,
1888) and in the volume *Merry Tales* (New York, 1892). The original MS, now in the
Huntington Library (HM 11610), contains the following unpublished note—addressed
probably to a printer in the house of Charles Webster & Company—ordering a trial impression unknown to bibliographers of Mark Twain:

Hartford, Aug. 8, /87.

Dear Van:
Please set me this up, & after you have got your proof as clean as you can, send *me* a

Freund der deutschen Sprache."[4] A few months later, in Vienna in
1898, he wrote out the anecdote called "Beauties of the German
Language," about compound words; and in March, 1899, still in
Central Europe, he made two more short speeches on the drollery
of the language.[5] A recent monograph by Dr. Edgar H. Hemming-
haus, in tracing the curve of Mark Twain's reputation in Germany,
has recalled the difficulty of rendering his puns and peculiarly
American humor into German.[6] But no special attention has been
paid hitherto to Mark Twain's attempt to turn some famous German jingles into English, and a preface he wrote for this little
volume has not been published up to the present time.

In 1935, the centenary of the humorist's birth, Harper and
Brothers published for children and for Mark Twain collectors a
slender book called *Slovenly Peter / (Struwwelpeter)/ or/ Happy
Tales and Funny Pictures/ Freely Translated/ By/ Mark Twain./
With Dr. Hoffmann's illustrations, Adapted from/ the Rare First
Edition, by Fritz Kredel.* It is based of course upon the familiar
rhymes first published in 1842 by the physician Heinrich Hoffmann.
The Preface to this volume, by Clara Clemens Gabrilowitsch, states
that her father made these translations in Berlin "that winter
[1891]," where, following "financial losses," the Clemens family had
taken a dismal flat; that Mark Twain kept up his spirits by rendering these rhymes of rebellious children, whose defiant spirit was not

---

proof & I will correct it & return it to you, & ask you to strike off two or three perfected
copies for me to forward to the "Century."

You needn't put in any small-caps or italics *any*where. I'll fix all that anew before
publication in the Century.

Keep the thing private. Don't let it get out of your hands.

Yrs truly
S L Clemens

Return the MS to me to read proof by.

On p. 14-E of this MS appears this explicit message signed "S L C":
Private:

Van, those "für's" are fur with dots over the u: *für.*

See Dr. Ada M. Klett, "Meisterschaft, or the True State of Mark Twain's German,"
American-German Review, VII, 10-11 (Dec. 1940), finds evidence that the manuscript
underwent correction "by some more or less competent hand" before publication, with the
suppression of Twain's most howling mistakes.

    [4] *Mark Twain's Speeches* (New York and London, 1910), pp. 42-51.
    [5] *Ibid.,* pp. 52-54 and 55; and Mark Twain's *Autobiography,* ed. A. B. Paine (New York
and London, 1924), I, 164-166.
    [6] *Mark Twain in Germany* (New York, 1939). Cf. Ulrich Steindorff, "Mark Twain's
Broad German Grin," New York *Times,* July 13, 1924, and Stuart Robertson, "Mark Twain
in German," *Mark Twain Quarterly,* II, 10-12 (Fall, 1937).

unlike his own; but that soon after their occupation of this flat he was called to America, where he found the financial outlook brighter, and "a month or two later" before returning to Germany in time for Christmas he cabled his family to move to better quarters. This account of Clemens's activities does not square with that given by Albert Bigelow Paine.[7] Since the former is a girlhood memory from the age of seventeen, and the latter a narrative supported by dated letters, one is prone to accept Paine as more trustworthy. According to Paine, an "attractive, roomy place" had been engaged by Mrs. Clemens in October, 1891, before her husband and three young daughters reached Berlin. Upon their arrival, and in the clear light of day, the neighborhood of No. 7 Körnerstrasse was found to be frowsy and not very quiet. Making a wry joke of their address among socially critical friends, the Clemenses weathered it out until the end of December, 1891; then, after paying the rest of their year's rent, they vacated the flat and moved to the Hotel Royal, Unter den Linden. Mark Twain indeed was none too prosperous, with the disaster of the Paige typesetting machine just breaking upon him, but he did not sail for a brief visit to America until mid-June, 1892, more than three months after they had quitted Berlin for the South of France. Mark Twain's own preface, it will be seen, is dated "Berlin, October, 1891," and must certainly have been written soon after his arrival from Lausanne in that month.

The manuscript of these translations, comprising twenty-six pages wholly in Mark Twain's hand, was sold in December, 1912, by a Boston bookseller to the late Willard S. Morse, Twain collector and bibliographer.[8] Morse submitted his purchase to Albert Bigelow Paine, who confessed that he had never heard of its existence, and called it a "unique item." To C. W. Fisk on December 17, 1912, Paine wrote:

"Struwel Peter" was a favorite of M. T.s & I am not surprised to know that he translated it . . . M. T. translated a good many such things for German practice—Mary's Little Lamb (into German) etc. I did not consider the items important enough to mention, though I did not *know* of "Peter"—

[7] *Mark Twain: A Biography*, II, 929-948.
[8] It came to him from the papers of Mr. William Cushing Brambury, who did not know just how or when his father had acquired it. This MS and the correspondence relating to it are now in the possession of Mrs. Willard S. Morse, Santa Monica, Calif., to whose kindness I am indebted for the quotations that follow.

A few months later, on May 1, 1913, Paine wrote to the new owner of the manuscript:

My opinion is that Mr. Clemens began it, expecting to print it, but by the time he had finished it he had realized that he had departed too far from the original for that; had burlesqued it too much, perhaps, and so gave it as a literary curiosity to some friend.

Confident that he possessed an item of great rarity, Mr. Morse applied to Harper for permission to print a limited edition, but the request was denied. Nevertheless, in March, 1915, he had twenty-five copies privately printed, but did not circulate them and apparently mislaid the entire lot.[9] But since the manuscript has remained untouched and apparently unseen among Mr. Morse's papers, in the many years following his death, it seems clear that one of these copies was recovered and served as the text for Mrs. Gabrilowitsch's edition. Missing from her volume is the following preface found in the Morse manuscript:[10]

Introduction.

Struwelpeter is the best known book in Germany, & has the largest sale known to the book trade, & the widest circulation. For nearly fifty years it has had its home in every German nursery. No man can divine just where its mysterious fascination lies, perhaps, but that it *has* a peculiar & powerful fascination for children is a fact that was settled long ago.

The book was not an intention—it was an accident. Dr. Hoffmann had among his child-patients some who raised war when he tried to insert the formidable medicines of the olden time into them; & to pacify them he used to snatch a pencil & dash off an absurd picture & a verse or two of descriptive doggerel & win a quick peace with them. These things accumulated on his hands & one day he pasted them together & made a Christmas book for his little son out of them. Grown people were taken with it, & persuaded him to publish it. The result astonished him; the book swept the country like a prairie fire—swept Europe, in fact, for it

[9] Willard S. Morse to Ulrich Steindorff, Oct. 2, 1924. Merle Johnson, *A Bibliography of the Works of Mark Twain*, New York and London, 1935, p. 110, states that these were photostats with a printed title page, and comprised "ten or so copies." The existence of a photostat of the manuscript among Morse's papers leads me to believe that his "edition" may have been in the form of photostats rather than a transcribed and printed text; but his statement that there were twenty-five copies is probably more trustworthy than the rather vague recall of Morse's agent whom Mr. Johnson interviewed.

[10] I find that the three last sentences of this preface are quoted by Merle Johnson, *op. cit.*, p. 110, from a privately printed edition issued in August, 1935, for the Limited Editions Club. This edition, which I have been unable to see, may print the entire preface as here given.

was soon translated into the principal languages of the continent, &
achieved popularity every where.

It was Dr. Hoffmann's opinion that the charm of the book lay not
in the subjects or the pictures, but wholly in the jingle. That may be
true, for rhymes that jingle felicitously are very dear to a child's ear. In
this translation I have done my best to fetch the jingle along.

Mark Twain

Berlin, October, 1891.

The translations which follow are indeed free. The original is
"seen darkly, as through a glass eye," as Mark Twain observed in
another connection. But the result is an increase of vigor. A trivial
though typical example may be taken from the story of Ugly
Frederick—a lad who, in the tradition of Hogarth's "Progress of
Cruelty," caught flies and dismembered them ("made hoppers of
them, minus wings," as Mark Twain phrases it). The climax of his
violence,

> Und höre nur wie bös er war:
> Er peitschte seine Gretchen gar!

which is rendered by the best-known English translation, issued by
John C. Winston, as

> And oh! far worse and worse
> He whipp'd his good and gentle nurse!

appears in Mark Twain as

> And worst of all that he did do,
> He banged the housemaid black and blue.

Cruel to a dog, Frederick is deservedly bitten and packed off to
bed to take bitter medicine, while the dog inherits the miscreant's
supper. Four lines in the German text and in more literal translations[10] are required to tell this last act, but Mark Twain expands
them into sixteen, with a footnote attached to his worst couplet—

> The dog's his heir, and this estate
> That dog inherits, and will ate.#

My child, never use an expression like that. It is utterly unprincipled

[10] As in the translation of *Struwwelpeter* by Annis Lee Furness, bearing the subtitle *The
Pictures and Verses as Remembered by the Children of Ralph Waldo Emerson* (Boston,
n.d.). Her father, the Reverend William Henry Furness, gave a copy of her translation to
his old friend and classmate Emerson, for Emerson's children, who years later, after the
original was lost, reconstructed it from memory. In this passage, and elsewhere, it follows
the German more timidly than does Twain.

& outrageous to say ate when you mean eat, & you must never do it except when crowded for a rhyme. As you grow up you will find that poetry is a sandy road to travel, & the only way to pull through at all is to lay your grammar down & take hold with both hands. *M. T.*

Current allusions are plentiful, as in the tale of three Nordic boys who deride a miserable Moor:

> The three they laugh and scoff and wink,
> And mock at that poor Missing Link,
> Because his skin is black as ink.

The original, needless to say, has no such Darwinian inflection of phrase—in telling a story of retribution that Nazis might well ponder today. In the "Story of the Thumb-Sucker" Mark Twain improves upon the description of Konrad's pain when his thumb is sheared off by the tailor, "Hei! Da schreit der Konrad sehr":

> While that lad his tongue unfurled
> And fired a yell heard 'round the world.

The vivacity of Mark Twain's version shows clearly in "The History of Hanns Stare-in-the-Air." In "Die Geschichte vom Hanns Guck-in-die-Luft" we read:

> Einst ging er an Ufers Rand
> Mit der Mappe in der Hand.
> Nach dem blauen Himmel hoch
> Sah er, wo die Schwalbe flog,
> Also dass er kerzengrad
> Immer mehr zum Flusse trat.
>   Und die Fischlein in der Reih'
>   Sind erstaunt sehr, alle drei.

The version remembered by Ralph Waldo Emerson's children runs, with less color than the original—

> Johnny took up his satchel one day
> And off to school he walked away.
> Which way he was going he didn't think,
> And it brought him down to the river's brink.
> Three little fishes at him did stare
> Wondering much what brought him there.

Vastly more spirited is Mark Twain:

> Once he snooped along the strand
> With his atlas in his hand,
> And his pug-nose tilted back
> So he could watch the swallow's track,
> And never got it through his gourd
> That he was walking overboard,
> Although the fishes, frightened, shout,
> "We three are orphans, please look out!"

Strongly stamped with the individuality of Mark Twain, *Slovenly Peter* offers the rare spectacle of the humorist turning his hand to verse. I am informed by sellers of children's books and attendants in children's rooms of public libraries that, in the six years since its publication, their young patrons in general have preferred the older, more conventional Winston translation to Mark Twain's *Struwwelpeter*. Perhaps they are more innately conservative than was Mark Twain himself.

Mark Twain's Lecture Tour of 1868–1869:
'The American Vandal Abroad'
Fred W. Lorch

IN A NUMBER of ways the tour of 1868-1869 was the most important in Mark Twain's entire career as a public lecturer. While it was not in a strict sense his first tour,[1] it was nevertheless his first extensive one, lasting an entire lecture season, and his first under the management of a lecture bureau. It opened up for him a rapid and exceedingly profitable way of earning a living—a matter of great importance to him; it assured him that he could please Eastern audiences as well as those in the Far West; it greatly increased his reputation as a humorist; and above all, it convinced him, as we shall see, that he could safely rely upon his own judgment in the selection and treatment of the materials of his lectures. It must be added, however, that it also revealed to him the exhausting hardships of constant travel and the painful loneliness of a full lecture season. There can be little doubt that his reluctance to engage himself to Redpath for later tours and his occasionally expressed hatred for the lecture platform had their earliest roots in the season of 1868-1869.

I

The subject which Mark Twain finally chose for the tour lecture was "The American Vandal Abroad," based on the *Quaker City* Holy Land excursion which he had participated in the preceding year. Surprisingly, the choice of the *Quaker City* material was not easy; nor was it his first choice, despite its freshness and the fact that his mind was full of it since he had just completed the manuscript of *Innocents Abroad,* based upon the same material. An examination of the newspaper record of the tour shows clearly

---

[1] Mark Twain's first tour was, of course, the brief one during the fall and winter of 1866-1867, after his return from the Sandwich Islands. For a detailed discussion of this, see Walter F. Frear's *Mark Twain in Hawaii* (Chicago, 1947).

that in the early stages of planning he had authorized Redpath
to advertise at least two other lectures: "The Sandwich Islands,"[2]
which he had given with much success during the season of 1866-
1867, and a new lecture on California.[3] Interesting, too, is the fact
that even after Mark Twain had decided upon the "Vandal" lecture,
he had trouble selecting a satisfactory title for it. Here again the
newspaper record proves helpful. At Newark, New Jersey, for
example, the title announced was "Brother Jonathan Abroad,"[4]
while at Norwich, New York, it was "American Vandals in the
Old World."[5]

It is apparent that the decision to use the *Quaker City* material
for his lecture caused Mark Twain a good deal of concern. And
that concern was rooted in the role which Mary Mason Fairbanks,
his literary guide of *Quaker City* days, attempted to play in the
preparation of the lecture. Actually Mark Twain faced two decisions: whether to use the *Quaker City* material rather than his
old "Sandwich Islands" lecture or the new lecture on California;
and whether to frame the *Quaker City* lecture (after his decision
to use it) according to his own judgment and desire rather than
submit to the dominating influence of Mrs. Fairbanks.

With regard to the first decision, there is considerable reason
for believing that he distrusted his ability to satisfy Mrs. Fairbanks
that he could lecture on the "Vandal" material without giving
offense.[6] He knew that she was displeased with the extremely
satiric and, in her opinion, ill-natured article about the *Quaker
City* excursionists which he had written for the New York *Herald*
the night the ship had reached port.[7] Nor was she, in all proba-

---

[2] Lansing, Michigan, *Republican*, Dec. 17, 1868.

[3] See this writer's "A Note on Mark Twain's Lecture on the Far West," *American
Literature*, XXIV, 377-379 (Nov., 1952). The discovery of the announcement of the
"California" lecture in the Charlotte, Michigan, *Republican*, Dec. 23, 1868, reveals Mark
Twain's early interest in the California material. No evidence has been found, however,
to show that Mark Twain ever lectured on California.

[4] *Daily Advertiser*, Dec. 8, 1868.

[5] Chenango *Union*, Dec. 9, 1868.

[6] See Mark Twain's letters, pp. 37-46 in *Mark Twain to Mrs. Fairbanks*, ed. Dixon
Wecter (San Marino, California, 1946).

[7] Printed in the *Herald*, Nov. 20, 1867. In a letter to a friend Mark Twain confided that "even Mrs. Fairbanks felt hurt" by it (*Mark Twain to Mrs. Fairbanks*, p. 2).
Though Mark Twain protested that the article was not ill-natured, it is obvious that he
knew it would sting, for after he had finished writing the *Herald* article he wrote his
mother that it would "make the Quakers get up and howl in the morning" (Samuel
C. Webster, *Mark Twain, Business Man*, Boston, 1946, p. 94).

bility, pleased with his lecture about the excursion which he had delivered in Washington, D. C., the preceding January. While this lecture, if one may judge from the extended portion printed in the Washington *Evening Star* of January 10, 1868,[8] was less ill-natured than the *Herald* article, it was nevertheless satiric in tone and contained passages in dubious taste.

The second decision—to frame the lecture according to his own desire and judgment—was in every way a decision of primary importance for Mark Twain. It constituted in a real sense an assertion of his freedom as a literary personality from the well-intentioned but misguided and emasculating influence of "mother" Fairbanks. There is no doubt that Mark Twain accepted and valued her advice to be "funny without being vulgar."[9] He was also convinced of the wisdom of avoiding profanity, slang, and other inelegancies of language.[10] But it is evident that he was not willing to surrender to her his judgment concerning the kind of lecture he was to give. It was probably his uneasiness on this score that caused him during the early stages of tour-planning to consider other lecture subjects rather than to risk using the "Vandal" material.

The extent to which Mrs. Fairbanks attempted to guide Mark Twain in the building of the Vandal lecture, and to influence its tone and character, is indicated in two letters. On September 24, 1868, he wrote to her, "Don't be afraid to write sermons—I am perfectly willing not only to receive them but to try to profit by them. Your advice about the building of the lecture I shall strictly follow. I shall try very hard to make it a creditable one. If diligent effort will do this I shall accomplish it."[11] A little later in the same letter he added significantly, "what I want a hundred times more than 'study' is a cheerful day—an untroubled spirit."[12] A few days later, in a letter dated October 5, we learn that she had sent him, but he had not yet received, a list of "main heads" for the lecture.[13]

[8] The title of this lecture, as printed in the Washington *Evening Star*, was "The Frozen Truth."

[9] *Mark Twain to Mrs. Fairbanks*, p. 18.

[10] *Ibid.*, p. 34.   [11] *Ibid.*, p. 37.

[12] Mark Twain's troubled spirit was the result of Olivia Langdon's rejection of his proposal of marriage. Her letter had reached him a few days earlier, leaving him in no mood to study.

[13] *Mark Twain to Mrs. Fairbanks*, p. 39.

Close examination of the two letters, especially of the passage quoted from the letter of September 24, reveals quite clearly the sort of lecture Mrs. Fairbanks was planning for her "cub."[14] It was to be an informative discourse in which his experience, gained on the Holy Land excursion, was to be enriched and extended by "study," presumably of European culture and art. It was to be a dignified performance, free from slang, vulgarity, and bad taste. Certainly it was to avoid satiric and ill-natured attacks on his fellow excursionists.

But before her letter with the main heads reached him, Mark Twain saw the folly of trying to write a lecture altogether alien to his own thought and personality. In a letter that gently but decisively freed him, he wrote her, "I wrote that *lecture* the day before your letter came. . . .That is to say I 'smouched' a lecture out of my book. I had planned the lecture *just about* as you did, and wrote and wrote and kept on writing till I saw that I was never going to weave a web that would suit me. So then I altered the tittle [*sic*] to 'American Vandal Abroad,' and began again."[15] Then, after briefly outlining his lecture, he asked placatingly, "now that isn't ill-natured, *is* it?"[16]

II

Mark Twain opened his tour on November 17 at Cleveland, Ohio. The choice of Cleveland for the premier performance was by no means accidental. Not only did "Mother" Fairbanks live there but so did other good *Quaker City* friends whom he could count on.[17] Furthermore, Mrs. Fairbanks's husband was the pub-

---

[14] In a letter to Mrs. Fairbanks (Oct. 31, 1868) Mark Twain referred to himself as "your cub" (*ibid.*, p. 47).

[15] *Ibid.*, pp. 43-44.

[16] *Ibid.*, p. 45. In a letter to Olivia Langdon dated Oct. 30, 1868 (*ibid.*, p. 47), Mark Twain said, "I have got Mrs. Fairbanks in a stew again.—I named that lecture just for her benefit. And I sent her an absurd synopsis of it that I knew would provoke her wrath. . . . I like to tease her because I like her so." As a matter of fact, the newspaper reports of the lecture lead one to believe that the synopsis was fairly accurate. Its absurdity, if it was absurd, lay rather in the suggestions it contained of episodes and allusions which might give personal offense to *Quaker City* passengers than in the actual content of the lecture. Not a single hint was discovered in the newspaper accounts that Mark Twain's references to American Vandals were personal or ill-natured. That Mrs. Fairbanks was disturbed by Mark Twain's use of the word "Vandal" in the title of the lecture can well be understood. But her fears proved groundless, for Mark Twain took special care to define the term in such a way as to remove all possibility of offense. As a matter of fact the definition was one of the passages most frequently quoted, and always with approval.

[17] Mr. and Mrs. Solon Severance, among others.

lisher of the Cleveland *Herald*. Certainly Mark Twain was fully aware of the importance of any help which the *Herald* might give in getting his first Eastern tour off to a good start, and he was not diffident in seeking such help. A few days prior to his arrival in Cleveland he wrote Mrs. Fairbanks, "I would like *you* to write the first critique on this lecture—and then it wouldn't be slurred over carelessly, anyhow."[18]

During the remainder of November he appears to have lectured only twice more, once in Pittsburgh, Pennsylvania, on November 19, and again in Elmira, New York, November 23. It was on the occasion of this visit to Elmira, which lasted at least a week, that Olivia Langdon accepted him as a suitor.[19]

The engagements in December also seem to have been spotty and infrequent, numbering probably not more than a dozen. January, however, was booked solid, the tour taking him to Ohio, Indiana, Michigan, Wisconsin, Illinois, and Iowa. During most of February he was again lecturing in such proximity to Elmira as to make frequent visits to that city possible, and the record shows that he availed himself of every opportunity. In all probability, the number of lectures during February did not exceed twelve. The tour finally came to a close at Lockport, New York, on March 3, 1869, after which Mark Twain, following a probable stopover

---

[18] *Mark Twain to Mrs. Fairbanks*, p. 46.

[19] Mark Twain's presence in the city and his connection with the Langdons (though the Langdon name is not mentioned) was noted in the Elmira *Daily Advertiser* of Nov. 24 as follows: "A JOKE ON A JOKER—We heard a little story yesterday which we think our readers will enjoy, and we propose, therefore, to give it to them right here in a few words and without the slightest degree of exaggeration. A distinguished author and lecturer, now on a brief visit to Elmira, (we prefer not to mention his name,) previous to taking a walk down town, yesterday, examined a thermometer hanging just outside the door, to see how the weather was. The mercury indicating a degree of frigidity considerably below zero, he returned indoors and proceeded to put on various extra garments proper for such an extremely cold day. Among the appropriate articles of clothing thus appropriated to guard against the inclemency of the weather, were two California overcoats, one bear skin cap, another cap made of hare to cover the bear one, one woolen muffler, one pair of buckskin nether garments, two pairs of knitted oversocks, one pair of double soled boots, one pair of cloth overshoes, and one pair of snowshoes. Taking on his arm another overcoat and a blanket shawl he sallied out. A brief hurried walk brought him to the office of the friend whom he is visiting, in a condition of much perspiration, and as full of wonderment as Jim Smiley when David [*sic*] refused to jump. The removal of the extra garments and the vigorous application of a full sized palm leaf fan having restored the gentleman to his ordinary state of coolness, his astonishment was also disposed by a remark from the gentleman who is the fortunate possessor of that Russian jaw-bone, to the effect that a broken thermometer can hardly be relied on as an index of the weather. This little true story was not included in Mark Twain's capital lecture last night, we believe."

at Elmira, hurried to Hartford, Connecticut, to see his publisher concerning his forthcoming book.[20]

Before presenting the reception which Mark Twain and his lecture "The American Vandal Abroad" received, one should point out briefly the extent of the reputation and popularity of the rising young humorist as the tour opened. His first great book, *Innocents Abroad*, it must be remembered, did not appear until several months after the tour closed.[21] Consequently, the fame that came to him following its publication still lay in the future. Nevertheless, an examination of the news files show that in the fall of 1868 Mark Twain was already well known. Prior to his trip to the Holy Land his "Jumping Frog" story had, of course, been widely reprinted in Eastern and Midwestern newspapers to the delight of many readers. During that trip and for a number of weeks after his return, his letters to the New York *Tribune* and to the San Francisco *Alta California* had also circulated widely. Then, during the spring and summer of 1868, a veritable stream of humorous articles came from his pen.[22] Most of these went the rounds of the press, reaching many of the communities where he later had lecture engagements. If in the fall of 1868 people knew little of the man, it is evident that they knew the name "Mark Twain," and liked what he wrote.

Despite his obviously growing reputation, however, the fact remains that Mark Twain had as yet no solid literary achievement to his credit. He was a mere newspaper humorist—fresh, vigorous,

[20] Despite Wecter's assertion that the 1868-1869 tour was a heavy one (*Mark Twain to Mrs. Fairbanks,* p. 48) and Paine's statement that Mark Twain made "most of his nights count" (*Mark Twain: A Biography,* New York, 1912, I, 373), the fact remains that the total number of engagements for the season was not high when compared with that of some of the later tours. This writer has identified forty-one towns in which he lectured. On Feb. 1, 1869, Mark Twain wrote Frank Bliss at Hartford that he had "now lectured thirty-five or forty times . . ." (*Mark Twain to Mrs. Fairbanks,* p. 68). On the basis of this writer's investigation, the number of lectures from Feb. 1 to the end of the tour numbered less than twelve. It appears, therefore, that the total number of engagements for the season did not exceed fifty. Paine's assertion that Mark Twain lectured between fifty and sixty times (*op. cit.,* I, 379), was close, but his estimate that Mark Twain's earnings for the season were "something more than $8000" was much too high. On the basis of his customary fee of a hundred dollars per lecture (he sometimes earned less), his gross earnings did not exceed $5000 for the season, an estimate which is supported by a statement which Mark Twain made to his sister in a letter on Jan. 14, 1869, when he had met over half of his engagements (S. C. Webster, *op. cit.,* p. 103).

[21] *Innocents Abroad* was published in July, 1869.

[22] These articles appeared originally in the New York *Herald,* the *Saturday Press,* the *Sunday Mercury,* the New York *Tribune,* and other newspapers.

promising, to be sure, and different from Artemus Ward, recently dead, but with nothing really substantial to recommend him to local lecture committees with the responsibility of providing a season's program of talent. It was this fact which accounted in large measure for the small number of engagements which Mark Twain secured during the latter part of November and most of December. That was why he needed so much the strong support of Mrs. Fairbanks and of a metropolitan newspaper like the Cleveland *Herald*. And it was not till the favorable notices of these papers filtered through the exchanges and came to the attention of the local committees that requests for his lecture came pouring into the offices of James Redpath, his agent.

In response to his request to give the lecture a good "push-off" Mrs. Fairbanks prepared the people of Cleveland for Mark Twain's appearance by printing a series of notices of his coming, together with numerous brief "reminders." These began about nine days prior to the lecture. Furthermore, she reprinted three of his articles—an essay on Horace Greeley, "The Jumping Frog" story, and a letter to the editors of the *Herald* with the title "A Mystery."[23] This latter item had to do with a person who had passed himself off as Mark Twain in Cleveland a few months earlier.

Mrs. Fairbanks's report of the lecture appeared in the *Herald* on November 18, the day following the lecture. Though not extensive, it was completely favorable. It contained precisely the sort of comment which would please the lecture committees, and it dispelled Mark Twain's fears that she would find his humorous lecture insufficiently dignified and instructive.

The course of lectures before the Library Association [she reported], was inaugurated last evening by the brilliant entertainment of the humorist "Mark Twain." Notwithstanding the unpropitious weather, and strong competition of counter attractions in the way of amusements, Case Hall was early filled with an assembly who were prepared to criticize closely this new candidate for their favor. A few moments sufficed to put him and his audience on the best of terms, and to warm him up with the pleasant consciousness of their approval. For nearly two hours he held them by the magnetism of his varied talent.

We shall attempt no transcript of his lecture, lest with unskillful

[23] These appeared between Nov. 12 and 16, 1869.

hands we mar its beauty, for beauty and poetry it certainly possessed, though the production of a profound humorist.

We know not which to commend, the quaint utterances, the funny incidents, the good-natured recital of the characteristics of the harmless "Vandal," or the gems of beautiful descriptions which sparkled all through his lecture. We expected to be amused, but we were taken by surprise when he carried us on the wings of his redundant fancy, away to the ruins, the cathedrals, and the monuments of the old world. There are some passages of gorgeous word painting which haunt us like a remembered picture.

We congratulate Mr. Twain upon having taken the tide of public favor "at the flood" in the lecture field, and having conclusively proved that a man may be a humorist without being a clown. He has elevated his profession by his graceful delivery and by recognizing in his audience something higher than merely a desire to laugh. We can assure the cities who await his coming, that a rich feast is in store for them, and Cleveland is proud to offer him the first laurel leaf, in his role as lecturer this side the "Rocky Slope."[24]

Albert Bigelow Paine's assertion that Mark Twain's "Vandal" lecture was immensely popular is accurate.[25] Crowded houses and enthusiastic audiences greeted him almost everywhere. With few exceptions the reporters commended the lecture both for substance and for the speaker's manner of delivery. Like Mrs. Fairbanks, they had expected humor, but it is quite apparent that they were unprepared for his eloquence and for the beauty of his descriptions of Athens and Venice and the Egyptian Sphinx. The succession of beautiful word pictures moved one reporter to compare it to "a string of pearls from which the string had been lost."[26]

Inevitably there were comparisons of Mark Twain with Artemus Ward, especially in his slow, quaint way of saying things. But it was noted with pleasure that the new humorist placed no dependence upon uncouth spelling and local vernacular. He had none of the "swagger of the traditional Yankee joker," and his lecture "was without a single low or ungrammatical phrase."[27] Furthermore, Mark Twain seems to have gone through the whole

[24] Mrs. Fairbanks could not resist, however, printing the description of the Egyptian Sphinx which "thrilled his audience with admiration" (Cleveland Daily *Herald*, Nov. 18, 1868).

[25] *Mark Twain: A Biography*, I, 373.

[26] Fort Wayne, Indiana, *Daily Gazette*, Jan. 4, 1869.

[27] Peoria, Illinois, *Daily Transcript*, Jan. 12, 1869.

season of lecturing without a single lapse into bad taste. The tute-
lage of Mrs. Fairbanks and his desire to please her, coupled with
his eagerness to win the approval of Eastern audiences, no doubt
served to hold him in check.

Widely noted, of course, was Mark Twain's distinctive drawling
manner of speech, usually described as agreeable,[28] and his dry,
dead-pan humor, with the fun invariably coming in at the end of
a sentence after a pause.[29] The language, it was observed, flowed
easily and gracefully. Every word was distinctly articulated and
clearly heard.[30] The slow, drawling speech, the dry humor, and
the dead-pan face at first fooled some audiences into believing they
were in for a boring evening. "The awakening from this error,"
observed an Indianapolis reporter, "comes so suddenly, so thoroughly and so pleasantly too, that from this point on to the close of the
lecture, the doubter at first, is a willing and delighted captive,
drinking in every word. . . ."[31]

In later lecture tours Mark Twain, more at ease on the platform
and less under the shadow of Mrs. Fairbanks, resorted to a number
of devices at the beginning of a lecture to put his audience in a
receptive frame of mind. These "starters," to use Mark Twain's
phrase, ranged from an awkward, shambling walk from the wings
to the rostrum, to humorous self-introductions. In the 1868-1869
tour, however, there is no evidence that he used any of these devices.
Nevertheless, his platform manner impressed some reporters as
peculiar, indicating that it was new to lecture audiences. He "hangs
around loose," reported the Chicago *Tribune,* "leaning on the desk
or flirting around the corners of it; then marching and counter-
marching in the rear of it."[32] The loose manner, like the slow
drawl, however, was generally regarded as agreeable.

If the reporters noted Mark Twain's platform manner and the
manner of his speech, they also frequently took note of his personal appearance and found it pleasing. Well-dressed and trim
looking, he had, in 1868-1869, a thick shock of curly, reddish
brown hair, a well-defined mustache, sharp twinkling eyes, and
intelligent features. The following description, while obviously a

[28] Decatur, Illinois, *Republican,* Jan. 14, 1869.
[29] Chicago *Tribune,* Jan. 8, 1869.
[30] Decatur, Illinois, *Republican,* Jan. 14, 1869.
[31] Indianapolis *Journal,* Jan. 5, 1869.
[32] Jan. 8, 1869.

humorous exaggeration, is nevertheless worth presenting as a picture of Mark Twain during the tour:

Beset with long legs, he is five feet ten inches in his boots, weight
167 pounds, body lithe and muscular, head round and well set on a
considerable neck, and feet of no size within the ken of a shoemaker,
so he gets his boots and stockings always made to order. Next to Grant
he wears the belt for smoking.... Drink never crosses the threshold of
his humorous mouth.[33] Fun lurks in the corners of it. The eyes are
deep set and twinkle like stars in a dark night. The brow overhangs
the eyes, and the head is protected from the weather by dark and curling
locks. The face is eminently a good one, a laughing face beaming with
humor and genuine good nature. He looks as if he would make a
good husband and a jolly father.[34]

That Mark Twain read the newspaper accounts of his lectures
with considerable interest is clear from his references to them in
letters to Mrs. Fairbanks and Olivia Langdon. Aside from the
report which Mrs. Fairbanks wrote about his opening lecture at
Cleveland, he seems to have been most favorably impressed by a
critical appraisal in the Charlotte, Michigan, *Republican,* signed
"Brownie." Since he regarded Brownie as "a very good judge"[35]
of his lecture, it is offered here, in part, as a means of revealing
what Mark Twain considered to be an accurate and discerning appraisal of his art as a public lecturer.

After holding the audience spell-bound . . . before the sphynx [*sic*],
with its melancholy gaze over the past ages, or after contemplating
some beautiful scene like Venice, its silent palaces, its bridges, and gon-
dolas; or Athens looked down upon by bright moonlight from the
Acropolis, he would . . . take to his native element of quaint humor.
Then came in his laughable matter-of-fact vandalisms, which, while
enjoyed, also served to heighten the previous enjoyment. He mingled
in a little of the grotesque and just enough of the terrible to heighten
the glow of his humorous descriptions, while these, in turn, served, by
contrast, to enrich the splendor of his great pictures. It was this artistic
changing of the excitement for different faculties and the different sides
of our nature, that so completely entertained, and rested, and kept the
attention of the audience constantly fixed. This is all art, the very

[33] Mark Twain's abstinence from intoxicating liquors was about six weeks old, from
the proceeding November 26 (*Mark Twain to Mrs. Fairbanks,* p. 50).
[34] Chicago *Tribune,* Jan. 8, 1869.
[35] *Mark Twain to Mrs. Fairbanks,* p. 66.

highest kind; that consummate art which conceals itself under the perfect simplicity and naturalness . . . which, in choosing language, gives us a medium of such chrystaline [*sic*] clearness that language, by the hearer, is never thought of—the art that prunes, rejects, condenses, polishes and elaborates sentences, imagery and thought.

This artist seems intentionally to avoid all effort at sublimity and pathos. For there was not a particle of either of these great powers in his lecture. This, too, the artist learns—to know where he might fail and where he can safely venture.

In wit, of the keen, cold, sparkling kind, he might, doubtless, have given us enough; but good taste and that sympathy which is the source of genial humor, taught him to refrain. Cutting wit, unless for the tough hide of vice or bigotry, ought not to be cultivated or indulged in. . . . In this lecture there was not an unkind cut. . . . There was not a word to disturb anyone's belief, religious or political. . . . But when Theodore Tilden comes we shall probably all of us get disturbed. Among our old and cherished opinions we can then expect earthquakes. . . . We will then learn the difference between a humorist and a reformer.[36]

Despite Mark Twain's popularity on the platform and the high praise accorded him by reporters, he did not altogether escape unfavorable criticism. At Detroit, for example, the reporter chided Mark Twain, mistakenly, of course, for an assumed drawl which the reporter believed spoiled the effect of his finest sentences even though it was very taking.[37] At other cities he was admonished to speak louder, a criticism which probably revealed his lack of experience in adjusting his voice to the varying sizes of the lecture halls. The harshest criticism of his manner of speech appeared in the Indianapolis *Daily Sentinel*. ". . . of all the miserable speaking ever heard," the reporter complained, "Mark Twain certainly can get up the poorest. Imagine a singsong snuffling tone from the nose, never varying six notes, and frequently mumbling out so that no one could understand it, and imagine that tone proceeding from a rather good looking young man, who wears good clothes, but is apparently afraid of making a gesture, and who generally keeps one hand raised above him and resting on a desk which no one but Goliath could have read from with ease, and you have Mark Twain." If Mark Twain would ask his advice, the reporter added, he would "urge him to quit lecturing."[38]

[36] Dec. 30, 1868.   [37] Detroit *Free Press*, Dec. 23, 1868.
[38] Indianapolis *Daily Sentinel*, Jan. 5, 1869.

There were other criticisms of a more serious nature. These had to do with the substance of Mark Twain's lecture and with humorous lectures in general. When the reporter on the Chicago *Tribune* expressed his opinion that there was nothing in Mark Twain's lecture, and that everything in it was sacrificed to make the audience roar, he spoke approvingly. He was willing to accept humor for its own sake. Others reported merely that the lecture was something to be enjoyed, not remembered.[39] A few, however, felt that it was mostly nonsense and that the audience laughed at small witticisms.[40] They regretted to see that the majority of "our people desire humorous lecturers, and will not turn out to hear a sound, able exposition of ideas, or a beautiful description of the country and scenery. . . . Nonsense, and not sense is what they want. . . ."[41]

It may be that in the first flush of his popularity and success Mark Twain was scarcely aware of these unfavorable comments, since they appeared infrequently and were not given special prominence. Furthermore, if one may accept his own statement, societies which had asked for his lecture before the tour began wanted it as a relief from "the heaviness of their didactic courses."[42] Consequently, he felt called upon chiefly to entertain. Even so, Mark Twain thought it wise to make a gesture in the direction of the didactic by supplying his lecture with a moral, "which is Let the Vandal continue to travel—it liberalizes him and makes a better man of him (though the moral is an entirely gratuitous contribution . . .")[43]

Nevertheless, the criticisms that his lecture was uninstructive and that he was a mere humorist on the platform were prospectively

[39] Davenport, Iowa, *Democrat*, Jan. 15, 1869.
[40] Iowa City *Republican*, Jan. 20, 1869; Ottawa, Illinois, *Republican*, Jan. 21, 1869.
[41] Genesco, New York, *Valley Herald*, March 2, 1869.
[42] *Mark Twain to Mrs. Fairbanks*, pp. 45-46.
[43] *Ibid.*, p. 45. While Mark Twain's lecture "The American Vandal Abroad" was reported at length in some newspapers, except for brief passages, none of the reporters seems to have attempted an extensive stenographic transcript of it. For that reason, and also because, according to Mr. Wecter (*ibid.*, p. 43), fifty-seven manuscript pages of the lecture are preserved among the Mark Twain Papers collected in the University of California Library at Berkeley, California, no attempt has been made to offer a composite version from the newspaper accounts. In *Mark Twain's Speeches* (New York, 1923), pp. 21-30, Albert Bigelow Paine prints an extract of considerable length. It is apparent, however, from an examination of the newspaper reports of the lecture, that once Mark Twain had his material well in mind, he departed from a fixed text as impulse and the exigencies of the occasion dictated.

significant. In the tours that followed, a rising crescendo of such charges troubled him deeply and provoked him eventually to a vigorous defense of the humorous lecture as entirely worthy of favorable public attention.

But during the tour of 1868-1869 Mark.Twain seems to have been untroubled by these criticisms. He knew, from the enthusiastic receptions which had been accorded to him by audiences everywhere and from the almost universally favorable press notices, that his tour had been a success. He had every right to believe, as several newspapers reported, that he was the most popular American humorist since Artemus Ward. Most important of all, however, he now knew that he was his own man on the platform and that he could follow his own genius as a public lecturer.

The Pilot and the Passenger:
Landscape Conventions and the
Style of *Huckleberry Finn*
Leo Marx

Nowadays it is not necessary to argue the excellence of *The Adventures of Huckleberry Finn*. Everyone seems to agree that it is a great book, or in any event one of the great American books. But we are less certain about what makes it great. Why is it in fact more successful than most of Mark Twain's other work? No one would claim that it is free of his typical faults. It descends here and there to sentimentality, buffoonery, and (particularly in the closing chapters) just plain juvenility. Nonetheless we persist in regarding the novel as a masterpiece. How are we to account for its singular capacity to engage us? One persuasive answer to the question has been to say that the book's excellence in large measure follows from the inspired idea of having the western boy tell his own story in his own idiom.[1] From that seminal idea, it may be said, many of the book's virtues—the convincing sense of life, the fresh lyricism, the wholeness of point of view—follow as the plant from the seed. This approach is persuasive, but it is easier to assert than to demonstrate. My purpose is to establish, on the basis of historical evidence and explicit critical values, certain ways in which the use of the narrator contributed to the novel's greatness.

The point to begin with is that it is Huckleberry Finn's story. And what he imparts to it, in a word, is style. The style is unique. To get a vivid impression of its uniqueness one need only compare the novel with *Life on the Mississippi* and *The Adventures of Tom Sawyer,* the other books in which Clemens re-creates the world of the Mississippi Valley. The three are linked in many ways, but above all by geography. In each the landscape is a primary source of unity and meaning. The same countryside, indeed sometimes

---

[1] Today this view is something of a commonplace, and there would be no point in attempting to assign priorities. Much of my appreciation of its importance, however, I owe to Henry Nash Smith, and to the illuminating study by Paul Steward Schmidt, "Samuel Clemens's Technique as a Humorist, 1857-1872," unpublished Ph.D. thesis, University of Minnesota, 1951.

the same scene, is described in each. Take, for example, the lyrical description of the dawn in *Huckleberry Finn,* the passage beginning, "Two or three days and nights went by; I reckon I might say they swum by, they slid along so quiet and smooth and lovely." This celebrated piece of writing, recently cited as exemplifying our national manner in prose,[2] may serve as a measure of stylistic achievement. As it happens, a similar description of the sunrise is to be found in each of the other Mississippi books. (All three are reprinted at the end of this essay, and to follow the argument they should be read at once.) Anyone who reads them in sequence will, I am confident, be struck by the superiority of the *Huckleberry Finn* version. I mean later to discuss the grounds for this judgment; here it is only necessary to recognize the difference. It is an impressive difference, and one which obviously turns upon narrative method or, if you will, style. The distinguishing mark of style in turn is language.

But these remarks do not answer the original question. To say that vernacular narration is a distinctive feature of *Huckleberry Finn* is one thing; it is quite another to account for Mark Twain's success with that technique. After all, we know that he used it elsewhere without comparable results. Moreover, it means nothing to contend that the novel is great because it is written in the native idiom unless, that is, we mean to impute some intrinsic or absolute value to the vernacular. That would be ridiculous. What we want to know, then, is why this method worked best for Clemens at this juncture. I assume that only a strong need can have called forth so original a style.

One of Clemens's persistent motives, clearly, was to convey a certain experience of his native landscape. *The Adventures of Huckleberry Finn* is, among other things, the fulfilment of a powerful pastoral impulse. Probably no one needs to be told that. But what is perhaps less obvious is that the vernacular style made possible the expression of emotions Clemens had long been working to put in words. The three attempts to depict the sunrise on the Mississippi reveal something of that liberating process. In each case the "theme" is the same: the observer's sense of beauty and harmony of nature. But for some reason, in the *Huckleberry Finn*

---

[2] "The Emergence of a National Style," *Times Literary Supplement,* Sept. 17, 1954, pp. xii–xiv.

version Clemens manages to create for us what, in the other two, he had only been able to describe. When, in reading the three passages consecutively, we come to the last, a sudden release of imaginative energy makes itself felt. The whole experience comes into bright focus. Sentences flow in perfect cadence, without strain or stilted phrase or misplaced word. It is as if the shift to the vernacular had removed some impediment to fullest expression.

I

What the impediment was Clemens reveals in "Old Times on the Mississippi." This series of articles written for the *Atlantic Monthly* in 1875 was his first sustained effort to represent the valley society he had known before the Civil War. In those chapters which now comprise the first volume of *Life on the Mississippi* his theme is "learning the river." Here the narrator recalls his initiation into a unique western mystery: Mississippi piloting. He makes clear that this vocation has to be learned by an apprentice on the spot; no books, no school, no theory can equip him. What he has to learn is a new language—indeed a language of nature. It is not simply the abstract technique of piloting, but a particular piece of western geography which he must possess. He has to "know the river" by day and by night, heading upstream and heading downstream. He must memorize the landscape. It is this knowledge which will forever distinguish him from the uninitiated. When ignorant passengers gaze at the face of the water they see "nothing but . . . pretty pictures."[3] But when the trained pilot looks at the river the river tells its "mind" to him. Nature, he explains, has been made to deliver him "its most cherished secrets." This experience is exhilarating, and in re-creating it Clemens managed to impart the exhilaration to his prose. (Notice that the second volume, which lacks the theme, is dull by comparison.) Yet—and here the problem arises—the narrator confesses that in acquiring the new lore he loses something too: the "grace, the beauty, the poetry" of the majestic river. It is gone. In learning the matters of fact necessary to his western vocation the pilot loses, or so he thinks, the capacity to enjoy the beauty of the landscape.

To illustrate his dilemma he compares two ways of experiencing a sunset on the river. It is a brilliant sunset. First he describes it

[3] (New York, 1906), p. 83. The account of the sunset is on pp. 82-85.

as, in his innocence, he once might have enjoyed it. At that time he would have observed "soft distances," "dissolving lights," and "graceful curves." The painter's terms are significant. In much of Clemens's work we find landscapes similarly framed, noble pictures seen as through a "Claude glass." For instance, Venice, in *Innocents Abroad,* is like "a beautiful picture—very soft and dreamy and beautiful."[4] Or of Lake Tahoe, in *Roughing It,* we are told that a "circling border of mountain domes, clothed with forests, scarred with landslides, cloven by cañons and valleys, and helmeted with glittering snow, fitly framed and finished the noble picture."[5] Clemens was working, needless to say, within the convention of the picturesque. Yet it should be added at once that he was not entirely comfortable in that mode. He often betrays his dissatisfaction by making comedy of the elevated style. In *Innocents Abroad* he allows a description of a Mediterranean vista to reach grandiose rhetorical heights. Then he quickly destroys the illusion with a revealing and self-conscious gag: "[Copyright secured according to law.]"[6] A similar impulse, in *Roughing It,* leads him to say, of a "majestic panorama," that "nothing helps scenery like ham and eggs."[7] Clemens was a writer of travel books and he recognized, as these remarks indicate, that the established rhetoric of landscape portrayal could not bear steady exposure to the immediate human fact. But if that style, at least when most elegant, was ludicrous, how was a writer to convey the loveliness of scenery? Clemens manifestly did not know. He resorted again and again to the conventional mode, using it straight as well as for burlesque.

Returning now to the sunset in "Old Times," we find that Clemens uses a language as trite as the paintings he must have had in mind. The pilot, discussing the lost beauty of the scene, says that he once would have enjoyed the sight of boughs that "glowed like flame" and trails upon the water that "shone like silver." This vocabulary is the literary counterpart of the painter's picturesque, an appropriately conventional medium for a conventional idea of beauty. In the presence of nature the pilot stands "like one bewitched" in a "speechless rapture." But this ecstasy, observe, was what he felt before his initiation. Afterwards, ". . . if that sunset scene had been repeated, I should have looked upon it without

---

[4] (New York, 1906), I, 281.   [6] I, 134.
[5] (New York, '906), I, 186.   [7] I, 148.

rapture, and should have commented upon it inwardly after this fashion: 'This sun means that we are going to have wind to-morrow; that floating log means that the river is rising, small thanks to it; that slanting mark on the water refers to a bluff reef which is going to kill somebody's steamboat one of these nights. . . . that silver streak in the shadow of the forest is the "break" from a new snag. . . .'" And so on. Beauty, the pilot learns, is for those who see only the surface of nature. Behind every perception of the beautiful there is a fact of another sort. And once he knows the facts "the romance and beauty . . . [are] all gone from the river."

Of course it may be said that this is merely another statement of a familiar modern conflict between two modes of perception, one analytic and instrumental, the other emotive and aesthetic. So it is. But to dispose of the issue thus is to miss the special significance the alternatives had for Sam Clemens. In *Life on the Mississippi* each of these ways of apprehending the river characterizes a particular mode of life. One might say a particular culture. One culture is exemplified by the uninitiated spectators and the ignorant novice pilot; the other is reflected in the melancholy wisdom of the older man who tells the story. There are many differences between these two ways of life, but the most important is the relation to nature fostered by each. The passengers are strangers to the river. They lack the intimate knowledge of its physical character a pilot must possess. As spectators, well-trained to appreciate painted landscapes, they know what to look for. They enjoy the play of light on the water. This aesthetic response to nature, given the American geography, Clemens inevitably associates with the cultivated, urban East. But the pilot, on the other hand, is of the West, and his calling such that he can scarcely afford to look upon the river as a soft and beautiful picture. He is responsible for the steamboat. To navigate safely he must keep his mind on the menacing "reality" masked by the trail that shines like silver.

The pilot's dilemma is a recurrent theme of our nineteenth-century literature. It was an age which attributed special meanings to the landscape, particularly in America. At the level of popular culture images of the landscape were used to depict a national destiny as glorious and beautiful as the surface of the Mississippi at

sunset.[8] The nation's scenic splendor was a sign of divine blessing.
At the same time, however, this chosen people was engaged in
transforming the landscape it celebrated, and in fact subjecting it
to the same instrumental method the pilot had learned. Hence it is
understandable, quite apart from the influence of European philosophy or literature, that many of our writers were concerned with the
penalties and perils attendant upon piercing Nature's mask. Melville's Ahab, driven by a compulsion to penetrate the ocean of mere
appearance, also fears he may find "naught beyond."[9] Like the
pilot, however, he cannot turn back. For both men the need arises
as an almost inescapable consequence of native callings. In *Walden*
we find the identical symbolic motif. Again the water's surface is
a metaphoric boundary between the beautiful and another possible
reality. When Thoreau, submitting faith to a test, fills a glass with
the "matchless and indescribable light blue" water of the pond, he
finds that it is in fact colorless.[10] Throughout the century the alleged values of nature, including its beauty, disappear when considered too curiously. When the pilot's keen eye penetrates the
silvery trail he sees the menacing snag. There are two ways of
regarding the Mississippi, just as, in *Moby-Dick* there are "gentle
thoughts" above the Pacific's surface, and murderous sharks and
leviathans below.[11] Ahab and the pilot are committed to knowing;
they can only lament the sacrifice, as Ahab put it, of "low enjoyment" for a "higher perception."[12] The bedeviling question of the
age, however, was whether that perception was indeed higher.

This was not, for Clemens, an abstract philosophical issue. It
would be wrong to think of him, standing at an artist's proper remove, simply manipulating an interesting theme. For him the
dilemma had a more compelling and practical urgency: it was a

---

[8] Henry Nash Smith calls my attention to this account of sunset on the river: "When
the sun went down it turned all the broad river to a national banner laid in gleaming bars
of gold and purple and crimson; and in time these glories faded out in the twilight and
left the fairy archipelagoes reflecting their fringing foliage in the steely mirror of the
stream" (Clemens and Warner, *The Gilded Age,* New York, 1906, I, 42).

[9] Chap. xxxvi, "The Quarter-Deck."

[10] Chap. ix, "The Ponds."

[11] Chap. cxxxii, "The Symphony."

[12] Chap. xxxvii, "Sunset." The rest of the passage is of some interest in view of
Melville's symbolization of the same conflict with the same images: "Oh! time was, when
as the sunrise nobly spurred me, so the sunset soothed. No more. This lovely light, it
lights not me; all loveliness is anguish to me, since I can ne'er enjoy. Gifted with the
high perception, I lack the low enjoying power. . . ."

matter of style. He faced it as a writer of prose, and it was as a writer (he was no theorist) that he finally came to grips with it. His solution, if that is the correct word, was implicit in the choice of Huckleberry Finn as narrator of his own adventures.

II

In 1875, when Clemens began work on the Mississippi material, the problem of landscape description became more acute. Writing about the country he had known as a boy and pilot was not quite the same as writing about Venice or Lake Tahoe. Here, for one thing, the picturesque convention was even less appropriate. We may guess that his feeling for his native landscape was such that he aimed at a greater fidelity to experience than the standard mode allowed. But what was the alternative? As he apparently felt, the choice was between the sentimental views of the passengers and the analytical attitude of the pilot, between a lush picture and mere matters of fact. It was an impossible choice. If *Huckleberry Finn* is any indication, what Clemens wanted was to affirm the landscape's beauty *in its actuality*. To do so, though he surely did not realize it, he had to do nothing less than fashion a literary style. The three versions of the dawn on the river help us to understand something of that process.

In *Tom Sawyer,* which he wrote soon after "Old Times," we see the new mode taking shape. Here we have certain obvious holdovers from the older landscape tradition in the hackneyed use of personification and the sense of the event as pictorial spectacle. "The marvel of Nature shaking off sleep and going to work unfolded itself to the musing boy." On the other hand, the effort to include sharp detail is a gauge of Clemens's need to break out of the painter's style. The microscopic focus upon the green worm is well outside the picturesque, which dealt with the general, not the particular; with the remote, not the near; and above all, with a genteel notion of the beautiful, not worms. In the older mode man was an onlooker or, in the pilot's language, a passenger. (Human figures are rare, or in any case of little consequence, in picturesque landscapes.) But the worm's journey over Tom blends the boy into the fabric of nature, and points toward the well-nigh baptismal immersion of Huck and Jim in the river. Nevertheless, here in *Tom Sawyer* the older tradition remains dominant and finally reasserts itself. The passage progresses to a coda of gaudy pictorial banality: "All Nature was wide awake and stirring, now; long lances of sunlight pierced down through the dense foliage far and near, and a few butterflies came fluttering upon the scene."

Clemens finished *Tom Sawyer* in 1875. "I perhaps made a mistake," he remarked to Howells, "in not writing it in the first person."[13] The following year he began *The Adventures of Huckleberry Finn*. After completing roughly four hundred manuscript pages (or about the first sixteen of forty-two chapters) his inspiration waned and he abandoned the project for seven years.[14] Then, in 1882, he made a trip back to the river as the basis for the second volume of *Life on the Mississippi*. He finished it in 1883. It is an uneven, hasty and loosely put-together volume. But it illuminates the complex relationship between history and style: "The majestic bluffs that overlook the river . . . charm one with the grace and variety of their forms, and the soft beauty of their adornment. The steep, verdant slope . . . is topped by a lofty rampart of broken, turreted rocks, . . . exquisitely rich and mellow in color—mainly dark browns and dull greens, but splashed with other tints."[15] Again we have a painting with all the picturesque niceties, not excepting the castle. There are sleepy villages, stealthy rafts, and white steamers too. It is a glimpse of the old river, a scene "as tranquil and reposeful as dreamland." But then, suddenly, the "unholy train comes tearing along . . . with its devil's war-whoop and the roar and thunder of its rushing wheels." The railroad, emblem of industrial power, is the demon of the entire volume. It destroys steamboating and the natural beauty of the valley. And in the same stroke it renders the established landscape convention obsolete. Clemens, in this remarkable passage, admits as much. He describes

[13] July 5, 1875, *Mark Twain's Letters*, ed. Albert Bigelow Paine (New York, 1917), I, 258. Actually, Bernard De Voto has demonstrated that an early version of *Tom Sawyer* was written in the first person. It is now called "Boy's Manuscript," and probably dates from the years 1870-1872. See *Mark Twain at Work* (Cambridge, Mass., 1942), pp. 3-9. The MS itself is reprinted on pp. 25-44. This MS seems to support my contention that first-person narration itself is no key to the superiority of *Huckleberry Finn*. De Voto rightly calls this first attempt at fiction "crude and trivial, false in sentiment, clumsily farcical, an experiment in burlesque with all its standards mixed" (p. 7). The fact is that Clemens here used the technique in a thoroughly mechanical fashion. Though the boy is supposed to be talking, his words do not actually reveal a boy's attitude, as in *Huckleberry Finn*, but rather that of a bemused adult observing childish behavior.

[14] For the chronology I am following De Voto, *Mark Twain at Work*.

[15] P. 432.

the train, in a metaphor whose concealed term surely is a picturesque canvas, "ripping the sacred solitude to rags and tatters." The second volume of *Life on the Mississippi* marks the passing of a way of life, a mode of apprehending nature, and by inference, a literary style.

III

The increasing obsolescence of the style becomes apparent when we compare the two accounts of the dawn which Clemens wrote after his return to the river.

The first is in *Life on the Mississippi*. The narrator pretends to be a reporter on the spot. What he gives us, however, is another formal landscape painting, "one of the fairest and softest pictures imaginable." Of course it may be said that the style has a certain appropriateness. Clemens in this case actually was a kind of reporter, an official visitor from the East. Yet the passage scarcely succeeds as reporting; it might pass for a description of the dawn on the Rhine or the Amazon. Nor does it fit another role the narrator intermittently assumes, that of the ex-pilot who knows the score. His command of piloting is carefully avoided in honor of the "picture," as if beauty really requires the suppression of knowledge. There is no danger, no thought of treacherous snags. All is beautiful, "soft and rich and beautiful." As compared with the dawn in *Tom Sawyer* this is writing of a conventional order.

Indeed it represents a regression to a divided universe in which beauty and reality are hermetically separated. Nothing makes this compartmentalization of life plainer than the paragraph which follows the sunrise passage. There we find that although no snags are permitted to mar the sunrise, they have not ceased to haunt the pilot.

We had the Kentucky Bend country in the early morning—scene of a strange and tragic accident in the old times. Captain Poe had a small stern-wheel boat, for years the home of himself and his wife. One night the boat struck a snag in the head of Kentucky Bend, and sank with astonishing suddenness; water already well above the cabin floor when the captain got aft. So he cut into his wife's stateroom from above with an ax; she was asleep in the upper berth, the roof a flimsier one than was supposed; the first blow crashed down through the rotten boards and clove her skull.

There is no way, within the convention, to treat the beautiful and the murderous rivers as one. The style imposes a hopeless bifurcation of experience. In the second half of *Life on the Mississippi,* consequently, the past and the present, the beautiful and the actual, the benign and the tragic are discrete compartments of life. The result is not literature but a disorderly patchwork.

What happens next is, for an understanding of the creative process, the most illuminating part of the story. For apparently the disheartening journey, so perfunctorily reported in the one book, inspired Clemens to go back to work on his masterpiece. It had re-invigorated the pastoral impulse. He had described how the older and by now idealized society of the valley was being torn apart by the new industrial power. Now the unfinished manuscript offered him a chance to render it whole.[16] In art he might achieve a unified vision of the world he had seen being destroyed in fact. But this was not simply a matter of turning his attention to the past. Just as important was the technique of vernacular narration he had fashioned. It was a style which at last made possible a genuine celebration of the landscape.

These circumstances help to explain the extraordinary lyrical intensity of *Huckleberry Finn,* of which the sunrise is but one example.

There are countless descriptions in literature of the sun coming up across a body of water, but it is inconceivable that a substitute exists for this one. It is unique in diction, rhythm, and tone of voice. Certainly when we place it alongside the earlier versions we see at once how vital point of view can be. In *Life on the Mississippi,* the narrator, who is also supposed to be on the scene, self-consciously pictures the dawn for a distant audience. He stands apart and reports; his explicit aim is to tell his readers why they should believe him when he says that the scene is "enchanting." Huck, on the other hand, is a participant, at times literally immersed

---

[16] According to De Voto, Clemens stopped work on the manuscript just after describing the steamboat—its "long row of wide-open furnace doors shining like red-hot teeth"— colliding with the raft. Clearly the boat is a monstrous embodiment of the forces menacing freedom in this idyllic valley society. The fact that Clemens stopped work at this point is highly suggestive. One might infer that the dilemma posed by the industrial transformation of the society had been acting upon his imagination from the first, but that he had not yet settled upon the literary form of his response. For a parallel in the genesis of Hawthorne's fiction, see "The Machine in the Garden," *NEQ,* XXIX, 27-42 (March, 1956).

in the river he is telling about. Hence the immediacy of his account. The scene is described in concrete details, but they come to us as subjective sense impressions. All the narrator's senses are alive, and through them a high light is thrown upon the preciousness of the concrete facts. Furthermore, Huck is not, as in the two earlier versions, committed to any abstract conception of the scene. He sets out merely to tell how he and Jim put in their time. Because he has nothing to "prove" there is room in his account for *all* the facts. Nothing is fixed, absolute, or perfect. The passage gains immensely in verisimilitude from his repeated approximations: "soon as night was *most* gone," "*nearly always* in the dead water," "a *kind of* dull line," "*sometimes* you could hear," "*but sometimes* not that way." Nature, too, is in process: "the daylight *come*," "paleness *spreading* around," "river *softened* up," "mist *curl* up," "east *reddens* up," "breeze *springs* up." Both subject and object are alive; the passage has more in common with a motion picture than a landscape painting.

Huck, moreover, "belongs" to this landscape in that his language is native to it. Perhaps this fact, above all, accounts for the exquisite freshness of these lines. Sunrises have not changed much since Homer sang of the rosy-fingered dawn, but here is the first one ever described in this idiom. What is distinctive about it, in other words, ultimately derives from the historical distinctiveness of the narrator, his speech, and the culture from which both emerge. But particularly his speech, for that is the raw material of this art, and we delight in the incomparable fitness of subject and language. Observe, for example, the three successive efforts to convey the solitude and silence at dawn. (It was the "sacred solitude" that the railroad tore to tatters.) Compare: "deep pervading calm and silence of the woods": "eloquence of silence": "not a sound anywheres—perfectly still—just like the whole world was asleep, only sometimes the bullfrogs a-cluttering, maybe." The first is merely commonplace; "eloquence of silence" is neat and fine, and it has the merit of compression and (to invoke a currently popular critical test) paradox. The phrase is so good, in fact, that it has often been used. Yet relative novelty is not the main point. There is nothing novel about "just like the whole world was asleep" either. On the contrary, both phrases are familiar; the difference is that our familiarity with one

comes from the written, indeed the printed, word, and the other
from the spoken word. One bears the unmistakable mark of a man
bent on making phrases; it is literary; the other sounds like a boy
talking. The same may be said of several other parallels, such as
"the birds were fairly rioting": "jubilant riot of music": "the song-
birds just going it." Much of the superior power of *Huckleberry
Finn* must be ascribed to the sound of the voice we hear. It is the
voice of the boy experiencing the event. Of course no one ever
really spoke such concentrated poetry, but the illusion that we are
hearing the spoken word is an important part of the total illusion of
reality. The words on the page carry our attention to life, not to art,
and that after all is what most readers want.

My purpose, I repeat, is not to exalt vernacular narration as a
universally superior technique. Each writer discovers methods best
suited to the sense of life he must (if he is to succeed) create. In
this case, however, the vernacular method liberated Sam Clemens.
When he looked at the river through Huck's eyes he was suddenly
free of certain arid notions of what a writer should write. It would
have been absurd to have had Huck Finn describe the Mississippi
as a sublime landscape painting.

Accordingly Clemens, in spite of his evident effort to convey
the beauty of the sunrise, permits Huck to report that "by and by
you could see a streak on the water which you know by the look
of the streak that there's a snag there in the swift current which
breaks on it and makes the streak look that way." He is endowed
with the knowledge of precisely those matters of fact which had
seemed to impair the pilot's sense of beauty. Huck now accepts that
fearful principle of nature responsible for the death of Captain Poe's
wife. Now at last, through the consciousness of the boy, the two
rivers are one. Mingled with the loveliness of the scene are things
not so lovely: murderous snags, wood piled by cheats, and—what
could be less poetic?—the rank smell of dead fish. Huck is not the
innocent traveler, yet neither is he the initiated pilot. He sees the
snags, but they do not spoil his pleasure. In his person Clemens
reaches back to a primal mode of perception undisturbed by the
tension between art and science. It does not occur to Huck to choose
between beauty and utility. His willingness to accept the world as
he finds it, without anxiously forcing meanings upon it, lends sub-

stance to the magical sense of peace the passage conveys. When the lights of the river form a continuum with the stars, the boy's sense of belonging reaches the intensity of a religious experience; the two on the raft face the mystery of the creation with the equanimity of saints: "It's lovely to live on a raft. We had the sky up there, all speckled with stars, and we used to lay on our backs and look up at them, and discuss about whether they was made or only just happened."

IV

The passion we feel here may only be compared with love. It is not the conventional sentiment of the early landscapes, but the love of an object as it exists, in all its gloriously imperfect actuality. Indeed, this sequence of Clemens's attitudes toward the landscape is comparable, in several respects, to an intricate love relationship. In all three of the Mississippi books his deep feeling for the landscape is evident. But at first, as the pilot in *Life on the Mississippi* reveals, a conflict blocks its full expression. He tells of a violent shift from one extreme conception of nature to another. At first the landscape is sheer perfection—soft, rich, and beautiful; then it suddenly comes to seem a merely indifferent, if not hostile, force. After having been submissive and adoring, he now is wary and aggressive. But in *Huckleberry Finn* there is no trace of either attitude. Here the narrator feels neither adoration nor hostility. The boy gives us a full account of his experience of nature, sensations unpleasant as well as pleasant, matters of fact and matters of feeling, objects attractive and repellent. At dawn, on the river, Huck knows neither anxiety nor guilt, but an intense feeling of solidarity with the physical universe.[17]

[17] How revealing that Clemens, who seldom if ever was able to depict a mature love relation, should have been able to express this passion only in the words of an adolescent! Those interested in a psychological analysis of his work should examine this highly suggestive material. Notice, for example, the unmistakable sexual connotations of the two attitudes toward landscape. On the beautiful surface nature has obvious feminine characteristics (softness, dimples, graceful curves), but the subsurface is represented by objects with strongly masculine overtones (logs, bluff reefs, menacing snags). In Melville the symbolism is explicit. For instance, in the passage from "The Symphony" (see p. 134 above), the air is "pure and soft" and has a "woman's look," while in the waters beneath the sea rush mighty leviathans and sharks, the "murderous thinkings of a masculine sea." Perhaps these sexual identifications are the key to the alternating submission and aggression noted in Clemens's treatment of the landscape (an object, finally, of love)—as if he were projecting an inner conflict. Henry A. Murray has made the point about Melville ("In Nomine Diaboli," *NEQ*, XXIV, 435-452, Dec., 1951). Of course Melville and

It is obvious that this capacity for realistic affirmation coincides with the disappearance, however temporary, of the earlier conflict. Needless to say, the conflict was no mere fiction. It was vital to Clemens, as it was endemic in a society at once so passionately committed to—and at war with—nature. As a writer, however, he felt the destructive consequences of this tension most acutely in his work. It was impossible to do justice to American experience by treating nature, in the conventional manner, as benign and beautiful. Clemens knew better, and his continuing impulse was to parody the accepted mode. To him the landscape, no matter how lovely, concealed a dangerous antagonist. He knew that nature had to be watched, resisted and—when possible—subdued. Unfortunately this often meant its obliteration as an object of beauty, hence of love. Nothing impressed this upon Clemens with such force as what he saw happening to the Mississippi Valley in 1882.

In the incomplete manuscript of *Huckleberry Finn,* to which he then returned with renewed imaginative vigor, he found a solution. Here was a tale told by a boy who—granted his age, his education, and the time he lived—could not possibly feel the anxiety Clemens felt. To Huck nature was neither an object of beauty nor the raw material of progress. Or, rather, it was both. He was as tough and practical as the pilot, and as sensitive to color and line as an artist; he kept his eye on dangerous snags, but he did not lose his sense of the river's loveliness. Moreover, he spoke a language completely unlike the stilted vocabulary of the literary cult of nature. His speech, never before used in a sustained work of fiction, was as fresh and supple as his point of view. The interaction of a narrative technique and the heightened emotion to which that technique lent expression helps account for the singular power of the sunrise passage. Behind the mask of Huck Finn, Clemens regained that unity of thought and feeling he felt himself, along with his contemporaries, to be losing.

Clemens were not alone, among our nineteenth-century writers, in presenting an apparent antithesis between (feminine) beauty and (masculine) reality. The subject would seem to warrant close examination, particularly in view of the frequency with which social scientists have noted the conflict between aggressive competitiveness and a desire to yield as peculiarly characteristic of American society. See, e.g., Franz Alexander, *Our Age of Unreason* (Philadelphia, 1942); Arnold W. Green, "The Middle-Class Male Child and Neurosis," *American Sociological Review,* II, 31-41 (Feb., 1946); Karen Horney, *The Neurotic Personality of Our Time* (New York, 1937).

But this is not to say that Clemens had suddenly thought his way out of the dilemma. We have only to read his later work to see that he had not. What he did was to discover a way around it—a sublimation, as it were, of the conflict. The discovery came to him not conceptually, but spontaneously, in the practice of his art. For all the intricacies of a problem at once psychological, philosophical, and historical, the "solution" was simple and primarily aesthetic. In one sense it consisted merely of placing himself behind the mask of a narrator for whom the problem did not exist. This device, however, was only the first step; it provided a point of view—an ideological, not an aesthetic truth. The more difficult task was to endow this viewpoint, for which there existed no appropriate literary style, with literary vitality, with life. He accomplished this by maintaining a fidelity to the experience of his narrator so disciplined that it cut beneath established conventions. The point of view became a style. Unfortunately, Clemens did not realize the dimensions of this achievement. But since his time many of our best writers, responding to pressures not unlike those he felt, have recognized the usefulness of the mode he devised.

Nor was the vernacular style useful only to depict landscape. Most of the book is as fine, in various ways, as the sunrise passage. Clemens not only fashioned a vital style, he sustained it. Its merit was the product not so much of technical virtuosity as of the kinds of truth to which it gave access. *The Adventures of Huckleberry Finn* contains insights neither a pilot nor a passenger could have had. It is a book, rare in our literature, which manages to suggest the lovely possibilities of life in America without neglecting its terrors.

MARK TWAIN: THE THREE DAWNS

I

When Tom awoke in the morning, he wondered where he was. He sat up and rubbed his eyes and looked around. Then he comprehended. It was the cool gray dawn, and there was a delicious sense of repose and peace in the deep pervading calm and silence of the woods. Not a leaf stirred; not a sound obtruded upon great Nature's meditation. Beaded dewdrops stood upon the leaves and grasses. A white layer of ashes covered the fire, and a thin blue breath of smoke rose straight into the air. Joe and Huck still slept.

Now, far away in the woods a bird called; another answered; present-ly the hammering of a woodpecker was heard. Gradually the cool dim gray of the morning whitened, and as gradually sounds multiplied and life manifested itself. The marvel of Nature shaking off sleep and going to work unfolded itself to the musing boy. A little green worm came crawling over a dewy leaf, lifting two-thirds of his body into the air from time to time and "sniffing around," then proceeding again—for he was measuring, Tom said; and when the worm approached him, of its own accord, he sat as still as a stone, with his hopes rising and falling, by turns, as the creature still came toward him or seemed inclined to go elsewhere; and when at last it considered a painful moment with its curved body in the air and then came decisively down upon Tom's leg and began a journey over him, his whole heart was glad—for that meant that he was going to have a new suit of clothes—without the shadow of a doubt a gaudy piratical uniform. Now a procession of ants appeared, from nowhere in particular, and went about their labors; one struggled man-fully by with a dead spider five times as big as itself in its arms, and lugged it straight up a tree-trunk. A brown spotted lady-bug climbed the dizzy height of a grass-blade, and Tom bent down close to it and said, "Lady-bug, lady-bug, fly away home, your house is on fire, your children's alone," and she took wing and went off to see about it—which did not surprise the boy, for he knew of old that this insect was credulous about conflagrations, and he had practised upon its simplicity more than once. A tumblebug came next, heaving sturdily at its ball, and Tom touched the creature, to see it shut its legs against its body and pretend to be dead. The birds were fairly rioting by this time. A catbird, the Northern mock-er, lit in a tree over Tom's head, and trilled out her imitations of her neighbors in a rapture of enjoyment; then a shrill jay swept down, a flash of blue flame, and stopped on a twig almost within the boy's reach, cocked his head to one side and eyed the strangers with a consuming curiosity; a gray squirrel and a big fellow of the "fox" kind came scurry-ing along, sitting up at intervals to inspect and chatter at the boys, for the wild things had probably never seen a human being before and scarce-ly knew whether to be afraid or not. All Nature was wide awake and stirring, now; long lances of sunlight pierced down through the dense foliage far and near, and a few butterflies came fluttering upon the scene.
—*The Adventures of Tom Sawyer*, Chapter XIV.

II

I had myself called with the four-o'clock watch, mornings, for one cannot see too many summer sunrises on the Mississippi. They are en-chanting. First, there is the eloquence of silence; for a deep hush broods everywhere. Next, there is the haunting sense of loneliness, isolation, remoteness from the worry and bustle of the world. The dawn creeps in stealthily; the solid walls of black forest soften to gray, and vast stretches of the river open up and reveal themselves; the water is glass-smooth, gives off spectral little wreaths of white mist, there is not the faintest breath of wind, nor stir of leaf; the tranquillity is profound and infinitely satisfying. Then a bird pipes up, another follows, and soon the pipings develop into a jubilant riot of music. You see none of the birds; you simply move through an atmosphere of song which seems to sing itself. When the light has become a little stronger, you have one of the fairest and softest pictures imaginable. You have the intense green of the massed and crowded foliage near by; you see it paling shade by shade in front of you; upon the next projecting cape, a mile off or more, the tint has lightened to the tender young green of spring; the cape beyond that one has almost lost color, and the furthest one, miles away under the horizon, sleeps upon the water a mere dim vapor, and hardly separable from the sky above it and about it. And all this stretch of river is a mirror, and you have the shadowy reflections of the leafage and the curving shores and the receding capes pictured in it. Well, that is all beautiful; soft and rich and beautiful; and when the sun gets well up, and distributes a pink flush here and a powder of gold yonder and a purple haze where it will yield the best effect, you grant that you have seen something that is worth remembering.—*Life on the Mississippi,* Chapter XXX.

III

Two or three days and nights went by; I reckon I might say they swum by, they slid along so quiet and smooth and lovely. Here is the way we put in the time. It was a monstrous big river down there—sometimes a mile and a half wide; we run nights, and laid up and hid daytimes; soon as night was most gone we stopped navigating and tied up—nearly always in the dead water under a towhead; and then cut young cottonwoods and willows, and hid the raft with them. Then we set out the lines. Next we slid into the river and had a swim, so as to freshen up and cool off; then we set down on the sandy bottom where the water was about knee-deep, and watched the daylight come. Not a sound anywheres—perfectly still—just like the whole world was asleep, only sometimes the bullfrogs a-cluttering, maybe. The first thing to see, looking away over the water, was a kind of dull line—that was the woods on t'other side; you couldn't make nothing else out; then a pale place in the sky; then more paleness spreading around; then the river softened up away off, and warn't black any more, but gray; you could see little dark spots drifting along ever so far away—trading-scows, and such things; and long black streaks—rafts; sometimes you could hear a sweep screaking; or jumbled-up voices, it was so still, and sounds come so far; and by and by you could see a streak on the water which you know by the look of the streak that there's a snag there in a swift current which breaks on it and makes that streak look that way; and you see the mist curl up off of the water, and the east reddens up, and the river, and you make out a log cabin in the edge of the woods, away on the bank on t'other side of the river, being a wood-yard, likely, and piled by them cheats so you can throw a dog through it anywheres; then the nice breeze springs up, and comes fanning you from over there, so cool and fresh and sweet to smell on account of the woods and the flowers; but sometimes not that way, because they've left dead fish laying around, gars and such, and they do get pretty rank; and next you've got the full day, and everything smiling in the sun, and the song-birds just going it!

A little smoke couldn't be noticed now, so we would take some fish off of the lines and cook up a hot breakfast. And afterwards we would watch the lonesomeness of the river, and kind of lazy along, and by and by lazy off to sleep. Wake up by and by, and look to see what done it, and maybe see a steamboat coughing along up-stream, so far off towards the other side you couldn't tell nothing about her only whether she was a stern-wheel or side-wheel; then for about an hour there wouldn't be nothing to hear nor nothing to see—just solid lonesomeness. . . .

Sometimes we'd have that whole river all to ourselves for the longest time. Yonder was the banks and the islands, across the water; and maybe a spark—which was a candle in a cabin window; and sometimes on the water you could see a spark or two—on a raft or a scow, you know; and maybe you could hear a fiddle or a song coming over from one of them crafts. It's lovely to live on a raft. We had the sky up there, all speckled with stars, and we used to lay on our backs and look up at them, and discuss about whether they was made or only just happened. Jim he allowed they was made, but I allowed they happened; I judged it would have took too long to *make* so many. Jim said the moon could 'a' *laid* them; well, that looked kind of reasonable, so I didn't say nothing against it, because I've seen a frog lay most as many, so of course it could be done. We used to watch the stars that fell, too, and see them streak down. Jim allowed they'd got spoiled and was hove out of the nest.—*The Adventures of Huckleberry Finn,* Chapter XIX.

Mark Twain's *Joan of Arc:*
The Child as Goddess
Albert E. Stone, Jr.

FEW NATURAL EVENTS in the history of American letters seem in retrospect less accidental than the wind which, one day in 1849, supposedly blew the stray leaf from a book about Joan of Arc across the path of a thirteen-year-old printer's apprentice in Hannibal, Missouri. Clearly Mark Twain himself, who came to believe in a world wholly determined from the beginning, regarded it as the first, if not the last, turning point in his life.[1] As he told the story years later, the random page fascinated the boy. It described the Maid's persecution in prison by the rough English soldiery who had stolen her clothes. Young Sam hurried home to ask his mother and brother whether Joan of Arc was a real person. For the first time, apparently, the remote past touched Sam Clemens.

From this casual beginning the worlds of history and literature opened simultaneously to Clemens. For the rest of his life Twain was absorbed by the past and by the urge to represent it through fiction. For a professional writer, this choice of theme sometimes ran counter to the expectations of Twain's audience; this was particularly true of the four medieval stories; none of these, except possibly *A Connecticut Yankee in King Arthur's Court,* was written primarily to make money.

Least of all *Joan of Arc.* "That is private & not for print, it's written for love & not for lucre, & to entertain the family with, around the lamp by the fire." So he described to Mrs. A. W. Fairbanks in January, 1893, the romance he was composing amid the "serene and noiseless life" which the Clemenses were momentarily

[1] See Dixon Wecter, *Sam Clemens of Hannibal* (Boston, 1952), p. 211; and Albert B. Paine, *Mark Twain, A Biography* (New York, 1912), I, 81-82. (Hereinafter cited as Paine). Neither biographer accounts for the fact that this episode, to which Twain often referred in later life, is unmentioned in "The Turning Point of My Life," in *What Is Man? and Other Essays* (New York, 1923), *The Writings of Mark Twain,* Definitive Edition, XXVI, 127-140. All references to Twain's published works herein cited will be to this edition, in which *Joan of Arc* comprises Vols. XVII and XVIII.

leading in Settignano, outside Florence.[2] At this time it was indeed
a sacrifice for Twain to write for love. He was in serious financial
difficulties with the omnivorous Paige typesetter, and his publishing
company and other business ventures were swallowing large portions
of the Clemens fortune. The Panic of 1893 was about to break out,
and this would shortly bring him to the brink of bankruptcy. Yet
in spite of these and other private anxieties, Twain took time from
more marketable work to begin his story of the Maid of Orleans.

On the face of it, *Joan of Arc*—or, more properly, *Personal
Recollections of Joan of Arc, By Sieur Louis de Conte (Her Page
and Secretary), Freely Translated out of the Ancient French into
Modern English from the Original Unpublished Manuscript in the
National Archives of France by Jean Francois Alden*—was an unusual *Festschrift* for Clemens to be writing. Behind him lay *Huckleberry Finn* and "1601"; a few years in the future he was to write
What Is Man? and *The Mysterious Stranger*. Neither the boisterous
humor of the past nor the bleak pessimism of the future prepares us
for *Joan of Arc*. Several questions about this, one of the least known
and least read of Twain's novels, seem to call for consideration. What
forces led him to the writing of such a novel in the 1890's? Since
his subject is an unusual one for the iconoclastic author of *The
Innocents Abroad*, how does Twain treat Joan as a fictional character? What role does the narrator, Sieur Louis de Conte, play in
the story? Does Twain reconcile the pessimistic determinism, already present in his work, with expressions of religious faith necessarily animating Joan's history? In other words, how does Mark
Twain *explain* Joan of Arc? These are some queries suggested by
his first and only novel about a young girl which have been overlooked in the present spate of Twain criticism. To seek their answers may illuminate the work of which Clemens himself remarked

[2] Mark Twain to Mrs. Fairbanks, Jan. 18, 1893, *Mark Twain to Mrs. Fairbanks,* ed.
Dixon Wecter (San Marino, 1949), p. 269. The history of the writing of *Joan of Arc*
Twain himself recorded in his *Notebooks:* "Every book from Huck Finn & Prince &
Pauper on, was read to the household critics chapter by chapter nightly as it was written.
Joan was thus read: the first half at the Villa Viviana [*sic,* properly Viviani] winter of
'92-3; the third quarter at Etretat [France] Aug. & Sept. '94—("wait till I get a hand-
kerchief, papa")—the final chapter in Paris Nov. Dec. 94 finished in the next month (Jan.
'95) I think" (unpublished *Notebook* #31 (II), last date indicated Jan. 6, 1897, Typescript, pp. 49-50). Permission has been granted by the Trustees of the Mark Twain
Estate to quote from this and other unpublished material in the Mark Twain Papers,
University of California, Berkeley. Copyright 1958, by Mark Twain Company.

in 1908, "I like the *Joan of Arc* best of all my books; & it *is* the best; I know it perfectly well."[3]

I

In a note made some time later, Twain remarked that fourteen years of labor went into *Joan of Arc*—twelve years of study and two of writing. Paine tells of a bibliography, compiled "not much later than 1880," of books about the young girl.[4] The interest first aroused by the stray page in Hannibal had thus been sustained, or at least renewed, during the Nook Farm years, though Twain had then been too preoccupied with business, entertaining, traveling, and writing other novels to do anything more with Joan than to study her story.

This cult Mark Twain shared with the nineteenth century. Before that time Joan of Arc had been wreathed in the mists of legend. Reviled by the Englishmen Holinshed and Shakespeare in the sixteenth century, neglected in the seventeenth, ridiculed by Voltaire in the eighteenth, and then idealized by Southey and Schiller in the early nineteenth century, Joan became, during Clemens's own lifetime, a figure of new fascination to writers and to readers.

Joan's modern popularity began in 1841. In that year appeared both J. E. J. Quicherat's remarkable collection of the records of the Maid's trial at Rouen in 1431 and Michelet's fifth volume of the *Histoire de France,* separately titled *Jeanne D'Arc.* Michelet's work had already been translated into English and published in America by 1845. It is possible, judging from the description in Paine, that the page Sam Clemens picked up in 1849 was from this very volume.[5]

---

[3] Paine, II, 1034.

[4] *Ibid.,* II, 958.

[5] "The 'maid' was described in the cage at Rouen, in the fortress, and the two ruffian English soldiers had stolen her clothes. There was a brief description and a good deal of dialogue—her reproaches and their ribald replies" (Paine, I, 81).

Michelet's version, in the American edition, tallies in part with this: "On the Sunday morning, Trinity Sunday, when it was time for her to rise, (as she told him who speaks,) and said to her English guards, 'Leave me, that I may get up.' One of them took off her woman's dress, emptied the bag in which was the man's apparel, and said to her, 'Get up.'—'Gentlemen,' she said, 'you know that dress is forbidden me; excuse me, I will not put it on.' The point was contested until noon; when, being compelled to go out for some bodily want, she put it on" (M. Michelet, *History of France, From the Earliest Period to the Present Time,* trans. G. H. Smith, New York, 1845, II, 164; all references hereinafter are to this edition, cited as Michelet).

Other writers—Lamartine, Dumas, Anatole France in France, J. R. Green, Janet Tuckey, Andrew Lang in England, John Lord and Francis Lodge in America—followed Michelet. Even Emily Dickinson, though she seemed secluded from popular currents in her father's house in Amherst, composed in 1861 a brief lyric in her honor.[6]

Such writers found a ready audience, too, among the readers of Clemens's generation. In the summer of 1885, for instance, Olivia Clemens reported in her diary that thirteen-year-old Susy was reading Schiller's *Jungfrau von Orleans* aloud to her and they were both finding it "delightful."[7] The culmination of these years of interest did not come until 1920, the year of Joan of Arc's canonization. But, as if to underscore the connection between the little saint and Mark Twain, Joan was beatified in 1909, a few months before Twain's death.

With many of these nineteenth-century writers Mark Twain was perfectly familiar. He owned and had read carefully copies of Michelet, Janet Tuckey, J. R. Green, and Dr. John Lord; of the eleven books cited in a preface to *Joan of Arc,* Twain owned at least seven, for they are preserved in the Mark Twain Papers.[8] These all bear copious underlinings and marginal comments in Twain's hand—unmistakable evidence of close and critical reading. Few men in his generation were as widely read in the lore of Joan of Arc as Twain himself.

The chief reason for Clemens's unusual breadth of knowledge was that the story of the Maid of Orleans touched him deeply. The image he constructed of her in his novel was the result of much thought; it answered not only to his intellectual interests but also to his personal emotional needs. Intellectually, Joan of Arc attracted

---

[6] For the treatment of Joan of Arc in nineteenth century history and letters, see Lord Ronald Gower, *Joan of Arc* (London, 1893), pp.289-319; and Helen H. Salls, "Joan of Arc in English and American Literature," *South Atlantic Quarterly,* XXXV, 167-184 (April, 1936). For the poem "A Mien to move a Queen," see *The Poems of Emily Dickinson,* ed. Thomas H. Johnson (Cambridge, Mass., 1955), I, 202-203.

[7] Olivia Clemens's journal, entry of July 2, 1885, p. 13. This journal is in the Mark Twain Papers.

[8] These include Marius Sepet, *Jeanne D'Arc* (Tours, 1887); Michelet, *Jeanne D'Arc* (Paris, 1873); Contesse de Chabannes, *La Vierge Lorraine: Jeanne D'Arc* (Paris, 1890); Monseigneur Ricard, *Jeanne D'Arc, La Vénérable* (Paris, 1894); Lord Ronald Gower, *Joan of Arc* (London, 1893); John O'Hagan, *Joan of Arc* (London, 1893); and Janet Tuckey, *Joan of Arc, "The Maid"* (London, 1880). Copies of Green and Lord were among the books sold at auction from Clemens's library, April 10, 1951.

Twain because she epitomized an age-old struggle of common folk against the twin institutions of cruelty and oppression, the Crown and the Church. In this respect, *Joan of Arc* repeats themes of *The Prince and the Pauper* and *A Connecticut Yankee.* Emotionally, the pull was even stronger. In Twain's eyes Joan was the incarnation of youth and purity and power. She was the unique instance in history of the young girl whose innocence not merely *existed* but *acted* in the gross world of adult affairs. She was the peerless human being, and it was of the utmost importance that she remain eternally a young girl.

To young maidens, hovering on the edge of adult experience, Mark Twain had a lifelong partiality. There were, first of all, his three daughters, in particular Susy Clemens. As Susy reached maidenhood she assumed a special place in her father's heart. Natural parental affection was reinforced by Susy's extraordinary gifts of sensitivity in speech and writing; in her thirteenth and fourteenth years Susy wrote a biography of her father which made him intensely proud of his daughter. In the wider Nook Farm life at Hartford was the Saturday Morning Club, a group of girls who met weekly at Clemens's home. For several exciting weeks in 1878 the Club listened to and criticized instalments of *The Prince and the Pauper.*[9] In later years this special fondness for young girls expressed itself in several ways. Paine tells of one Bermuda holiday which Clemens spent largely in the company of Margaret Blackmer, aged twelve. The lonely old man, whose infant son, favorite daughter, and beloved wife were all dead, found the child so charming that he organized the Angel Fish Club, or The Aquarium. To this select group he elected only himself and a dozen teen-aged girls whose youthful beauty reminded him of the pretty tropical fish.[10]

Even more suggestive of the psychological depths underlying this interest in girlhood is the fragmentary, posthumous "My Platonic Sweetheart," composed in 1898. This story purports to be a true account of a dream Twain had recurrently throughout his adult life. In it, Clemens, always seventeen, has for a lover a fifteen-year-old maiden "girlishly young and sweet and innocent." The pair of "ignorant and contented children" move across a phantom land-

[9] William W. Ellsworth, *A Golden Age of Authors* (Boston, 1919), p. 224.
[10] See Paine, III, 1435-41, and Twain's *Notebooks,* # 38 (1905), entry of June, 1908, Typescript, 3, Mark Twain Papers.

scape conversing in eloquent, cryptic phrases which lose their meaning to the awakened dreamer. Twain comments on his dream:

She was always fifteen, and looked it and acted it; and I was always seventeen, and never felt a day older. To me she is a real person not a fiction, and her sweet and innocent society has been one of the prettiest and pleasantest experiences of my life. I know that to you her talk will not seem of the first intellectual order; but you should hear her in Dreamland then you would see![11]

The timeless and sexless quality of Twain's devotion to girlhood is explicit here. That he regarded Joan of Arc also specifically as a "platonic sweetheart" is clear from his treatment of the Maid in his romance. There is, for example, no hint of sexual development in his growing heroine, in spite of the interesting fact that Michelet, whom Twain followed often very closely, comments upon this very aspect of Joan's history. "She had the divine right to remain," Michelet observes at one point, "soul and body, a child. She grew up strong and beautiful; but never knew the physical sufferings entailed on women." In a footnote the French historian quotes from the testimony of several Domremy women to the effect that Joan never menstruated.[12] Twain knew this passage, for in the margin of his own copy of Michelet he wrote, next to this paragraph: "The higher life absorbed her & suppressed her physical (sexual) development."[13] Anyone familiar with Clemens's skittishness about sex in his books, not to mention the social attitudes of his day, will not be surprised at his silence on this score. Still, it is a detail that throws light upon Joan's strictly childish appeal for Twain. The notion that the Maid was believed to have remained a child in body as well as in spirit must have pleased him and added force to his iterations of her immaculate girlishness.

Similar sentiments about girlhood animate the whole of *Joan of Arc,* in which the aged narrator, Sieur Louis de Conte, in addition to being an actual historical personage, is the most transparent of personae. Twain discovered the "young man of noble birth" with

[11] XXVII, 303. The details of this story are so numerous and suggestive they have not failed to attract the attention of psychologists, amateur and professional. For an interesting discussion of the less platonic aspects of Twain's dreams, see A. E. Jones, "Mark Twain and Sexuality," *PMLA,* LXXI, 595-616 (Sept., 1956).

[12] Michelet, II, 133.

[13] Mark Twain's personal copy of Michelet, *Jeanne D'Arc* (Paris, 1873), p. 10, Mark Twain Papers. Copyright 1958, Mark Twain Company.

the convenient initials in Michelet's history and translated a minor figure into the central intelligence around which his story is structured. By so doing the novelist introduced himself and his private feelings into the stream of history.

II

Joan of Arc is the most historical of all Mark Twain's novels and shows on every page its debt to the history books he read so carefully. "I have never done any work before that cost so much thinking and weighing and measuring and planning and cramming, or so much cautious and painstaking execution," he wrote H. H. Rogers in January, 1895, as he was finishing the book in Paris. Speaking of the final scenes in Rouen, he went on:

> Although it is mere history—history pure and simple—history stripped naked of flowers, embroideries, colorings, exaggerations, inventions—the family agree I have succeeded . . . . The first two-thirds of the book were easy; for I only needed to keep my historical road straight; and therefore I used for reference only one French history and one English one—and shoveled in as much fancy work and invention on both sides of the historical road as I pleased. But on this last third I have constantly used five French sources and five English ones and I think no telling historical nugget in any of them has escaped me.
>
> Possibly the book may not sell, but that is nothing—it is written for love.[14]

Twain's boyish sense of accomplishment is reflected also in the itemized list of "Authorities examined in verification of the truthfulness of this narrative" printed in a preface to *Joan of Arc*. Besides Quicherat's *Condamnation et Réhabilitation de Jeanne D'Arc* and Fabre's *Procès de Condamnation de Jeanne D'Arc,* Twain lists six biographies by Frenchmen and three by Englishmen. Since we have his personal copies of seven of these, it is clear that Twain was neither boasting to his friend Rogers nor trying to hoodwink the reading public.

At one point in the novel Sieur Louis observes, "the office of history is to furnish serious and important facts that *teach."* (XVIII, 63). As usual, the page speaks for his creator. Twain's

---

[14] Mark Twain to H. H. Rogers, dated (erroneously) April 29, 1895, *Mark Twain's Letters,* ed. A. B. Paine (New York, 1917), II, 623-624. Wecter corrects Paine's error in the month in *Mark Twain to Mrs. Fairbanks,* p. 275.

careful display of his documentation is proof that *Joan of Arc* was written to teach others about the most perfect human that ever lived. Children especially (though not exclusively) seem to be the audience Twain had in mind, as William Dean Howells was the first to point out.[15] For an ex-newspaperman whose career opened with satiric squibs against Sunday school books, this fact is somewhat ironic.

Now, as was the case with *The Prince and the Pauper,* Clemens's commitment to historical "truthfulness" involves him in the effort to deal impartially with Joan of Arc. Certain of the writers he has leaned upon try to write realistically and rationally about the Maid; others, in their sympathy and prejudice, make scant effort to do so. Michelet and Sepet, though both staunch Armagnac sympathizers, are of the first group. Michelet, in particular, seems to have influenced Twain more than any of the eleven writers he lists. On internal and external evidence he is the "one French history" Twain told Rogers he used for the first two-thirds of his romance.[16]

It is chiefly from Michelet that Twain derives the inspiration for what realism *Joan of Arc* possesses. The French historian places Joan in the context of political and religious events of her day. He sees her as the manifestation on the one hand of the medieval Virgin cult and the spirit of French nationalism on the other. Joan's successes are related to contemporary military and political realities. When the girl-general is fearful, imprudent, or opportunistic Michelet usually says so. Although patriotic and absurdly Anglophobic,

[15] W. D. Howells, *My Mark Twain* (New York, 1910), p. 151.

[16] Besides furnishing Twain with the most complete treatment of Louis de Contes (as his name is spelled in *Jeanne D'Arc*), Michelet is directly cited several times in the text (XVII, 191; XVIII, 18, for example). The wording of Joan's reply to the Archangel (XVII, 69), her leavetaking from her Domremy playmates (XVII, 89), and numerous other specific details seem closer to Michelet than to any other source. Clemens's marginalia in his French copy of Michelet indicate a close and early reading; many of the opening passages are translated in the margin as if Twain had read Michelet first and was not sure of his French. In his copies of Gower and De Chabannes, Clemens has written Michelet's name in the margin as if testing certain passages against Michelet's version. An illustration from one edition (not Twain's one of 1873) of *Jeanne D'Arc* was tucked inside Twain's copy of Sepet.

More general in its influence is Michelet's blend of candor, humor, anticlerical bias, and sympathy for Joan. At one place the Frenchman remarks, "To travel at such a time with five or six men-at-arms was enough to alarm a young girl. An English woman, or a German, would never have risked such a step; the *indelicacy* of the proceeding would have horrified her" (Michelet, II, 135). In his French copy Twain wrote indignantly next to this passage: "How stupid! A *Joan of Arc* would do it, no matter *what* her nationality might be. That spirit has no nationality." Copyright 1958, Mark Twain Company.

Michelet expresses the spirit of the nineteenth century—rational, anticlerical, nationalistic. Mark Twain's *Joan of Arc* partakes of this spirit.

But Twain's letter to Rogers also mentions as a historical guide "one English one." That book, I believe, is Janet Tuckey's *Joan of Arc, "The Maid."* This little volume, which, to judge from the underlinings and comments, Twain read as carefully as any other source, is manifestly designed for a family, even a childish, audience. Miss Tuckey's Maid is a less impartial and candid creation than Michelet's. Language and the details of military life are less graphic. Unsupported legends find an uncritical welcome, and in the process Joan becomes an angel whose final end is a pathetic victimization of ideal innocence. Miss Tuckey's book is also of the nineteenth century—it is saccharine, churchly, genteel. Twain's romance likewise partakes of this spirit.

For, faced with dissimilar, almost opposing, images of Joan of Arc, Clemens has not decided between them: he has accepted and used both. To do so, of course, fits with the twin tendencies towards sentimentality and realism which characterize virtually all of Twain's fiction. Furthermore, to be both blunt and gentle, pious and anticlerical, cynical and awe-struck in the face of Joan's history fits the character of Twain's alter ego, Sieur Louis de Conte. Through his eyes we see the saint's life and death unfold; he supplies, consequently, the novel's unifying structure, the means by which Twain has altered and embellished the historical narrative.

III

One of the characteristic features of Mark Twain's fiction is his dramatic use of a narrator. *Joan of Arc* derives much of its power from the character who tells the story. Although it is not clear from the early Domremy chapters, Louis de Conte bears a striking resemblance to the narrators Twain created many years earlier both for *Roughing It* and "Old Times on the Mississippi": that is, he is two people at once. Louis is both the fifteen-year-old boy who leaves Domremy to follow Joan and the old cynic who relates the tale many years later. This double role is made explicit in such a comment as this:

My wound gave me a great deal of trouble clear into the first part of October; then the fresher weather renewed my life and strength. All this time there were reports drifting about that the King was going to ransom Joan. I believed these, for I was young and had not yet found out the littleness and meanness of our poor human race, which brags about itself so much, and thinks it is better and higher than the other animals. (XVIII, 109)

The stripling who hears and believes the rumors is carefully differentiated from him who speaks; he is brother to the greenhorn in the opening chapters of *Roughing It* and the cub of "Old Times," just as the old misanthrope is a parallel figure to the old timers in each of the earlier works.[17]   It is as if a middle-aged Mark Twain were looking back at himself, the thirteen-year-old boy, Sam Clemens, and commenting on his own naïveté. In this sense *Joan of Arc* is a double initiation. At the same time that a saint is being made of an innocent village maiden her page is becoming an embittered old man.

One reason, however, for the weakness of *Joan of Arc* as a novel is that Twain does not sufficiently dramatize these two narrators or the process by which "the boy" (as Clemens identified him in early marginal notes in his reading) is transformed into the misanthrope. Louis's initiation is already over when he records Joan's career. As a result, the novel, already somewhat desiccated by historical fact and occasional footnotes, loses that freshness which Huck Finn, for example, was able to give to the account of his initiation.

In the opening chapters these effects of the page's disenchantment are less apparent, and this section is in many respects the most successful part of the novel. Certainly it is most completely of Twain's own manufacture. Always at home in treating childhood, Clemens expands the village scenes far beyond the accounts of Michelet or Tuckey. His narrator becomes almost a believable boy and Joan a real girl as the history of their life in the woods and fields is told. The specifically pastoral quality of these chapters is likewise Twain's own idea. Ignoring those sources which point out that the D'Arc family were not simple farmers but prosperous villagers, and that Joan was not often afield, Twain casts Joan almost exclusively in the role of shepherdess.[18] In so doing Twain

[17] Henry Nash Smith, "Mark Twain as an Interpreter of the Far West: The Structure of *Roughing It*," in *The Frontier in Perspective* (Madison, Wis., 1957), pp. 205-228.

[18] See Michelet, II, 132; Tuckey, p. 25; Gower, p. 5; O'Hagan, p. 39 on this point. O'Hagan, for instance, writes, "She attended almost wholly to the house, but rarely going

draws a distinct line between her life in the open fields, where all is idyllic peace beneath the Fairy Tree, and that of the village, where violence and evil can and do occur.

Perhaps the most graphic instance of the violent realism of Louis's recollection of village life occurs when the Burgundians raid Domremy. Twain developed this episode from brief references in the histories. Both Michelet and Miss Tuckey dismiss the event in a sentence or two, but Clemens constructs an extended scene of wartime pillage. To the bare facts supplied by the records Twain adds such details as the "wrecked and smoke-blackened homes" to which Joan and her friends return to discover "in the lanes and alleys carcasses of dumb creatures that had been slaughtered in pure wantonness . . . ." The climax is reached as Joan and the others reach the village square:

At last we came upon a dreadful object. It was the madman—hacked and stabbed to death in his iron cage in the corner of the square. It was a bloody and dreadful sight. Hardly any of us young people had ever seen a man before who had lost his life by violence; so this cadaver had an awful fascination for us; we could not take our eyes from it. I mean, it had that sort of fascination for all of us but one. That one was Joan. She turned away in horror, and could not be persuaded to go near it again. (XVII, 53)

The village lunatic, Joan's friend, along with every other outcast person and animal in Domremy, is wholly Twain's creation. His gory death repeats the pattern of violence which all of Twain's childish characters confront. Joan of Arc, in spite of her carefree life in the fields, is no more spared the sight of blood than is Tom or Huck or Prince Edward or Theodor Fischer.

De Conte's account of Joan's childhood is a mixture of pastoral idyll and realistic, even gruesome, picture of medieval village life. But as saint and secretary leave Domremy to fulfill their fates at Orléans, Rheims, and Rouen, the balanced tone of Twain's romance changes. The credulous, boyish side of the narrator's mask is discarded and with it the depiction of outdoors life as innocence. The unhappy old man takes over the story. At the same time the pastoral idyll gives way to blatant melodrama. Whereas Joan and her

---

to the fields to keep her father's sheep." Twain here chooses to follow the Countess de Chabannes, whose opening chapter is entitled "La Bergère."

companions are pictured in the village with considerable individuality (especially in their speech), in later scenes all the characters tend to be projected as stereotypes. Joan herself, of course, is the virtuous heroine. The Paladin is her comic bodyguard with the heart of gold. Cauchon and Loyseleur, the Bishop and Priest who control the trial at Rouen, are the arch-villains. The sometimes absurd excesses of melodramatic simplification are suggested by Louis's description of Bishop Cauchon:

> . . . I asked myself what chance an ignorant poor country-girl of nineteen could have in such an unequal conflict; and my heart sank down low, very low. When I looked again at that obese president, puffing and wheezing there, his great belly distending and receding with each breath, and noted his three chins, fold above fold, and his knobby and knotty face, and his purple and splotchy complexion, and his repulsive cauliflower nose, and his cold and malignant eyes—a brute, every detail of him—my heart sank lower still. (XVIII, 123-124)

The radical degree to which Twain conceived this novel as melodrama—and undercut thereby his own claim to "historical truthfulness"—is aptly suggested by a note he made on the flyleaf of one of the history books he read. "Have several of her playmates," he scribbled, "come all the way, hoping somehow to save her—she glimpses them when she knows she is en route to the stake & they don't—a little later they crowd in & get a glance—it is then that the boy closes with Oh, my God!"[19] History would not allow this Tom Sawyer scheme to be carried out, but in places where the facts are hazier Clemens gratuitously added scenes that were often lurid with passion, mystery, or sentiment.[20]

The tensions between Twain's intellectual aims and his emotional predilections, the pull of "truthfulness" against the image of

[19] Penciled notation, flyleaf, Countess de Chabannes, *La Vierge Lorraine, Jeanne D'Arc,* Mark Twain Papers. Copyright 1958, by Mark Twain Company.

[20] One such interpolation is the whole of Book II, Chapter XIX, a ghost story complete with candles at midnight, a haunted room, and groans behind a wall, climaxing in the discovery of "a rusty sword and a rotten fan" (XVII, 245). This episode was evidently added to the narrative after an evening at the Villa Viviani. Olivia Clemens noted in her journal, "Yesterday Mme. Villari and Mrs. Charles Leland called and we sat around the fire telling ghost stories. Mme. Villari told of friends of hers taking to pieces an old house to rebuild, in tearing down the walls they came upon a room that they did not know existed, it was entirely walled up, all that was found in this room was a fan and a sword" (Olivia Clemens Journal, entry "Florence, Italy, 1892-3," p. 29, Mark Twain Papers). Copyright 1958, by Mark Twain Company.

Joan as his "platonic sweetheart," as it were, are everywhere evident in *Joan of Arc*. The sentimental innocence of the boy, though more palpable in the Domremy chapters, runs all through the narrative; we see it particularly in the melodramatic touches. Side by side with this maudlin sentiment, however, exists the mocking laughter of the old secretary, whose cynicism is directed not at Joan but at himself and at all men. Sieur Louis de Conte, being so thoroughly of two minds about Joan's life, is indeed an ambiguous interpreter of its meaning.

IV

"What can we say to it in the last year of this incredulous old century, nodding to its close?" asked William Dean Howells of the "preposterous," "impossible" facts of the Maid's life as his friend Mark Twain had presented them.

We cannot deny it. What was it all? Was Joan's power the force dormant in the people which her claim of inspiration awoke to mighty deeds? If it was merely that, how came this poor, ignorant girl by the skill to lead armies, to take towns, to advise councils, and to change the fate of a whole nation? . . . Could a dream, an illusion, a superstition, do this?[21]

Such was the fundamental question *Joan of Arc* raised for Howells, nor could he go on to give Twain's answer to the matter of Joan's power, because there was no such clearcut answer in the novel. Howells could see that Joan was more to Twain than the expression of French nationalism, but he could not tell, judging from the novel alone, whether her power came from a divine source or from the girl's own soul.

At this level of "meaning," *Joan of Arc* is indeed a perplexing mixture. A devotional exercise for a Roman Catholic girl couched in profoundly Protestant terms, it is also a celebration of the world's most perfect human by an oldish man who has lost his faith in mankind. The novel is, moreover, a case history of a religious mystic whose puissance seems to emanate from her own intuition rather than from the temporary indwelling of holy Voices. These ambiguities are implicit in the structure of *Joan of Arc* not simply because the historical Joan was, and is, an enigma, but also because Sieur Louis de Conte cannot resolve his own doubts.

[21] W. D. Howells, *My Mark Twain*, p. 155.

Actually, in the course of the story Louis offers three explanations of Joan's life and accomplishments. First, she may be considered purely as the amanuensis of supernatural powers which, because of her heritage, her reliance upon saints and sacraments, her allegiance to the Pope, are to be regarded as specifically Christian and Catholic. This, the grave churchmen of Poitiers are glad to confess, is the answer to "that elusive and unwordable fascination, which was the supremest endowment of Joan of Arc." Though the priests appropriate Joan's power and declare "This child is sent of God," Sieur Louis himself will not admit that Joan's superhuman abilities are a Catholic Christian's special gift from Heaven, for in his world-weary eyes the Church is a very fallible institution. Even before the dreadful disenchantment of the trial at Rouen, Louis's name for the doctors of the Church is the "holy hair-splitters." Frequently the secretary (whose boyish faith as he hid in the woods and watched the Archangel approach Joan was unquestioned) has the chance to make Christian explanations for the events he witnesses. He seldom does so, for to the old man the Church is not the exclusive channel through which the Maid is empowered to do her mighty miracles. "She could have reminded these people," Louis observes on one occasion, "that Our Lord, who is no respecter of persons, had chosen the lowly for his high purposes even oftener than he had chosen bishops and cardinals" (XVIII, 205). In the jaundiced eyes of her servant, at any rate, Joan cannot be adequately explained as Catholic Christian. Her faith does not explain her power, but rather the reverse.

A second, and stronger, possibility is that the child's mysterious mastery over the adult world derives, as Howells and Michelet believed, from the people. "To the Dwarf, Joan was France, the spirit of France made flesh . . ." de Conte remarks, and then adds, "and God knows it was the true one" (XVII, 225). On another occasion Louis calls Joan "a mirror in which the lowly hosts of France were clearly reflected" (XVIII, 29). And yet, as the romance moves towards its tragic conclusion, this theory is more and more eroded by the facts of life as Louis comes to know them. This same dwarf, who both believed Joan to represent the people and was one of them himself, turns out to be a cruel and bloodthirsty soldier. Colonel Sherburn's shooting of old Boggs in *Huckleberry Finn* is no more disgusting a demonstration of human brutality than the scene in which the Dwarf strangles a Burgundian soldier. Yet these soldiers are little better than the king himself, who is "a sceptered ass" to Louis. From the top to the bottom of French society the page finds nothing but venality, cruelty, weakness. At the end we are prepared to discount the page's assertions of Joan as the spirit of France as the credulous hopes of the young boy; what the old man later learns undercuts and all but denies this explanation of Joan of Arc.

A third possibility suggests itself finally as the key to Joan of Arc's life. Her power is not intellectual—it defies rational explanation by the best university minds; nor is it social—the people is a great beast, the Church simply a group of people. Her supernatural deeds must, then, emanate from some mysterious source anterior to reason and to human institutions. That this source is mysterious is everywhere insisted upon by Twain's commentator.

Who taught the shepherd-girl to do these marvels—she who could not read, and had had no opportunity to study the complex arts of war? . . . It is a riddle which will never be guessed. *I* think these vast powers and capacities were born in her, and that she applied them by an intuition which could not err. (XVII, 304)

The translator of Louis's history, Samuel L. Clemens, can no more elucidate the matter clearly than the old page. "Joan of Arc, a mere child in years, ignorant, unlettered, a poor village girl unknown and without influence . . . laid her hand upon this nation, this corpse, and it rose and followed her." So runs the Translator's Preface. Clemens himself, in his own voice, falls back on wonder (as, curiously enough, does Michelet, for all his rational nationalism). Nowhere in the records Twain has combed can he isolate a sufficient First Cause for the career of this "noble child, the most innocent, the most lovely, the most adorable the ages have produced."

But has the novel not already suggested one source? If the church or the people cannot, may not the Fairy Tree "explain" Joan of Arc? This Tree is the central symbolic vehicle for Mark Twain's pastorale. Mentioned in passing by all his historical sources, the Fairy Tree is the haunt of the fairies who befriend Joan and the other children until banished by the superstitious village priest.

Beneath the Fairy Tree, too, Joan is first visited by the Archangel
Michael. The boys and girls of Domremy sing a hymn to the Tree
whose words, entirely Twain's creation, evoke the mood of Joan's
life. Since it plays so central a role in establishing the theme of
Joan of Arc it is worth quoting in its entirety.

L'Arbre Fée de Bourlemont
Song of the Children

Now what has kept your leaves so green,
    Arbre Fée de Bourlemont?
The children's tears! They brought each grief,
    And you did comfort them and cheer
Their bruisèd hearts, and steal a tear
      That, healèd, rose a leaf.

And what has built you up so strong,
    Arbre Fée de Bourlemont?
The children's love! They've loved you long:
    Ten hundred years, in sooth,
They've nourished you with praise and song,
And warmed your heart and kept it young—
    A thousand years of youth!

Bide always green in our young hearts,
    Arbre Fée de Bourlemont!
And we shall always youthful be,
    Not heeding Time his flight;
And when, in exile wand'ring, we
Shall fainting yearn for glimpse of thee,
    Oh, rise upon our sight!
                    (XVII, 13-14)

This sacred song is referred to at key points in the narrative so
often that it comes to resemble an operatic *motif*. The Tree and
song together constitute Clemens's most notable addition to the Joan
of Arc legend.

It is not easy to say whether the Fairy Tree means more to Joan
of Arc, dead at nineteen, or to Sieur Louis, who lives unhappily on
into old age. For both, the Tree signalizes happiness, unity with
nature, the past. The most touching demonstration of its appeal to
both comes at an unlikely point in the story, at the banquet following King Charles's coronation at Rheims. After the speech-making,

it is the weak-willed King's happy thought to surprise Joan with the singing of the children's song.

Then out of some remote corner of that vast place there rose a plaintive voice, and in tones most tender and sweet and rich came floating through that enchanted hush our poor old simple song "L'Arbre Fée de Bourlemont!" and then Joan broke down and put her face in her hands and cried. Yes, you see, all in a moment the pomps and grandeurs dissolved away and she was a little child again herding her sheep with the tranquil pastures stretched about her, and war and wounds and blood and death and the mad frenzy and turmoil of battle a dream. (XVIII, 55)

The Tree is the talisman of Joan's oneness with nature; it asserts that she is "born child of the sun, natural comrade of the birds and of all happy free creatures" (XVIII, 124-125). It gives her the "seeing eye," "the creating mouth," those innate, mysterious qualities which neither the Doctors, nor the soldiers, nor Joan's own page can otherwise account for. A vision of the Tree appears to Joan in prison and aids her as much as the Holy Voices to meet death. For the Fairy Tree is the sign of Paradise. It is a pagan sign, not specifically Christian, being associated with children, fairies, open fields, and animals of the forest rather than with Saint Catherine and Saint Margaret. Furthermore, it signifies a Paradise existing eternally in the past, not a future Christian heaven.

Mark Twain would not have us think that Joan and her companions are less devout Catholics for their allegiance to the Fairy Tree, so clearly a pagan nature symbol. Their childish faith and love encompass both modes of grace. Just as the Archangel appears to Joan under the branches of the Tree, so do the two visions of paradise coexist at her death in Joan's innocent soul. The Fairy Tree that rises upon her sight in prison shares its power with the Cross, in sight of which she dies.

The Fairy Tree is the comprehensive symbol through which Joan's life approximates for Twain the pattern of myth. Her sacrificial death (so like Christ's) completes the cycle of the nature goddess begun by a pastoral childhood, continued through an heroic, miraculous career, and climaxed by the Passion at Rouen. Through her death—and clearly this is the significance of her life to Louis de Conte—Joan of Arc escapes from time, from old age, from loss of faith. The vision of the Fairy Tree redeems life.

This interpretation of his heroine clearly fitted Mark Twain's own spiritual condition which, in the 1890's, was in many respects identical in its pessimism and nostalgia with that of his spokesman. That he could represent Joan simultaneously as Christian, democrat, and nature goddess, and yet not exclusively as any of these, argues a spiritual ambivalence, a tension among skepticism, determinism, and faith which was, by 1896, far from being resolved.

Joan of Arc both exemplifies this dilemma and offers a way out. Sieur Louis, with his mixture of irony, resignation, and rage at the human race, is the literary spokesman for the philosophical contradictions (if one may so grace the simplicities of Clemens's thought) of *What Is Man?* More significant, however, is Joan of Arc herself. The Maid embodies and transcends all contradictions. Depicted as girlishly human in speech and manner, Joan escapes the stain of depraved humanity by her indestructible innocence. A devout Catholic, Joan's loyalty to her Voices places her in righteous opposition to that fallible institution, the Church. Her bond with the Fairy Tree, on the other hand, establishes a link with nature, with a pre-rational source of knowledge, with a pre-institutional source of piety, with an eternal world of values not subject to the pains, disappointments, doubts, and contradictions of adult life. For it is *adult* life which creates ambiguities for Sieur Louis de Conte. *Joan of Arc,* though it culminates in the victimization of childhood, affirms that state as the only form of life worth living—and dying—for.

V

Twain was not alone in his spiritual confusions nor was he the only artist in the 1890's who found in childhood, in a romantic return to nature, in a mixture of Christian and pagan imagery, resolution of the loss of faith and the crippling effects of scientific determinism. At the same time as Mark Twain was composing *Joan of Arc,* Henry Adams was working his way toward a private cult of the Virgin. William Dean Howells, in *A Boy's Town* (1890) had just celebrated childhood in terms even more nostalgic than *Joan of Arc.* Stephen Crane, in the imagery of *The Red Badge of Courage* and "The Monster," was mixing pagan and Christian symbols in an attempt to replace by art the lost Methodism of his unworldly father. Further afield, the artists and architects of the White City at Chicago were carefully blending Christian and pagan motifs and ornaments and Frederick L. Olmstead was introducing nature into that plan with his "wooded isle" landscape arrangement. In France, where Twain completed *Joan of Arc,* a similar mixing of themes was taking place in certain symbolist poems and on the canvases of Paul Gauguin.

Joan of Arc has, to be sure, no direct tie with *Mont-Saint-Michel and Chartres, The Red Badge of Courage,* the Columbian Exposition, or the paintings of Gauguin. Yet a common pattern may perhaps be discerned in these manifestations of *fin-de-siècle* art. Certain artists, of whom Mark Twain was one, were simultaneously struggling to assert spiritual values in the face of massive forces making for religious decay. Some of these forces may be identified as scientific determinism, the ugly spread of industrialism, imperialism, worship of wealth. What concerns readers of *Joan of Arc* is not the nature of these forces but rather the form of the response. In this historical romance Twain utilizes some of the ideas abroad in the air of his time. Like Adams, he worships a Virgin whom he has, along with his friend Howells and, to a lesser degree, Stephen Crane, made into a child. He merges the image of a Roman Catholic saint with that of a primitive nature goddess much as Saint-Gaudens would mix pagan and Christian elements in the decoration of a frieze or Gauguin would place a halo about the head of a half-naked Tahitian maiden. Thus, though *Joan of Arc* was Clemens's private act of devotion, it partook of certain of the spiritual and artistic currents in the Western world of 1896.

What strikes the casual reader as an incongruity in Mark Twain's career shows, upon inspection, to have an appropriate inevitability. Far from being an unlikely topic for him to hit upon, Joan of Arc had all the earmarks of a predetermined subject for his pen. At a particular moment in his life Twain found that the Maid of Orleans gave him a means of dramatizing his own, and his age's, spiritual dilemma without the embarrassing obligation to resolve the dilemma. For, after all, Joan was "the *Riddle* of the Ages . . . . All the rules fail in this girl's case." To the aging man who was both a realist and romantic in his writing, a determinist and a moralist in his thinking, an agnostic and yet a deist in his worship,

Joan of Arc permitted a temporary haven. That haven lay in the
timeless past of childhood, symbolized by the Fairy Tree of Bourlemont, a kind of Jackson's Island in the fifteenth century, where
even death at the stake was but a necessary stage in the cycle of a
girl goddess.

The Composition and Structure of
Tom Sawyer
Hamlin L. Hill

T HE STRUCTURE OF *The Adventures of Tom Sawyer* has for some time marked a point of divergence among Twain scholars. Walter Blair's study "On the Structure of *Tom Sawyer*" suggested that the book was organized as the story of a boy's maturation, presented to the reader through four lines of action—the Tom and Becky story, the Muff Potter story, the Jackson's Island adventure, and the Injun Joe story—each of which begins with an immature act and ends with a relatively mature act by Tom.[1] Blair's interpretation has been accepted by Dixon Wecter, who agreed that "Tom and Huck grow visibly as we follow them,"[2] by Gladys Bellamy,[3] and E. H. Long.[4] But it has been ignored by DeLancey Ferguson, who claimed that "*Tom Sawyer*, in short, grew as grows the grass; it was not art at all, but it was life."[5] It was disclaimed by Alexander Cowie, who stated that *Tom Sawyer* "lives in small units, which when added up (not arranged) equal the sum of boyhood experience."[6] And most recently, Roger Asselineau dismissed Blair's hypothesis as a mere tour de force when he suggested, "This attempt at introducing logic and order into a book which had been rather desultorily composed was interesting, but not fully convincing. Such *a posteriori* conclusions, however tempting, smacked of artificiality and could only contain a measure of truth."[7]

These, then, are the two poles: that *Tom Sawyer* has a narrative plan and exhibits what was for Twain a high degree of literary craftsmanship; or that it is a ragbag of memories, thrown together

---

[1] Walter Blair, "On the Structure of *Tom Sawyer*," *Modern Philology*, XXXVII, 75-88 (August, 1939).

[2] "Mark Twain," *Literary History of the United States*, ed. Robert E. Spiller *et al.* (New York, 1953), p. 930.

[3] *Mark Twain as a Literary Artist* (Norman, 1950), pp. 334-335.

[4] *Mark Twain Handbook* (New York, 1957), pp. 316-318.

[5] *Mark Twain: Man and Legend* (Indianapolis, 1943), p. 176.

[6] *The Rise of the American Novel* (New York, 1948), p. 609.

[7] *The Literary Reputation of Mark Twain from 1910 to 1950* (Paris, 1954), p. 58.

at random with little or no thought to order or structure. My suggestion is that the original manuscript, now in the Riggs Memorial Library of Georgetown University, Washington, D. C.,[8] holds the solution to the problem of the book's structure and that a more intensive examination of it than DeVoto made in *Mark Twain at Work*[9] provides the secret of Mark Twain's methods of composition of *Tom Sawyer*.

I

Twain's own statements about the book's composition support the "ragbag" theory. He began work on *Tom Sawyer* itself, as distinguished from its several precursors,[10] probably in the summer of 1874. By September 4, he "had worked myself out, pumped myself dry,"[11] so he put the manuscript aside until the spring or summer of 1875, and on July 5, 1875, announced its completion.[12] Years later, he described the crisis which presumably came in September, 1874:

At page 400 of my manuscript the story made a sudden and determined halt and refused to proceed another step. Day after day it still refused. I was disappointed, distressed and immeasurably astonished, for I knew quite well that the tale was not finished and I could not understand why I was not able to go on with it. The reason was very simple—my tank had run dry; it was empty; the stock of materials in it was exhausted; the story could not go on without materials; it could not be wrought out of nothing.[13]

And Brander Matthews, reporting a discussion with Twain, confirmed this haphazard method of composition:

He began the composition of "Tom Sawyer" with certain of his boyish recollections in mind, writing on and on until he had utilized them all, whereupon he put his manuscript aside and ceased to think about it,

---

[8] I am grateful to Mr. Joseph Jeffs of the Riggs Memorial Library for making a microfilm of the manuscript available to me. I also thank the Mark Twain Estate for granting permission to quote previously unpublished notations in the manuscript, which are copyright 1959, by the Mark Twain Company.

[9] Bernard DeVoto, *Mark Twain at Work* (Cambridge, Mass., 1942), pp. 3-18. Cited hereafter as MTAW.

[10] See MTAW, pp. 3-9.

[11] *Mark Twain's Letters*, ed. Albert B. Paine (New York, 1917), p. 224.

[12] *Ibid.*, p. 258.

[13] *Mark Twain in Eruption*, ed. Bernard DeVoto (New York, 1940), p. 197.

except in so far as he might recall from time to time, and more or less unconsciously, other recollections of those early days. Sooner or later he would return to his work and make use of memories he had recaptured in the interval.[14]

The manuscript provides many examples of this plot development through recollection and association.

While writing or reading over the early parts of *Tom Sawyer,* Twain apparently remembered ideas and incidents from his earlier writings or his own boyhood which he felt might be of use to him later. Accordingly, he wrote notes and suggestions in the margins of his manuscript, mentioning material which would either be utilized later in the book or be discarded.[15] A few of these notations are so cryptic that I have been unable to identify them: "The dead cigar man" on manuscript page 210, "The old whistler" on page 85, and "Silver moons" on page 322. But in most cases his intention is perfectly clear.

Among the marginal reminders which Twain discarded was the name of a steamboat, the *City of Hartford,* which he wrote on manuscript page 89, opposite the Sunday school superintendent's speech (Chapter IV). Evidently his first thought was to utilize an anecdote from his May, 1870, "Memoranda" column for this speech. The episode went thus:

"Just about the close of that long, hard winter," said the Sunday-school superintendent, "as I was wending toward my duties one brilliant Sabbath morning, I glanced down toward the levee, and there lay the City of Hartford!—no mistake about it, there she was, puffing and panting, after her long pilgrimage through the ice. . . . I should have to instruct empty benches, sure; the youngsters would all be off welcoming the first steamboat of the season. You can imagine how surprised I was when I opened the door and saw half the benches full! My gratitude was free,

[14] Brander Matthews, *The Tocsin of Revolt and Other Essays* (New York, 1922), p. 265.

[15] DeVoto (MTAW, p. 6) mentions only one of these many marginal notations, the one on the first page of the manuscript: "Put in thing from Boy-lecture." The reference was probably to a lecture Twain proposed for the 1871-1872 lecture season. In the *American Publisher,* a magazine published by the American Publishing Company, Twain's publisher, and edited by Orion Clemens, Twain's brother, Orion revealed, "We have the pleasure to announce that Mark Twain will lecture in New England during the ensuing fall, and later, in the Western States. The subject is not yet decided upon. He has *two* new lectures, one an appeal in behalf of Boy's Rights, and one entitled simply 'D.L.H.' " (*American Publisher,* I, 4, July, 1871).

large, and sincere. I resolved that they should not find me unappreciative.
I said: 'Boys, what renewed assurance it gives me of your affection. I
confess that I said to myself, as I came along and saw that the City of
Hartford was in—'
"'No! But is she, though!'
"And as quick as any flash of lightning I stood in the presence of
empty benches! I had brought them the news myself."[16]

In the margin of a page for Chapter VIII (MS p. 210), he wrote
"Rolling the rock," a reference to the Holliday's Hill episode which
he had utilized in *The Innocents Abroad* (Chapter LVIII) and which
he rejected for *Tom Sawyer*. And three pages later Twain noted,
"candy-pull," apparently toying with the idea of having "Jim Wolfe
and the Cats" make an appearance in the book.[17] He also suggested
to himself on page 464, "Becky had the measles," and "Joe drowned."
One suggestion which was not eliminated entirely but was greatly
altered in the book appeared on manuscript page 161: "burnt up the
old sot." The story recalled the time that Clemens gave a tramp
some matches which "the old sot" used to burn up the jail and
himself, and Twain referred to it in *Life on the Mississippi* and the
Autobiography[18] as well as *Tom Sawyer*. The character corresponding to the tramp was Muff Potter, and Tom did smuggle "small
comforts" to Muff in jail and was bothered with nightmares, just
as young Sam Clemens was in 1853. But since burning Muff
Potter would have made it necessary to omit the trial chapter, Twain
used only those portions of the story which we find in the book.

Some of the marginal notations bore fruit immediately. On
page 15 Twain wrote "coppers" and on page 19 mentioned that the
"new boy" whom Tom was challenging "took two broad coppers
out of his pocket and held them out with derision" (Chapter I).
On page 409 he wrote "storm" and on page 432 began describing
the storm on Jackson's Island (Chapter XVI).

[16] Memoranda," *Galaxy*, IX, 726 (May, 1870), reprinted in *Mark Twain at Your
Fingertips*, ed. Caroline T. Harnsberger (New York, 1948), pp. 30-31.
[17] "Jim Wolfe and the Cats" was frequently reprinted. According to Merle Johnson,
A Bibliography of Mark Twain (New York, 1935), p. 229, it appeared in the *Californian*,
the New York *Sunday Mercury*, the "Buyer's Manual of 1872," "Beecher's Readings and
Recitations," and in book form in *Mark Twain's Speeches* (New York, 1910), pp. 262-264,
and *Mark Twain's Autobiography*, ed. Albert B. Paine (New York, 1924), I, 135-138.
[18] *Life on the Mississippi*, Chapter LVI, and *Autobiography*, I, 130-131. See Dixon
Wecter, *Sam Clemens of Hannibal* (Boston, 1952), pp. 253-256, for a succinct account of
the actual incident.

Several of the notes were not incorporated into the manuscript until much later. In the margin of a page of Chapter viii (ms p. 209), he wrote, "Cadets of Temp.," a suggestion for including material which would appear in Chapter xxii of the book. On the next page, 210, he wrote, "Learning to smoke" and "Burying pet bird or cat." The first note was amplified in Chapter xvi, where Huck instructs Tom and Joe Harper in the art of smoking; and the other received brief mention in Chapter xxii: "He drifted listlessly down the street & found Jim Hollis acting as Judge in a juvenile court that was trying a cat for murder, in the presence of her victim, a bird" (ms p. B-12).

In another hand, probably Mrs. Clemens's, there was a note on page 160 (Chapter vi) which read, "Take of[f] his wig with a cat." Twain himself reiterated the suggestion on page 573 (Chapter xxiii, but written before the graduation ceremony chapter), noting "(Dropping cat)."[19] Finally, in Chapter xxi, the humorist incorporated the incident of lowering a cat from the ceiling to remove the schoolmaster's wig.

Incidentally, the graduation chapter, although it utilized these notes, was greatly assisted by a book Twain possessed: *The Pastor's Story and Other Pieces; or Prose and Poetry* by Mary Ann Harris Gay, of which seven editions were published between 1858 and 1871.[20] It was this author and this book which Twain acknowledged in his note at the end of the graduation chapter: "The pretended 'compositions' quoted in this chapter are taken without alteration from a volume entitled 'Prose and Poetry, by a Western Lady'—but they are exactly and precisely after the school-girl pattern and hence are much happier than any mere imitations could be." The elocutions in this chapter, "Is This, Then, Life?," "A Missouri Maiden's Farewell to Alabama," and "A Vision," were not, then, as Dixon Wecter suggested,[21] Twain's own satiric efforts. On the contrary, the humorist pasted actual pages torn from Mary

---

[19] This and one other note of Livy's, considered below, are the only comments I have found in the manuscript which are by his wife; neither smacks of censorship. Mr. Fred Anderson, curator of the Mark Twain Papers, has suggested that since the language of these two notes does not sound like Mrs. Clemens, she may well have written them at her husband's dictation, perhaps while they were reading the manuscript aloud together.

[20] See L. H. Wright, *American Fiction, 1851-1875* (San Marino, 1957), p. 131.

[21] Wecter, *Sam Clemens of Hannibal*, p. 257, speaks of saccharine poetry "which he later satirized in *Tom Sawyer*, when at school exercises a 'slim, melancholy girl' arose and recited 'A Missouri Maiden's Farewell to Alabama.' "

Ann Gay's book in his manuscript. His page A-14 (547-548) is
actually pages 31 and 32 of her selection, "Is This, Then, Life?"
His pages A-16 (550) and A-17 (551) are her pages 118 and 119,
"Farewell to Alabama," written, her footnote explained, in imita-
tion of Mr. Tyrone Power's "Farewell to America." And finally,
Twain's page A-19 (553) was her pages 189 and 190, "A Vision."

All this material supports the theory that *Tom Sawyer* was
structureless. The author's own statements suggested that he wrote
those memories of his childhood which came to mind, waited until
he remembered some more, and then added them to his manuscript. The marginal notations show that as he wrote he thought
of other incidents by association and made his notes to keep them
in mind. In one instance the associative link between the material
he was writing and the marginal note is apparent. On page 209
he was describing Tom Sawyer's daydream of returning to St.
Petersburg as a pirate wearing a "crimson sash." A red sash was
the enticement which the author could not resist as a boy when
joining the Cadets of Temperance, and, remembering this, he
wrote the "Cadets of Temp." note in his margin. This was sheer
opportunism, but it was the way he collected the material for the
book—from immediate memory and from brief notes in his margins
which he would later expand.[22]

[22] On at least one occasion, however, Twain wrote some separate notes relating to his
book. In the Aldis Collection of the Yale University Library there is a single page of
notes for the graveyard scene:

> Potter & Dr.
> objects to job
> quarrell [*sic*]
> fight
> Potter knocked down with Tom's

shovel.

> Joe rushed in & stabs Dr.
> Potter insensible
> Joe will bury Dr in Tom's hole &

will make Potter think *he* is accessory.

> Finds treasure—goes & hides it
> —returns & finds P up.
> No use to bury body, for Potter

thinks *he* did it.

> When boys leave, they carry their
> tools with them & will never tell.
> Somewhere previously it is
> said Joe lives in the cave.

Since Injun Joe has been substituted for Pap Finn (who originally played this part in the
manuscript [see MTAW, p. 17]), and since the graveyard and the treasure scenes have
been combined, this was probably a note for a lecture or a dramatization.

II

On the other hand, some of the material in the manuscript supports the "maturation" theory. In the margin of manuscript page 276, in the hand I believe is Mrs. Clemens's, there appeared, "Tom licked for Becky." Twain repeated the suggestion on page 464: "T takes B's whipping." And in Chapter xx, he expanded the note into one of the chapters which Blair suggests are crucial,[23] delaying the use of his wife's note until fairly late in the book. Conversely, he manipulated the Cadets of Temperance episode to emphasize Tom's immaturity. He first mentioned the Cadets of Temperance in a brief paragraph of a letter for the *Alta California*:

. . . And they started militia companies, and Sons of Temperance and Cadets of Temperance. Hannibal always had a weakness for the Temperance cause. I joined the cause myself, although they didn't allow a boy to smoke, or drink or swear, but I thought I never could be truly happy till I wore one of those stunning red scarfs and walked in procession when a distinguished citizen died. I stood it four months, but never an infernal distinguished citizen died during the whole time; and when they finally pronounced old Doctor Norton convalescent (a man I had been depending on for seven or eight weeks,) I just drew out. I drew out in disgust, and pretty much all the distinguished citizens in the camp died within the next three weeks.[24]

In *Tom Sawyer* (Chapter xxii), the material was almost as short:

Tom joined the new order of Cadets of Temperance, being attracted by the showy character of their "regalia." He promised to abstain from smoking, chewing, and profanity as long as he remained a member. Now he found out a new thing—namely, that to promise not to do a thing is the surest way in the world to make a body want to go and do that very thing. Tom soon found himself tormented with a desire to drink and swear; the desire grew to be so intense that nothing but the hope of a chance to display himself in his red sash kept him from withdrawing from the order. Fourth of July was coming; but he soon gave that up—gave it up before he had worn his shackles over forty-eight hours—and fixed his hopes upon old Judge Frazer, justice of the peace, who was apparently on his death-bed and would have a big public funeral, since he was so high an official. During three days Tom was

[23] "On the Structure of *Tom Sawyer*," pp. 84-87.
[24] *Mark Twain's Travels with Mr. Brown*, ed. Franklin Walker and G. Ezra Dane (New York, 1940), p. 146.

deeply concerned about the Judge's condition and hungry for news of it. Sometimes his hopes ran high—so high that he would venture to get out his regalia and practice before the looking-glass. But the Judge had a most discouraging way of fluctuating. At last he was pronounced upon the mend—and then convalescent. Tom was disgusted; and felt a sense of injury, too. He handed in his resignation at once—and that night the Judge suffered a relapse and died. Tom resolved that he would never trust a man like that again.

The four months of membership were shortened to less than a week in *Tom Sawyer*, making Tom much less steadfast than young Clemens. And the overwhelming desire to drink and swear made Tom much more irresolute and immature. Both changes tended to emphasize the boy's inability to abide by his decisions at this point in the book.

But the most important support for Blair's interpretation occurs on the first page of the manuscript. Here Twain wrote a long note, never before discussed, which merits careful study:

1, Boyhood & youth; 2 y & early manh; 3 the Battle of Life in many lands; 4 (age 37 to [40?],) return & meet grown babies & toothless old drivelers who were the grandees of his boyhood. The Adored Unknown a [illegible] faded old maid & full of rasping, puritanical vinegar piety.

This outline was written, if not before he began the book, before he reached page 169 of his manuscript. Before that page, the "new girl" was referred to as "the Adored Unknown" (Chapter III of the published book). And on that page the name "Becky Thatcher" appeared for the first time (Chapter VI). If Becky had been "christened" when Twain wrote this outline, it seems likely that he would have used her name in it. The marginal note represents, then, a very early if not the earliest plan for the plot of the new novel. The book was to be in four parts, clearly progressing from boyhood to maturity and ending with Tom's return to St. Petersburg and a puritanical Becky. The "return" idea was a recurrent one, appearing in Twain's notebooks several times.[25] Rudimentary though it is, this outline assumes enormous importance, for the only "theme" it conveys is one of the maturation of a person

[25] See MTAW, p. 49, and *Mark Twain's Notebook*, ed. Albert B. Paine (New York, 1935), p. 212.

from boyhood to manhood. It is obviously crucial to determine exactly when this plan was discarded, because if Twain composed the book by this formula the "maturation" theory stands vindicated.

Even after the book was finished, Twain was uncertain about the wisdom of having stopped with Tom's youth. "I have finished the story and didn't take the chap beyond boyhood," he told Howells. "See if you don't really decide that I am right in closing with him as a boy."[26] But the decision to alter the original outline was not made until after September 4, 1874, and perhaps as late as the spring of 1875.

Page 403 of the manuscript, where the change is noticeable, appears toward the end of Chapter xv. Tom, Joe Harper, and Huck have run away to Jackson's Island to become pirates. Joe and Huck, homesick and ready to return to St. Petersburg, have been "withered with derision" by Tom, who has no desire to go back to civilization. The cannons on the ferry boat have failed to bring up the boys' bodies. Just as in *Huckleberry Finn,* the stage has been set, the devices prepared, for an imminent departure. After the other boys go to sleep, Tom scrawls a note to Joe Harper on a piece of sycamore bark and leaves it, together with his "schoolboy treasures of almost inestimable value." This leavetaking from Joe thus sounds much more final than would be necessary merely for Tom to deliver a note to his aunt. Tom writes another note for Aunt Polly, returns to his home in St. Petersburg, and at page 403 is standing over his sleeping aunt.

Preparations were thus made for Tom to begin his "Battle of Life in many lands," to leave both St. Petersburg and his comrades who were about to return there. But Mark Twain's manuscript shows that he pondered the wisdom of having Tom depart. Aware that a critical point in the story was at hand, he sprinkled the page with signs of his indecision. Deliberating what course to take, he wrote at the top margin, "Sid is to find and steal that scroll," and "He is to show the scroll in proof of his intent." In the left margin, he wrote two further lines and cancelled them. Across the page itself he wrote, "No, he leaves the bark there, & Sid gets

[26] *Mark Twain's Letters,* pp. 258-259. See also his letter of June 21, 1875, to Howells (MTAW, p. 10, n. 2).

it." Then he suggested, "He forgets to leave the bark." This was the point at which he had "pumped myself dry"[27] and found that "at page 400 of my manuscript the story made a sudden and determined halt and refused to proceed another step."[28]

If the note was merely to contain the message, "We ain't dead— we are only off playing pirates," the author's ruminations over what would happen to it were completely out of proportion. If Tom left Jackson's Island to deliver this message and then return, the bequest of his proudest possessions to Joe Harper was equally absurd. If, as one of the notes suggested, he was to forget to leave the scroll after swimming part of the river and sneaking under his aunt's bed, he would be completely unbelievable. But if the bark was to contain a farewell message to Aunt Polly and was to be stolen by Sid, this scene might prepare for Tom's return at age thirty-seven to St. Petersburg. Though the possible development of the plot is conjectural, it is plausible to suggest an identification scene, perhaps a court trial, in which the stolen bark would be the crucial evidence.[29] Almost literally, the piece of bark with a scrawled message separated the reader from something very similar to *Adventures of Huckleberry Finn*; the scroll of sycamore bark became the key to the further progress of *Tom Sawyer* that the resurrected raft would later be in Twain's masterpiece.[30] Used in one way, the plot would continue on the course Twain outlined on the first page of his manuscript; used in another, the direction of the novel would be altered.

Twain chose not to have Tom start his travels. The boy returns the scroll to his jacket pocket, where Aunt Polly discovers it a few chapters later. It was undoubtedly after he made his decision that he also turned back to page 401 and inserted a paragraph: "This was Wednesday night. If the OVER [then on the back of the page] bodies continued missing until Sunday, all hope would be given over, & the funeral would be preached on that morning.

[27] Sept. 4, 1874, *Mark Twain's Letters*, p. 224.

[28] *Mark Twain in Eruption*, p. 197.

[29] Court trials with surprise witnesses and sensational evidence were the ingredients of one of Mark Twain's favorite plots. They occurred in "Ah Sin," "Simon Wheeler, the Amateur Detective," and several of the trials analyzed in D. M. McKeithan, *Court Trials in Mark Twain and Other Essays* (The Hague, 1958), pp. 10-114.

[30] See Walter Blair, "When Was *Huckleberry Finn* Written?" *American Literature*, XXX, 1-25 (March, 1958), and Henry Nash Smith, "Introduction," *Adventures of Huckleberry Finn* (Boston, 1958), p. ix.

Tom shuddered." *Now* the stage was set for the boys' return to their own funeral.

In several places the author reminded himself marginally to insert Aunt Polly's discovery of the message: on page 409 he jotted down, "The piece of bark at Aunt Polly's," and on page 464, "Aunt P's bark." Finally, on manuscript page 512 he related her discovery of the scroll and rounded off the awkward solution of that problem. He never explained Tom's similar message to Joe or his strange bequest of his "treasures" to his friend. Whether from expediency, indifference, or, most likely, the realization that Tom Sawyer was not the boy to send off on the "Battle of Life in many lands," Twain decided not to start Tom's journeying. Evidence that he realized Tom's shortcomings for such a role is offered by his own statement to Howells that "by and by I shall take a boy of twelve and run him on through life (in the first person) but not Tom Sawyer—he would not be a good character for it."[31] The decision committed him to center the book in his protagonist's boyhood in St. Petersburg.

Even though Twain thus determined the direction of his plot on manuscript page 403, the second half of the book gave him some problems in organization. For two hundred pages, beginning at manuscript page 533 and therefore in the late spring and summer of 1875, he juggled and rearranged his chapters extensively. For the two hundred pages following page 533 the manuscript is paginated thus (brackets indicating cancelled page numbers):

		A-1	to	A-24		
		B-1	to	B-13		
	[534]	573	to	[642]	694	
[535]	[643]	695	to	[345]	[653]	705
	[654]	706	to	[669]	721	

The two inserts, A-1 to A-24 and B-1 to B-13, related the graduation ceremonies and the Cadets of Temperance episode (Chapters xxi and xxii). The latter chapter may have been composed separately when the author wrote a note about it the previous fall; but since a marginal note referring to the graduation chapter occurred at page 573, that material must have been composed after the note (in Chapter xxiii) was written. Obviously neither insert was

[31] *Mark Twain's Letters*, p. 259.

placed in its present position until after Twain had written beyond them to page 722 (Chapter xxx). The third section listed above contained Chapters xxiii through the first paragraph of xxix. The fourth contained eleven pages of Chapter xxix relating some preliminary details about the picnic. The final section related the last paragraphs of Chapter xxix, those concerning Huck, Injun Joe, and Widow Douglas. From the pagination it appears that Twain originally intended the picnic section to follow the scene in which Tom took Becky's whipping.[32] Then Muff Potter's trial was substituted. While writing of the aftereffects of Muff's trial, Twain cancelled a passage which was to lead to the capture or death of Injun Joe. In Chapter xxiv, just before the final sentence of the published book, he wrote regarding Tom's apprehension of Injun Joe's revenge: "But Providence lifts even a boy's burden when it begins to get too heavy for him. The angel sent to attend to Tom's was an old back-country farmer named Ezra Ward, who had been a schoolmate of Aunt Polly's so many. . . ." The page (ms p. 600) ended and Twain discarded whatever other pages carried the idea further. Ezra Ward became an enigma, the only clue to his intended function in the story being the cryptic marginal note, "Brick pile." At this spot, probably, Twain replaced whatever plan he had for Injun Joe with the "buried treasure" chapters culminating in Joe's death in the cave. For he began writing the treasure chapters (xxv-xxix) immediately after cancelling the "Ezra Ward" material. These chapters then followed the trial chapter, and the beginning of the picnic was placed in Chapter xxix. At this point, apparently realizing the climactic possibilities of the cave chapters, Twain placed the two sections on the graduation exercises and on the Cadets of Temperance between the whipping scene and Potter's trial. This manipulation of material which was written more or less at random was accurately described by Brander Matthews:

When at last he became convinced that he had made his profit out of every possible reminiscence, he went over what he had written with great care, adjusting the several instalments one to the other, sometimes trans-

[32] The first three pages of the picnic material were originally numbered "535" to "537." The next eight pages were "338" to "345." The two-hundred-page drop in pagination was apparently inadvertent. There is no indication in the manuscript that this material might have belonged at page 338; Twain was making preparations for the picnic in Chapter xviii, ms pp. 487-490.

posing a chapter or two and sometimes writing into the earlier chapters the necessary preparation for adventures in the later chapters unforeseen when he was engaged on the beginnings of the book.[33]

Furthermore, this rearrangement of his material tends to support the theory that Twain was working with the deliberate intention of showing Tom's maturation. The school graduation depicting the high jinks at the expense of the school master and the pain-fully amateurish orations, and the Cadets of Temperance material revealing a youthful, irresolute Tom Sawyer were inserted in a relatively early spot in the manuscript, forcing three of the four chapters which Blair suggests are crucial into later positions.[34] The trial of Muff Potter was followed by the treasure chapters which portrayed a superstitious and fanciful pair of boys, and be-fore this line of action was completed in Chapter xxix by "showing Huck conquering fear to rescue the widow,"[35] the author inserted some preliminary paragraphs originating the picnic scene, para-graphs which had originally been intended for Chapter xxi. Next came Huck's bravery (ms pp. 706-721), completing the Injun Joe line of action. Finally the picnic material developed into the ad-ventures in the cave, which not only completed the Tom and Becky line of action but also showed Tom at his most manly. Though terms like *maturation, boyhood, youth*, and *early manhood* are ambiguous and ill-defined, nevertheless the rearranging of these climactic chapters allowed Twain to present Tom in a group of critical situations toward the end of the book where maturer judg-ment and courage were vital. These events required a Tom Sawyer who was nowhere apparent in the idyllic first half of the book.

III

In composing *Tom Sawyer,* then, Twain faced and solved two problems. First, when he was about half way through his manu-script, he paused at a crucial point and determined to keep his story centered in youth in St. Petersburg. An early scheme had included taking Tom on a "Battle of Life in many lands," and the

[33] Matthews, p. 266.

[34] "On the Structure of *Tom Sawyer*," p. 87: "And well in the second half of the book, in a series of chapters—xx, xxiii, xxix, xxxii—come those crucial situations in which he acts more like a grownup than like an irresponsible boy."

[35] *Ibid.*, p. 85.

moment for his departure was reached on manuscript page 403. Even though he altered the structure of the novel then, the author was nevertheless progressing through several stages of childhood mentioned in his outline, a progression which would be, as Blair observed, a "working out in fictional form . . . of a boy's maturing."[36]

Then in 1875, in the second half of the book, Twain very deliberately shifted his chapters so that climactic actions were placed after childish and immature incidents. Though the various anecdotes and episodes which he mentioned in his margins came to him chaotically and without formal significance, the humorist's selectivity and rearrangement of the material provided him with the structure he envisioned, roughly, in his early outline of the book. The marginal notations were identical with the working notes of *Huckleberry Finn*: though they were a ragbag of memories, the book which resulted was not structureless.

The manuscript of *Tom Sawyer* thus provides convincing evidence to corroborate Blair's interpretation of the book. The original outline indicated that it was begun with a definite structure in the author's mind. And the rearrangement of the later material shows that, instead of growing "as grows the grass," the book was considerably altered to conform to a bisected version of the outline when Twain determined to keep it, as he stated in the "Conclusion," "strictly a history of a *boy* . . . the story could not go much further without becoming the history of a *man*."

[36] *Ibid.*, p. 84.

The Sober Affirmation of Mark Twain's Hadleyburg
Clinton S. Burhans, Jr.

To SAY THAT "The Man That Corrupted Hadleyburg" is one of Twain's finest and most significant works would probably provoke little argument among serious students of his writing. Curiously, however, there are almost no independent studies of this story, and where it is considered in general studies of Twain's art, it is usually given little more than passing attention as a cynical and pessimistic story reflecting the deepening despair of his later years. I think the story deserves more serious consideration by Twain critics, and I offer this essay as a beginning.

Praising the Hadleyburg story, A. B. Paine calls it "a tale that in its own way takes its place with the half-dozen great English short stories of the world,"[1] and DeLancey Ferguson declares that while "the short story, as an art form, was not Mark's metier . . . in 'The Man That Corrupted Hadleyburg' he came near to perfection."[2] In contrast, Gladys Bellamy, though recognizing the story's power, feels that "for the thoughtful reader there is a mischief in it that keeps it from being altogether satisfying." She considers the story marred by inconsistencies stemming from two conflicting characteristics of Twain's mind—his determinism and his moralism. Twain, she says, establishes a deterministic framework to explain the motivation and behavior of his characters and then violates it illogically with "an implied theme of divine justice— the great theme of the judgment of God as it operates through the consciences of Mr. and Mrs. Richards. . . . There is no continuity of motivation, no steadiness of emotional effect, no philosophical unity to the story. In it the moralist gives an out-of-bounds blow to the determinist, and Hadleyburg settles itself on a philosophic quicksand."[3]

[1] A. B. Paine, *Mark Twain: A Biography* (New York, 1912), III-IV, 1068.
[2] DeLancey Ferguson, *Mark Twain: Man and Legend* (New York, 1943), p. 278.
[3] Gladys Bellamy, *Mark Twain as a Literary Artist* (Norman, Oklahoma, 1950), pp. 308-309.

It seems to me, however, that Miss Bellamy's usually brilliant insight fails her here, for in this story Twain is consistent both logically and aesthetically. On the surface, the story is an attack on human greed and hypocrisy, but at its deeper levels it reflects Twain's return to the unresolved problems which had perplexed him in Huck Finn's moral conflict and an exploration of the possibility that experience can unify man's moral perceptions and his motivating emotions. In this context, Twain's concept of determinism, especially environmental determinism, or training, does not conflict with his moralism; on the contrary, his moralism functions here in terms of his determinism. Moreover, his view of conscience in this story[4] is not, as Miss Bellamy implies, that of the conventional religious moralist; it is far more complicated than this, synthesizing as it does the principal elements in his earlier concepts of conscience.

Twain's determinism in "The Man That Corrupted Hadleyburg," far from being inconsistent with his moralism, is the source of its real values. In his concern in this story with the relations between conscience and the heart, he views the moral values of conscience as determined by environment, by training; and one of his major aims is to show that such training in moral values must be empirical, not merely prescriptive. The people of Hadleyburg try to preserve the honesty which has made them famous by training it into their young. They forget, however, that originally this honesty was not just an abstract ideal, but a principle developed and maintained empirically in constant action against the forces and temptations of dishonesty and therefore rooted by experience firmly among the motivating impulses of the heart. "It was many years ago," Twain writes. "Hadleyburg was the most honest and upright town in all the region around about. It had kept that reputation unsmirched during three generations, and was prouder of it than of any other of its possessions."[5]

---

[4] Critical opinions on this aspect of Twain's story diverge widely. At one extreme, Alexander Jones feels that "in such works as 'The Man That Corrupted Hadleyburg,' he assumed the existence of an inner moral standard which enables man to determine what is right, and this is essentially in agreement with the doctrines of Shaftesbury" ("Mark Twain and Religion," Ph.D. dissertation, University of Minnesota, 1950, p. 223). At almost the other extreme, however, Leon Howard declares that Twain "implicitly denied the existence of an internal, incorruptible moral sense in his story 'The Man That Corrupted Hadleyburg'" (*Literature and the American Tradition*, New York, 1960, p. 219).

[5] Mark Twain, *The Man That Corrupted Hadleyburg and Other Stories and Essays*

So proud are the people of Hadleyburg of their reputation and so fearful of the slightest threat to it that they try to safeguard it not by the continued practice of honesty but rather by an attempt to exclude all temptations to dishonesty. The town "was so proud of it," Twain declares, "and so anxious to insure its perpetuation, that it began to teach the principles of honest dealing to it babies in the cradle, and made the like teachings the staple of their culture thenceforward through all the years devoted to their education. Also, throughout the formative years temptations were kept out of the way of the young people, so that their honesty could have every chance to harden and solidify, and become a part of their very bone" (p. 1). Hadleyburg has tried to create an environment in which the principles of honesty can be trained into the young without the dangers involved in practicing them against inimical temptations. The fame of the town, the people feel, will thereby be secure.

But Hadleyburg's training is defective and artificial on at least two counts: in the first place, it is impossible to shield men forever from all temptations to dishonesty, and when inexorably they do arise, men unpracticed in recognizing and resisting them will succumb, as Richards does in failing to clear Burgess—a failure which foreshadows the fall of Hadleyburg. And in the second place, Hadleyburg forgets that man is determined by heredity as well as by environment, that human nature is potentially petty and selfish as well as noble and kind. Thus, when the town becomes obsessed with vanity over its empty and now unearned reputation, its preoccupation with preserving that reputation by excluding the temptations to dishonesty not only fails but also leaves other vices free to develop unchecked. When Richards tells his wife that "'we have been trained all our lives long, like the whole village, till it is absolutely second nature to us to stop not a single moment to think when there's an honest thing to be done,'" she refutes him prophetically:

Oh, I know it, I know it—it's been one everlasting training and training and training in honesty—honesty shielded, from the very cradle, against every possible temptation, and so it's *artificial* honesty, and weak as water when temptation comes, as we have seen this night. God knows I never had shade nor shadow of a doubt of my petrified and inde-

structible honesty until now—and now, under the very first big and real
temptation, I—Edward, it is my belief that this town's honesty is as
rotten as mine is; as rotten as yours is. It is a mean town, a hard,
stingy town, and hasn't a virtue in the world but this honesty it is so
celebrated for and so conceited about; and so help me, I do believe that
if ever the day comes that its honesty falls under great temptation, its
grand reputation will go to ruin like a house of cards. There, now, I've
made confession, and I feel better; I am a humbug, and I've been one
all my life, without knowing it. (pp. 15-16)

Obsessive vanity and insulated disuse, then, have made Hadleyburg's honesty artificial and hypocritical: much like Huck Finn's
attitude toward slavery, it is largely an untested abstraction; it is
almost entirely divorced from the townspeople's hearts. In short,
the training of the people of Hadleyburg has shaped their consciences to an awareness of the moral ideal of honesty, but it has
given them no experience in following the directions of conscience
and therefore no true knowledge of its values.

Seeing in the people of Hadleyburg what they cannot see in
themselves or, like the Richardses, see too late, the vindictive stranger
directs his ingenious revenge at their most vulnerable spot—the
greed for wealth and social position in hearts whose inexperience in
resisting temptations to dishonesty has left them no answering
passion for true honesty. That Hadleyburg falls, that all of the
Nineteen succumb, is therefore not surprising. Nor is their subsequent sense of guilt, as reflected in the Richardses, at all inconsistent. Both are corollaries of Twain's concept of determinism;
ironically, paradoxically, Hadleyburg's fall is determined by the
abstract training which the people had counted on to keep them
forever incorruptible; and their consciences, whose moral perceptions also stem from that training, cause them to feel guilt and
shame.

In the end, of course, Hadleyburg learns the meaning of its
mistakes: that only through experience can the moral perceptions
of conscience be united with the emotions which motivate man.
Moreover, this is also the significance of the story's central conflict
as Twain develops it through the Richardses. From the beginning
he defines this conflict largely in terms of the relationship between
the Richardses' consciences and their hearts, an evolving relationship
synthesizing most of his earlier concepts of conscience.

At times, Richards's conscience operates like Tom Sawyer's; that is, it makes moral distinctions and influences him to commensurate action. Learning that the town is planning to punish the Rev. Burgess for something which only Richards knows he did not do, Richards warns him. " 'When the thing was new and hot,' " he tells his wife, " ' and the town made a plan to ride him on a rail, my conscience hurt me so that I couldn't stand it, and I went privately and gave him notice, and he got out of the town and staid out till it was safe to come back' " (pp. 9-10). But Richards's training in honesty has been only prescriptive, and his conscience affects his actions only to the point at which they conflict with the desire for the good opinion of the town, which is the principal element in his basic emotion of self-approval. He warns Burgess privately, and almost at once regrets having saved him; he fears the town will find out and turn its dislike of Burgess against him. For, as Twain points out in the contemporaneous *What Is Man?*, "Corn-Pone Opinions," and "The United States of Lyncherdom," "the Sole Impulse which dictates and compels a man's every act: the imperious necessity of securing his own approval, in every emergency and at all costs,"[6] usually involves not only the disposition to do whatever will gain public approval but also "man's commonest weakness, his aversion to being unpleasantly conspicuous, pointed at, shunned, as being on the unpopular side."[7]

Reflecting Hadleyburg's defective training in honesty, Richards's moral ideals are in this crisis almost entirely separated from his motivating emotion of self-approval.[8] In addition to making him regret having saved Burgess, this basic emotion violates his conscience and prevents him from clearing the clergyman of the unjust accusation against him. " 'I am ashamed,' " Richards admits. " 'I was the only man who knew he was innocent. I could have saved him, and—and—well, you know how the town was wrought up—I hadn't the pluck to do it. It would have turned everybody against me. I felt mean, ever so mean; but I didn't dare; I hadn't the manliness to face that' " (pp. 8-9). Here, then, though its moral values and demands as well as the emotions it contends with are the re-

[6] Mark Twain, *What Is Man? and Other Essays* (New York, 1917), p. 29.
[7] Mark Twain, *Europe and Elsewhere* (New York, 1923), p. 243.
[8] The emphasis on public opinion in Richards's desire for self-approval can also be laid to his Hadleyburg training, to an environment, that is, in which the reputation for honesty, the public image of the town, has become an obsession.

verse of Huck Finn's, Richards's conscience functions much like Huck's in that it exerts almost no influence on his actions but does punish him with a sense of guilt when he fails to obey it.

The stranger's bag of gold evokes in the Richardses and in the rest of the Nineteen the same conflict between the moral guidance and the demands of their consciences and the urgings of their emotions. Despite the warnings of his conscience, each is driven by his desires for wealth, security, and social position to rationalize and then to lie about his right to the gold. "All night long," Twain writes, "eighteen principal citizens did what their caste-brother Richards was doing at the same time—they put in their energies trying to remember what notable service it was that they had unconsciously done Barclay Goodson. In no case was it a holiday job; still they succeeded" (p. 28). Like Adam and Eve in Twain's version of their temptation and fall, the Nineteen "could not understand untried things and verbal abstractions which stood for matters outside of their little world and their narrow experience."[9]

The town meeting reveals the dishonesty of the rest of the Nineteen, but for the Richardses it means only more temptation and further conflict between the values and entreaties of their consciences and their passion for public favor. Twice again they are tempted and twice again they fall. When they think their dishonesty is going to be disclosed, they rise to confess and to plead for the town's forgiveness; but when the generous Burgess silences them and then fails to read Richards's note, they are "faint with joy and surprise" and no longer disposed to confess. "'Oh, bless God,'" whispers Mary Richards, "'we are saved!—he has lost ours—I wouldn't give this for a hundred of those sacks!'" (p. 50). Their desire for public approval completely overcomes the demands of their consciences that they confess and justly "suffer with the rest" (p. 49), and once more they succumb to the temptation to dishonesty.

Nor is this all, for they compound their dishonesty when the town proposes to auction off the stranger's bag of gold and give the proceeds to them. Again, their consciences point out the Richardses' deceitfulness and urge them to confess: "at the beginning of the auction," Twain writes, "Richards whispered in distress

[9] Twain, *Europe and Elsewhere*, pp. 344-345.

to his wife: 'O Mary, can we allow it? It—it—you see, it is an honor-reward, a testimonial to purity of character, and—and—can we allow it? Hadn't I better get up and—O Mary, what ought we to do?—'" She, too, understands the moral implications and requirements of their position and replies, "'it is another temptation, Edward—I'm all in a tremble—but, oh, we've escaped *one* temptation, and that ought to warn us to — . . . O Edward . . . we are *so* poor!—but—but—do as you think best—do as you think best.'" This, however, is precisely what he does not do; "Edward fell," Twain declares, "—that is, he sat still; sat with a conscience which was not satisfied, but which was overpowered by circumstances" (pp. 55-56), circumstances of wealth and an intoxicating public admiration.

As the incitements to dishonesty become more tempting, then, conscience in the Richardses, as in the Hadleyburg they reflect, diminishes as an effective moral and ethical force; and finally, much as Twain defines it in *What Is Man?*, it has no moral and ethical function at all. For a while the consciences they have violated cause the Richardses to feel some last glimmerings of guilt and shame and regret: Richards decides to resign his position at the bank, feeling that he can no longer trust himself with other people's money; and both he and his wife are made profoundly miserable by Stephenson's note praising their honesty. But these feelings soon die, and the Richardses' sense of guilt becomes a matter not of morality but of exposure; "within twenty-four hours after the Richardses had received their checks," Twain writes, "their consciences were quieting down, discouraged; the old couple were learning to reconcile themselves to the sin which they had committed. But they were to learn, now, that a sin takes on new and real terrors when there seems a chance that it is going to be found out. This gives it a fresh and most substantial and important aspect" (p. 64).

Fearing the exposure of their dishonesty, the Richardses are no longer concerned with the moral values and responsibilities of their situation. The separation between their ideal of honesty and their motivating emotions is now complete, and their consciences lose all moral and ethical function and become in effect identical with the Richardses' self-approval in its passion for public approval. Conscience now moves the Richardses only to a suspicion that others know about their dishonesty and to fear that someone will disclose it, particularly the suspicion that Burgess knows of Richards's failure long ago to reveal his innocence and the fear that he intends to revenge himself by exposing them.[10]

Tortured beyond endurance, the Richardses sicken and die, but not from any Divine punishment reflected in the agonies of a guilty conscience. They die because they cannot abide the knowledge that their good name may be destroyed and that they may be held up to an even greater obloquy than the rest of the Nineteen. In short, they are no longer aware of sin and guilt as matters of moral principle and individual responsibility; self-approval is their conscience, and its demand for public favor renders them obsessed, like the town they mirror, with the name of honesty at the cost of its essence, which would mean, as Richards realizes in the town meeting, confessing publicly that they have been as dishonest as the others.

Before the Richardses die, however, Twain reveals that they have not suffered barrenly. Their racking fear that their dishonesty will be exposed has rooted the knowledge of that dishonesty deeply in their hearts; through experience, the self-approval which is their conscience has learned moral and ethical responsibility and now makes moral distinctions which result in commensurate action. In Richards, as Twain in Huck Finn implies they must, conscience and the heart, moral perception and motivating emotion, at last function together. Richards's ideal of honesty is rooted in his heart, in the self-approval which governs his actions, and he dies an honest man.

Concerned anew with moral values, he destroys the checks which have cost him so dearly; " 'they came from Satan,' " he tells the nurse. " 'I saw the hell-brand on them, and I knew they were sent to betray me to sin' " (p. 67).[11] His self-approval now de-

---

[10] The change in the nature and function of conscience in Richards is illustrated in this change in his attitude toward Burgess. Earlier, his conscience had led him to feel ashamed of his failure to clear Burgess; now, however, it moves him only to fear Burgess as a threat to his reputation for honesty.

[11] The evolution in Richards's conscience and its relation to his heart is reflected in this change in his reason for wanting to destroy the checks. When his conscience had lost its moral functions and become identical with his amoral desire for self-approval, he considered the checks a temptation not in moral terms but only as a threat to his reputation; thus, he declares that " 'we mustn't be tempted' " and wants to burn the checks because

mands behavior consistent with moral rectitude, and he wants the essence of honesty, not its mere reputation. With his last breath, he admits his guilt—not privately, as in what he had told his wife about Burgess, but openly in a public avowal. " 'I want witnesses,' " he declares. " 'I want you all to hear my confession, so that I may die a man, and not a dog. I was clean—artificially—like the rest; and like the rest I fell when temptation came. I signed a lie, and claimed the miserable sack' " (p. 68). Moreover, though he thinks Burgess has exposed him, Richards admits his cowardly failure to save the clergyman from undeserved disgrace.

Experience has made Richards's conscience a highly complex faculty in which moral perception and direction and the motivating emotion of self-approval work together to produce real honesty— honesty which is not simply allegiance to an abstract principle, but honesty expressed in practice against the temptations of dishonesty.[12] Nor is this lesson lost upon Hadleyburg, which learns fully and well what the Nineteen and particularly the Richardses exemplify: the town's new motto, "Lead Us Into Temptation," is not an invitation to sin, but a means to grapple with it empirically. Whatever its new name may be, Hadleyburg is truly "an honest

---

they are " 'a trick to make the world laugh at *us*, along with the rest' " (p. 61). Now, however, he destroys them as a temptation which conflicts with his renewed and more profound moral perceptions.

[12] This view that the real knowledge of abstract moral values is determined by environment, or training, that only empirically can the essential unity of conscience and the heart be secured, is a central element in Twain's moralism and appears in a variety of forms throughout his generally inconsistent moral thought. In addition to its vital influence on many of his finest literary works, it is suggested in such philosophical writings as *What Is Man?*, especially in the idea that the heart can be trained to act by higher ideals, and implied in many remarks throughout Twain's writing. Thus, in a letter to Henry Ward Beecher in 1885, Twain exclaims, "how I do hate those enemies of the human race who go around enslaving God's people with *pledges*—to quit drinking instead of to quit wanting to drink" (*Mark Twain's Letters*, A. B. Paine, ed., New York, 1917, II, 459). The Connecticut Yankee feels that the common man in King Arthur's England needs "a new deal," and he would like to start a revolution for that purpose. "But I knew," the Yankee reflects, "that the Jack Cade or the Wat Tyler who tries such a thing without first educating his materials up to revolution grade is almost absolutely certain to get left" (*A Connecticut Yankee in King Arthur's Court*, New York, 1917, p. 108). And in his essay "My First Lie, and How I Got Out of It," Twain writes that when he was a baby he got the attentions he wanted by crying as though a pin were sticking him. Soon, however, a safety-pin put an end to his infantile dishonesty. "But," he argues, "is that reform worth anything? No; for it is reform by force and has no virtue in it; it merely stops that form of lying; it doesn't impair the disposition to lie, by a shade. It is the cradle application of conversion by fire and sword, or of the temperance principle through prohibition" (*The Man That Corrupted Hadleyburg*, p. 160).

town once more, and the man will have to rise early that catches it napping again" (p. 69).

"The Man That Corrupted Hadleyburg" is therefore neither as inconsistent nor as pessimistic as it is usually considered. In it are reflected the major aspects of Twain's conflicting moral thought— moral values as abstract, moral values as empirical; conscience as the reflector of moral values, conscience as the amoral emotion of self-approval—but these conflicting ideas are reconciled by Twain's determinism into a formal and thematic unity which generates substantial beauty and power. Moreover, the story is in fact less pessimistic than soberly optimistic; it ends, after all, not with the greed, hypocrisy, and cynicism of the town meeting, but with the development of a significant conscience in Richards and in the affirmation of Hadleyburg's new motto. And if Twain shows man as a deterministic creature driven by vanity and greed, he also shows that this is neither the complete nor the final answer to the question of man, that the experience of living can determine man to his salvation as well as to his perdition.

In "The Man That Corrupted Hadleyburg," then, Twain declares with Milton that "I cannot praise a fugitive and cloistered virtue, unexercised and unbreathed, that never sallies out and sees her adversary, but slinks out of the race where that immortal garland is to be run for, not without dust and heat. Assuredly we bring not innocence into the world, we bring impurity much rather: that which purifies us is trial, and trial is by what is contrary. That virtue therefore which is but a youngling in the contemplation of evil, and knows not the utmost that vice promises to her followers, and rejects it, is but a blank virtue, not a pure; her whiteness is but an excremental whiteness. . . ."[13] Again, Twain argues with Conrad's Stein that " 'the way is to the destructive element submit yourself, and with the exertions of your hands and feet in the water make the deep, deep sea keep you up. . . . In the destructive element immerse. . . .' "[14] In "The Man That Corrupted Hadleyburg," Twain's divergent moral and ethical ideas merge in a view of man which places Twain within a great and a positive tradition.

[13] Maynard Mack, ed., *Milton* (New York, 1953), p. 81.
[14] Joseph Conrad, *Lord Jim* (London, 1953), p. 156.

Alias Macfarlane: A Revision of Mark Twain Biography
Paul Baender

MARK TWAIN has perhaps received more causal analysis than any other American writer. Regional and economic factors, guilts and frustrations imposed by his family life, several kinds of sexual motives—all these have served to explain the man and his works; and far from any abatement of the genetic approach, recent years have produced in it a considerable sophistication and expertise. It is therefore surprising that a certain supposition of influence has never been challenged. This is the belief that while working in Cincinnati in 1856-1857, young Sam Clemens was so impressed with the pessimistic doctrine of a man named Macfarlane as to adopt it for his own in later years. There are two sources for this notion. The first to become public was Albert Bigelow Paine's discussion of the Clemens-Macfarlane relationship in his biography (1912). After describing their conversational evenings in the Cincinnati boarding house, and after a summary of Macfarlane's pessimism, Paine reflects: "They were long, fermenting discourses that young Samuel Clemens listened to that winter in Macfarlane's room, and those who knew the real Mark Twain and his philosophies will recognize that those evenings left their impress upon him for life."[1] The other source is a brief manuscript which Paine included in his edition of Twain's autobiography (1924).[2] It was the basis of Paine's account in the biography, with one important exception: Twain says nothing whatever about Macfarlane's influence on him.

I

But many later critics have drawn Paine's conclusion. They have read the manuscript as an autobiographical fragment in which

[1] *Mark Twain: A Biography* (New York, 1912), I, 115.

[2] *Mark Twain's Autobiography,* ed. Albert Bigelow Paine (New York, 1924), I, 143-147. The manuscript is DV 224(8) in the Mark Twain Papers. All quotations are from the manuscript, which differs in a few places from Paine's emended text. So far as is known, Twain referred to Macfarlane only in this manuscript, and no other information about him is available.

Mark Twain revealed a source of his late opinions on man and human history. The persistence of this interpretation is surprising because one would not expect it to last in the climate of theory fostered by Brooks, DeVoto, and others with a psychoanalytic orientation. In that climate one would expect the idea of Twain's indebtedness to a chance acquaintance in Cincinnati for the opinions of *What Is Man?* and *The Mysterious Stranger* to be discarded as a relic from the age of John Townsend Trowbridge, when a young carpenter might meet his turning point while reading Emerson over lunch. Nor does one need a Brooks-DeVoto tradition to doubt that the older man could influence the young Sam Clemens so crucially in so short a time, or that Mark Twain in his sixties could isolate such an influence without oversimplification, or that he could restate Macfarlane's pessimism without using his own vocabulary of contempt, which was already well developed by the time he wrote about Macfarlane. And yet as recently as 1961 a survey for the general reader that says it "takes into account all the biographical research ... since A. B. Paine's monumental authorized biography" also says Macfarlane "inspirited [Mark Twain] with the germ of the deterministic pessimism to which he held more and more staunchly as he aged."[3]

Few people if any would have inferred this indebtedness without Paine's interpretation of the manuscript, but it is doubtful he was altogether responsible. Later critics repeat the Macfarlane story, and enjoy repeating it, with an air of superiority and condescension quite foreign to Paine. They appear to believe in the influence because it helps put Mark Twain in his place as one of those writers whose "ideas" need not be taken seriously. To this argument they may bring aspects of his traditional characterization. There is the Mark Twain whose philosophic culture was naïve, shallow, and overly subject to personal motives. All of these faults show up in the Macfarlane episode, where young Clemens, not long out of Missouri and easily impressed, swallows once and for all the presumptuous opinions of a provincial eccentric only less ignorant than he. Then there is the elderly Mark Twain who became rigorous about the "damned human race" partly from grief and dis-

[3] Frank Baldanza, *Mark Twain: An Introduction and Interpretation* (New York, 1961), pp. v, 15.

appointment but also because he was dogmatic. Thus, the tenacity of his pessimism in the later years may measure not a degree of conviction so much as an habituation of bias, and thus the Macfarlane influence seems all the more probable from its early place in his life.

There is also Mark Twain the self-made man, who as a youth was bright but underprivileged and had to struggle to educate himself on his own. And so the Macfarlane episode takes its place beside the image of Sam Clemens teaching himself French and reading a little Voltaire while piloting on the Mississippi. But if critics reason from this characterization to a belief in Macfarlane's influence, their procedure is just the reverse of Paine's. To Paine the influence of Macfarlane was proof of Clemens's sensitivity and a credential of his right to become a self-made man. Not long before publishing the Twain biography Paine told how Thomas Nast "engaged certain impecunious college men ... to read and discuss solid books of history and science" and thus "make up for a lack of school education."[4] Years later he would tell how the young Theodore Vail used to meet with an educated friend to "discuss the problems of life and death, and broaden his philosophies, which hitherto had been confined within orthodox limits."[5] All three men demonstrated a capacity to range beyond conventional limits of opinion, and Paine—a Midwestern farmboy who had become a professional writer in New York—saw in this a harbinger of the truly exceptional man, as compared with the specious success who might change his locale and his class but whose ideas never left home. And though Paine says Macfarlane's ideas "left their impress ... for life," his tone is respectful, as if in so fully accepting Macfarlane's influence Clemens showed he recognized a significant independence of mind and knew how to profit by the example when making his way in the world.

Thus, Paine led other critics to accept a proposition of fact but not his evaluation of it. Worse, they have used the Macfarlane episode not to elevate Mark Twain but to criticize him. While Paine imagined an archetypal spot of time wherein an obscure adult passed the burden of responsibility to a youth who would become famous, later critics find the same incident an example of

[4] Th. Nast: His Period and His Pictures (New York, 1904), p. 121.
[5] In One Man's Life (New York, 1921), p. 50.

Mark Twain's irresponsibility. Like his boyhood traumas and adult neurosis, the Macfarlane affair reduces his pessimism to a derivative.

II

Paine started the course of this irony by grouping the "Macfarlane" manuscript with several autobiographical pieces Twain wrote in 1897 and 1898. Here was his basic mistake. The manuscript contains autobiographical material,[6] yet I maintain that its purpose was rhetorical and that the manuscript properly belongs to a genre of polemic Mark Twain experimented with in his last three decades. I do not argue that Paine or the later critics were right or wrong in their evaluations but that they were irrelevant in making them. The question should not be how much Twain owed Macfarlane, or whether such an indebtedness affected his stature as a philosopher, but for what reasons he used the Macfarlane evoked in the manuscript as a voice for his own opinions.

The manuscript begins as Twain's description of a memorable eccentric he met in Cincinnati when he was "just turned twenty." This was Macfarlane, a man of forty and the only interesting person in the boarding house he patronized. While the other residents were lively and frivolous, he was somber, quiet, reticent about his personal life, yet willing to talk seriously with young Clemens. Macfarlane never mentioned his trade or background, except to say he had picked up his learning for himself. From his rough hands Clemens inferred he was a mechanic of some sort.

Macfarlane's command of his dictionary was remarkable. He could spell and define every word with which Clemens tried to stump him. He was equally familiar with the Bible, his other favorite book, and in general he considered himself a "philosopher and thinker." He talked sincerely on large issues, and though his mind was untrained he "hit by accident upon some curious and striking things"; for instance, a theory of evolution the same as Darwin's "but with a difference." At this point, to characterize the difference, Twain drops his manner of genial reminiscence and delivers an alleged summary of Macfarlane's philosophy, as follows:

---

[6] Twain was indeed in Cincinnati for several months in his early twenties. And the "earlier friend in Philadelphia, the Englishman Sumner," appears to have been a real person; see "Jul'us Caesar," DW 12, in the Mark Twain Papers.

Macfarlane considered that the animal life in the world was developed in the course of æons of time from a few microscopic seed-germs, or perhaps *one* microscopic seed-germ deposited upon the globe by the Creator in the dawn of time; and that this development was progressive upon an ascending scale toward ultimate perfection until *man* was reached; and that then the progressive scheme broke pitifully down and went to wreck and ruin!

He said that man's heart was the only bad heart in the animal kingdom; that man was the only animal capable of feeling malice, envy, vindictiveness, vengefulness, hatred, selfishness, the only animal that loved drunkenness, almost the only animal that could endure personal uncleanliness and a filthy habitation, the sole animal in whom was fully developed the base instinct called *patriotism,* the sole animal that robs, persecutes, oppresses, and kills members of his own immediate tribe, the sole animal that steals and enslaves the members of *any* tribe.

He claimed that man's intellect was a brutal addition to him and degraded him to a rank far below the plane of the other animals, and that there was never a man who did not use his intellect daily all his life to advantage himself at other people's expense. The divinest divine reduced his domestics to humble servitude under him by advantage of his superior intellect, and those servants in turn were above a still lower grade of people by force of brains that were still a little better than theirs.

Here the manuscript abruptly ends, without a peroration or a return to the personal matter with which it begins.

In itself the manuscript suggests three reasons why Paine grouped it with Twain's autobiographical writings of the 1890's. First, the handwriting appears to be that of the middle or late nineties.[7] Second, like several autobiographical pieces of the period, the manuscript begins as a recollection of an unusual personality. Like James Lampton, Jane Clemens, Petroleum V. Nasby, and Ralph Keeler—all of whom Twain wrote about in the nineties— Macfarlane has eccentricities which apparently evoke nostalgia, amusement, pity, and respect in the author, and which he seems to think will evoke similar responses in a reader. Finally, the philosophy attributed to Macfarlane was also Twain's, as Paine well knew. And so, putting the three observations together in a simple way, he may have concluded that the manuscript was entirely

[7] The paper suggests a date around 1894 or 1895, since it contains a watermark so far found only among correspondence and manuscripts of those years. The autobiographical fragments of 1897-1898 are of different paper.

autobiographical and that Twain was about to admit a source of his pessimism. His failure to admit it could have been an accident, if the abrupt end of the piece meant it was incomplete.

Whatever his preliminary reasoning, Paine's belief in the influence of Macfarlane ultimately depended on something Mark Twain did not say, and it failed to account for important aspects of what he did say. Twain's summary of Macfarlane's philosophy is put in terms that are often nearly the same as those he used elsewhere (though more violently) when speaking in the first person—compare "The Character of Man" and "The Lowest Animal."[8] Yet in his summary he uses the past tense almost always ("He *said* that man's heart *was* the only bad heart"), as though to seem a disengaged reporter of someone else's opinions. Also the manuscript was not a memorandum to himself or a private disclosure to friends and relations, but a public composition meant for the general reader of the 1890's. Had Twain published it such readers might have sensed his indorsement of the pessimism beneath his pose of disengagement, yet unlike Paine they could not have known how long or with what passion it was his own doctrine. And if the work was in fact incomplete, a plausible inference from the equable tone of Twain's summary is that he would have concluded with an affectation of judicious assent, pretending to admit to the general reader that Macfarlane's opinions had more merit than he realized in his youth. In any case, as it stands, the manuscript does not chronicle but conceals the history and temper of Twain's pessimism, and it appears to be an argument by means of disguise rather than a personal memoir. If it is this, a line of interpretation different from Paine's is necessary.

Thus, I suggest that the "Macfarlane" piece belongs to a group of works which have in common Twain's use of outsiders as voices for his own opinions. The group is more numerous than is generally known, since several relevant manuscripts and the outlines of others Twain contemplated have not yet been published. Among those that have been are *The Mysterious Stranger,* "The Man That Corrupted Hadleyburg," "Corn-Pone Opinions," and "The War Prayer." In all such works a character from outside a normal society is introduced to impart wisdom the society badly

[8] *Mark Twain's Autobiography,* II, 7-13, and *Letters from the Earth,* ed. Bernard DeVoto (New York, 1962), pp. 222-232.

needs but cannot discover. For the wisdom consists in a disenchanted view of mankind that subverts the natural complacencies of the society, and only a mind free of communal illusions can possess the wisdom or dare to utter it. The outsider never succeeds in humbling the society's egotism or in curbing its selfishness, for it must continue to be what it is—a mass of slavish, cruel, malicious creatures beneath the dignity of other animals. The outsider's failure is rhetorical insofar as Twain believed it might inspire his readers' education, yet he also believed the polarity between society and outsider represented an actual split between public opinion and the facts of life. Every society needed to think well of itself, and it gladly ignored anyone who frustrated that need, even when (and especially when), as in the late nineteenth century, he might have legitimate implications of science on his side.

Twain's chief argumentative problem was to account for the outsider. If men were naturally cruel, how could any man be decent enough to deplore their cruelty? If men were conditioned by society, who could resist its comforting illusions? In certain polemics Twain assumed no human being could be exempt, and in them his wise outsiders were creatures of different species. In *The Mysterious Stranger* it was an angel. In an unpublished manuscript of 1889 it was a dog by the name of "Newfoundland Smith" who listed the same indictments Twain attributed to Macfarlane, e.g.: "Malice resides in no animal but one—Man. Envy is found in no animal but one—Man."[9] Compare "Macfarlane": "man was the only animal capable of feeling malice, envy." Late in 1898 Twain thought of using an ant to deliver the doctrine of *What Is Man?* He imagined a "Visit to & talks with politicians & professors, soldiers & slaves among the ants. One had written a book on human beings— proves Selfishness, No Merit &c.... Court gazette, telling which Equerry dined with the queen &c.—satirize all human grandeurs & vanities."[10] The element of fantasy in these devices was by no means a concession of fantasy in the moral ideal. By the late 1880's Twain seriously believed in the moral superiority of the "lower

[9] Copyright © 1966 by the Mark Twain Company. The manuscript is "Letters from a Dog," DV 344 in the Mark Twain Papers.
[10] Copyright © 1966 by the Mark Twain Company. The citation is to typescript notebook 32(II), p. 52, in the Mark Twain Papers. "Selfishness" was a provisional title for *What Is Man?* in 1898. "No Merit" refers to Twain's argument in Chapter 1 that virtuous actions do not confer personal merit.

animals," and he chose them for his philosophic outsiders because
they might accuse mankind in a lofty tone of unhurt outrage which
was imaginatively true to their character.

In other works, the outsiders are men, and to make their free
minds plausible Twain gave them special personal traits or membership in groups hardly susceptible to the standard beliefs of society. In the unpublished "Indiantown" story he characterizes Orrin
Lloyd Godkin as

> an educated bachelor of forty, and the next richest planter . . . his com-
> plexion . . . was ghostly, spectral, ghastly. It was wholly colorless. . . .
> It was the cold, hard, smooth, polished, opaque, tintless and horrible
> white of a wax-figure's hands. . . . Out of this dreadful mask looked a
> pair of sloe-black eyes; alert, intelligent, searching, wistful, and very
> human eyes.[11]

Despite his "very human eyes," Godkin's appearance implies a death
of feeling that has liberated him from the gentleness and compunc-
tion that might compromise the sardonic philosophies of ordinary
men. Later Twain says Godkin "always spoke in light and airy
disparagement of the human race; and also as if it were a species
in which he had no personal concern; in fact he . . . complacently
spoke of its members as 'those foreigners.' "[12] And in a note to the
story Twain says Godkin will claim "all men are made exclusively
of selfishness"[13]—again the doctrine of *What Is Man?* The other
tactic of plausibility shows up as early as an 1882 notebook. The
entry is a philosophic dialogue between two Negroes, one of whom
asserts God's responsibility for man's sins, another favorite thesis
of Twain's later years:

> [God] could a made de mankind so *dey* wouldn't ever want to rip &
> cuss & kill folks, & git drunk & so on, 'f he'd a wanted to. But he didn't
> *want* to. Dat's de pint!—he didn't *want* to. He made most all of 'em

[11] Copyright © 1966 by the Mark Twain Company; DV 302g in the Mark Twain
Papers. Note that Macfarlane and Godkin are both forty years old. Compare John Hay's
statement to Twain: " 'A man reaches the zenith at forty, the top of the hill. From that
time forward he begins to descend' " (*Mark Twain: A Biography*, II, 563); and Twain's
own statement: "The man who is a pessimist before 48 knows too much; if he is an
optimist after it, he knows too little" (*Mark Twain's Notebook*, ed. Albert Bigelow
Paine, New York, 1935, p. 380).

[12] "Indiantown." Copyright © 1966 by the Mark Twain Company.

[13] Copyright © 1966 by the Mark Twain Company; DV 302h in the Mark Twain
Papers.

so dey'd be a set of ornery blame' scoun'ls,—& now you reckon he gwine to roas' 'em all to everlast'n for what He done his own seff? No, *sir*— He's 'sponsible—shore's you's bawn he is.[14]

Similarly, in 1901 Twain uses the slave Jerry to introduce the argument of "Corn-Pone Opinions": " 'You tell me whar a man gits his corn-pone, 'en I'll tell you what his 'pinions is.' "[15] Fortunately excluded from the white culture, these pariahs enjoy a skeptical perspective on its illusions which well-born folk like Orrin Lloyd Godkin can acquire only through eccentricity and a somewhat fanatic resolve.

The "Macfarlane" manuscript represents this sort of outsider polemic, and it uses both means of plausibility. Twain tells us that the people in the Cincinnati boarding house were "full of bustle, frivolity, chatter, and the joy of life, and were good-natured, clean-minded, and well meaning." Yet Macfarlane, like Orrin Lloyd Godkin, stood apart from the crowd. He was "a serious and sincere man. He had no humor, nor any comprehension of it. He had a sort of smile, whose office was to express his good nature, but if I ever heard him laugh the memory of it is gone from me." He maintained a façade of politeness but lapsed into intimacy only with Clemens, and even he discovered very little about Macfarlane's background. On the other hand, while his withdrawal suggests the aristocratic self-containment of Col. Sherburn, Barclay Goodson, and Orrin Lloyd Godkin, Macfarlane's low occupation preserved him from middle-class culture, much like Twain's Negro philosophers. He spent twelve hours a day at some mechanical job so unimportant to him that no one knew what it was. He evidently cared nothing for advancement, inasmuch as he spent his free time on his offbeat learning and philosophy. And his philosophy could hardly inspire anyone to adopt middle-class imperatives of belief or action. The sum of these characteristics made Macfarlane an aristocratic proletarian, proud though humble, an uncompromising cynic who could do little with his wisdom.

Macfarlane, the Negroes, and other low-class outsiders have

[14] Copyright © 1966 by the Mark Twain Company; typescript notebook 16, p. 41, in the Mark Twain Papers.

[15] On January 31, 1901, Twain writes in a notebook: "Hoecake opinions (bread & butter) on religion & politics." Copyright © 1966 by the Mark Twain Company; typescript notebook 34, p. 5, in the Mark Twain Papers. This was a germinal note for "Corn-Pone Opinions," but Twain had not yet found the final phrase to attribute to Jerry.

antecedents in Twain's early period. Mr. Brown, for example, the raffish companion in the travel letters of 1866-1867, mocked the pretensions of genteel culture from a skeptical perspective roughly similar to the slave's in "Corn-Pone Opinions." Yet Twain used Mr. Brown to attack the manners of the culture, not its fundamental assumptions, and in this role Brown was no solitary and ineffectual outcast. He embodied a common-sense detestation of sham and snobbery that the author expected his readers to share, and judging from the gross attacks on clergymen and other starchy persons in Western papers during the 1860's, one must assume he knew what to expect. When he had Mr. Brown object to "milk and mush preacher travels" by "pious bushwackers from America,"[16] he was writing out of a cultural rapport with his California audience, in that he knew just how far they would be pleased to tolerate vulgarity with a healthy motive. The outsiders in this situation were the admirers of pious and sentimental travel books, against whom the author, Mr. Brown, and the readers united in disrespect.

But by the 1890's Mark Twain was most concerned with the premises of societies, not their manners; and on this issue he had no audience rapport. He was disturbed at the apparent ease with which people continued to believe life was good, the universe well-disposed, and mankind on the whole an admirable species. He was living into an age when he himself could believe none of these things and yet when they seemed unquestionable among the mass of his countrymen. Fearing ostracism should he speak his mind, Twain started many diatribes, completed few, and suppressed every one that revealed the extent and fervor of his disenchantment. Though he also suppressed most of the outsider polemics, he developed them in part to state his position with least risk to his career. In two, "Macfarlane" and "Corn-Pone Opinions," he even tried to expound his pessimism and maintain a familiar relation with his readers at the same time. Writing as the elderly Mark Twain engaged in genial reminiscence, he pretended to come upon the doctrines of Macfarlane and Jerry by an accident of recollection. "Corn-Pone Opinions" had a relatively innocuous subject—conformity—which he discussed at length in his own voice, yet the use of Jerry made his interest appear occasional rather than chronic.

[16] Walter Francis Frear, *Mark Twain and Hawaii* (Chicago, 1947), p. 372.

The more open and dangerous doctrine of "Macfarlane" required a greater play of geniality and a more thorough grounding in the outsider's character. Hence, the humorous description of Macfarlane's somberness and self-sufficiency, and the introduction of his ideas as "curious and striking things," as though Mark Twain shared the perspective of his readers and was simply mediating between them and an amusing eccentric he once happened to know.

Yet the resulting isolation of Macfarlane was designed to embarrass not him but public complacency in the nineties. He was an old-style provincial who used a free mind without fear or prejudice, and his using it to recognize the basest facts of human nature showed the dishonesty in a progressive theory of history. Late nineteenth-century optimists thought they were in the van of civilization, and they had made Darwin serve their optimism less than three decades after he seemed to destroy it. They regarded the past as a preparation for themselves, and reformers differed only in thinking tomorrow might be better than today. But back in the 1850's, in a cheap Cincinnati boarding house, an ascetic laborer might have anticipated Darwin without seeing or needing any cause for optimism. His period and class did not count against him, for his cynical perceptions were those of honest men in any time or situation. Yet the wisdom could never become popular, and anyone who discovered it might only help a few others discover it for themselves. Indeed, Paine caught the pattern of Mark Twain's rhetoric though he was mistakenly literal in applying it. Twain proposed the communication of a painful wisdom from an aging and humble man to an ambitious youth, and from him to others when, in his turn, full maturity brought a recognition of the wisdom. The communication was always precarious because men did not wish to learn that their dignity and high purpose had to take account of their worst tendencies.

Mark Twain's Later Dialogue:
The 'Me' and the Machine
John S. Tuckey

ALTHOUGH THE LAST PERIOD of Samuel L. Clemens's literary work has been regarded as one of despair, there has recently been an increasing recognition of complexities in the later writings. It is true that there is still a rather prevalent notion that Clemens arrived at despair and then, during his last ten or twelve years, substantially remained there—though he was seldom consistent for very long in much else. And it has often been said that the later writings lack significance because their author had lost his belief in the dignity of man and the value of human life.[1] One is likely to find allusions to *The Mysterious Stranger* and to *What Is Man?*, such words as "pessimism" and "despair," and perhaps the phrase "the damned human race" (a phrase, incidentally, that no one seems able to document in the writings), and then a rounding off with a facile finis, ringing down the curtain on a supposedly finished Mark Twain. But this notion of a sustained despair is beginning to look like a disposable myth of Mark Twain criticism. Louis J. Budd has observed that Clemens "was less consistent than ever during his last years,"[2] and that while he had "his nihilistic moods," he "kept add-ing to the confusion with occasional statements of faith."[3] Cole-man O. Parsons has noted that Clemens liked to have two final words, "a hopeful and a hopeless one."[4] And it may be added that these expressions of faith and of hope were something more than occasional and random ones. In Clemens's thought they were philosophically based, even as were his more despairing views. For he had not one but two philosophies; or one might say more par-

[1] For a balanced discussion of this critical viewpoint, see Edward Wagenknecht, *Mark Twain: The Man and His Work,* 3d ed. (Norman, Okla., 1967), p. 214.

[2] *Mark Twain: Social Philosopher* (Bloomington, Ind., 1962), p. 188.

[3] *Ibid.,* pp. 207-208.

[4] "The Devil and Samuel Clemens," *Virginia Quarterly Review*, XXIII, 603 (Autumn, 1947).

ticularly, two psychologies—the somewhat older positivistic one, already in vogue when he had been maturing, which viewed human beings as mechanisms, entirely the products of their environment, and the newer one, emphasizing the forces of the unconscious and the significance of dreams. And one can find in the writings a continuing dialogue that he carried forward with a growing awareness of the ways in which these two psychologies enlisted his own divided sympathies and convictions. The two psychologies of course had quite different implications concerning the possibilities for human freedom and survival.[5] And the central issue of Clemens's dialogue was one that is still before humanity: whether man is essentially an automated or an autonomous being; whether he is a slavish and perishable mechanism or a free and immortal spirit.

The psychology that regarded the psyche as essentially and entirely a mechanism became, in the terms in which Clemens understood it, his "gospel," the view that he eventually elaborated in *What Is Man?* This view was, so to speak, first in possession of the field, and it was not until the late 1890's, after the just then developing new psychology had begun to come into its own, that he found an alternate position, an actual basis for a more hopeful outlook regarding the human situation. Thus it is especially in the later period that one finds the aforementioned dialogue. That does not, however, mean that it is absent from the earlier writings. For Clemens was intuitively making his own way toward the newer psychology. His work of the 1870's and 1880's shows the long foreground of his interest in dreams, in illusions, and in evidences of special powers of mind such as "mental telegraphy," by which he meant telepathy. In the 1880's he was already following avidly the investigations of the London Society for Psychical Research, as a regular reader of its publications. Even if he had as yet no adequate basis for a doctrinal formulation of a second position, it appears that he was looking for one. Walter Blair has observed that "for all his talk [as in the paper

[5] The differences are probably greater than the deliberately limited approaches of modern psychology (except for the still not generally credited parapsychology) have so far allowed to become evident. See for example William James's observation that, although he hoped to "force . . . materialistic minds to feel more strongly the logical respectability of the spiritualistic position," he intended to keep his "psychology . . . positivistic and non-metaphysical," although this was "certainly only a provisional halting-place," in *The Principles of Psychology*, Authorized Edition (New York, 1890; reprinted in 1950), I, 181-182.

on determinism that he had read to his Hartford club] about believing man 'merely a machine automatically functioning,' Mark had not been completely converted by his own eloquence,"[6] and that in *Huckleberry Finn* it may be seen that "against all his logic Mark Twain was fighting for a faith."[7] Mr. Blair perceives the same fight going on in some of Clemens's other works of the 1880's. In *A Connecticut Yankee in King Arthur's Court*, for example, Clemens at one point wrote what looks like an authorial intrusion into the Yankee's narrative, a passage expressing both his acceptance of determinism and his desire to fight against it:

We have no thoughts of our own, no opinions of our own; they are transmitted to us, trained into us. All that is original in us, and therefore fairly creditable or discreditable to us, can be covered up and hidden by the point of a cambric needle, all of the rest being atoms contributed by, and inherited from, a procession of ancestors that stretches back a billion years. . . . And as for me, all that I think about in this plodding sad pilgrimage, this pathetic drift between the eternities, is to look out and humbly live a pure and high and blameless life, and save that one microscopic atom in me that is truly *me*: the rest may land in Sheol and welcome for all I care.[8]

I believe it can be shown that Clemens was still fighting during those late years that have often been considered his time of hopeless resignation. And, since a number of the later works can now be dated with some accuracy, it seems possible to consider more or less sequentially some phases of the battle.

I have suggested that by the late 1890's he was finding more of a basis for opposing his own reluctantly held deterministic position. In an extended notebook entry of January 7, 1898—actually, a short essay of about 1,500 words—he proclaimed that he had "struck upon a new 'solution' of a haunting mystery"[9]—one that he had

[6] *Mark Twain and Huck Finn* (Berkeley, 1960), p. 343.

[7] *Ibid.*

[8] Definitive Edition, XIV, 150. This edition, used for this and subsequent references to the published works unless otherwise noted, is *The Writings of Mark Twain*, 37 vols. (New York, 1922-1925), hereinafter cited as *Writings*.

[9] *Mark Twain's Notebook*, ed. Albert B. Paine (New York, 1935), p. 348. This passage may also be seen in the holographic notebooks, as well as in typescript copies, in the Mark Twain Papers collection at the General Library of the University of California, Berkeley; see Typescript 32(I), p. 1. I am grateful to the Mark Twain Estate for the opportunity to study the notebooks and other materials in the collection, and to Henry

concerned himself with much earlier when writing "The Recent
Carnival of Crime in Connecticut." That story he now regarded as
a crude "attempt to account for our seeming *duality*—the presence
in us of another *person*; not a slave of ours, but free and independent, and with a character distinctly its own."[10] He went on to consider the new solution: "The French [evidently Pierre Janet and
others of the school of Jean Martin Charcot] have lately shown
(apparently) that that other person is in command during the
somnambulic sleep; . . . but that *you* [i.e., the person awake] have
no memory of its acts. . . . To this arrangement I wish to add this
detail—that we have a *spiritualized self* which can *detach itself*
and go wandering off upon affairs of its own"[11]—a self having a
common memory with the waking self, since the latter could remember dreams. "[M]y dream self," he supposed, "is merely my
ordinary body and mind freed from clogging flesh and become a
spiritualized body and mind, and with the ordinary powers of both
enlarged in all particulars a little, and in some particulars pro-
digiously."[12] Asserting "I do actually make immense excursions
in my spiritualized person," he conjectured, "When my physical
body dies, my dream-body will doubtless continue its excursions
and activities without change, forever."[13] To be sure, his use here
of the word "doubtless" suggests not certainty but a need to reassure
himself, and the whole passage represents his wishful thinking at
least as much as it does his actual convictions. And Albert B. Paine
was surely right in thinking that Clemens had already begun to
fictionalize the idea when, at the end of the notebook entry, he
wrote, "The time that my dream-self first appeared to me . . . it
was dressed in my customary clothes."[14] Still, the entry is something
more than a pleasing fancy or a warm-up for fiction: it is recog-
nizably a layman's attempt at analysis of the psyche, inspired by
what he had been hearing of the experiments and theories of pro-

---

Nash Smith and Frederick Anderson for many valuable suggestions. For specific confirmation of the dating of the presently considered passage, which was dated a year
earlier by Paine, I here express my thanks to Mr. Anderson and to Howard G. Baetzhold.
    [10] *Ibid.*
    [11] This passage was published with slight inaccuracies in *Notebook*, p. 349; I have
quoted from the Typescript, 32(I), pp. 3-4.
    [12] Typescript, 32(I), p. 4; see also *Notebook*, p. 350.
    [13] Typescript, 32(I), p. 5; see also *Notebook*, p. 351.
    [14] Typescript, 32(I), pp. 6-7; see also *Notebook*, p. 352.

fessionals, and one by which he tried to work out a basis for a belief in human survival after death. Having within the past several years lived in Paris, London, and Vienna, major centers for psychological research, he had many opportunities to know of recent developments. But his principal source may have been William James's *The Principles of Psychology*, which Clemens had read and had commented upon in earlier notebook entries.[15] James discusses at length Pierre Janet's work with the subject Léonie, a somnambulist found to have three distinct selves.[16] In other chapters James considers the "spiritual self" and also presents the testimonies of a number of persons whose hallucinatory experiences had been as far-ranging and as remarkable as those Clemens attributed to his dream self, and had seemed as real.[17] And in discussing the perception of reality, he goes about as far as Clemens in recognizing the possible reality of what we call dreams:

The world of dreams is our real world whilst we are sleeping, because our attention then lapses from the sensible world. Conversely, when we wake the attention usually lapses from the dream-world and that becomes unreal. But if a dream haunts us and compels our attention during the day it is very apt to remain figuring in our consciousness as a sort of sub-universe alongside of the waking world. Most people have probably had dreams which it is hard to imagine not to have been glimpses into an actually existing region of being, perhaps a corner of the "spiritual world."[18]

It is of interest that the notebook passage was written some few months after Clemens had, in August, 1897, been writing the first and most rigorously deterministic part of the existing manuscript of *What Is Man?* It is also interesting that this notebook entry was made at just about the time that he had been composing the first part of *The Mysterious Stranger*—that is, of the "Eseldorf" version that was used for most of the story as posthumously published in 1916. Both sides of the dialogue are represented in the published story, although it is of course the pessimistic "gospel" that chiefly is expressed. It is only in the concluding chapter—which

[15] Typescript 31(I), pp. 6, 11.
[16] James, I, 385-390 and passim.
[17] *Ibid.*, I, 296; II, 114-133.
[18] *Ibid.*, II, 294 n.

was written for the later "Print Shop" version[19]—that the stranger reveals himself to be the dream self of the narrator. Clearly, when he came to the writing of the "Print Shop" manuscript Clemens meant to explore and assess the relationship of the dream mind to the other levels of consciousnsess. In that version there is much about the waking self, the somnambulistic self, and the dream self or immortal self, and these aspects of the psyche are individualized as characters in the story.[20] Clemens was working out what he had envisioned in the note of January, 1898. It is evident that he had not so much taken occasion to do so in the earlier-written "Eseldorf" manuscript, most of which was composed in 1899 and 1900; instead, he made the story an exposition and a fictional portrayal of such pessimistic views as he had advanced in *What Is Man?* It is likely that the dark events of war and of world politics at the close of the nineteenth century prompted him to put aside for a time any extensive following up of the more hopeful implications concerning the human condition and, in the face of seeming fresh proofs that mankind was unworthy of freedom and of survival, draw out the lesson on human worthlessness. But by the time that he was writing most of the "Print Shop" manuscript—in 1903 and 1904—he was no longer under quite so black a shadow: the Boer War, the Spanish-American War, and the Boxer uprising and subsequent military actions in China were past events; the Russo-Japanese War had yet to become a further cause for disillusionment. There were, on the other hand, compelling personal reasons for employing literary strategies that might yield a hopeful answer to the problem of survival. Most of the "Print Shop" manuscript was written while his wife Olivia was in her last illness, and there is some evidence, which I have considered in a monograph,[21] that it was probably at about the time of her death, which came on June 5, 1904, that he wrote, as an anticipated conclusion, the chapter that was used to complete the published story. That chapter does work out at least a minimal survival for the individual—if at the cost of letting all

---

[19] The course of composition of *The Mysterious Stranger* and some related manuscripts is discussed in John S. Tuckey, *Mark Twain and Little Satan: The Writing of "The Mysterious Stranger"* (Lafayette, Ind., 1963), pp. 9-81.

[20] Most of the "Print Shop" manuscript remained unpublished until it was published in full in a volume of the Mark Twain Papers: William M. Gibson, ed., *Mark Twain's Mysterious Stranger Manuscripts* (Berkeley and Los Angeles, 1969).

[21] *Mark Twain and Little Satan,* pp. 62-64.

else go to Sheol while preserving his essential self. The boy narrator learns that the world and all of his experiences of it have been
"a grotesque and foolish dream," and that he alone exists and will
forever "remain a *thought*, the only existent thought, . . . inextinguishable, indestructible."[22] Before dissolving into nothingness, the
mysterious stranger reveals that he is merely a projection of the
boy's own thought: "I am but a dream—your dream, creature of
your imagination." Moreover, *"Life itself is only a vision, a dream."*
When his dream self tells him, *"Nothing exists save empty space—
and you!"* the lad echoes, "I!"[23] And it is the essential "I" that remains, that is saved. Of course one could suppose that it was again
Clemens's hope and not necessarily his firm belief that here found
expression. Nevertheless, the conclusion develops great emotional
force; furthermore, it amounts to an assertion of a philosophical
position, that of an absolute solipsism. Although from a common-
sense point of view it is easy to treat such a position as an absurdity,
it may be considered a legitimate countering of a view of man as a
mere machine in a mechanical universe—a view that may also be
made to look absurd enough. Either position appears to leave something out of account if not opposed and corrected by the other. It is
not surprising that E. S. Fussell should have found, in *The Mysterious Stranger*, a "tension that Twain could never organize" and "a
failure to arbitrate the claims of subjective and objective phenomena."[24] His observations tend to confirm that Clemens had a
real commitment to both positions.

It was in the following year of 1905 that the dialogue came into
sharpest focus and was carried as close to any final resolution as
Clemens would ever be able to bring it. In that year he no longer
had any immediate need, in behalf of a loved one, for assurances of
the preciousness and permanency of individuals. Yet it was again
the problem of survival that he addressed, in a novel that he began
almost at once upon settling at Dublin, New Hampshire, on May 20,
for a summer of writing. The novel was *Three Thousand Years
among the Microbes*. Unlikely as it might seem, there are parallels
and linkages between this book and *Huckleberry Finn*. It was in

[22] *The Mysterious Stranger, Writings*, XXVII, 138-140.
[23] *Ibid.*, p. 138.
[24] Edwin S. Fussell, "The Structural Problem of The Mysterious Stranger," *Studies
in Philology*, XLIX, 104 (Jan., 1952).

August, 1884, when he had been reading proofs of Huck's story, that he had recorded in his notebook a concept of the human situation that anticipated the microbe story: "I think we are only the microscopic trichina concealed in the blood of some vast creature's veins, and it is that vast creature whom God concerns Himself about and not us."[25] Furthermore, the microbic narrator, a cholera germ, calls himself "Huck," and the human "planet" he inhabits, a chronically drunken and odoriferous tramp named Blitzowski, is reminiscent of Huck Finn's degenerate father Pap. The tramp has other Hannibalesque features. For instance, he contains "many rivers (veins and arteries)" that "make the Mississippi . . . trifling . . . by comparison."[26] And the situation of Huck Finn, who rafts upon the Mississippi, is paralleled by that of the germ "Huck" who journeys in Blitzowski's veins. Moreover, even as Huck Finn is much of the time fleeing from some threat of violence and possible destruction, so is "Huck" the microbe much concerned with the problem of survival. Clemens may be seen improvising various devices that may allow "Huck" to avoid the destruction of his essential "me." For example, it is disclosed that as a microbe he has eternal youth—*almost:* his body is still keeping human time, a week of which lasts for a thousand microbe years; thus while his germ comrades grow old and die, he does not perceptibly age. Of course this stratagem does not actually dispose of death but merely postpones it. But still more hopefully "Huck" finds that with his microbic sight he can distinguish individual atoms, and that each one is an individual, alive and indestructible. And he rhapsodizes that *"there is no such thing as death."*[27] Yet it soon appears that not even these considerations can really provide any lasting reassurance. His atoms will all survive, but will *he?* Reflecting that "D. T. will fetch Blitzy" some time, bringing about the end of the world he inhabits, he muses, "My molecules would scatter around and take up new quarters . . . but where should *I* be? . . . There would be no more *me."*[28] And he continues his fearful reasonings:

[25] *Notebook,* p. 170.

[26] *Three Thousand Years among the Microbes,* in *Mark Twain's "Which Was the Dream?" and Other Symbolic Writings of the Later Years,* ed. John S. Tuckey (Berkeley, 1967), p. 437.

[27] *Ibid.,* p. 447.

[28] *Ibid.,* p. 458.

[M]y details would be doing as much feeling as ever, but I should not be aware of it, it would all be going on for the benefit of those others, and I not in it at all. I should be gradually wasting away, atom by atom, molecule by molecule, as the years went on, and at last I should be all distributed, and nothing left of what had once been Me.... And to think what centuries and ages and aeons would drift over Me before the disintegration was finished, the last bone turned to gas and blown away! I wish I knew what it is going to feel like, to lie helpless such a weary, weary time, and see my faculties decay and depart, one by one, like lights which burn low, and flicker, and perish, until the ever-deepening gloom and darkness which—oh, away, away with these horrors, and let me think of something wholesomer![29]

It seems likely that in writing the latter part of this passage Clemens was imaginatively back in Hannibal, seeing again the fiery death of the hapless drunken tramp who had burned up in the jailhouse one night while the horror-stricken young Sam had watched, remembering that he had earlier that day provided the man with some matches.[30] His own life may have seemed fatefully linked to that of this tramp, even as was "Huck" the microbe's to that of his tramp-planet Blitzowski. For that matter, the name "Blitzowski" translates as "man of lightning" or "blazing one"— a man afire. Clemens may have been looking full-faced at the most terrible image of death that was in his disaster-laden memory. And at this point the outlook for survival might seem to have perished with the expiring flickers of flame: apparently the "me" could not be saved. Some three days after he had done his last work on the microbe story, he wrote, on June 26, his "Apostrophe to Death":

> O Death, O sweet & gracious friend,
> I bare my smitten head to Thee, & at thy sacred feet
> I set my life's extinguished lamp & lay my bruisèd heart.[31]

One might think that here indeed was the finis to Clemens's hope; that this at least was confirmed resignation. Yet such was still not quite the case. A few days later, on June 30, 1905,[32] he had reread

---

[29] *Ibid.*

[30] See *Mark Twain's Autobiography*, 2 vols. (New York, 1924), I, 130-131; also *Life on the Mississippi, Writings*, XII, 455.

[31] In Arthur L. Scott, *On the Poetry of Mark Twain* (Urbana, Ill., 1966), p. 127.

[32] Clemens's marginal note on p. 432 of the "Print Shop" holograph provides this date. For other datings of Clemens's work of the later years I have relied on various evidences

his unfinished "Print Shop" story, for which he had already written
the chapter that would immortalize the conscious "I" of the narrator, and was carrying it toward that planned conclusion. He did
not quite bring the story through to that point, however, for he put
it aside about July 12, after Frederick A. Duneka of Harper &
Brothers had visited him to see whether he could provide something
for the next winter's book trade.[33] Clearly, *The Mysterious Stranger*
was not what Duneka was looking for. Clemens turned to work
on "Eve's Diary." But in August he did some further work on
What Is Man?—and by paper and ink comparisons as well as other
evidences the parts he then wrote can be identified. The earlier-
written parts are, despite their having been written in the form of
a Platonic dialogue, hardly a real dialogue in that only one viewpoint is effectively presented. The Young Man is hardly more than
a foil for the mechanistic monologue of the Old Man, the cynical
expositor of determinism. It is in the parts added in 1905 that
there emerges, if only briefly, some real dialogue. In a section entitled "A Difficult Question," the Old Man and the Young Man
consider "Who is the Me?" And when the crux of the argument
is at last reached, it rather astonishingly turns out that the Old
Man, who always before has been so sure of his position, is in a
state of uncertainty:

> O. M. . . . You say the mind is wholly spiritual; then you say "I have
> a pain" and find that this time the Me is mental *and* spiritual
> combined. We all use the "I" in this indeterminate fashion,
> there is no help for it. . . . The intellect and the feelings can act
> quite *independently* of each other; we recognize that, and we
> look around for a Ruler who is master over both, and can serve
> as a *definite* and *indisputable* "I" and enable us to know what we
> mean . . . when we use that pronoun, but we have to give it up
> and confess that we cannot find him.[34]

And the Old Man makes no effective denial, offers no rebuttal,
when his young companion propounds the key question—proposes

such as his correspondence, dictations, notes, and marginalia; internal evidences of successive stages of revision of the manuscripts; paper, ink, and handwriting comparisons of the
manuscript materials. In making such investigations I drew heavily upon the expert
knowledge and unfailing helpfulness of the Literary Editor of the Mark Twain Papers,
Frederick Anderson.

[33] See *Mark Twain and Little Satan*, p. 69.

[34] *What Is Man?*, *Writings*, XXVI, 97-98.

that which, if true, must discredit the "man is a machine" philosophy:

Y. M. Maybe the Me is the Soul?

O. M. Maybe it is. What is the Soul?

Y. M. I don't know.

O. M. Neither does any one else.[35]

And that, it seems, is where we finally come out—with an unresolved dialogue on the unresolved question of the nature and destiny of man. Evidently it was where Clemens himself was still coming out in 1907. His biographer Albert B. Paine has reported his remarks:

"As to a hereafter, we have not the slightest evidence that there is any—*no* evidence that appeals to logic and reason. I have never seen what to me seemed an atom of proof that there is a future life."

Then, after a long pause, he added:

"And yet—I am strongly inclined to expect one."[36]

Logic and reason tended to support his "gospel," but there still was a good likelihood that the "me" would escape from the trap of the Old Man's logic; that it would turn out to be the Soul. But no certainty, either optimistic or pessimistic, about the matter was attainable in this life. That was clearly still his thought in the last year of his life, when he wrote to Elizabeth Wallace on January 26, 1910, not without some humor:

Do I "know more" than I knew before? Oh, *hell* no! There was nothing to learn (about hereafters and other-such undesirables), there has never *been* anything to learn and know about those insulting mysteries. I am happy—few are so happy—but I get none of this happiness from "knowing more" of the unknowable than I knew before.[37]

For Clemens, the question of which would finally prevail, the "me" or the machine, was still unresolved—and he was in the last analysis not confirmed in despair, not barred from seeing and representing human life as having value and significance.

[35] *Ibid.*, p. 98.

[36] *Mark Twain: A Biography*, 4 vols. (New York, 1923), IV, 1431.

[37] Samuel L. Clemens to Elizabeth Wallace, January 26, 1910. A copy of this letter is in the Mark Twain Papers. Published in part in Elizabeth Wallace, *Mark Twain and the Happy Island* (Chicago, 1913), p. 137; however, the part here quoted has not been previously published, and for permission to use it I thank Frederick Anderson and the Mark Twain Estate. Copyright © 1969, Mark Twain Company.

Pudd'nhead Wilson: A Parable of Property
George M. Spangler

THE STRIKING LACK OF AGREEMENT about the merits of Mark Twain's *Pudd'nhead Wilson* is unquestionably related to the equally striking disagreements over interpretation of the novel, related in the crucial sense that all the thematic analyses so far presented leave important aspects of the novel unaccounted for. The result is that those who are inclined to praise the novel dismiss certain parts as finally inconsequential evidence of Twain's predictably careless technique, while those who have serious reservations about its merits stress its lack of coherence, its lack of an action adequate to embody what appear to be the author's chief concerns. Although interpretations vary widely, ranging from the view that its theme is the conflict between appearance and reality to the assertion that it has "no clear meaning,"[1] two interpretative emphases are most common. First, there are those critics who stress racial themes, especially slavery and miscegenation, and second, those who argue for the centrality of the theme of environmental determinism and see slavery as simply a metaphor for Twain's more general concern with the influence of "training" on the individual.[2]

Although both these approaches yield valuable insights, both are finally unsatisfactory because they leave too many important questions unanswered—except by alluding to Twain's uncertain artistry.

[1] These views are presented respectively in Edgar T. Schell, " 'Pears' and 'Is' in *Pudd'nhead Wilson*," *Mark Twain Journal*, XII (Winter, 1964–1965), 12–14, and Warner Berthoff, *The Ferment of Realism* (New York, 1965), p. 72.

[2] The racial interpretation is most elaborately presented in James M. Cox, *Mark Twain: The Fate of Humor* (Princeton, 1966), pp. 225–246. Racial themes are also stressed in P. S. Foner, *Mark Twain: Social Critic* (New York, 1958); Robert A. Wiggins, *Mark Twain: Jackleg Novelist* (Seattle, 1964); and Barbara A. Chellis, "Those Extraordinary Twins: Negroes and Whites," *American Quarterly*, XXI (Spring, 1969), 100–112. The case for environmental determinism is best presented in Henry Nash Smith, *Mark Twain: The Development of a Writer* (New York, 1967), pp. 171–183; and Leslie Fiedler, "As Free as Any Cretur . . . ," in *Mark Twain: A Collection of Critical Essays*, ed. H. N. Smith (Englewood Cliffs, N.J., 1963), pp. 130–139. Similar emphasis also appears in DeLancey Ferguson, *Mark Twain: Man and Legend* (Indianapolis, 1963); and Louis J. Budd, *Mark Twain: Social Philosopher* (Bloomington, Ind., 1962).

If Twain's purpose was to condemn slavery, racism, and miscegenation, why did he grant so much respect and even, at a key point,
sympathy to the FFV gentlemen and their code of honor; and why
did he allow such sympathetic figures as Wilson and Roxy to accept unquestioningly the values of these leaders of a guilty society?
On the other hand, if Tom is the victim and avenger of racial injustice, why did Twain present him as a moral monstrosity, an un-
mitigated villain throughout the narrative? Why, finally, did
Twain allow Roxy's racist explanation of Tom's behavior to go
unchallenged? Similarly, the interpretative stress on environmental
determinism raises as many questions as it answers. If the novel
illustrates the debilitating effects of the training of a corrupt society,
why did Twain present Tom as being far beyond the community in
viciousness? Why did he present Tom's contempt for the code of
honor which the town endorses as major evidence of Tom's base-
ness? If training is all, Tom should express the values of his environment; but he specifically does not in the key matter of the duel and
in his response to the twins, and in fact generally stands apart from
the environment that is supposed to have shaped him. Clearly what
is necessary is a thematic analysis that can answer these questions in
terms of what is shown in the novel and thus demonstrate a coherence in *Pudd'nhead Wilson* that has too often been denied.

The key to such an analysis is the idea of property, more particularly the obsession with property as a vitiating and reductive
influence on human beings. Written when Twain's financial condition was at its worst, *Pudd'nhead Wilson* is a parable dealing with
the faults of the Gilded Age, faults of which Twain himself was
often guilty. It is a book pervaded from start to finish with the very
obsession with property which is its theme, yet fully in control of
the revelation it offers about the moral and spiritual consequences of
this obsession. At both the beginning and the conclusion of the
book the importance of the theme of property is revealed with stark
clarity. The basis for the narrative is the fact that human beings may
be sold as property, and its starting point is Roxy's recognition, itself
the result of an incident involving petty theft, that her master may
sell her child down the river at any time. "A profound terror had
taken possession of her. Her child could grow up and be sold down

the river! The thought crazed her with horror."[3] Her response is to exchange her child and her master's, the fact of plot which is central to the subsequent narrative. Similarly, in the final pages the property theme is underscored, this time through Twain's bitter parody of thinking in terms of property. After Tom is convicted of murder and sentenced to imprisonment for life, the creditors of the Percy Driscoll estate offer their view of the situation.

They rightly claimed that "Tom" was lawfully their property and had been so for eight years; that they had already lost sufficiently in being deprived of his services during that long period, and ought not to be required to add anything to the loss; that if he had been delivered up to them in the first place, they would have sold him and he could not have murdered Judge Driscoll; therefore it was not he that had really committed the murder, the guilt lay with the erroneous inventory. Everybody saw that there was reason in this. (p. 203)

Inconsistent with the story—if the false heir was not part of the inventory, his substitute certainly was and the creditors had had the benefit of his disposal—this passage defines in the manner of parody what has been the consistent theme of the novel, viz., the distortions of reason, feeling, and morality that result when economic motives are the primary source of human action. If the creditors' logic is absurd, it is also, in a paradoxical sense, correct, for mistaken attitudes about property are in fact the cause of murder and much other evil in this novel.

In the body of the story Twain's focus is on the false Tom, a character whose increasingly vile acts cannot be understood in terms of race or environmental determinism. Rather Tom makes sense only as a nearly allegorical figure of the obsession with property to the exclusion of all other human concerns. Spoiled by too much as a child, threatened by too little as a man, Tom in the end becomes property. His final condition is merely the expression of what his behavior has implied all along: as his singleness of purpose is reductive, so he himself is finally reduced. A nasty child from the start, Tom in his first words makes clear the essence of his bad nature: "He would call for anything and everything he saw, simply

[3] Mark Twain, *Pudd'nhead Wilson,* in *The Writings of Mark Twain* (New York, 1929), XVI, 18. Subsequent page references to this volume of the Stormfield Edition will be included in the text.

saying, 'Awnt it!' (want it), which was a command" (p. 27). When
he reaches manhood, his principal vice and the cause of all of his
difficulty, gambling, is consistent with his acquisitiveness as a child.
Apparently not tempted by sex, alcohol, or other traditional vices,
he cannot, on the other hand, resist gambling, even though he knows
that the revelation of his losses will cause the judge to disinherit him.
Indeed his fear of being disinherited is the crucial emotional fact
of his life and the only source of his vows to reform himself. Moreover, his determination to hide his gambling losses leads directly to
his overt crimes: the robberies, the betrayal of Roxy, the murder of
the judge.

The point is perfectly clear, indeed has the clarity of allegorical
pattern: neither when he assumes that he is white nor when he
knows that he is legally black does Tom reveal for more than a
moment any motive other than the economic one. No moral standard and no personal tie of love, loyalty, or simple gratitude have
any force for him. When knowledge of his true birth presents him
with a subtle problem of identity, his response is merely a determination to resolve this problem, like all his others, with economic means.
Furthermore, in the singleness of his commitment to property
values, Tom stands apart from the rest of the community, however
deeply it, too, is involved in his kind of thinking. For in the respect it grants to the cosmopolitanism of the visiting Italian twins
and to the aristocratic code of honor, Dawson's Landing shows its
capacity to appreciate values that are not simply materialistic. Tom,
on the other hand, has no such appreciation; he is instinctively
hostile to the twins, and his response to Luigi's insult shows that the
code of honor is completely unintelligible to him. Twain's characterization of Tom then makes no consistent sense so long as it is seen
as embodying some statement about race or training. When, however, this central figure of the parable is recognized as the type of
the obsession with property as it reduces human beings and poisons
human relations, both characterization and narrative reveal a coherence that they at first may not appear to have.

Structurally the foil to Tom is Pudd'nhead Wilson; as Tom
degenerates morally and is finally convicted of murder and sold
into slavery, Wilson gradually gains status in the town and ends
as a hero when his file of fingerprints allows him to reveal Tom's

true identity. As Tom falls Wilson rises, and in fact the rise of the one depends on the fall of the other. Moreover, this structural contrast has a crucial analogue in the sharp divergence of the values of the two characters. If Tom typifies obsession with property, Wilson is largely dissociated from property, particularly from material success. Wilson is, in fact, long a conspicuous failure, unable to practice law, a profession for which he is well trained. The reason for his lack of success in Dawson's Landing is his fatal display of humor when he first arrives in town. He remarks that he wishes he owned half of a noisy dog so that he could kill his half. His hearers forthwith decide that he is a fool, a pudd'nhead, and the nickname they give him ruins his chances for a successful legal practice. Taken literally, the incident is incredible—Wilson's little joke is of the very sort the town loafers could understand—but in this parable about property it is clear enough: Wilson's low status is the result of his apparent failure to respect and understand the laws of property. Thus for years Wilson must content himself with the respect of only Judge Driscoll and Roxy (a sign of course of his true merit), until he at last wins favor through his association with the duel between Judge Driscoll and Luigi and becomes a hero through his exposure of Tom.

The contrast between the values of Tom and those of Wilson is fully revealed in their discussion of the legal action Tom brought against Luigi instead of fighting a duel with him. Defending Luigi against Tom's charge was Wilson's first chance to practice his profession in the town and thus perhaps the first step toward at long last establishing himself as a lawyer. Yet when Wilson discovers that Judge Driscoll did not know of Tom's action, he is ashamed of his part in the trial, and he tells Tom that he would have kept the matter out of court until the judge had been informed and had had a "gentleman's chance" to avoid the disgrace of having a member of his family take such a matter to court. Tom finds Wilson's attitude incomprehensible.

"You would?" exclaimed Tom, with lively surprise. "And it your first case! And you know perfectly well there would never have been any case if he had got that chance, don't you? And you'd have finished your days a pauper nobody, instead of being an actually launched and recog-

nized lawyer today. And you would really have done that, would you?"
(p. 110)

What seems incredible to Tom, who has only one standard of value,
is matter of fact for Wilson because he has values in the face of
which considerations of personal success and status are inconsequential. Himself symbolically dissociated from property, Wilson
sees in Tom "a degenerate remnant of an honorable line" who has
no other commitment.

Indifferent to material success and respectful of the aristocratic
code, Wilson also stands for other values that Tom could not comprehend. Though as well educated as Tom, he is not meanly ambitious in Tom's manner; he is open and frank, not devious like
Tom; his sense of humor is kindly, not cutting like Tom's. His
interest in fingerprinting and other such scientific advances and
his membership with the judge in their two-member Freethinker's
Society reveal his intellectual curiosity, which also allows him to
appreciate the Italian twins whom Tom only envies. Once again
the point is clear: if this tale is primarily an attack on a corrupt
community, Twain's sympathetic portrayal of Wilson, who uncriti-
cally accepts the values of the community and who is finally and tri-
umphantly accepted into it, is a serious flaw which threatens the coherence of the book. But if *Pudd'nhead Wilson* is above all a
protest against exclusively materialistic values, the reason for the
status Twain gave Wilson is evident, for it is Wilson, the imma-
terialist, who stands most apart from and ultimately vanquishes
Tom, the figure of unqualified devotion to property.

Unlike Wilson, who serves continuously as a foil to Tom, Roxy
becomes deeply involved for a time in her son's economic way of
thinking. When she returns to Dawson's Landing after eight years
of working on a riverboat, she is the victim of a bank failure which
has robbed her of her savings and taught her that "hard work and
economy" are not enough to make her secure and independent.
Faced with poverty, she pathetically thinks that Tom will give her
a little money, "maybe a dollar, once a month, say." But when she
discovers what a complete monster he has become, she is willing to
blackmail him with the threat that she will reveal his true parentage.
Understandably indifferent to property rights, she has no objection

to Tom's stealing and is generally willing to aid his plots to remain the heir of the Judge. For a time, that is, economic considerations shape her relation with her son, not simply because of her need, but also because of her desire to be close to a child who does not exist on any other level.

That love is the cause of her apparent acquiesence to Tom's values is movingly suggested in her demand that he recognize her maternity: " 'You'll call me ma or mammy, dat's what you'll call me—leastways when dey ain't nobody aroun'. *Say* it!' " (p. 72). Later, her feeling for Tom becomes patent when she suggests that he sell her in order to pay his gambling debts. Heroic as her sacrifice is, it is still a matter of trying to function at Tom's level, and when she learns that he has betrayed her trust by selling her *down* the river, her attitude changes greatly. Yet she does not simply denounce him; she also accepts responsibility for what he is: " 'You is de low-downest orneriest hound dat was ever pup'd into dis worl'—en I's 'sponsible for it!' " (p. 161). Moreover, she demands that he tell the Judge the truth about his debts and ask for money to buy her freedom, even though, as Tom protests and she realizes, such a confession will mean disinheritance. Having suffered the consequences of meeting Tom at his level, she attempts to force him to a higher one where he will be honest with Judge Driscoll and recognize his obligation to her. But Tom of course is incapable of such a change; instead he plans to rob the Judge and ends by murdering him.

Roxy then, despite her temporary acceptance of Tom's standards, is redeemed by her capacity for love, self-sacrifice, and moral awareness. In comparison to Tom, who has economic motives solely, she is very heroic indeed. Recognizing a similar sort of comparative merit is also the key to understanding Twain's attitude toward the town aristocrats and their code of honor, which has caused commentators so much difficulty. That a problem of ambivalence on Twain's part exists is evident from two early passages of characterization, which had better be quoted in full. About Judge Driscoll Twain writes,

He was very proud of his old Virginian ancestry, and in his hospitalities and his rather formal and stately manners he kept up its tradition. He was fine and just and generous. To be a gentleman—a gentleman without stain or blemish—was his only religion, and to it he was always faithful. He was respected, esteemed, and beloved by all the community. (p. 3)

Since the Judge as a freethinker makes no claim to religious orthodoxy, the passage must stand as praise unqualified by irony. Yet two paragraphs later Twain sounds the ironic note in his description of the Judge's best friend, Pembroke Howard:

He was a fine, brave, majestic creature, a gentleman according to the nicest requirements of the Virginia rule, a devoted Presbyterian, an authority on the "code," and a man always courteously ready to stand up before you in the field if any act or word of his had seemed doubtful or suspicious to you, and explain it with any weapon you might prefer from brad-awls to artillery. (p. 4)

The difference of tone between these two passages is not a matter of distinguishing between the Judge and his friend, for if Twain first presents the Judge in the language of praise, he subsequently provides evidence for a case against him. For example, the Judge's swoon when he learns that Tom took an insult to court instead of the dueling ground has the tone of burlesque. Further, the Judge is not only an aristocrat, he is also a democratic politician and something of a Babbitt. As politician, he is quite willing to buy votes and use innuendo against his opponent, and as Babbitt he escorts the twins around Dawson's Landing, pouring out "an exhaustless stream of enthusiasm" for its paltry "splendors." Finally, he is dozing over his cash and accounts when Tom comes to rob him, a scene which suggests the economic base of his status, one perhaps similar to that of his brother and Tom's presumed father who died a bankrupt because of his speculations in land.

Yet, in spite of these hints, Twain's portrayal of the Judge is not finally negative. Because the sympathetic Roxy and Wilson endorse the duel while the vicious Tom rejects it, the reader is allowed to admire the courage and integrity the Judge displays in the service of his code. More important, just before the duel Twain shows the Judge once more writing a will in Tom's favor, even though he vowed to disinherit Tom after hearing of his cowardice.

"This may be my last night in the world—I must not take the chance. He is worthless and unworthy, but it is largely my fault. He was entrusted to me by my brother on his dying bed, and I have indulged him to his hurt, instead of training him up severely, and making a man of him. I have violated my trust and I must not add the sin of desertion to that." (p. 118)

Like Roxy, the Judge accepts more responsibility for Tom than is properly his, and also like her, displays an affection which Tom cannot comprehend. Then, to make perfectly sure of his readers' response, the author portrays the Judge's friend Howard fully endorsing the Judge's humane act and, a few pages later, shows Tom, who has overheard the Judge's change of heart, regretting that the Judge has not been killed in the duel. This contrast of attitudes makes perfectly clear the Judge's moral and emotional superiority to Tom. For all his faults, the Judge, like Roxy, has a capacity for feeling and moral judgment that places him far above Tom. His aristocratic code, despite its endorsement of violent foolishness, allows for values far superior to Tom's, and even at its worst, it fosters an integrity that Tom's materialism does not. If it is a dubious center of value for the town, it is also clearly better than the values Tom embodies.[4]

As well, the code is preferable to the democracy the town practices. The townspeople not only accept and admire the aristocratic ways of the Judge, they also make a farce of their practice of democracy. Their politics amount to no more than the division between the rum and the antirum parties, and the meeting of the Sons of Liberty ends in a drunken brawl of "raging and plunging and fighting and swearing humanity." The Judge is at his worst, not when he is fighting a duel, but when he runs for office confident that he can win by buying votes and slandering his opponent. The satire of democracy is only a small part of *Pudd'nhead Wilson,* but it is consistent with the main thrust of the book—its relentless attack on the obsession with property. Viewed from this perspective, some of the most striking items in Wilson's *Calendar* become comprehensible.

July 4. Statistics show that we lose more fools on this day than in all the other days of the year put together. This proves, by the number left in

---

[4] F. R. Leavis makes this distinction between the code and certain admirable human qualities it fosters in his introduction to the Grove Press edition of *Pudd'nhead Wilson* (New York, 1955), pp. 9–31.

stock, that one Fourth of July per year is now inadequate, the country has grown so. (p. 147)

The irreverence of this reference to Independence Day is repeated in the final and most conspicuous entry in the *Calendar:* "October 12, the Discovery. It was wonderful to find America, but it would have been more wonderful to miss it" (p. 201). Even if it were the only evidence of Twain's attitude available, this book would suggest a Twain writing in reaction to the Gilded Age, in reaction to a period in which democracy seemed to be a failure and obsessive acquisitiveness, of the kind Tom represents, prevailed. In comparison, the ability of Roxy and Judge Driscoll to love, the disinterestedness and immaterialism of David Wilson, and even the aristocratic code—all associated with a bygone age—are very attractive indeed.

Even the extraordinarily unwieldy twins have their place in this parable about property. Representative through their cosmopolitanism and their artistic skills of yet another realm of value that Tom cannot understand, they, too, have experienced financial hardship: " 'We were seized for the debts occasioned by their [parents'] illness and their funerals, and placed among the attractions of a cheap museum in Berlin to earn the liquidation money. It took us two years to get out of that slavery' " (p. 45). It is this kind of slavery that Twain is talking about in *Pudd'nhead Wilson*—slavery to property, to economic motives, which, as in the case of Tom, finally reduces one to property, to slavery.

Biographically related to Twain's own financial distress and historically to an America dominated by robber barons, the book, far from being incoherent or inconsistent, is remarkable among Twain's works for its unity, a unity which derives from its pervasive concern with the theme of property, particularly the perils of an obsession with property to the exclusion of all other human values and needs.

Mark Twain's Masks of Satan:
The Final Phase
Stanley Brodwin

PERHAPS THERE IS NO MORE intriguing—or perplexing—phase in Mark Twain's life and art than the final one, the 1890's and early 1900's. During these years, according to Bernard DeVoto, Twain threshed out his "symbols of despair" from a wide variety of material much of which was left incomplete, though virtually all of it saturated with a bitter or "black" satiric mood.[1] And DeVoto's hypothesis that Twain sought to free himself from an intolerable burden of guilt through the dream-philosophy of Philip Traum, the mysterious stranger, remains one that still must be considered fruitful, though it has set off some impressive countertheories.[2] Yet there is no easily perceived, clearly defined artistic direction in this phase of Mark Twain's work as a whole. What we do see is that Twain's mind and art were coiled around a number of stakes driven into the heart of a dominant symbolic and thematic complex: fallen man with all his attendant personal, social and political evils; an "absurd" universe grotesquely deterministic and dream-like at the same time; the problem of personal (psychic) identity; and a Satan-figure, who, ironically, very likely developed out of a persistent Mark Twain character-type, the sometimes "innocent," sometimes devious stranger striving either to "con" or to "reform" the people and society around him. The Satan-figure has received serious critical attention, since it is he who is at the center of the "Mysterious Stranger" manuscripts—the uncompleted "last testament" of Mark Twain.[3] But there were several Satans for

[1] See Bernard DeVoto, *Mark Twain at Work* (Cambridge, Mass., 1942), pp. 105–130.

[2] A good sampling of the criticism on *The Mysterious Stranger* is in *Mark Twain's The Mysterious Stranger and the Critics,* ed. John S. Tuckey (Belmont, Calif., 1968). See particularly Part Four, the essays by Coleman O. Parsons, Gladys C. Bellamy, Roger B. Salomon, Albert E. Stone, H. N. Smith, and James M. Cox.

[3] We now have these manuscripts in a definitive edition: *Mark Twain's Mysterious*

Mark Twain, each one a mask or persona embodying a different aspect of his thought in a particular work, as well as his satiric or comic voice and style. To study Mark Twain's protean Satan is to study the trajectory of a great writer's intellectual and artistic attempts to find "salvation" in an apparently unsalvageable world.

Mark Twain cast Satan into four basic roles,[4] each requiring a separate characterization so that the created mask could express the proper tone and philosophic stance for the immediate story or sketch at hand. Interestingly, there seems to be no strict chronological development which would indicate that Twain had a clear "plan" when to employ one Satan mask or another. The creative ferment of these decades, producing so many reworked and unfinished projects, very likely made it impossible for Twain to formulate a consistent strategy in his uses of Satan. But the figure haunted his imagination which was fueled by his reading of *Paradise Lost,* Voltaire's *Zadig,* Goethe's *Faust,* the Apocrypha and other works. Neverthless, the following Satan figures stand out in the wide range of his work.

First, there is the conventional tempter and "Father of Lies," in "The Man that Corrupted Hadleyburg" (1899).[5]

Second, in "That Day in Eden (A Passage from Satan's Diary)" and "Eve Speaks" (ca. 1900), Satan is a sympathetic commentator on the tragedy of man's fall, but one who fails to make Adam and

---

Stranger Manuscripts, ed. with an Introduction by William M. Gibson (Berkeley, Calif., 1969), whose texts I will use in this paper unless otherwise indicated. Indispensable, too, is John S. Tuckey's *Mark Twain and Little Satan: The Writing of "The Mysterious Stranger"* (Lafayette, Ind., 1963).

[4] See Gibson's "Introduction," pp. 14–16. Professor Gibson sees Satan as forming a "Square Deific." He is a "rebel," and "the truth-speaker . . . banished from heaven"; the "Father of the Old Testament and Missouri Presbyterianism"; and the "supernal Power not so much indifferent to men as wholly unaware of them" (p. 15). Gibson is here expanding the formulation presented by Coleman O. Parsons in "The Devil and Samuel Clemens," *Virginia Quarterly Review,* XXIII (Autumn, 1947), 582–606. I am clearly indebted to the formulations of both scholars. However, my emphasis is on the separate characterizations of Satan Twain gives us, especially as they relate to particular variations of mood and theme. I am also concerned with the relationships of comedy, satire, and tragedy as they are reflected in these Satan-masks. I feel that my category, "Satan-as-failure," has not been delineated by critics, despite its strong thematic presence in Twain's treatment of the figure. Of course, I am not attempting in this article to give a comprehensive listing and analysis of all of Mark Twain's references to Satan, but only those that suggest meaningful patterns and ideas.

[5] Though most critics have seen the "stranger" as Satan in this story, the most complete demonstration is by Henry B. Rule, "The Role of Satan in 'The Man that Corrupted Hadleyburg,' " *Studies in Short Fiction,* VI (Fall, 1969), 619–629.

Eve understand the concepts which would have saved them. The idea of Satan-as-failure crops up again in a number of unpublished pieces and in "Sold to Satan" (1904), all of which contain burlesque and serio-comic portraits of and attitudes toward the Tempter. "Sold to Satan," in particular, comically establishes the "ancestral" relationship between Twain and the Devil.

Third, in *Letters from the Earth* (1962),[6] Satan becomes a mischievous, sarcastic questioner of God's ways, writing secret letters to St. Gabriel and St. Michael about the absurdity of man, God's experiment.

Fourth, in "The Mysterious Stranger" stories (1897–1908), Satan is presented (with some variations) as a force of spiritual though amoral "innocence" charged with divine-like creative power. Though man, himself, is consistently viewed as a base creature in each of the three main versions, it is clear that Mark Twain's imagination was gripped by the relationships among the universe, Satan, and man.

I

"The Man that Corrupted Hadleyburg" embodies Twain's cynicism concerning the damned human race in the character of the vengeful stranger. In this Western version of the fall, the lines of action are determined, both artistically and philosophically, by Satan—or Howard L. Stephenson, as he is called.

Stephenson, a "ruined gambler" (XXIII, 4),[7] begins the action of the story by translating his anger at Hadleyburg into a plan for corrupting it. "Bitter" and "revengeful" (XXIII, 2), he is actually as guilty of spiritual pride as his victims. In the mythical ramification of the biblical story, Satan also falls through pride and is thereby able to recognize and penetrate to the pride in Adam and Eve. Stephenson does indeed expose an inherently sinful Hadleyburg. His last "gamble" pays off. Critics have therefore read the tale as Mark Twain's "affirmation"[8] of his belief in man's ability to learn

[6] Edited by Bernard DeVoto (New York, 1962). Hereafter referred to in my text as *LE*. For a brief background to these letters from Satan, see Albert B. Paine, *Mark Twain: A Biography* (New York, 1912), III, 1531–1532. The pieces were written in 1909.

[7] *The Writings of Mark Twain*, ed. A. B. Paine, 37 vols. (New York, 1923). Unless otherwise noted, all references will be to this Stormfield Edition.

[8] See Clinton S. Burhans, "The Sober Affirmation of Mark Twain's Hadleyburg," *American Literature*, XXXIV (Nov., 1962), 375–384.

and accept the truth about himself. From that point of view, Satan's role is easily interpreted as that of a "savior."[9] But the many complex ironies in the story suggest another interpretation. Satan-Stephenson, as in the traditional Christian view, wins only to lose, since at the end he is duped into thinking Richards was in fact incorruptible. At the same time, the ending of the story in which we find the citizens of Hadleyburg willing to confront temptation and not be caught "napping" (XXIII, 69), again, does not necessarily suggest any real *moral* change in them that would justify reading the conclusion as a genuine version of the *felix culpa*. We can see this by examining the complex and ironic relationships Stephenson triggers, but which entrap him, too.

One of the most piercing ironies in the story derives from the relationship between Edward Richards and Burgess, a relationship Stephenson exploits after Mary and Edward discover the sack of "gold" (actually lead discs) left by Stephenson. Their initial response is to keep it and to burn the note which orders the money to go to the man who gave advice to Stephenson, whose exact words are recorded in a sealed envelope. Mary and Edward momentarily control themselves and assume that the advice was given by Barclay Goodson, the good samaritan, now dead. Of course, Goodson had not been brought up in Hadleyburg. They then wonder why the stranger made the hated Burgess the one to deliver the wealth, and they discuss the fact that Edward was guilty of not clearing Burgess from some (unnamed) accusation which destroyed his reputation. The implication, as the story progresses, is that Stephenson somehow knows this, but counts on Burgess's repaying Edward with kindness. This Burgess does, for in the grand revelation scene in which he reveals the letters of eighteen of the town's "incorruptible" families, he holds back Edward's note containing the secret advice: "You are far from being a bad man: Go, and reform" (XXIII, 22). By preventing the Richardses' disgrace, Burgess unwittingly exposes them to a second temptation. They accept the proceeds from the sack the town had auctioned off. But our elderly Adam and Eve are destroyed by guilt, for they become obsessed with the idea that Burgess was kind only to expose them later in

[9] Rule, "The Role of Satan in 'The Man that Corrupted Hadleyburg,'" p. 620. Like Burhans, Rule sees the story as Twain's version of the *felix culpa*. I agree, but as I try to demonstrate, the fall was not all *that* fortunate or affirmative.

revenge for Richards's earlier failure to help him. Although Richards had warned Burgess to leave town so as to avoid being tarred and feathered, he did not clear him. The dying Richards therefore convinces himself that Burgess "repented of the saving kindness which he had done me, and he *exposed* me" (XXIII, 68). But Burgess had not exposed the Richardses, and is ironically hurt by them again. He will be more hated than ever now. Stephenson's plan succeeds because he has insight into both the weaknesses and the strengths of his victims. He is, so to speak, a *psychological* determinist, capable of creating a situation in which people can be emotionally manipulated toward his desired end: mutual physical or spiritual destruction. This Satan has insight into *guilt,* just as, in "The Mysterious Stranger" fables, "44" can read minds. Stephenson emerges, in part, as a demonic mask for Mark Twain's own obsession with guilt, turned here to destructive rather than creative purposes. One of the consequences of such power, however, is to risk exile, a frequent condition for many of Twain's characters other than Satan. In "Hadleyburg," Twain gives us Burgess and Halliday, perhaps as pointed contrasts to Stephenson, for they are both good men who have grown embittered in their social exile.

Halliday is described as "the loafing, good-natured, no-account, irreverent fisherman, hunter, boys' friend, stray-dogs' friend, typical 'Sam Lawson' of the town" (XXIII, 18). He also becomes, in part, the author's satiric voice, a grown-up Huck Finn. The change in the people is not noticed "except by Jack Halliday, who always noticed everything; and always made fun of it, too, no matter what it was" (XXIII, 19). Here we see an Adamic figure developing a "Satanic" characteristic, that inability to believe in the essential goodness of others. If he exists at all, the "good" man is pushed towards exile, with its embitterment and estrangement. However unwilling, man may come to share a common vision with his Arch-Enemy. "The Mysterious Stranger" stories may be read as a demonstration of this idea, as well.

It is given to the Richardses to recognize the larger tragic dimension of the situation Stephenson created. Confronting his lie-filled life, Edward realizes that the money "came from Satan. I saw the hell-brand on them, and I knew they were sent to betray me to sin" (XXIII, 67). And again: "like the rest I fell when temptation came" (XXIII, 68). Still, this confession, however "realistic" and "affirmative" it may be, serves only to create yet another lie: that Burgess had exposed him. To the end, Richards is trapped in lies, whether motivated by greed or by what he felt was the truth of man's nature.

Mary, too, has her insight. When Edward rationalizes that it "was so ordered" (XXIII, 15) that the money be sent to them, she replies:

Ordered! Oh, everything's *ordered,* when a person has to find some way out when he has been stupid. Just the same, it was *ordered* that the money should come to us in this special way, and it was you that must take it on yourself to go meddling with the designs of Providence—and who gave you the right? It was wicked, that is what it was—just blasphemous presumption. (XXIII, 15)

Her point is clear, and reflects Mark Twain's own view of the matter. Man invokes Destiny or a form of determinism to bolster his own selfish rationalizations. The next step is to meddle with Providence. For what *is* ordered is man's pride which leads him to destined ends in spite of himself. The revised motto of Hadleyburg, "Lead Us Into Temptation" (XXIII, 69), is not merely a recognition that morality must be continually tested by experience, though of course that is an important theme in the fable. The deeper meaning seems to be that the only way to confront destiny is to surrender to it. At least man will not be caught "napping" when he falls, but fall he must. But the grand irony is that Satan will not see the proof of this. He, too, is a victim of the lie, and writes to Richards that he is *"a disappointed man. Your honesty is beyond the reach of temptation"* (XXIII, 62). This appears so only because, as the reader knows, Burgess did not tell the truth at the court. Satan is justified in thinking that all men will fall when tempted, but the reality of it eludes him. Also eluding him will be the consolation that Hadleyburg has not really changed. Certainly, Hadleyburg will be shrewder, more careful, more alert, in the future. The citizens welcome temptation, not because any profound moral change has taken place in them, but because they are now "experienced." Twain's implication, I believe, is that expediency will still be the basis of morality, a conviction he often expressed throughout his writings. To be sure, a morality based on "enlightened" expediency is better than the sham, self-righteous attitudes of the Hadley-burgians before the fall, and must not be despised. But it is not authentic moral reform. One thinks of an early Twain quip: "the serene confidence which a Christian feels with four aces."[10] No doubt Stephenson, the ruined gambler, would have bitterly recognized the truth of that description.

II

The Satan we meet in *Letters from the Earth* is quite different from Stephenson. Where the latter was a portrait of a quietly sinister, embittered manipulator of human souls, the Satan of *Letters* is drawn as a questioning, intellectual Archangel, unafraid to voice his opinions about God. Predictably, he is sarcastic about God's experiment, man, and vicious in describing God's Laws of Nature which compel creatures to be dominated by certain characteristics that define their being. God banishes him on account of "his too flexible tongue" (*LE*, p. 6), but he is used to this. Satan flies into space and eternal night, and then finally decides to observe man. In this description it is possible to see Mark Twain defining himself and his role in life. He had no trouble in identifying himself with this kind of Satan, who is but a fuller extension of the type of spiritual exile developed in the figures of Pudd'nhead Wilson and Halliday. What follows is eleven letters written to Michael and Gabriel, embodying the most explicit condemnation of God, the Bible and man of which Mark Twain was capable.

As is to be expected, God creates Adam and Eve insufficient to stand, and, when they fall, He carries out the sentence of death against them. Satan's comment is sharply ironical: "As you perceive, the only person responsible for the couple's offense escaped; and not only escaped but became the executioner of the innocent" (*LE*, p. 20).[11] This is the essence of Mark Twain's case against God.

10 From a "Letter to a Young Gentleman in Missouri Who Wanted Information on the Nevada Territory," *Territorial Enterprise*, 1863. Quoted in *Mark Twain's Frontier*, ed. James E. Camp and X. J. Kennedy (New York, 1963), pp. 30–31. I am quoting "out of context," of course, but the amusing description applies.

11 See also Mark Twain, "Reflections on Religion," ed. Charles Neider, *Hudson Review*, XVI (Autumn, 1963), 352: "God alone is responsible for every act and word of a human being's life between cradle and grave."

God is the devil, while Satan is the bitterly ironic sympathizer of man. God sends forth Adam and Eve "under a curse—a permanent one" (*LE*, p. 20). And it was of the consequences of this curse that Mark Twain wrote and over which he agonized much of his creative life. It is significant, too, that Satan is not involved in this fall. There is only the traditional serpent, as in the biblical account, to tempt man. Moreover, this serpent offers man what he naturally (according to God's laws) must have: knowledge. By contrast, Mark Twain tells us, "the priest, like God, whose imitator and representative he is, has made it his business from the beginning to keep him *from* knowing any useful thing" (*LE*, p. 17). Even the serpent emerges sympathetically.

Yet the full force of Twain's attack centers on the New Testament. The gift of the God of the Old Testament was death, and death to a life that is only a "fever-dream . . . embittered by sorrows. . . . a nightmare-confusion of spasmodic and fleeting delights . . . interspersed with long-drawn miseries," was "sweet," "gentle," and "kind" (*LE*, p. 44). What the New Testament and the figure of Jesus do is to create hell, so that man cannot claim "the blessed refuge of the grave" (*LE*, p. 44). In Mark Twain's embittered mind and personal theology, "The palm for malignity must be granted to Jesus, the inventor of hell . . ." (*LE*, p. 45).[12] The Sermon on the Mount becomes a collection of "immense sarcasms" (*LE*, p. 54), in the light of the fact that man cannot by temperament and the permanent curse upon him turn the other cheek or be meek and humble. Above all, it is a God who cannot fulfill these moral precepts and who makes a mockery of man's life by demanding that humanity must. Such is the view of Satan-Mark Twain concerning these key aspects of traditional Western theology. The rather obvious Satan mask here functions only to voice a polemic. Hell, for this Satan, is having to watch the workings of a cruelly absurd Divine Plan. Satan shifts from a demonic glee to an almost tragic indignation as he observes the victimization of man and the cosmic insanity of his Judge.

[12] In his *Notebook*, ed. A. B. Paine (New York, 1935), p. 290, Twain wrote: "There seems to be nothing connected with the atonement scheme that is rational. If Christ were God, He is in the attitude of One whose anger against Adam has grown so uncontrollable . . . that nothing but a sacrifice of life can appease it, & so without noticing how illogical the act is going to be, God condemns Himself to death . . . and wipes off that old score."

III

The next Satan-mask is curiously two-sided, though the two sides are joined by a single motif: Satan-as-failure. In "That Day in Eden" and "Eve Speaks," Satan becomes a tragic failure whose predicament enlists our sympathies, and in a group of unpublished short works he emerges as a vulgar—even grotesque—fool. He may appear quite polished in "Sold to Satan," but nevertheless admits to his past silly blunders. One of the story's main concerns, however, is to demonstrate the "ancestral" relationship between the narrator (Twain) and himself.

Satan's failure in the Adamic pieces comes about not as a result of any flaw in Satan, himself, but as a consequence of an insoluble situation created by the Deity: Adam and Eve can in no way understand God's prohibitions. Nothing Satan can do will make them grasp the meanings of words whose substance they have never experienced. Satan must watch helplessly as they eat of the Tree of Knowledge and acquire the "disaster" (XXIX, 344) that is the Moral Sense. Therefore Twain invests Satan's narrative with a pathetic tenderness:

Poor ignorant things, the command of refrain had meant nothing to them, they were but children, and could not understand untried things and verbal abstractions which stood . . . outside of their . . . narrow experience. Eve reached for an apple!—oh, farewell, Eden and your sinless joys, come poverty and pain, . . . envy, strife, malice and dishonor, age, weariness, remorse; then desperation and the prayer for the release of death, indifferent that the gates of hell yawn beyond it! (XXIX, 345)

After the fall, Satan simply comments that the change in Eve "was pitiful" (XXIX, 345), and then describes in a quietly lyrical way, the onrush of old age in the First Couple. And, at the end of "Eve Speaks" when Eve discovers the death of Abel, Satan returns as the Consoler: "Death has entered the world, the creatures are perishing; one of The Family is fallen; the product of the Moral Sense is complete. The Family think ill of death—they will change their minds" (XXIX, 350). By using Satan as his compassionate mask, and keeping the Deity narratively detached from the account of the fall and primal murder, Twain is able to "humanize" Satan, contrasting his sympathy—even compassion—for man, with the Deity's distantness and absurd prohibition.

A wholly different emphasis on Satan's failures emerges from a group of unpublished fragments in the Mark Twain Papers and the short novel "The Refuge of the Derelicts" (1905–1906). In this novel, Admiral Stormfield sympathizes with Satan over his failure to tempt Christ and his inability to prevent bishops from breaking their contracts with him. In these matters, Satan comes off somewhat as an incompetent. More ironically, the Admiral, complaining that Satan "only" converted "nine tenths of the human race," ponders the question: "Is he one of life's failures? . . . *One* of them? why, he's It!"[13] In another piece (untitled, ca. 1909), "little Sammy" mocks Satan's reputation for "commercial" ability, using again the example of Christ in the Wilderness. How could a place no more than "a hundred miles in diameter"[14] tempt God? This subject seems to have gripped Twain as early as the 1880's when he wrote "Bible Citations in proof [of?] a real devil," nine pages of short, exegetical notes on over twenty-three New Testament references to a real or substantive devil. Matthew 4 is again the central illustration. The note on Matthew 4:8 contains a biting remark on America:

They . . . go to the mountains—an *exceedingly* high mountain from whose top all the vast Roman Empire was easily visible . . . also America. [This is the *real* discovery of America, & the devil ought to have credit of it, not Columbus.] The D offers to give all . . . these to C to worship him. He is now both . . . dishonest & foolish, since he owns . . . no part of this territory, yet offers it to a personage whom he suspects owns it all.[15]

Twain could never quite free himself from reading the Bible with fundamentalist passion even as he ridiculed it in the name of reason. But neither could he escape seeing irony in all things. In these fragments he characterizes Satan indirectly by discussing his actions rather than by dramatizing them. Satan appears stupid in dealing with God and priests, but effective with man, becoming, as Twain wrote in "Concerning the Jews" (1899), "spiritual head of four fifths of the human race and political head of the whole of

---

[13] In *Mark Twain's Fables of Man,* ed. with an Introduction by John S. Tuckey (Berkeley, Calif., 1972), p. 195. References to this volume in the present section will appear in the text, cited by page.

[14] In the Mark Twain Papers, Berkeley, California: DV# 30, p. 9 of the holograph.

[15] In the Mark Twain Papers, Berkeley, California: DV# 81, Typescript, p. 2.

it . . ." (XXII, 265); he could be compassionate or destructive; and Twain's own relationship to him could oscillate between ironic "respect" or contempt or horror. If Satan occasionally fails to teach man the true nature of reality, he nearly always awakens and reveals some inner corruption or lie within him. As with Adam, Twain assumed the spiritual "kinship" between Satan and himself.[16] "Sold to Satan" dramatizes this relationship perfectly.

"Sold to Satan" is a clever burlesque exploiting the discovery of radium by the Curies. Twain inserts in it a comic temptation scene built around the themes of science, American big business tactics, and the spiritual consanguinity between himself and Satan. Here is a courteous, apparently successful Tempter who is made of radium worth millions on the market. Only Satan's polonium shield—still undiscovered by science—prevents him from blowing up the world. Indeed, Satan is an eerie forecast of The Ultimate Bomb. But it is the economic temptation that first works on the narrator, who sees what an "original" idea it would be to "kidnap Satan, and stock him, and incorporate him, and water the stock up to ten billions— just three times its actual value—and blanket the world with it!" (XXIX, 328). Satan tells him:

"Do you know I have been trading with your poor pathetic race for ages, and you are the first person who has ever been intelligent enough to divine the large commercial value of my make-up."

. . . .

"Yes, you are the first," he continued. "All through the Middle Ages I used to buy Christian souls at fancy rates, building bridges and cathedrals in a single night in return, and getting swindled out of my Christian nearly every time that I dealt with a priest—as history will concede—but making it up on the lay square-dealer now and then, as *I* admit; but none of those people ever guessed where the *real* big money lay. You are the first." (XXIX, 328–329)

The interesting conceit here is that, instead of Satan tempting man with some external precious thing, it is Satan himself—pure power which can run all the world's "machines and railways a hundred million years" (XXIX, 331)—who is the overwhelming temptation to economic and technological man. The narrator cries: "Quick—

---

[16] For a good compilation and discussion of Twain's references and allusions to this kinship, see Allison Ensor, *Mark Twain and the Bible* (Lexington, Ky., 1969), pp. 24, 40–61 passim.

my soul is yours dear Ancestor; take it—we'll start a company!"
(XXIX, 331). The narrator then gets a lesson in "modern" physics
while Satan demonstrates his power by lighting cigars with his
fingertips and his wit by casting backhanded compliments at
Madame Curie for having discovered his (and Hell's) natural element. Only when Madame Curie isolates polonium, will the narrator be able to clothe himself in it and take possession of the
radium located in a firefly cemetery. The story concludes: "Stock
is for sale. Apply to Mark Twain" (XXIX, 338).

Clearly, then, Mark Twain sees himself in this tale as a mirror-
image of Satan (or *vice versa*), since both have an immediate, intu-
itive sense of what the other wants and the knowledge of how to
get it. In getting the power that is radium, the narrator fulfills the
Gilded Age dream that so many of Mark Twain's characters
dreamed—to make the biggest "killing" and the grandest "effect"
ever. The burlesque is as much a satire and exposure of Twain's
own character as it is of man's crude exploitation of scientific discoveries. The witty and business-like attitudes of both the narrator
and Satan sharpen the disparity between their "styles" and moral
natures. "Sold to Satan" gives us a single mask whose transparency
allows the reader to see that the separate entities—the Tempter and
the Tempted—are one and the same.

IV

Perhaps the most significant role of Satan for Mark Twain is
to be found in "The Mysterious Stranger" complex. It is in this
group of stories that Twain reached an identification of himself as
a creative artist with the divine-like creative powers of an unfallen
Satan. It is here that we receive his final condemnation of the
damned human race and attempt to describe the nature of the universe. And, as DeVoto originally suggested, these works reflect
Twain's striving for some salvational ideal. By contrast, the other
masks of Satan we have observed are constructions whose function
is to voice the tragicomic relationship between man and God,
sometimes compassionately, more often cynically or satirically. But
these Satan-masks did not escape Twain's criticism, either, as the
failure theme attests. That is why, in all likelihood, these Satans do
not offer "solutions" to the massive moral and theological problems

inherent in the "human condition." This may also be the reason why Twain was never able to achieve an esthetically and intellectually complete version of "The Mysterious Stranger" idea. Dream psychology, determinism, the myth of the fall—all these explanatory "solutions" to universal problems were deeply ingrained in Twain's mind. On an intellectual level, "The Mysterious Stranger" stories represent Twain's attempts to make these conflicting "philosophies" seem harmonious and persuasive. To do this, Twain employed a version of one of his most profound patterns—the contrast and relationship between a putative Huck Finn-Tom Sawyer narrator who has not yet dreamed of "lighting out" for the territory, and an "Adamic" Satan who utterly transcends the human condition. It is this pattern that creates whatever unity the stories possess and into which dreams, determinism, and the fall are woven. And lurking in almost every line, there exists an emotional force which derives from Mark Twain's confronting himself in an inner dialogue between the "earthly" man and the "divine" artist.

Insofar as the stories represent projections of this inner dialogue going on within Mark Twain, himself, their real meanings and tensions can be located in his need to "liberate," psychically and philosophically, his creative Self from the noncreative claims of what he called in a letter to Howells, his "mud image." The letter, dated February 23, 1897, the period during which the Satan figure was to emerge dominantly, deals with Twain's mood after the death of Susy. He writes that he is "Indifferent to nearly everything but work." Yet he must persist:

This mood will pass, some day—there is history for it. But it cannot pass until my wife comes up out of the submergence. She was always so quick to recover herself before, but now there is no rebound, & we are dead people who go through the motions of life. Indeed I am a mud image, & it puzzles me to know what it is in me that writes, & that has comedy-fancies & finds pleasure in phrasing them. It is a law of our nature, of course, or it wouldn't happen; the thing in me forgets the presence of the mud image & goes its own way wholly unconscious of it & apparently of no kinship with it.[17]

The "thing" in him—clearly his creative power that in some way

17 *Mark Twain-Howells Letters,* ed. Henry Nash Smith and William M. Gibson (Cambridge, Mass., 1960), II, 664–665.

"forgets" (is *indifferent* to?) his mud image—is the salvation here, ultimately finding expression in the Satan of "The Mysterious Stranger" stories. In "real" life, these two aspects of being are mysteriously embodied, to use Theodore Dreiser's phrase, in "Mark the Double Twain." In "The Mysterious Stranger" stories they confront one another as separate entities, characterized by a kind of love-hate or love-fear relationship. And in the first of the stories, "The Chronicle of Young Satan," Philip Traum says that

> Man is made of dirt—I *saw* him made. I am not made of dirt. Man is a museum of disgusting diseases, a home of impurities; he comes to-day and is gone to-morrow, he begins as dirt and departs as a stench; I am of the aristocracy of the Imperishables. And man has the *Moral Sense*. (p. 55)

Adamic man *is* what his name means: earth. His evil-creating Moral Sense is an inextricable part of this dirt origin. The need to be liberated from this condition is touched upon in "No. 44, The Mysterious Stranger," when Emil Schwarz, August Feldner's Dream-Self, cries out against his being an embodiment of man:

> oh, free me from *them*; these bonds of flesh—this decaying vile matter, this foul weight, and clog, and burden, this loathsome sack of corruption in which my spirit is imprisoned, her white wings bruised and soiled—oh, be merciful and set her free! (p. 369)

He goes on to bemoan the fact that he is a "servant!—I who never served before; here I am a slave—slave among little mean kings and emperors made of clothes, the kings and emperors slaves themselves, to mud-built carrion that are *their* slaves!" (p. 369)

   Mud, dirt, "earth-shod,"—these terms are at the center of Mark Twain's metaphor for fallen man. To be "free," "Imperishable," without the Moral Sense, describes unfallen creative Satan. The tension and relationship between the two provides, as I have suggested, the unifying pattern in all three versions. Seen from this perspective, the other key themes in the stories find significant, but supportive roles. The kind of determinism that characterizes fallen man or the mud image is a fixed, mechanical process well suited to man's nature. Mechanical determinism becomes, in effect, a covering definition for fallen man. It becomes a way of *knowing* him. Yet, as we shall see, that determinism is itself, when examined, intrinsically absurd in its workings and results. The determinism that characterizes unfallen Satan is really a species of idealism, that is, it describes the nature of the universe and its manifestations as dream —as unreal ontologically speaking, though "real" enough in appearance. Satan's mission is to teach man this "truth." The creative powers of Satan become a vital way by which this truth is to be conveyed. This is a fascinating inversion of the Gospels in which Jesus uses his divine powers to heal, teach, and create faith and preparedness for the Kingdom to come. For Mark Twain-Satan the Kingdom to come ends in nothing but an escape into solipsistic idealism, a consequence of a metaphysical irreconcilability in a universe in which the primal drama has always been strife between Flesh and Spirit. The earth-bound narrators of "The Mysterious Stranger" stories find themselves in the very center of this struggle which began historically and theologically in the Garden of Eden.

The "Paradise" of Eseldorf is the final fictional *locus* of this drama for Mark Twain. And it is in the "Schoolhouse Hill" version that the problem of the fall is treated most explicitly. This is significant especially in the light of the fact that the other two versions mainly stress the problems of dreams and determinism. It is true that all three versions portray the creative powers of Satan, although the young "44" of "Schoolhouse Hill" is made remarkable (at least at the outset) by his learning abilities rather than his cosmic gifts. Toward the end of this unfinished story "44" does indeed perform the miracle of saving people who are trapped in a mysterious snowstorm from death. The other two versions play considerably more on his ability to create and destroy life, and to manipulate and reveal the past and the future. Similarly, "44"'s indifference to human suffering is lightly touched upon in "Schoolhouse Hill" but intensified in the other two. In all three versions man is presented as small-minded and corrupt. In all three the Satan-figure tries to teach "truths" to ignorant man. What, then, is the "truth" in "Schoolhouse Hill"? It is simply that man's entrapment in flesh and human history with all its moral perversities is nothing but an absurd, primal error. This is what "44" tells Mr. Hotchkiss in their discussion of biblical events. He says: "There was no tempter until my father ate of the fruit himself and became one. Then he tempted other angels and they ate of it also; then Adam and the woman." The elder Satan is very upset for "he could

do nothing but grieve and lament" (p. 215). According to "44,"
Satan gave no warning to Adam because he had an "erroneous"
idea of what the fruit could do once eaten: "His error was in
supposing that a knowledge of the difference between good & evil
was *all* that the fruit could confer" (p. 216). Young Satan elaborates:

"Consider the passage which says *man is prone to evil as the sparks to
fly upward*. Is that true? . . . ."
"Indeed it is—nothing could be truer."
"It is not true of the men of any other planet. It explains the mystery.
My father's error stands revealed in all its nakedness. The fruit's office
was not confined to conferring the mere knowledge of good and evil, it
conferred also the passionate . . . eager and hungry *disposition to* DO *evil*.
Prone as sparks to fly upward; in other words, prone as water to run
down hill—a powerful figure, and means that man's disposition is wholly
evil, . . . inveterately evil, and that he is as undisposed to do good as
water is undisposed to run *up* hill. Ah, my father's error brought a
colossal disaster upon the men of this planet. It *poisoned* the men of this
planet—poisoned them in mind and body. . . ."
"It brought death, too."
"Yes—whatever that may be . . . ." (p. 216)

"44" then goes on to say that he will try to lift part of the "burden
of evil consequences" (p. 217) from man, although the evil is now
"permanent." At that point the discussion breaks off and is not
referred to again. But its implications for the entire "Mysterious
Stranger" complex seem to me to be considerable. First, the passage
is another remarkable instance of Mark Twain's intellectual struggle
with the idea of the fall.[18] Some new elements present themselves
here that are not to be found in his earlier treatment of the myth,
but fit into the general pattern of Mark Twain's thinking on the
subject. The idea that the fall was an "error" on the part of a
guilt-struck Satan is a new perspective, though it serves once again
to reinforce Twain's picture of a tragically victimized Adam and his
descendants. For not only is Adam an innocent victim, but the
whole "temptation" situation is a lamentable mistake. Adam *and*

---

[18] Many critics of Twain have commented on his concern with Adam but very few in-
depth studies have been made on the subject. See my article "The Humor of the Absurd:
Mark Twain's Adamic Diaries," *Criticism*, XIV (Winter, 1972), 49–64; and Thomas Werge,
"Mark Twain and the Fall of Adam," *Mark Twain Journal*, XV (Summer, 1970), 5–13.
Also see Ensor for an overall account of Twain's Adamic references. See too, my unpublished
dissertation, "Mark Twain and the Fall of Man," Columbia University, 1967.

Satan have been fooled by God, and are therefore natural objects of sympathy for Mark Twain. Satan had only wished to give man moral discrimination; instead he gave him a permanent disposition to evil. To underscore this, Twain plays with biting wit on the passage in Job 5:7: "Man is born unto trouble, as the sparks fly upward." The substitution of "prone to evil" for "born unto trouble" reveals one of Twain's habitual responses to the problem of human suffering.

Secondly, the idea of the fall as an "error" reinforces—even provides the grounds for—the metaphysics of dreams and determinism which permeate the other two versions of "The Mysterious Stranger." It is the fall which *creates* the conditions of a world characterized by imprisonment in flesh and the ironbound consequences flowing from this state. The fact that the fall was an "error" only provides more "proof" for an absurd universe. It therefore is reasonable to assume that the philosophic "positions" presented in "The Chronicle of Young Satan" and "No. 44, The Mysterious Stranger," are organically tied to the Adamic myth and spring from it as final descriptions of man's fate.

The first "position" made explicit in "The Chronicle" may be termed "deterministic nihilism," a description that covers all the mechanistic, but purposeless aspects of existence.[19] By changing the life-events of Nikolaus, Lisa, and Fischer, the weaver, Satan only teaches the narrator, Theodor, the futility of knowing one's history in advance. Theodor says, "Satan had shown me other people's lives and I saw that in nearly all cases there would be little or no advantage in altering them" (p. 147). Not only do Satan's lessons "prove" man's life to be contemptible and miserable, but also that there is no redemption from this misery. One "determined" life turns out to be no better than any other "determined" life. It is clear that life has no meaning. Though Satan does say that "Some few will profit in various ways by change" (p. 132), this does not really offer any consolation to Theodor or qualify the meaninglessness significantly. The very Heaven mortals yearn for and may

19 Many excellent insights into Twain's determinism are developed by Ellwood Johnson, "Mark Twain's Dream Self in the Nightmare of History," *Mark Twain Journal*, XV (Winter, 1970), 6–12. Johnson argues persuasively that "The two thematic developments [in *The Mysterious Stranger*] may be termed ideational determinism (thesis) and mechanistic determinism (antithesis); these are brought together and resolved in solipsistic determinism" (p. 7).

receive is ruled over by a God who has no "compassion" in "His hard heart" (p. 129). This is said by the embittered Frau Brandt whose prayers to God went unheeded. The irony is that she should have prayed for the death of her child. Theodor sees into mankind's dilemma: "Ah! that poor woman! It is as Satan said, we do not know good fortune from bad, and always mistaking the one for the other. Many a time, since then, I have heard people pray to God to spare the life of sick persons, but I have never done it" (p. 129). All that could possibly be called "redemptive" is death. And yet one of Satan's prime demonstrations even undercuts the dubious consolation of death. For early in the story, in explaining to Nikolaus that the "Fall did not affect me nor the rest of the relationship" (p. 49), Satan casually squashed two little workmen he had created and then "wiped the red from his fingers . . . and went on talking . . ." (p. 49). Their lives were meaningless—an illusion—and so were their deaths. Finally, Satan teaches the boys that mankind "duped itself from cradle to grave with shams and delusions which it mistook for realities, and this made its entire life a sham" (p. 164). There is no way, then, for man to reach any kind of "truth" or positive meaning in existence. There is only the negative meaning that all is sham or meaninglessness precisely because man cannot distinguish appearance from reality, good fortune from bad, and the value of one deterministically shaped life from another. Such are the true consequences of the fall.

If this is true, it explains Mark Twain's mask or portrait of Satan. He must be completely freed from any mortal element in order to dramatize unequivocally man's fate. His indifference to human suffering can then be made to function as an artistic device which would make his teachings "believable." The excitement the boys feel in Satan's company is based on not only his tricks and effects, but also, more importantly, on his irreverence and aura of transcendence emanating through his cosmic power. These elements make possible, at best, the grounds for a condescending relationship between the Immortal and the Mortal. Mark Twain has provided us with no middle ground, as it were, for both to inhabit meaningfully. This radical polarization in character only underscores what little hope Twain had that a redemptive ideal could be found in a world ultimately "empty and soundless" (p. 403). Knowing this, Satan says that "No sane man can be happy, for to him life is real, and he sees what a fearful thing it is. Only the mad can be happy, and not many of those" (p. 164).

The second position developed in "No. 44, The Mysterious Stranger," is that of the much-discussed solipsism presented in the famous dream-ending Twain wrote in 1904. This passage was written four years after Twain had stopped work on "The Chronicle" and six years after "Schoolhouse Hill." Yet it was written four years *before* the scene of the historical pageant "44" shows August and then dissolves, leaving an "empty & soundless world." This surely indicates that both positions maintained their hold on Twain's mind, and that he could not separate, intellectually, the two. William M. Gibson suggests that the pageant-ending might have been intended as an alternate to the dream-passage.[20] If so, it does not seem to reflect any real philosophic confusion in Twain's mind, though it certainly presented him with an artistic choice to make. Twain's philosophic task was to integrate or harmonize his view that existence is essentially meaningless and determined at the same time, with his view that reality is a dream dreamed by a "vagrant Thought" (p. 405)—the isolated Self. However artistically unfinished "No. 44, The Mysterious Stranger" is, Mark Twain did work out a meaningful, though not totally logical, pattern of ideas. The key to the pattern lies in the final mask of Satan and his dream-philosophy.

This mask embodies the marriage of two major preoccupations and themes in Twain's work: the Adamic myth and the problem of identity in its relationship to a dreamed and/or deterministic world. Thus, "44" is a Satanic Dreamer, a version of the Superintendent of Dreams in the fragment "The Great Dark."[21] The Superintendent is a "trickster" who uses and manifests the basic absurdity of dreams, in themselves. What makes most dreams absurd is that they always reflect the horror of reality and man's fate as they are archetypically dramatized in the Adamic myth. This thematic marriage becomes strikingly clear in the long fragment called "Which Was It?" (1902). George Harrison, a major character, reflects on his father's crime of paying off debts with counterfeit money and the excuse he constructs for himself:

20 Gibson, "Introduction" to *Mark Twain's Mysterious Stranger Manuscripts*, p. 11. Also see pp. 26–33, on the ideas and problems involved with the ending.

21 In *Letters from the Earth*. DeVoto's notes on the story contain the idea that the Superintendent of Dreams is "clearly an unconscious anticipation of Satan in *The Mysterious Stranger*" (p. 299).

He [the father] argued with Rev. Mr. Bailey about temptations, and said a character that hadn't been exposed to them and solidified by fighting them and *losing* the fight was a flabby poor thing and couldn't be depended upon in an emergency. He said a temptation successfully resisted was good, but a fall was better. He said he wouldn't go so far as to put temptations in the way of a child of his, but had always been willing to see them come; and said a person wouldn't ever be safe until he had tried and *fallen*.[22]

Later in the story, after the son has experienced a long series of calamities as a result of a murder he commits to save his family from debt, he analyzes his predicament by drawing a tree entitled the "genealogy of a lapse." The root of the tree is called "False Pride," the trunk, "Disaster," and on the limbs are eleven fruits or crimes (p. 241). For George, each crime was a consequence of a preceding crime revealing a deterministic pattern. But Twain had planned to have George awaken to find that all was a nightmare, anyway. The awakening from the nightmare of the fall was no doubt a desperate wish-fulfillment for Mark Twain. Actually, his sense of a fallen world went so deep that he ironically could not believe in the forms of salvation offered by the "Judeo-Christian" tradition. Moreover, it was a belief that found dubious consolation in philosophic determinism, since genuine moral and spiritual reform seemed illusory. The picture is that of a fallen world that cannot be redeemed, deterministically structured yet at the same time chaotic and a "sham" through which man wanders in a kind of schizoid dream-state, never knowing quite who and what he is. The solipsistic view of Satan-Mark Twain can be seen now as a direct emotional and intellectual spin-off from the idea or perception that there is a Cosmic Contradiction at the heart of things.[23] That is why Satan, after describing these contradictions to August in terms of a God who "mouths justice, and invented hell—mouths mercy, and invented hell" (p. 405), says: "You perceive, *now*, that these things

---

22 "Which Was It?" in *Mark Twain's Which Was the Dream? and Other Symbolic Writings of the Later Years*, ed. with an Introduction by John S. Tuckey (Berkeley, Calif., 1967), p. 195.

23 John S. Tuckey in his *Mark Twain and Little Satan*, p. 64, describes some notes written by Twain at Florence at the same time the dream-ending was written. The notes tell of a man whose "foible" it was to believe that life was a dream and himself a foolish thought in it. This does not, it seems to me, qualify the essential seriousness and pessimism inherent in the solipsistic conclusion. But for another approach to the idea of the "Absurd" in Twain's work, see Richard Boyd Hauck, *A Cheerful Nihilism: Confidence and "The Absurd" in American Humorous Fiction* (Bloomington, Ind., 1971), chapter 5.

are all impossible, *except* in a dream" (p. 405, "except" in my italics). This seems to me to be the crucial line in the argument of the dream-passage. Because the world is fallen, trapped in flesh and mud, and beset by insoluble moral and metaphysical contradictions, it must be a dream. This is the inverse of Tertullian's *"certum est, quia impossible."* For Twain, reality has no inner logic to make it believable as an objective-existent structure with a meaningful *telos*. The universe, therefore, comes closest to the nature of a dream-nightmare. "44" wonders why August did not see the analogy before: "Strange, indeed, that you should not have suspected that your universe and its contents were only dreams, visions, fictions! Strange, because they are so frankly and hysterically insane—like all dreams" (p. 404). Then, "44" proceeds to list his examples of cosmic contradictions. But he has made the key analogy: "insane—like all dreams." His next step—though a *non sequitur,* yet emotionally, existentially, true—is to say that this insane reality *is* a dream. He moves from analogy to identification, from simile to metaphor. Nevertheless, "44" cannot escape the fact that some one mind must be making or perceiving the identification. He tells August that "Nothing exists but You. And you are but a Thought . . . wandering forlorn among the empty eternities!" (p. 405). And "Thought" had been defined as "inextinguishable, indestructible" (p. 404). The exhortation by "44" to "Dream other dreams, and better!" is not the consolation it seems.[24] It may be possible to dream less insane dreams than man is now dreaming, but little else. Every dream will end by revealing the Self's forlorn state amid empty eternities. True, there is the consolation of being "set . . . free" (p. 404) as "44" says. August is indeed set free, at least intellectually, from being a mud image. Not only is he set free from the "nightmare of history" *qua* history, but also from the nightmare implicit in the conditions of the Adamic myth. Still, what good would it be for August to dream other dreams in a human context? To be truly

24 But see John S. Tuckey's "Mark Twain's Later Dialogue: The 'Me' and the Machine," *American Literature,* XLI (Jan., 1970), 532–542. Tuckey gives some evidence for the view that Twain was struggling against his deterministic philosophy of *What is Man?* Thus, the "dream self" might suggest man's essentially spiritual nature and the final chapter of *The Mysterious Stranger* evidence that Satan is a reflection of man's own creative powers. For Tuckey, Mark Twain was not totally pessimistic. One can easily agree that Twain sought release from his despair and that that was in itself an affirmative search. But his "dialogue" was never resolved. And Twain still asserts that, though all reality is the product of a single, creative dream self, it is still *nothing but a dream,* with no ultimate meaning.

"saved," August's thought-reality would have to be precisely the same as "44"'s. August would have to dream himself—actually be —a god. Earlier in the story, "44" had told him that "a man's mind cannot *create*—a god's can, and my race can. That is the difference. *We* need no contributed materials, we *create* them—out of thought. All things that exist were made out of thought—and out of nothing else" (p. 333).

A god can create out of a thought-stuff which is pure essence; man can only create by associating external realities received through the senses into set forms as a machine does. Man does not enjoy *true* creativity. Only unfallen Satan can experience this. Ultimate salvation is to be set free from the consequences of the fall and to become a god. Mark Twain's remarkable irony is that the cardinal sin of pride is salvation itself. Unlike Howard L. Stephenson and the other Satan-masks, this Tempter is translated through a new dream into a genuine Savior. The concept is best understood as a revelation of Mark Twain's spiritual and philosophic anguish in his final years, rather than as serious metaphysics. But as a metaphorical description or radical theological concept it resonates forcefully with the truth of man's existential confrontation of a reality that he can make little sense of and that always throws him back on himself to find truth. As such, it is a serious theological statement, replete with symbols and paradox and the striving for transcendence. In turning the theology of the Adamic myth upside down, Mark Twain created his most outrageous protest against God's world and mediated it through a Satan no longer angry, only free and detached. Though tentatively and incompletely worked out in "The Mysterious Stranger" stories, Mark Twain had come to the "position" that salvation lay outside of man, in the inevitable triumph of Satan.

Mark Twain the Tourist:
The Form of *The Innocents Abroad*
Bruce Michelson

W HILE MOST READERS AGREE that *The Innocents Abroad* is organized by some kind of consistent narrative stance, just what
that stance is remains a mystery and a cause of argument. *The Innocents* has lasted a century as the most popular travel book ever written by an American, and in the course of that century this particular
American, this "Mark Twain" who guides us through Europe, has
been hailed and damned with a baffling variety of names. Flag-
waving Yankee-Philistine, hater of Americans and American ways,
exacting and sober critic of civilization, boor and yahoo, ferocious
democrat, sycophant before royal fools, pilgrim of real or hypocritical or parodistic piety—the long list gives little hope of ever settling
the question.[1] Even so, understanding the narration and the structure
of *The Innocents* can be made much easier if we recognize a mistake
common to most of these opinions: the mistake of listening too
closely to one voice among the many which present themselves in
the narrative—and of consequently missing the one voice behind
them all.

Solving the identity problem can be fairly simple, provided one is
willing to trust Mark Twain a little and take *The Innocents* to be,
in one sense, exactly what he says it is. Repeatedly his book announces
itself as "the record of a pleasure trip,"[2] of the "Great Pleasure Excursion,"[3] of America's historic first "picnic on a gigantic scale";[4] that
is, an account not merely of travel but of travel for the fun of it, of

---

[1] For a comprehensive if somewhat irascible survey of critical comment on *The Innocents Abroad*, see Arthur L. Scott, *"The Innocents Abroad* Revaluated," *Western Humani-
ties Review*, VII (Summer, 1953), 215–223. More recent important studies of the book are
cited in the notes below.

[2] *The Writings of Mark Twain* (New York, 1911), I, xxxvii. All subsequent citations of
The Innocents Abroad refer to this edition, the famous red-bound version of the "Author's
National Edition" of Mark Twain's Works, Volume I of which opens with the "Biographical
Criticism" by Brander Matthews.

[3] Ibid., p. 45.

[4] Ibid., p. 45.

that modern, familiar kind of play which we call "tourism." This
much the book says outright, and this much we should be able to
concede at the start. The next step is to understand the meaning of
the obvious. We need to consider what tourism is, and the special
circumstances which dictated the form and style of Mark Twain's
first real book, in order to make a clearer statement of the principles
which hold it together and give it lasting life.

Few authorities would dispute the proposition that touring, traveling for pleasure, is a kind of play. To use a typology widely accepted
now, touring for pleasure is a form of *paidia*, play of the free and
improvisatory sort, as opposed to *ludus*, the formal, structured game.[5]
We must recognize, however, that by nature paidia is quite different
from other kinds of improvisation. Paidia requires a spirit of make-
believe, and therefore, as in any other form of true play, something
is always at stake in true paidia. Improvisatory *play* is always a
challenge to the player to maintain for some given interlude the
fictive world of the play itself.[6] Play is a relative phenomenon which
must be actively sustained against an intrusive, circumscribing "reality," and the player is a player only so long as his play-world can
hold out. In the paidia of pleasure touring, the object is to sustain an
imaginative engagement and thereby to transform a various and
sometimes tedious real world into a world of novelty, fantasy, and
adventure.[7] This much is already known to anyone who has ever
traveled for the fun of it and known the moment when a pleasure

---

[5] This typology was the invention of Roger Caillois, whose study *Man, Play, and Games*
(New York, 1961) ranks second only to Huizinga's *Homo Ludens* as a study of play as a
cultural and aesthetic phenomenon. Caillois intends not so much to quarrel with Huizinga
as to make the discussion of play more precise. These writers share the view that play is a
distinct kind of human behavior, and avoid what Huizinga called the "ontological short-
circuit" of assuming that all literature, all life is one enormous game. Of course I am making
the same assumption, and I take it as obvious that Mark Twain did as well, considering how
often he lamented the difference between his work and the "serious" writers he admired.
Those interested in ingenious arguments that literature and life are all play should consult
Jacques Ehrmann, ed., *Play, Games, and Literature*, Yale French Studies, XLI (New Haven,
Conn., 1968).

[6] Johan Huizinga, *Homo Ludens* (Boston, 1955), pp. 10–11; Caillois, pp. 4, 9–10.

[7] Caillois on play as make-believe: ". . . the player on the one hand lacks knowledge of
how to invent and follow rules that do not exist in reality, and on the other hand the game
is accompanied by the knowledge that the required behavior is pretense, or simple mimicry.
This awareness of the basic unreality of the assumed behavior is separate from real life and
from the arbitrary legislation that defines other games. The equivalence is so precise that
one who breaks up a game, the one who denounces the absurdity of the rules, now becomes
the one who breaks the spell, who brutally refuses to acquiesce in the proposed illusion . . ."
(pp. 8–9).

excursion becomes a chore; to understand the importance of the play-impulse, we need only to have toured a little ourselves.

In his landmark study of Mark Twain's works,[8] James M. Cox has done more than anyone else to end the long, hollow argument that the narration of *The Innocents Abroad* reveals this or that sort of conventional personality. Cox stresses that the central purpose of the book is to entertain us, and therefore to exercise that "humor" which for Cox is the essence of Mark Twain's genius. Among the narrative methods of *The Innocents* Cox locates impersonation, comic exaggeration, burlesque. The varying and sometimes contradictory voices of the "Mark Twain" who guides us through Europe are poses for the sake of our amusement:

Although much of Mark Twain's burlesque has its roots in indignation, it moves the reader not toward guilt but toward a laughter arising from recognition of the absurdity of the world; and the laughter is not an acceptance of, or a guilt toward, but a relief *from* responsibility. The achievement of Mark Twain's burlesque is thus to redeem or at least to recover the journey from the condition of funeral procession and make it a genuine pleasure trip. . . . *The New Pilgrim's Progress* as *The Innocents* was subtitled, was Mark Twain's account of an attempt to recover the joy of the earthly life which the betrayals of the spirit have almost annihilated. . . . What he must constantly do in order to restore the threatened excursion is to invent burlesque distortions which literally make fun of the various forms of piety. (pp. 44–45)

As Cox sees it, Mark Twain's purpose—to give pleasure—answers the question about the narrative voice. This view of the book seems to me correct as far as it goes; but I believe it needs to go farther. Mark Twain's prevailing device for entertaining his audience in *The Innocents* is a persona who vigorously and consistently seeks to entertain *himself*. Twain tells us that he is on the voyage not to be one of the "pilgrims" but one of the "boys," sharing their avowed purpose of having a good time. It may seem trivial to insist on this, to hold that Twain styles himself more as a player of his own games than as our entertainer. The distinction is important, however, as it allows us to answer many questions which arise when we reject conventional descriptions of Mark Twain the traveler and guide. The first question is whether there really is in the book any identity worth

[8] *Mark Twain: The Fate of Humor* (Princeton, N.J., 1966).

talking about, and therefore any real structure and coherence in the narrative. Is the "Mark Twain" of *The Innocents* only a hollow and frivolous mask, a thin excuse for an essentially disjointed monologue? Unless we recognize the implications of Twain's self-presentation as a player, in both his touring and his narration, we cannot properly answer such a question. Cox's answer is that the narration of the book defines itself in the very confidence of the prose, that *The Innocents* consistently shows us a Mark Twain in full control of his literary effects, manipulating his "impersonations" sometimes to puzzle us, but always to present himself as the master of our revels and a champion in the cause of plain speaking.[9] Cox's case is ingenious and persuasive—but it is not clear how a smooth, effortless style makes for a narrative identity while mere "impersonation" in his judgment does not. Nor is it clear, for that matter, how the vernacular style itself can be told from just another impersonation. Nor does Cox's conclusion reconcile with Twain's talent for pure and simple banality, a talent which makes itself all too obvious in *The Innocents*. And finally such an explanation of the book fails to reflect adaquately the circumstances from which it came.

The phrase "Mark Twain" rode into the national vernacular on the back of a certain frog, not as the name of just another sketch-writer, but as the pen-name of "The Wild Humorist of the Pacific Slope," as he was billed, in tall black type, on posters all across the country.[10] Americans came to know "Mark Twain" as a clown of genius, and such a name was sure to bring more business in the bookshops. But what sort of audience was Clemens gathering? The readers he had won expected clowning. Many of them would want only clowning and therefore be disposed to find it in whatever "Mark Twain" might subsequently write. We know that Clemens much regretted his public image as the great national clown, as the "phunny phellow" he sometimes called himself, with a wry sadness. The regret shows in that famous letter to Howells, praising an *Atlantic* audience which did not "require a 'humorist' to paint himself stripèd and stand on his head every fifteen minutes."[11] The regret is clear even in that letter which announces his resolve to be the national humorist, a letter to his brother Orion in 1865. To read these words is to sense Twain's

[9] Ibid., p. 40.
[10] See Justin Kaplan, *Mr. Clemens and Mark Twain* (New York, 1966), pp. 32–37.
[11] Ibid., p. 146.

deep, frustrated wish to be that serious artist someday which he believed a clown's identity would simply not allow:

I *have* had a "call" to literature of a low order—*i.e.,* humorous. It is nothing to be proud of, but it is my strongest suit, & if I were to listen to that maxim of stern *duty* which says that to do right you *must* multiply the one or the two or the three talents which the Almighty entrusts to your keeping, I would long ago have ceased to meddle with things for which I was by nature unfitted & turned my attention to seriously scribbling to excite the *laughter* of God's creatures. Poor, pitiful business! Though the Almighty did His part by me—for the talent is a mighty engine when supplied with the steam of *education*—which I have not got, & so its pistons & cylinders & shafts move feebly & for a holiday show & are useless to any good purpose.[12]

There is certainly no joy here; and no reason to suppose that Mark Twain had given up all hope of being the "serious" writer even as he played the clown. Surely his later achievements make it obvious that he proved capable of doing both. To observe something, then, of the challenge which faced Mark Twain in writing *The Innocents Abroad:* he had to transform "Mark Twain" the sketch-writer into "Mark Twain" the author, the author of a long book if he were to sell it by subscription. He had to please that mass audience which his sketches had found him—and yet he had to do something to frustrate the buffoon implications of his own joking and his public name. It was no small trick, to amuse and yet to nurture a reputation as something more than the Great American Clown. The finesse with which *The Innocents Abroad* met this multiple challenge is a wonder. It is a wonder of adaptation, however, and not of invention, for marvel as we should at the fitness of Mark Twain's strategy, we should marvel as well at its resemblance to those very writings he was seeking to surpass.

The pleasure that Mark Twain's early sketches still give us is strongly vicarious, coming of our witnessing acts of absorbing, imaginative paidia, much as one would be pleased to watch the play of a child caught up in fantasy. The fun which endures in "The Celebrated Jumping Frog" consists not simply of a license to laugh at Jim Smiley or at Wheeler and his cornered visitor. We respond at

---

[12] *My Dear Bro, A Letter from Samuel Clemens to His Brother Orion,* ed. Frederick Anderson (Berkeley, Calif., 1961), pp. 6–7.

least as much to the richness of Wheeler's vernacular and to the
obvious relish with which he tells the tale—a relish delightfully incongruous with his deadpan face. Perhaps Wheeler does have some
malicious design on his listener, wants to "put him on" after the
tall-tale fashion. Or perhaps Wheeler is too drunk to know what he
wants to do. But whatever his initial intentions might be, he falls
quickly and completely under the spell of his own childlike self-
indulgence. His language reveals a man spinning his yarn with such
gusto that he loses track—as we do—of where the truth ends and
the fantasy begins:

Well, thish-yer Smiley had rat-tarriers, and chicken cocks, and tomcats
and all them kind of things, till you couldn't rest, and you couldn't fetch
nothing for him to bet on but he'd match you. He ketched a frog one day,
and took him home, and said he cal'lated to educate him; and so he never
done nothing for three months but set in his back yard and learn that frog
to jump. . . . He got him up so in the matter of ketching flies, and kep'
him in practice so constant, that he'd nail a fly every time fur as he could
see him. Smiley said all a frog wanted was education, and he could do
most anything—and I believe him.[13]

Many of the best Southwestern tall tales have this same kind of
appeal. Their mode of narration denies that they are merely or even
predominantly put-ons, intended only to "sell" the gullible audience.
These tales are additionally acts of play for a narrator who tells them
for the pleasure of spinning them out; and because the narrator seems
to enjoy himself, our pleasure, as listeners, is the richer. The story-
teller's good time is of course never so obtrusive as to spoil our fun.
Fantasy is properly the narrator's pleasure; and the discovery of that
pleasure is properly our own. When a narrator plays innocently and
unobtrusively in this manner, his spirit is infectious, and the reader
finds his delight in seeing the paidia of make-believe succeed.

If Mark Twain's early successes did not teach him this principle,
his early failures, the ones which precede *The Innocents,* probably
did. *The Innocents* followed soon after two long and unsuccessful
travel writings, the "letters" from the Sandwich Islands (finally to
appear as a book in 1938) and the *Alta California* letters from
Europe, the letters from which *The Innocents* eventually grew.[14] In

[13] *Writings,* XIX, 30.
[14] These letters were eventually collected in *Mark Twain's Travels with Mr. Brown,* ed.
Franklin Walker and G. Ezra Dane (New York, 1940).

neither work does Mark Twain present himself as a freewheeling and imaginatively engaged person at play. He contrives instead two *un*imaginative characters, possessed not of a play-impulse but only of a set of stock responses; these characters fail precisely because they are so consistent, so tediously unplayful. The "Mark Twain" of these letters is ever the effusive innocent; the gruff, irreverent "Mr. Brown" who for obscure reasons accompanies him is every bit as predictable. The problem is the incongruity between the consistent characterization and the fact that Brown and Twain are supposed to be on a pleasure trip. Descended of Don Quixote and Sancho, Twain and Brown are out of place. Fit for a comic quest or a mock pilgrimage on which some single-mindedness and seriousness might make sense, these pilgrims are sent instead on a holiday. The true tourist must be willing to play, and to improvise amusements wherever he should find himself. The epitome of the playful tourist, moreover, is the improvising traveler who will risk improvising himself, who will surrender his everyday consistencies and seriousness to his powers of make-believe, and forgo being his reasonable, normal self for as long as the play shall last. He who plays without giving up his nonplay identity does not really play at all.[15] Twain and Brown may take a physical holiday from the everyday world, but they refuse to take any holiday from themselves—and that is the essence of their failure. They give no impression that they enjoy their travels, and while we may find some cause to laugh at them, we are denied the pleasure of sharing with them any intensive and fictive fun.

This is why the self-contradictions of the "Mark Twain" who leads us through Europe in *The Innocents Abroad* serve the book much better than would the consistencies of some more conventional comic character. The form of the book and its narration come naturally out of the essence of tourism, out of the play of improvisation and make-believe. For Twain's discovery of the player's identity, the *Quaker City* trip itself deserves some credit. When Mark Twain called the voyage "The New Pilgrim's Progress" he was not being wry about its historical importance. With or without his company, the excursion was a memorable event. The first invasion of the old world by the American "guided tour" was so unprecedented an act that the

---

15 For a provocative discussion of the loss of identity in play, see Bernard J. Bergen and Stanley D. Rosenberg, "The New Neo-Freudians: Psychoanalytic Dimensions of Social Change." *Psychiatry*, XXXIV (Feb., 1971), 19–37, especially 36–37.

steamship and its passengers were objects of wonder—and suspicion. At Leghorn, local authorities detained the ship in the harbor for several days, having never seen the like and fearing some dark ulterior purpose. They were right to be uneasy. The *Quaker City* contained the vanguard of the largest and richest invasion of wandering pleasure-seekers in history. The Americans were coming to turn Europe into one vast amusement park, to transform every gallery, palace, cathedral, and house of state into a hometown sideshow, to gape at the "foreigners" and have themselves a good time. The millions back home waited to hear of the great national pleasure adventure from someone who had gone along in the proper spirit. No Quixote and grumbling side-kick would do for such a book. To suit the American audience he knew, the subject he undertook, the demands of his art, and the hopes he held for his own future, Mark Twain had no better choice than to assume the role of the American gone out to play.

To understand how this role works in *The Innocents Abroad* requires that we consider both the play of the tourist and the play of the narration. The former is easily recognized. I have noted that pleasure touring, as paidia, is very different from travel as a pilgrimage. As it turns out, Mark Twain's distinctions are every bit as exact as my own—and perhaps more so. Sorting the *Quaker City* voyagers into factions at the start of his book, Twain groups with the "pilgrims" not only the somber and the puritanical, but also the passive and the unimaginative travelers. Membership in "the boys" is closed to anyone who lacks a play-impulse and an interest in make-believe, anyone who allows himself to be led wherever guides and customs and commonplace-responses would have him go. "The boys" will not consent to be physically or imaginatively docile in the presence of Europe; they dedicate themselves to making Europe both the plaything and the play-ground; and whenever one entertainment flags they are quick to find or contrive another. With her quarantines, impatient and humorless police, bewildering streets, bad restaurants, sadistic barbers, treacherous pool tables, and impossible native languages, Europe conspires to keep its visitors to the deep-worn paths of pilgrimage. The challenge to the playful tourist is to escape the conspiracy and the trodden ways, to frustrate the demand for conventional reverence, and to sustain the makeshift, fictive fun of a true holiday. The discoveries and imaginative inventions of Mark Twain the tourist consistently convey a sense of a young man out to squeeze pleasure out of an uncooperative world. We know him not to be "serious" of course, in the facades he and his friends assume to puzzle their guides. The boys love to dash Europe's expectations, to hold their Yankee poker-faces against all urging and intimidation, to change the faceless and formal world of the pilgrim into a vital, unpredictable, imaginative, human encounter. Corralled by their Italian "Ferguson" into worshiping at a statue of Columbus, Twain and his friends save the moment by masquerading as idiots:

"Christopher Columbo—the great Christopher Columbo. Well, what did *he* do?"
"Discover America!—discover America, oh ze devil!"
"Discover America. No—that statement will hardly wash. We are just from America ourselves. We heard nothing about it. Christopher Columbo —pleasant name—is—is he dead?"
"Oh, corpo di Baccho!—three hundred year!"
"What did he die of?"
"I do not know!—I cannot tell."
"Small-pox, think?"
"I do not know, genteelmen!—I do not know *what* he die of!"
"Measles, likely?"
"May be—may be—I do *not* know—I think he die of somethings."
"Parents living?"
"Im-posseeble!"
"Ah—which is the bust and which is the pedestal?" (I, pp. 370–371)

In such episodes the playful boys become "round" for us much as Simon Wheeler did, that is, convincingly round in their play. Furthermore, when he is played *with* in such a manner, the bewildered guide becomes real himself. Twain and his companions are players to the core, and their paidia goes much farther than an occasional prank. The zest they show for tourism is amazing. Scrambling up every tower and mountainside, testing echoes, wandering the fair and foul quarters of every town, declaiming for the Czar, trekking the Holy wastes on mules and reluctant horses, gaping and fantasizing in every gallery, grotto, and catacomb, Mark Twain the tourist and his small circle of playful companions put all guidebook travelers and all unimaginative pilgrims to shame.

But the more important question is how the role of the player influences Mark Twain's narration. Of course we can locate many moments when the narrator and the tourist seem to become one: there are numerous "stretchers" in the book which suggest both a traveler delighting in make-believe and a narrator relishing a reminiscence. When we hear of Mark Twain devouring an especially noisy beggar in Rome, or splitting a Moslem to test the edge of Godfrey's sword, we have both a traveler and a narrator indulging in the play of make-believe, and our pleasure is reinforced. But beyond these "stretchers" a more interesting organizing principle remains to be seen in the narration, a principle which reconciles the style of the book to the pleasure trip of the tourist, which explains many of the incongruities which critics have long debated, and which underlies the book's lasting appeal.

The number of narrative voices which critics hear in *The Innocents* seems to be getting smaller;[16] as I have noted, Cox's excellent recent study of the book records only one. He defines the narration as burlesque impersonation, a "fusion of burlesque and mock innocence" which "animates Mark Twain's perspective, equipping him with a burlesque stance toward experience which gives unity of vision to the immense variety of scenes and experiences he encounters."[17] John Gerber remarks that such a description seems to make Twain out as something of a "charlatan," pandering to his masses with whatever will amuse.[18] Gerber is correct: "burlesque impersonation" does not serve well to characterize Mark Twain's narration in this book.

The test of the "burlesque" reading is Mark Twain's banality. What is accepted as true of his writings in general is true also of his first book, namely that he did at times lapse into bad taste with no joke intended. To recognize that Twain can slip in this way does not deny his achievement, nor does it explain away all puzzling moments in *The Innocents*. But consider a passage in which the American tourist, on a Paris boulevard, rhapsodizes on a French Emperor:

NAPOLEON III, Emperor of France! Surrounded by shouting thousands, by military pomp, by the splendors of his capital city, and companioned by kings and princes—this was the man who was sneered at, and reviled, and

---

[16] See Franklin Rogers, *Mark Twain's Burlesque Patterns as Seen in the Novels and Burlesques* (Dallas, Tex., 1960), p. 56; Gladys Bellamy, *Mark Twain as a Literary Artist* (Norman, Okla., 1950), pp. 184–191. Rogers apparently hears three voices in the narration, Bellamy two.

[17] Cox, p. 42.

[18] "Mark Twain," in *American Literary Scholarship: An Annual/1966,* ed. James Woodress (Durham, N.C., 1968), p. 55.

called Bastard—yet who was dreaming of a crown and an empire all the while; who was driven into exile—but carried his dreams with him; who associated with the common herd in America, and ran foot-races for a wager—but still sat upon a throne, in fancy; who braved every danger to go to his dying mother—and grieved that she could not be spared to see him cast aside his plebeian vestments for the purple of royalty; who kept his faithful watch and walked his weary beat a common policeman of London —but dreamed the while of a coming night when he should tread the long-drawn corridors of the Tuileries. . . . (I, 173)

This is mawkish stuff, but we have no reason to think of it as burlesque. The passage comes in the first quarter of the book, too early for the reader to be "set up" to expect anything but sincerity here. Furthermore, revising *The Innocents* for an 1871 British edition, Clemens dropped all this about Napoleon III as the "representative of the highest modern civilization," the empire having toppled to the Prussians in six weeks. Were the praise meant as a joke, the emperor's debacle would only have sharpened the edge. But this narrator was not joking; and therefore the passage was dropped.[19]

The point is that Mark Twain's narrative voice engages not in burlesque so much as in paidiac make-believe. Readers have long recognized too many changes in tone, from mock-theatrics to plausible ones, from one political position to its opposite, for burlesque to explain them all. But paidia, a fictive, improvisatory play which both embraces and surpasses burlesque, does provide us with at once a broader and a more accurate description of Mark Twain's narration. Twain the tourist constantly affirms his dedication to improvising amusement; Twain the narrator does very much the same thing. Paidia is play for its own sake, freely begun and terminated or altered, and by no means required to be either consistent or consistently funny. When Kenneth Lynn praises *The Innocents* as an accurate portrait of what a real American tourist might feel,[20] he is responding, I think, to Clemens's diligence in sustaining the play of make-believe in action and narration alike. When Mark Twain the narrator pretends to be the gullible, wide-eyed innocent, or the

[19] Arthur L. Scott, "Mark Twain's Revisions of *The Innocents Abroad* for the British Edition of 1872," *American Literature*, XXV (March, 1953), 43–61. Tony Tanner discusses the unintentional banality of such passages in Twain's works in *The Reign of Wonder: Naivety and Reality in American Literature* (Cambridge, Eng., 1965).

[20] *Mark Twain and Southwestern Humor* (Boston, 1960), pp. 154–155.

worldly skeptic, or the imp, or the fool, or the child, or anyone else, sometimes he intends to make us laugh; but *always* he intends to present himself as one caught up in the play of make-believe. All the apparently incongruous impersonations in the book are absorbed into the larger stance of constant imaginative engagement, a stance which the role of the tourist welcomes the narrator to assume. The book is more than a pleasure tour through Old World Landscapes. It is a pleasure tour through modes of narration. It ranges through sentimentality and parody, patriotism and anti-Americanism, whimsy and plodding factuality; the persistent, overriding assertion of the prose being that "I Mark Twain am out to have myself a good time." And we are meant to enjoy his narrator's pleasure trip, his tour through the world of literary voices, just as we enjoy his tour of foreign lands.

The Innocents Abroad is a stylistic experiment with the principle of improvisatory play. And it works. The book remains alive and popular, and the mode of narration does not trouble most readers. Mark Twain makes good his escape from buffoonery by assuming the one role which could encompass buffoonery and allow something more. Trusting their better instincts, readers have for generations been willing to do just what Clemens intends them to do: to take all the narrative modes of the book as modes of one voice, the voice of the playful traveler, and as imaginative episodes in an ongoing quest for fun. How well this technique suits *The Innocents* becomes even clearer when we compare the book to *A Tramp Abroad* (1870) or *Following the Equator* (1899), both of which are conventional and nearly forgotten. The trouble with each of these later travel books is that the "Mark Twain" we find in them is a traveler but not a tourist. It is often said that *A Tramp Abroad* fails because its humor is diverted into satire and seriousness; to put it more accurately, the failure comes not because this "Mark Twain" is occasionally inconsistent, but because the humor and satire and sobriety of this narrator are not reconciled by the play-impulse. Actually, the best moments in the work, the stories of Jim Baker and Jimmy Finn, of Nicodemus Dodge and Riley the Washoe reporter, are all imaginative flights *away* from the trip at hand and home to times of more genuine pleasure.

The same point can be made about *Following the Equator,* but little is gained by doing so. Once we understand the grounds on

which most of *The Innocents Abroad* succeeds, we need to recognize
the limits of that success. The common opinion of the book is that
it deteriorates severely after Mark Twain arrives in the Middle East.
The weariness of the "boys," the unpleasantness of the landscape, and
the necessity for constant piety are the usual explanations for the
trouble.[21] These explanations make sense, and each of them is implicit in the broader observation that when Twain leaves Europe for
the Holy Land, he leaves the world of the tourist for the world of the
pilgrim. The journey falls into the hands of the "serious" travelers,
and in their world free make-believe is no longer easy. In Europe,
the narrator may have what fun he likes with the sacred objects he
sees and the miracles he is told about, for most of these are of the
Roman church, and fair game therefore for a nineteenth-century
American Protestant and his predominantly Protestant audience. But
in the Holy Land almost everything Mark Twain encounters is so
sacred as to be imaginatively untouchable. Flights of fancy have no
place on a pilgrimage. The narrator becomes ill at ease, his predicament being especially clear on his visit to the Church of the Nativity:

I have no "meditations," suggested by this spot where the very first "Merry
Christmas!" was uttered in all the world, and from whence the friend of
my childhood, Santa Claus, departed on his first journey to gladden and
continue to gladden roaring firesides on wintry mornings in many a distant land forever and forever. I touch, with reverent finger, the actual spot
where the infant Jesus lay, but I think—nothing.

You *cannot* think in this place any more than you can in any other in
Palestine that would be likely to inspire reflection. Beggars, cripples, and
monks compass you about, and make you think only of bucksheesh when
you would rather think of something more in keeping with the character
of the spot.

I was glad to get away, and glad when we had walked through the
grottoes where Eusebius wrote, and Jerome fasted, and Joseph prepared
for the flight into Egypt, and the dozen other distinguished grottoes, and
knew we were done. (II, 384–385)

Should we gather that Mark Twain is struggling lamely here to
play at piety, or that the paidiac narrative stance has been overcome
by a world both venal and relentlessly holy? Actually the answer
makes little difference. The point is that in these closing chapters

---

[21] See, for example, Henry Nash Smith, *Mark Twain: The Development of a Writer*
(Cambridge, Mass., 1962), pp. 32–33.

Mark Twain's play of make-believe has come to an end, and so has the remarkable vigor and coherence of the book. Twain's narration does manage a few moments of imaginative escape—the "Tomb of Adam" soliloquy being the most famous instance—but in general he seems passive, roaming listlessly from shrine to shrine as the mere traveler, not as the tourist, grumbling more at the imaginative indulgences of others than indulging himself. He speaks repeatedly of his weariness of the excursion, and of his powerlessness, as either traveler or narrator, to continue his fictive play:

It hardly seems real when I find myself leaning for a moment on a ruined wall and looking *listlessly* down into the historic pool of Bethesda. I did not think such things *could* be so crowded together as to diminish their interest. But, in serious truth, we have been drifting about, for several days, using our eyes and ears from a sense of duty than any higher and worthier reason. And too often we have been glad when it was time to go home and be distressed no more about illustrious localities. (II, 358–359)

As Mark Twain's play fares, so fares *The Innocents Abroad*. The book's special kind of coherence, its life, and its perennial popularity all owe to the ability of "Mark Twain" the traveler and "Mark Twain" the narrator to amuse themselves in the play of make-believe; and when the play fails, the book fails too. To see the structure of the work in this way is to begin to wonder about Mark Twain's work as a whole. It is common knowledge that Samuel Clemens was all his life a dedicated game-player and game-inventor; we know too that the best of his fiction is very often about characters who make games of make-believe out of worlds of peril and moral consequence—and who suffer because they do so. And we understand enough about the nature of play now to begin to consider its thematic and structural importance in Mark Twain's major writings, to see whether there is some way of expressing more clearly the link we sense between Clemens's personality and Mark Twain's literary forms, and of understanding better how order and energy are reconciled in his greatest writings.

The Meaning of *A Connecticut Yankee*
Everett Carter

INTERPRETATIONS of Mark Twain's fiction about knight errantry, *A Connecticut Yankee in King Arthur's Court*, have changed with successive generations of American commentators. Like the Spanish readers of *Don Quixote*, American readers of *A Connecticut Yankee* have divided into "hard" critics who have seen the book as an attack on sentimentalism about the past, and, increasing in number, those "soft" critics who have read it as either ambivalent or as an attack on technology and the American faith in material progress.[1] The terms "hard" and "soft" are those of a scholar commenting upon the division between schools of commentaries on *Don Quixote*, the "hard" critics of Cervantes' masterpiece insisting upon its defense of reality, the "soft" critics interpreting the work as a defense of the dauntless power of the imagination to remake reality nearer to the dream.[2]

The new "soft" reading of *Don Quixote* has been essential to interpretations of Spanish culture; Unamuno, the first of the "soft" critics of our century, suggested that Don Quixote, rejecting the miserable real for the hopeless dream, is the symbol of what is good, holy, and tragic in the Spanish soul. The fact that one modern American commentator[3] has suggested that the Yankee's enemy, Merlin, plays a similar role in Mark Twain's romance is an index of how far criti-

---

[1] Among the "hard" critics are Louis Budd, *Mark Twain, Social Philosopher* (Bloomington, Ind., 1962), Howard Baetzhold, *Mark Twain and John Bull* (Bloomington, Ind., 1970) and most social historians who have alluded to the work as a summary of nineteenth-century faith in technology; see, for example, Carl N. Degler, *The Age of Economic Revolution, 1876–1900* (Glenview, Ill., 1967), p. 198. Among the "soft" critics have been: Alan Guttman, "Mark Twain's Connecticut Yankee: Affirmation of the Vernacular Tradition?" *New England Quarterly*, XXXIII (June, 1960), 232–237; Henry Nash Smith, *Mark Twain: The Development of a Writer* (Cambridge, Mass., 1962), and *Mark Twain's Fable of Progress* (New Brunswick, N.J., 1964); James M. Cox, "*A Connecticut Yankee in King Arthur's Court*: The Machinery of Self-Preservation," *Yale Review*, L (Autumn, 1960), 89–102; and Kenneth Lynn, *Mark Twain and Southwestern Humor* (Boston, 1959).

[2] Oscar Mandel, "The Function of the Norm in Don Quixote," *Modern Philology*, LV (Feb., 1959), 154–163.

[3] Cox, "*A Connecticut Yankee in King Arthur's Court*, The Machinery of Self-Preservation," p. 100.

cism has come from the nineteenth-century assumptions that *A Connecticut Yankee* was a satire on English chivalry. Like the controversy over *Don Quixote,* the controversy about the Yankee has been
couched in terms that leave no doubt that for twentieth-century readers there is something eponymous about Hank Morgan. Hank is not
only a Connecticut Yankee; he is *The* Yankee, and his fate, like the
fate of Cervantes' hero and of the book in which he appears, is more
than a falling out among scholars; it has something to do with a
country's feeling about itself and its role in the Western world. In
1889, most readers, the illustrator Dan Beard among them, thought
they were reading a book about a Yankee's praiseworthy attempt to
make a better world. In the second half of the twentieth century,
some critics, among them our most influential, have seen it as a pre-
monition of what they assume is an American danger to the world:
a story that ends in massive destruction of a large number of the
inhabitants of an underdeveloped country is obviously suggestive to
the modern mind.

My purpose here is to try to find out what is the probable meaning
of *A Connecticut Yankee.* In doing so, I accept both the terminology
and the method of E. D. Hirsch's *Validity in Interpretation.* Hirsch
urges the distinction between "meaning" and "significance," with
"meaning" restricted to the meaning that the author meant.[4] I address
myself to this meaning alone. About significance I shall not comment. No one is going to convince the modern readers who see the
book as a reinforcement of their dread of American technological
progress that it is anything other. I shall not try. I shall simply try to
answer the question: "What, in all probability, and on the basis of
all the internal and external evidence, did Mark Twain mean by the
total fiction *A Connecticut Yankee in King Arthur's Court?*"

In evaluating the external evidence which bears upon the novel's
meaning, the first problem to resolve is the probable attitude of Mark
Twain towards his narrator, Hank Morgan. Did Mark Twain identify with and sympathize with Hank? Or did he create a narrator
whom the reader must criticize, whose attitudes the reader is directed
to reject? The answer to this question need not suppose constant
authorial identification with the narrator: Mark Twain, after all, had
been completely one with Huck Finn's "sound heart" and yet he had

---

[4] E. D. Hirsch, Jr., *Validity in Interpretation* (New Haven, Conn., 1967).

satirized minor aspects of Huck's attitude. All that need be asked is "did the writer generally identify with and approve of his narrator and the general course of his narrator's behavior?"

The external evidence that Mark Twain disbelieved in Hank's values consists of a statement to Dan Beard that the Yankee is "an ignoramus."[5] The context of this expression is a description of the protagonist in so favorable a light that Beard made his portraits of the Yankee uniformly sympathetic, although obviously Beard's Yankee is far from refined. Mark Twain, himself a philistine, would not have regarded this as a serious shortcoming. However, he made Hank even more philistine than himself, and Hank's blindness to the beauties of medieval painting and tapestry provides one of the relatively rare instances of Twain's satirizing his protagonist.

Against this lone piece of dubious evidence outside the work itself which might indicate the author's adverse attitude towards the narrator, there are arrayed several indications that Mark Twain sympathized deeply with his Connecticut Yankee. The notebook entries that announce the first glimmerings of the idea for the book, and Twain's working notes for the development of the plot identify the author with the protagonist, suggest he is like Mark Twain's hero, Ulysses S. Grant, and use the first person in outlining the story: "I gave a knight a pass to go holy-grailing.... I did everything I could to bring knight-errantry into contempt." After saying that "the whole tribe" will be away on the quest, Twain asks: "Is here my chance to push a R R along, while they are out of my way?"[6] After writing the first thirty-two chapters, he paused to think about the conclusion of his book, and he wrote himself a memorandum: "I make a *peaceful* revolution and introduce advanced civilization."[7]

Even more directly, Mark Twain is on record as approving of his protagonist. The circumstances which led to his expression of approval were these: Howard Taylor had asked for and had received

[5] Quoted in A. B. Paine, *Mark Twain: A Biography* (New York, 1912), p. 887.

[6] The Mark Twain Papers, Box 41 #4, Bancroft Library, University of California, Berkeley. The working notes will be published as one of the appendices to the forthcoming MLA-CEAA edition of *A Connecticut Yankee in King Arthur's Court*, ed. Bernard L. Stein, with an Introduction by Henry Nash Smith, Berkeley, [1978]. Permission to quote unpublished excerpts from the papers has been kindly granted by the trustees of the Mark Twain Estate, Frederick Anderson, curator.

[7] The Mark Twain's Papers. This material will be published in *Mark Twain's Notebooks and Journals* (cited hereafter as *NB&J*), *Volume III, 1883–1891*, ed. Robert Pack Browning, Michael B. Frank, and Lin Solamo (Berkeley [1978]), p. 415.

permission to rework the novel for the stage. When Twain read the
dramatization he was disappointed, and he focused his criticism on
Taylor's failure to do justice to the Yankee. "The new play," Twain
wrote his daughter, "has captured but one side of the Yankee's
character—his rude animal side, his circus side; the good heart & the
high intent are left out of him. . . . I told Taylor he had degraded
a natural gentleman to a low-down blackguard."[8]

The external evidence seems weighted in Hank's favor; the internal evidence which bears upon Mark Twain's attitude towards his
narrator concerns the Yankee's philistinism and his seemingly inhuman attitude towards the chivalry he is trying to destroy. His
philistinism is announced at the beginning: Hank describes himself
as "nearly barren of sentiment . . . or poetry. . . ."[9] He stands amid
medieval glories of sculpture, painting, and tapestry and complains
that there is no "insurance-chromo, or at least a three-color-God-Bless-
Our-Home over the door."[10] But this lack of a refined aesthetic sense
is a minor flaw (and probably not a flaw, at all, in the eyes of Mark
Twain). More serious are the several instances where Hank sounds
close to megalomania in his desire to reform the medieval world.
When he declares, near the end, referring to the massed knights, "We
will kill them all,"[11] he seems like the Hitler to whom one "soft"
commentary has come close to comparing him. "There is a time,"
Hank says, "when one would like to hang the whole human race.
. . ."[12] He describes with apparent relish the "steady drizzle of microscopic fragments of knights and hardware and horse-flesh"[13] that
result from his use of dynamite. He considers using "a person of no
especial value"[14] to place a bomb down a well. He hooks up a re-
petitively bowing hermit to a machine and, after he wears him out,
he unloads him on Sir Bors de Gans. Finally he approves (although
he had not himself prepared) the electrified fences that wipe out
England's chivalry.

These constitute an almost complete list of the charges against

---

[8] *The Love Letters of Mark Twain*, ed. Dixon Wecter (New York, 1949), pp. 257–258.

[9] *A Connecticut Yankee in King Arthur's Court*, ed. Hamlin Hill, San Francisco, 1963 (Facsimile of the first edition of 1889), p. 20. (Subsequent references to *A Connecticut Yankee* will be to this edition.)

[10] *A Connecticut Yankee*, pp. 83–84.

[11] *Ibid.*, p. 556.

[12] *Ibid.*, p. 395.

[13] *Ibid.*, p. 355.

[14] *Ibid.*, p. 275.

Hank. If we add to them his willingness to cheat in business, to hang some musicians who play off-key, and to murder a boring would-be humorist, we have the complete indictment. But there is evidence to support a contention that the author did not consider these actions as fundamentally immoral or as more than occasionally and humanly foolish. In the instance of Hank's apparently callous actions, Twain either agreed with their necessity or, in less important cases, took it for granted that his audience would understand the comic-epic tone which permits us to laugh unreservedly at the obliteration of Tom in a Tom and Jerry cartoon, without agonizing about the realities of pain. For example, when Hank asks Clarence if some committee members had made their report (they had just walked over a land-mine), Clarence answers that it was "Unanimous."[15] Until the final pages, when Twain's rage against aristocratic privilege got out of hand, Twain was working confidently in the comic world of frontier humor where overstatement about death and destruction was a stan-dard mode of evoking laughter. Many of the seemingly inhuman reactions of Hank take this form, a form linked to the author's own perhaps tasteless but nevertheless comic hyperbole.

Others of Hank's actions are meant to be taken seriously, and in these instances there is a weight of evidence to indicate Twain's sym-pathies with his protagonist. When planning the activities of the nar-rator, he not only used the "I," but in the writing sometimes forgot that he was using a specious rather than an actual first-person. Hank's enormous pride when the first newspaper comes out, and as he watches the favorable reaction of a reader, is not the feeling of a Connecticut factory foreman, but rather that of a Missouri journalist: "Yes, this was heaven; I was tasting it once, if I might never taste it more."[16] When Hank expresses his views of England and Russia, they are views that Mark Twain held and which were, according to the two most thorough accounts of the genesis of *A Connecticut Yankee,* the major impulses for the revival of his interest in the narrative in 1887–1888;[17] Hank's words are usually paraphrases of Twain's letters and notebook entries during those years. He could look into the fu-

---

[15] *Ibid.,* p. 543.
[16] *Ibid.,* p. 344.
[17] Howard G. Baetzhold, "The Course of Composition of *A Connecticut Yankee," Ameri-can Literature,* XXXIII (Jan., 1961), 456–461 and John B. Hoben, "Mark Twain's *A Connecticut Yankee:* A Genetic Study," *American Literature,* XVIII (Nov., 1946), 197–218.

ture, says Hank, and see England "erect statues and monuments to her unspeakable Georges and other royal and noble clothes-horses, and leave unhonored the creators of this world—after God—Gutenberg, Watt, Arkwright, Whitney, Morse, Stephenson, Bell."[18] Said Mark Twain in a speech in Baltimore in January, 1889, "Conceive of the blank and sterile ignorance of that day, and contrast it with the vast and many-sided knowledge of this. Consider the trivial miracles and wonders wrought by the humbug magicians and enchanters of that old day, and contrast them with the mightly miracles wrought by science in our day of steam and electricity."[19]

From the opening of the tale to its end, Mark Twain treated his alter-ego sympathetically, weighting plot and characterization heavily in his favor. When, at the beginning, Clarence unwittingly dooms him to seeming certain death by his well-meaning acceleration of the date of execution, Hank is considerate of the boy's feelings even at the moment that would tempt most men to relieve their own feelings in recrimination: "I had not the heart to tell him," says Hank, "his good-hearted foolishness had ruined me."[20] When Hank comes upon a dying woman in a peasant's hut, he comforts her, and stays with her even when he knows she is dying of small-pox. "Let me come in and help you—you are sick and in trouble,"[21] are his words. His aim in urging the king to travel incognito and his motivation for allowing himself to be kept in the chain-gang, is to open the king's eyes to the horrors of slavery. When they are opened, and the king says he will abolish the evil institution, Hank says he is "ready and willing to get free, now,"[22] for his mission has been accomplished. A thoroughly middle-class husband and father, Hank is properly concerned for the good name and well-being of his wife and child. He marries Sandy because he is "a New Englander and in my opinion this sort of partnership [their unwedded companionship] would compromise her."[23] Their marriage results in "the dearest and perfectest comradeship that ever was."[24] The illness of their child compels his absence at the crucial moment of his new country's history: the child is sick;

---

[18] *A Connecticut Yankee*, p. 420.
[19] The Mark Twain Papers, Box 41, DV #21.
[20] *A Connecticut Yankee*, p. 74.
[21] *Ibid.*, p. 370.
[22] *Ibid.*, p. 458.
[23] *Ibid.*, p. 524.
[24] *Ibid.*

the good father unhesitatingly takes her to the sea-shore. Dan Beard, the illustrator of the first edition, underscored the firm position of the Yankee at the heart of middle-class values with his full-page illustration of a benign and solicitous Yankee, standing next to a beautiful and adoring Sandy, both holding the recumbent "Hello Central," while on the wall behind them is the inevitable framed embroidery of "God Bless Our Home."[25]

Most important of all, Twain sympathetically gave Hank a fatal, but entirely praiseworthy weakness: a reluctance to use violence when the opinion of the sansculotte Mark Twain of 1888 was that bloodshed is the only means of accomplishing major social change. It is "the immutable law," says Hank, echoing sentiments Mark Twain had confided to Howells, "that all revolutions that will succeed must *begin* in blood, whatever may answer afterward. . . . What this folk needed, then, was a Reign of Terror and a guillotine, and I was the wrong man for them."[26] In the end, it is Hank's humanitarianism (viewed by Clarence as his "mistimed sentimentalities")[27] that causes his final tragic sleep. Clarence reports that Hank proposed to go out to help the wounded knights; Clarence strenuously opposes the project; Hank insists, and it is on this errand of mercy that he is treacherously stabbed by one of the knights. Clarence, in what are almost the final words of the epilogue, calls Hank "our dear good chief."[28]

Hank, the eponymous Yankee, then, is a good and trustworthy narrator whose weaknesses are occasionally satirized but who usually carries the burden of authorial attitudes. This fact about the narrator is central to the answer of the next and the most important question: the meaning of *A Connecticut Yankee* with regard to the progress of mankind through the application of reason to the physical and social world, an application that has resulted in the technological society. When Hank engages in his duel with Merlin and with knight errantry, the duel is not simply a conflict between two men, but between two ways of life, between two cultures with their attendant deities, "a mysterious and awful battle of the gods": the god of science

---

[25] Mark Twain was delighted with his illustrator: "What luck it was to find you!" he wrote Beard. "There are hundreds of artists who could illustrate any other book of mine, but there was only one who could illustrate this one." *Mark Twain's Letters*, ed. A. B. Paine (New York, 1917), II, 511.

[26] *A Connecticut Yankee*, p. 242.

[27] *Ibid.*, p. 558.

[28] *Ibid.*, p. 571.

on the one hand, the god of superstition on the other. "I was a champion . . . ," Hank says, "but not the champion of the frivolous black arts, I was the champion of hard unsentimental common-sense and reason."[29]

There are three pieces of external evidence that might support a proposition that *A Connecticut Yankee* is not a book in praise of commonsense and reason, but is rather an attack on these and a defense of a lost world of the imagination. One is a notebook entry written very early in the gestation of the work when Twain predicted that his Yankee would mourn "his lost land" and would be "found a suicide."[30] A second piece of external evidence is the fact that Twain was outraged, in August or September, 1887, by the Langdon family's sharp business practices, a concern which led him to write a section, unused in the final version, satiric of nineteenth-century commercialism. The third piece of external evidence is the most famous: Twain's letter to Howells, after the dean of American letters had read and praised the book: Twain replied that there were many things left unsaid, that if he were to say them it would take "a pen warmed-up in hell."[31]

All three pieces of evidence are ambiguous, but all three more logically support a view that the meaning of the work is a defense of the American nineteenth century than the reverse. The early notebook reference to Hank's longing for a sixth-century, a "new" and "virgin" England can be read as a reference to the century and the country as Hank had reformed them, a land and a time that held the memories of his wife and child, a time and a land that, in the same entry, he contrasts with the degradation not of nineteenth-century America, but of nineteenth-century England. Concerning his anger at Andrew Langdon's sharp business practices: Twain's awareness of the curse of financial greed had long been a motive of his satire; since *The Gilded Age,* sixteen years before, he had deplored this disease in a system that he otherwise considered far superior to those of other lands and times. To satirize those ancient evils which persisted into the present was consistent with his reformist purposes; it was this meliorist urge that Dan Beard pointed up by using the face of Jay

---

[29] *Ibid.*, pp. 497–498.

[30] *NB&J*, III, 216.

[31] *Mark Twain-Howells Letters*, ed. Henry Nash Smith and William M. Gibson (Cambridge, Mass., 1960), II, 613.

Gould on the body of the medieval slave-driver, and that William Dean Howells and Clarence Stedman noticed in their reviews. What is more significant than the fact that Twain continued to criticize the shortcomings of his contemporary society is the fact that, in the final version of *A Connecticut Yankee,* he decided to omit a specific satire of this example of a contemporary evil.

The third, and more often quoted bit of external evidence consists of that cry to Howells that he would need a "pen warmed-up in hell" to say the unsaid things of *A Connecticut Yankee.* There is little reason to believe that the unsaid things would have been attacks on common-sense, republicanism, and technology. There is every reason to believe that the unsaid things were further scathing attacks on monarchy, foreign despotisms, and aristocratic pretensions. Exactly two months after his cry for a hell-warmed pen, he crowed to Howells that "These are immense days. . . . There'll be plenty to sneer & depreciate & disenthuse—on the other hand, who can lift a word of the other sort, in the name of God let him pipe up! I want to print some extracts from the Yankee that have in them the new ⟨sweet⟩ breath of republics."[32] The same week he wrote the hell-warmed pen letter, he wrote to Sylvester Baxter to gloat over the fall of the Brazilian monarchy, and to link the last chapters of *A Connecticut Yankee* with that happy demise.[33] Within three months he wrote to his English publisher: "I wanted to say a Yankee mechanic's say against monarchy and its several natural props."[34] From 1885 to 1889 his notebooks and letters are full of rage against English arrogance, Russian tyranny, commercial speculation and greed, and those prolongations of medieval prejudices into the nineteenth century which made the South and the slavery system the subject of nostalgic sentimentalizing. These had been the evils against which Twain had been fulminating for years; he had never expressed the need for a weapon with which to attack technological progress and liberal democracy, while he had often raged against royalty, aristocracy, and hereditary privilege. To take the angry satirist's cry for a pen warmed in hell as a cry for a tool with which to attack republican progress would be an improbable introduction of a new and unexpected attitude; to take the phrase as a reference to his hatred of those past and

---

[32] *Mark Twain-Howells Letters,* II, 621.
[33] *Mark Twain's Letters,* II, 520.
[34] *Mark Twain's Letters,* II, 524–525.

foreign institutions about which he had frequently expressed himself
would be a more probable inference.

The letter to his English publisher constitutes one of six direct,
unambiguous statements of authorial purpose, six declarations of intent which provide a substantial body of support for a reading of
A Connecticut Yankee as a defense of democracy, technology, and
progress. Every time Mark Twain expressed himself about what he
meant in writing the book, he tried to say bluntly that he was defending the American nineteenth century and attacking a brutish and
inhumane past. The letter to the English publisher not only made the
identification between author and narrator: "I wanted to say a Yankee mechanic's say . . . ," but it went on to declare: ". . . the book
was not written for America; it was written for England. So many
Englishmen have done their sincerest to teach us something for our
betterment that it seems to me high time that some of us should substantially recognize the good intent by trying to pry up the English
nation to a little higher level of manhood in turn."[35] Twain's changing the name of the Yankee from the neutral "Robert Smith" to a familiar form of the name of the pirate who harried English trade
routes is, in this context, no reflection on the character of Hank
Morgan, but is rather the humorist's signal of the direction of his
satire. Twain's angry response to English criticism of America, and
his defense of his country, was one of his preoccupations in the years
he was writing *A Connecticut Yankee*; he has left notes for a talk
attacking English and defending American society: ". . . If you
scrape off our American crust of shabby politicians," the unfinished
draft reads, "you will find a nation underneath of as sterling a character, & with as high purposes at heart. . . ."[36] The draft did not
complete the terms of the comparison, but the meaning is unambiguous. Equally unequivocal is the introduction to several excerpts from
A Connecticut Yankee which appeared in the *Century Magazine* in
November, 1889. There Twain described the work as "a bitter struggle for supremacy . . . , Merlin using the absurd necromancy of the
time and the Yankee beating it easily and brilliantly with the more
splendid necromancy of the nineteenth century—that is, the marvels
of modern science." After a few chapters, Twain wrote a summary of

[35] *Ibid.*
[36] The Mark Twain Papers, Box 41 #5.

the plot: "Meantime the Yankee is very busy; for he has privately set himself the task of introducing the great and beneficent civilization of the nineteenth century, and of peacefully replacing the twin despotisms of royalty and aristocratic privilege with a 'Republic on the American plan.'. . . ."[37] In 1906, he dictated his memories about the book; they were that he had been ". . . purposing to contrast that English life . . . with the life of modern Christendom and modern civilization—to the advantage of the latter, of course."[38]

In addition to these declarations of purpose in letter, introduction, and memoir, Twain wrote three prefaces that announce the intended meaning of the work. One, published as an appendix in A. B. Paine's biography, accounts for the fact that he chose England, and not Russia (or Belgium) as the object of his satire. "I have drawn," he wrote, "no laws and no illustrations from the twin civilizations of Hell and Russia. To have ventured into that atmosphere would have defeated my purpose: which was to show a great & genuine progress in Christendom in these few later generations, toward mercifulness— a wide and general relaxing of the grip of the law."[39] This was one of his tries at an introduction; another emphasized that his attack was not only upon the false worship of the English past, but upon the sentimentalizing of history in general: "The strange laws," this unpublished preface went, "which one encounters here and there in this book, are not known to have existed in King Arthur's time, of course, but it is fair to presume that they did exist, since they still existed in Christian lands in far later times—times customarily called, with unconscious sarcasm, 'civilized and enlightened.' The episodes by which these laws are illustrated in this book are not invention, but are drawn from history; not always from English history, but mainly from that source. Human liberty—for white people—may fairly be said to be one hundred years old this year; what stood for it in any previous century of the world's history cannot be rationally allowed to count."[40] This seems clear enough, but even more to the point was another unpublished preface that was directed at the reader who might make the mistake of preferring the past to the present: "One

[37] "A Connecticut Yankee in King Arthur's Court by Mark Twain," *Century Magazine*, XXXIX (Nov., 1889), 74, 77.

[38] Autobiographical Dictation of December 5, 1906, The Mark Twain Papers.

[39] The Mark Twain Papers, Box 41 #10.

[40] The Mark Twain Papers, Box 41 #7.

purpose of the book," Mark Twain wrote, "is to entertain the reader
—if it may have the happy luck to do that. Another is, to remind him
that what is called Christian Civilization is so young and new that it
had not yet entered the world when our century was born. . . . If
any are inclined to rail at our present civilization, why there is no
hindering him; but he ought to sometimes contrast it with what went
before, & take comfort—and hope, too."[41]

In the face of this evidence of authorial purpose, few commentators
have implied that Mark Twain intended to write an attack on progress and technology. Instead, modern revision of the work's meaning
has either ignored the question of authorial intent (after all, academic
critics had been warned off by the dread of committing "the intentional fallacy") or has argued that authorial intent was subverted by
the act of creation: behind the new commentaries has hovered the
critical idealogy which insists upon the independence of the work of
art: "trust the tale, not the teller." The tale, for the "soft" critics, tells
us that the Yankee is at least a well-meaning fool or at most an author-
itarian villain whose obsession with technology brings about the destruction of civilization. This interpretation was proposed in 1950, by
Gladys Bellamy who summarized the work as meaning that a "too-
quick civilization brings disaster,"[42] thus placing blame for the ending on Hank. The new reading received its most influential formulation in 1962 when Henry Nash Smith described the working of Mark
Twain's unruly genius: "He had planned a fable illustrating how the
advance of technology fosters the moral improvement of mankind,"
Smith wrote. "But when he put his belief to the test by attempting to
realize it in fiction, the oracle of his imagination, his intuition, the
unconsciously formulated conclusions based on his observation and
reading, his childhood heritage of Calvinism, at any rate some force
other than his conscious intention convinced him that his belief in
progress and human perfectibility was groundless." The support for
this view came, as it must, from a close reading of the romance with
special attention to the ending: "The raw aggression expressed in
Mark Twain's description of the slaughter of the knights reveals a
massive disillusionment and frustration."[43] James Cox had earlier

[41] The Mark Twain Papers, Box 41 #12. The three prefaces will appear as Appendix C
in the MLA-CEAA edition.
[42] Bellamy, *Mark Twain as Literary Artist*, p. 314.
[43] Smith, *Mark Twain*, pp. 169–170.

agreed that a subconscious obsession took over the meaning of the work, and argued that the Yankee became an "anti-mask," a burlesque caricature of the Enlightenment, a symbol of the "machine madness" which possessed Mark Twain, and that he had to kill by killing its embodiment in Hank Morgan. While admitting that Twain's disenchantment with the machine did not come until five years after finishing *A Connecticut Yankee,* Cox argued that the successive postponements of the completion of Paige's typesetter caused the book to become "more than a mere prophecy of the disaster toward which the machine obsession was tending; it was an acting out beforehand of the experience itself." Cox's analysis goes on to suggest that in viewing the final triumph of Merlin, one is "almost" led to believe that the necromancer is "the prototype of the artist who emerges from humiliation and shame to exercise his magic powers at the last."[44]

While occasionally concerned with internal evidence drawn from other portions of the book, these revisions of *A Connecticut Yankee*'s meaning have usually concentrated on the conclusion: the catastrophic scenes of the slaughter of the knights, the destruction of the technological civilization, the triumph of Merlin, the thirteen-century-long sleep of the Yankee, and his sad death while calling out for his lost life in the sixth century. Any interpretation of the meaning of the romance must address itself to the construction of the plot of *A Connecticut Yankee* with particular attention to its development towards this ending: towards the electrocution of the knights, the dynamiting of the factories, and the defeat of the Yankee. What were the causes of the Yankee's failure? Who and what was responsible for the downfall of his civilization?

To support a contention that this ending constitutes a subconscious inversion of the author's conscious intention, several necessary conditions would have to be proven. One is that there was a sudden shift, an undermining of the author's meaning as the work progressed, a reversal of previous mood and tone. The second is that the ending was unusually, even unbearably painful for the author: certainly a subconscious fear that exploded previous convictions and that subverted conscious desires would be something to which he would be

---

[44] Cox, "*A Connecticut Yankee in King Arthur's Court:* The Machinery of Self-Preservation," p. 100.

loathe to return. A third is that the sadness of the ending, the change
from comedy to tragedy, was a statement about human institutions
and not about man's cosmic fate, a statement about society and not
about metaphysics. An ending that described common-sense, reason,
and technology as destructive forces inside of history would be truly
a subversion of authorial intent; a plot whose denouement showed
an awareness of the immutable human condition, condemned to
eventual earthly separation from home and love, would be a shift in
mood, but not a change in social commitment: within the larger,
inescapable terms of human existence, this ending might say, men
can still make choices that will make society better or worse; the
crucial point is whether the Yankee offered a better choice than that
which was offered in the past.

First the question: was the ending an unforeseen reversal of previous plans for the novel? It seems not to have been. From the beginning, as we have seen, Mark Twain planned an ending in which the
Yankee would "mourn his lost land." In Chapter 8, "The Boss," a
chapter written in the summer of 1887[45] a full eighteen months before
he wrote the ending, Mark Twain put in Hank's mouth the following prediction about the conclusion of his adventure: "Yes, in power
I was equal to the king. At the same time there was another power
that was a trifle stronger than both of us put together. That was the
Church. I do not wish to disguise that fact. I couldn't if I wanted to.
But never mind about that, now; it will show up in its proper place,
later on."[46] Then, in September, 1888, still nine months before he
wrote the conclusion, Twain made the entry in his notebook where
he both identified himself with the protagonist, and then summarized
the ending: "I make a *peaceful* revolution and introduce advanced
civilization. The Church overthrows it with a 6 year interdict."[47]

The frustration of England's premature progress, the failure of the
Yankee to reform the medieval world was the ending Mark Twain
had decided upon possibly as early as 1885, probably as early as 1887,
and certainly by the autumn of 1888. It was no sudden change, no
turning of a creator's subconscious against his conscious wishes. Furthermore the very form of the ending—the carnage of the knights,
electrocuted by charged barbed wire and mowed down by machine

---

[45] Baetzhold, "The Course of Composition of *A Connecticut Yankee*," p. 199.
[46] *A Connecticut Yankee*, pp. 96–97.
[47] The Mark Twain Papers. This material will be published in *NB&J*, III, 216.

guns—had been one of the earliest incidents Mark Twain had devised; he had written of precisely this kind of battle in 1886, when no more than three chapters had been completed. Some of these "adventures of Sir Robert Smith of Camelot" were read before the Military Service Institute of Governor's Island on November 11, 1886. According to a reporter's version, Sir Robert Smith "took a contract from King Arthur to kill off, at one of the great tournaments, fifteen kings and many acres of hostile armored knights. When, lance in rest, they charge by squadrons upon him, he, behind the protection of a barbed wire fence charged with electricity, mowed them down with Gatling guns that he had made for the occasion."[48] After finishing the book in 1889, Twain gave another reading of it before a military audience, this time the cadets of West Point. He included the scene of the Battle of the Sand-Belt, and in his reading notes—a paste-up of pages from the first edition—he identified the 52 loyal "boys" with the audience before him, substituting the word "cadet" for "boy" when the latter first appeared, and ended his reading with a description of the military victory: ". . . the campaign was ended, we fifty-four were masters of England! Twenty-five thousand men lay dead around us." Then he crossed out the remaining paragraphs that dealt with Hank's wounding and his defeat.[49]

The carnage at the end, then, is no aberration but a conventional mode of frontier hyperbole in which Mark Twain frequently indulged, which he had planned for three years to be part of his novel, and which he read with obvious relish before audiences properly appreciative of the progress of military weaponry; one may deplore its childish ferocity or its possibly misplaced admiration, but one can scarcely use it to prove a sudden reversal of authorial intent, or a pathological change in customary style. Above all, since Mark Twain conceived the scene early and returned with relish to it late, he was obviously untraumatized by its possible implications for his belief in the blessings of technology.

The ending, then, was both planned by and was untraumatic for its author; it was something Mark Twain had decided upon early, and with unusual care for an author who was self-admittedly a poor

---

[48] Howard G. Baetzhold, "The Autobiography of Sir Robert Smith of Camelot: Mark Twain's Original Plan for *A Connecticut Yankee*," *American Literature*, XXXII (Jan., 1961), 459.

[49] The Mark Twain Papers, Box 41 #1.

constructor of plots. But there is certainly a difference in tone between the ending of *A Connecticut Yankee* and almost everything Mark Twain had written before; all of his previous works had concluded "happily": *The Gilded Age* with Washington Hawkins coming to his senses; *The Prince and the Pauper* with the regaining of the Prince's position and with the improved fortunes of the pauper; *Tom Sawyer* with the finding of Injun Joe and the winning of the reward; *Huckleberry Finn* with the freedom of Jim from slavery and of Huck from his father's tyranny; *Life on the Mississippi* with paeans to Northern progress. The sense of weariness and sadness at the end of *A Connecticut Yankee* is a changed tone. Very early in its writing, Mark Twain knew that the Yankee would have to lose and began to prepare his readers for his hero's downfall. The crucial question is: to what causes did the book assign the Yankee's failure? Were they causes inherent in the Yankee's beliefs or moral structure? Did Hank cause the terrible ending of *A Connecticut Yankee?* Or did Mark Twain take care to assign the reasons for the disaster to other elements of history? And what did this assignation of guilt tell us about forces in history that should be encouraged, and those discouraged, in order to achieve a better society?

Mark Twain made Hank but a minor, and morally guiltless, cause of the final catastrophe: he was too humane in his efforts to reform an evil society. With Hank absent, drawn from his post by the needs of a sick child, forces that the romance identifies as evil and reactionary, and that Hank (still according to the authorial voice) had been too soft-hearted to make impotent, these forces nullify his reforms. In self-defense and in defense of a small besieged band of loyal followers, victims of an unprovoked aggression by armored soldiers who outnumber them 500–1, soldiers who would torture and kill them and then reinstitute serfdom and slavery, Hank uses advanced technology to destroy the enemy. There is no evidence that Twain thought Hank's self-defense reprehensible. The major causes of the disaster, as Twain described them, are, first, the growing corruption of the Round Table, specifically the adultery of Launcelot and Guenever, and second, and most important, the opening that this corruption made for the exercise of the decisive cause: the power of an absolute church.

The corruption of the Round Table was fixed as a moving force in the denouement from the beginning of the conception of *A Connecticut Yankee*. Immediately after he outlined the burlesque of knight-errantry for the Military Institute of Governor's Island in 1886, Twain reassured Mrs. A. W. Fairbanks that he would not besmirch the work she loved, the *Morte Darthur,* and its "beautiful" characters.[50] He did not keep his promise with regard to the whole of Malory's romance; it comes in for pretty rough treatment in Chapter XV; but as a counterpoint to the broad burlesque of knight errantry and of its chronicler, Mark Twain introduced and intermittently sustained the serious traditional subplot concerning the gallant and praiseworthy members of the chivalric orders: Galahad, Launcelot, and, above all, the king himself. The king is more than a king, says Hank, he is "a man."[51] Galahad, the Yankee tells us, has a "noble benignity and purity."[52] Launcelot has "majesty and greatness,"[53] and it is he who comes riding to Hank's rescue—on a bicycle. The part of the *Morte Darthur* that Mark Twain seized upon was the tragic and fatal adultery that resulted in the waste of Malory's admirable characters; in *A Connecticut Yankee* it was this crime against nineteenth-century middle-class morality that leads directly to the death of that portion of the chivalry of England that was praiseworthy, leaving only the dregs of aristocracy to be destroyed by Hank and Clarence and their fifty-two loyal cadets.

The adultery is suggested as early as the third chapter, upon Hank's first view of the Knights of the Round Table. He sees the queen fling the kind of "furtive glances at Sir Launcelot that would have got him shot in Arkansas, to a dead certainty."[54] A few moments later, the court explodes in a riot of indecency, using language that "would make a Comanche blush." Hank is stripped, and stands before the knights and ladies "naked as a pair of tongs." Queen Guenever, says Hank, "was as naïvely interested as the rest."[55] Dan Beard obligingly emphasized the meaning of this scene by drawing a small picture of Guenever, looking anything but naïve, as she presumably appraises the object before her. In Chapter XXVI, written during the summer of 1886, Hank describes the mournful look of King Arthur, when

[50] *Mark Twain to Mrs. Fairbanks,* ed. Dixon Wecter (San Marino, Calif., 1949), p. 258.
[51] *A Connecticut Yankee,* p. 458.
[52] *Ibid.,* p. 44.
[53] *Ibid.*
[54] *Ibid.,* p. 45.
[55] *Ibid.,* p. 57.

Hank suggests that he tell Guenever that he is going away. "Thou forgettest," says the king, "that Launcelot is here; and where Launcelot is, she noteth not the going forth of the king, nor what day he returneth." Hank then observes: "Yes, Guenever was beautiful, it is true, but take her all around she was pretty slack."[56] When Hank returns from his trip of mercy to find his partially reformed country in ruins, Clarence tells him of the Civil War that resulted when Arthur found out about Guenever's and Launcelot's adultery; it is a tale of the destruction of all of the worthy knights, of the death of Arthur, and of the queen's retirement to a nunnery. Moral slackness had destroyed what was good in knight errantry.

Sexual immorality, however, was but a contributory cause of the disaster; it had been but the weakening of the body politic, making it susceptible to the final fatal disease. The disease, announced by Mark Twain in both notebook and text, was the power of the absolute church. It was a power exercised when both the adultery of court life and the morally opposite fidelity of Hank to wife and family made it possible for the Church to exercise its latent strength. While Hank is away, caring for his child, the Church, stronger than both Hank and the king, makes its move; the Church, Hank says sadly when he returns from France, was going to "*keep* the upper hand, now, and snuff out all my beautiful civilization. . . ."[57] Again, Dan Beard obliged by visualizing these lines in a full-page illustration of a smirking monk placing a bishop's miter over a bright candle labeled "19th Century," and entitling the drawing: "Snuffing Out the Candle."

The failure of the Yankee, then, is accounted for: minor blame is assigned to Hank for the venial sin of sentimentality, major blame to the mortal sins of Launcelot and Guenever and, most important, of the reactionary church. In only one place in the narrative is there the suggestion that progress through technology itself is the wrong course for humanity. This is the paragraph where Hank, describing his hidden factories, uses the analogy of a volcano, and compares them to the lava's "rising hell": "Unsuspected by this dark land," Hank says, "I had the civilization of the nineteenth century booming under its very nose! . . . There it was . . . as substantial a fact as

---

[56] *Ibid.*, p. 333.
[57] *Ibid.*, p. 528.

any serene volcano, standing innocent with its smokeless summit in the blue sky and giving no sign of the rising hell in its bowels."[58]

Comparing technology to a hell, the metaphor seems on the face of it to be loaded with negative feelings about the beneficence of applied science. Perhaps. One might also observe that "hell" did not always have negative connotations for an author who would rather be consigned to the Puritan hell than the Puritan heaven, who asked for his pen to be warmed in the infernal regions, and who might quite typically have described what was going to happen to aristocracy and church as, from their standpoint, a diabolical eruption. Furthermore the possibly negative import of the metaphor is contradicted by the surrounding allusions where technology is associated with light, and backward England with darkness.

The metaphor of the volcano is the one piece of internal evidence that might support the view that the cause of the disaster was technology itself; everywhere else there is the suggestion that Hank's prescription for the cure of social ills—the prescription of the faith in progress through reason, common sense, and applied science—is sound. What is perhaps true, although the internal evidence is far from clear, is that the general metaphysical framework in which this belief was embedded began to show signs of stress by the time Mark Twain was finishing *A Connecticut Yankee*. This framework had been built of a certain view of human nature—that it is essentially good—, and a corresponding view of universal law—that it too is moral and tends to work by assuring the betterment of human institutions over the course of history. Both optimisms are questioned by the conclusion of Mark Twain's fiction.

The disappointment Hank suffers when he returns to find not only the chivalry of England massed against him, but the people of England as well, revives his (and Mark Twain's) latent ambivalence towards the common man and towards the doctrine of his natural goodness. Where at the beginning of his adventures in medieval England, Hank used the word "muck" literally, to describe the streets of Camelot,[59] Hank uses the term at the end of the novel to describe the people themselves: "Imagine such human muck as this; conceive of this folly!"[60] This constitutes the "massive disillusionment" to

[58] *Ibid.*, p. 120.
[59] *Ibid.*, p. 29.
[60] *Ibid.*, p. 551.

which revisionist criticism of *A Connecticut Yankee* refers. It is incontestable that the Yankee is disappointed, and that his faith in humanity has been shaken. However, it had never been a faith without an admixture of both doubt and realism; earlier in the work, Hank had faced the problem posed for his hope of progress by the complex nature of man, and had come out of the experience with a renewed, if chastened, conviction that in the main there is enough good in human nature to justify a hope for society's improvement. The situation was this: travelling incognito, Hank and the king had come upon a frightful example of the operations of the archaic customs of England, laws that had resulted in mass cruelties and executions. Hank found that the peasants support the lords. "The painful thing," he observed, ". . . was the alacrity with which this oppressed community had turned their cruel hands against their own class. . . . It was depressing to a man with a dream of a republic in his head." Then, as it often did, the distance between narrator and author collapsed, and Mark Twain began to talk of his own experiences, experiences in the American South outside the range of a descendant of New England blacksmiths and horsedoctors: "It reminded me of a time thirteen centuries away, when the 'poor whites' of our South . . . were . . . pusillanimously ready to side with slave-lords . . . for the upholding and perpetuating of slavery." There was a redeeming factor, however, a small one, but enough to modify Hank's pessimism: "secretly the 'poor white' did detest the slave-lord and feel his own shame." This was enough "for it showed that a man is at bottom a man. . . ."[61] That this is straightforward and not ironic is made clear a moment later when Hank describes the bravery of one of the peasants and declares: "There it was, you see. A man *is* a man, at bottom. Whole ages of abuse and oppression cannot crush the manhood clear out of him." Yes, he continues, "there is plenty good enough material for a republic in the most degraded people that ever existed. . . ." Then, as mask and author once more abruptly coalesce, he adds: "—even the Russians." At this pont, the most extended discussion of the problem of the moral nature of man in *A Connecticut Yankee,* Hank concluded: "there was no occasion to give up my dream yet a while."[62] The abandonment of the dream would be

[61] *Ibid.,* pp. 387–388.
[62] *Ibid.,* pp. 390–391.

forced not by the nature of man, but by the nature of radically corrupt human institutions.

The second part of the metaphysical structure that supported the American belief in progress was an attitude toward the power behind history, be it God, Nature, or Universal Law: the sense that the movement of events was both purposeful and, in the long run, moral. There is some support for the proposition that Mark Twain's shaky allegiance to this faith was undergoing stress, and that the stress is reflected in the ending of *A Connecticut Yankee*. When the Yankee is described in Twain's notebook as "mourning his lost land," when in the frame of the narrative he smiles "one of those pathetic, obsolete smiles of his,"[63] when, in his dreams, he still wanders "thirteen centuries away," his unsatisfied spirit ". . . calling and harking all up and down the unreplying vacancies of a vanished world,"[64] we seem to have taken a long step toward the final pessimisms of *The Mysterious Stranger*. If, in his longing for his vanished world, Hank is longing for Camelot as Camelot, and if he feels himself a stranger in the nineteenth century as the nineteenth century, then, indeed, *A Connecticut Yankee,* as fiction, subverted its author's announced intention.

That this is not true can be proven by an examination of the portrait of medieval England as we find it in *A Connecticut Yankee*. The sixth century landscapes are idyllic, but its villages are vile and the life of its people is a hell for all but noble and aristocrat. It is a pastoral land whose dream-like beauty is, for Hank, "as lonesome as Sunday."[65] In the course of his incognito wanderings, Hank comes upon a telegraph station of his underground army of progress. "In this atmosphere of telephones and lightning communication . . . ," Hank says, "I was breathing the breath of life again after long suffocation. I realized then, what a creepy, dull, inanimate horror this land had been to me all these years."[66]

The apparently idyllic land contained a culture that made a horror out of natural goodness. Even the most favored of the aristocrats were prevented from enjoying it. The most eloquent description of pre-technological England, a description full of sentimental cliches

[63] *Ibid.,* p. 22.
[64] *Ibid.,* p. 524.
[65] *Ibid.,* p. 27.
[66] *Ibid.,* p. 305.

like "sylvan solitudes,"[67] comes at the beginning of the chapter called "Slow Torture," a chapter devoted to the intolerable life inside a coat of armor. A second flowery passage describing "blessed God's untainted dew-freshened, woodland-scented, air" comes after the description of Morgan le Fay's tortured victims, and is followed by Hank's description of the suffocation of mind and body in "the moral and physical stenches of that intolerable old buzzard-roost."[68]

This pretechnological England, naturally beautiful, humanly terrible, was transformed by Hank without, apparently, harming the landscape. Like "another Robinson Crusoe,"[69] he invented, contrived, created, and made a good society. "Consider the three years sped," he said proudly. "Now look around on England. A happy and prosperous country, and strangely altered. Schools everywhere, and several colleges. . . . Slavery was dead and gone; all men were equal before the law; taxation had been equalized. The telegraph, the telephone, the phonograph, the type-writer, the sewing machine, and all the thousand willing and handy servants of steam and electricity were working their way into favor. . . ." The list of accomplishments goes on, and ends with: "I was getting ready to send out an expedition to discover America."[70]

There is reason to believe, then, that Hank's longing is not for a pretechnological Eden, but for an England that the Yankee, like Robinson Crusoe, had made bearable by the exercise of his ingenuity. However, more powerful motives than nostalgia operated at the end of *A Connecticut Yankee* to give the comedy its serious turn. One was Mark Twain's consideration of a cyclical, repetitive theory of the movements of history. While the immediate cause of the downfall of Hank's society was the immorality of the Queen, Clarence suggests, without contradiction, that the end would have come "by and by,"[71] and would be caused by Hank himself. Merlin's taunt: "Ye were conquerors, ye are conquered,"[72] has the ring of the mockery of the goddess of Fortune, the deity of an inevitable turning back upon itself of all human enterprise.

[67] *Ibid.*, p. 141.
[68] *Ibid.*, p. 231.
[69] *Ibid.*, p. 85.
[70] *Ibid.*, pp. 512–513.
[71] *Ibid.*, p. 531.
[72] *Ibid.*, p. 570.

The second tragic motive, and a more important one, was Mark Twain's growing awareness, at the age of fifty, of the inevitable private failures of men, whatever the fate of their societies. Men must die; men must be separated from their earthly loves. Except for those fortunate, or self-deluding, enough to have a traditional religious faith, men must face the fact that time is man's enemy, cutting him away from his worldly affections. Hank's final delirium is entirely about these private sadnesses; he raves about Sandy and about their child, not about politics or technology. The bathetic ending of *A Connecticut Yankee* has nothing to do with the relative merits of republics or monarchies, progress or tradition. This is the human condition, says the novel's ending; but given the unalterable limits of this condition, man can still ask the question: what should man then do? And the answer *A Connecticut Yankee* gives, just as Mark Twain's tract *What Is Man?*, written years later, would give, is that within the severe restrictions and limitations of man's condition, he can try to act for human, for worldly improvement.

The available evidence, then, external and internal, suggests that the meaning of *A Connecticut Yankee* is, as the author repeatedly said it was, that the American nineteenth century, devoted to political and religious liberalism and to technology, was better than the traditional past. The efforts of modern men to continue a progress towards a fulfillment of material goals is shown to be a worthy mission of man. Mark Twain's fictional excursion into history was, as he insisted it was, for the purpose of saying to the reader: you've been poor following European models; you've become rich following American models; rich is better. Twentieth-century interpreters who find an opposed significance in the work must ask themselves whether that significance is an "appropriate" extension of authorial meaning.

The Lonesomeness of Huckleberry Finn
Paul Schacht

WHAT DOES "lonesomeness" mean to Huckleberry Finn? In recent years at least three critics have addressed this question directly—or would seem to have done so. Two of them analyze Huck's unhappy relation to society; one, his supposed emotional instability.[1] The three critics all make reference to several indispensable passages, reprinted just below, in which Huck himself speaks of "lonesomeness." Nevertheless, as if their ears were too finely tuned to implications and suggestions to register plainer meanings, the three adopt and develop ideas of lonesomeness that have little if any connection with Huck's word. These ideas do not lack interest or value, but so intelligent a narrator as Huck deserves to be understood on his terms as well as analyzed on ours; if we are to discuss *his* lonesomeness, we must begin with his words and the meanings he seems to give them. We shall discover, if we begin there, that "lonesomeness" has less to do with society or neurosis than with Nature; that it has a significant though perhaps recondite relation to a play by Shakespeare; and that it can help us to a new understanding of another important word in *Huckleberry Finn*: "freedom."

Three "Lonesomeness" Passages

I. At the Widow's

I felt so lonesome I most wished I was dead. The stars was shining, and the leaves rustled in the woods ever so mournful; and I heard an owl, away off, who-whooing about somebody that was dead, and a whippowill and a dog crying about somebody that was going to die; and the wind was trying to whisper something to me and I couldn't make out what it was, and so it made the cold shivers run over me. Then away out in the woods I heard

[1] Joel Jay Belson, "The Nature and Consequences of the Loneliness of Huckleberry Finn," *Arizona Quarterly*, 26, No. 3 (Autumn 1970), 243–48; Levi A. Olan, "The Voice of the Lonesome: Alienation from Huck Finn to Holden Caufield," *Southwest Review*, 48, No. 2 (Spring 1963), 143–50; Campbell Tatham, " 'Dismal and Lonesome': A New Look at *Huckleberry Finn*," *Modern Fiction Studies*, 14, No. 1 (Spring 1968), 47–55.

that kind of a sound that a ghost makes when it wants to tell about something that's on its mind and can't make itself understood, and so can't rest easy in its grave and has to go about that way every night grieving. I got so down-hearted and scared, I did wish I had some company.

II. On the River

A little smoke couldn't be noticed, now, so we would take some fish off of the lines, and cook up a hot breakfast. And afterwards we would watch the lonesomeness of the river, and kind of lazy along, and by-and-by lazy off to sleep. Wake up, by-and-by, and look to see what done it, and maybe see a steamboat coughing along up stream, so far off towards the other side you couldn't tell nothing about her only whether she was stern-wheel or side-wheel; then for about an hour there wouldn't be nothing to hear nor nothing to see—just solid lonesomeness. . . . So we would put in the day, lazying around, listening to the stillness.

III. At the Phelps Farm

When I got there it was all still and Sunday-like, and hot and sunshiny— the hands was gone to the fields; and there was them kind of faint dronings of bugs and flies in the air that makes it seem so lonesome and like everybody's dead and gone; and if a breeze fans along and quivers the leaves, it makes you feel mournful, because you feel like it's spirits whispering—spirits that's been dead ever so many years—and you always think they're talking about *you*. As a general thing it makes a body wish *he* was dead, too, and done with it all.[2]

In the second passage above, Huck speaks of the river's "lonesomeness," not his own; and in the third passage, the droning of bugs and flies makes "it seem" (not "you feel") "lonesome": in both places Huck evidently means the words "lonesome" and "lonesomeness" to describe not a state of mind but a quality of Nature. As we read these passages, we may at first want to accuse Huck, as one critic does, of "projecting" his feelings onto Nature, of mistaking his own aloneness for an emanation from the circumjacent world.[3] Perception can never go on wholly independent of emotion, of course, and at times, as in the Widow Douglas passage, the two may well be inseparable. But it cannot be right to say that Huck sees only what he feels, for surely he never feels *less* alone than when, on the raft with Jim, he senses "the lonesomeness of the river." On the

[2] Clemens, *Adventures of Huckleberry Finn,* ed. Sculley Bradley, Richmond Croom Beatty, and E. Hudson Long (New York: Norton, 1961), pp. 8–9, 96, 171. Subsequent references, included in the text, are to this edition.

[3] Tatham, p. 49.

river Huck passes beyond subjectivity to the apprehension of something external and real. A few excerpts from Clemens's autobiographical *Life on the Mississippi* (1883) will verify Huck's objec-
tivity. "We met two steamboats at New Madrid," begins Chapter
XXVII. "Two steamboats in sight at once! An infrequent spectacle
now in the lonesome Mississippi. The loneliness of this solemn,
stupendous flood is impressive—and depressing." Chapter XXVII
goes on to present descriptions of the Mississippi from five English
visitors to America, at the end of which Clemens summarizes,
"The tourists, one and all, remark upon the deep, brooding loneliness and desolation of the vast river." Finally, a few chapters later
Clemens says this of Mississippi sunrises: "They are enchanting.
First, there is the eloquence of silence; for a deep hush broods everywhere. Next, there is the haunting sense of loneliness, isolation,
remoteness from the worry and bustle of the world."[4] In each of
these instances "loneliness" is primarily a property of place, a thing
outside and independent of its observers. The word does indeed
imply a relation between perception and emotion, but the very
opposite of that contained in the term "projection"; the *Oxford
English Dictionary* makes clear the real relation in its definition of
"lonesome": "Causing feelings of loneliness, making one feel
forlorn." Clemens and Huck perceive a quality in the natural world
which induces in them a mood to fit. For Huck, the word "lonesomeness" apparently describes both the reality without and the
mood within.

Huck is as sensitive and precise a recorder of impressions as any
narrator in literature, so when he calls the Phelps farm "lonesome,"
we may assume he has been struck there by the same quality that
impressed him on the river, a quality that is more clearly than
ever—in its present connection with sunshine, insects, wind, and
leaves—an effect of Nature as much as of population. Yet the
moment we equate the "lonesomeness" of the farm with that of the
river, we face a problem. Why should the one make Huck wish
he "was dead . . . and done with it all," while the other evokes a
kind of lazy contentment? We meet a similar problem in *Life on
the Mississippi,* where the loneliness of the river is by turns "depres-

4 Clemens, *Life on the Mississippi* (1883; rpt. New York: Harper and Bros., 1917), pp.
225, 229, 258.

sing" and "haunting" according as it distresses or enchants Clemens. But Clemens's adjectives begin to solve our problems with Huck. If we take them for emblems of Huck's two reactions to "lonesomeness"—"depressing" aptly describes the farm, and "haunting" is consistent with Huck's depiction of the river—a provocative similarity arises between what at first seemed radically different experiences. For in disheartening Huck, the Phelps farm turns his mind to spirits, suggesting the presence, in this "depressing" setting, of something palpably "haunting." It may be, then, that Huck's responses to the farm and river have a buried kinship as important as their superficial differences. Until we can sort the elements that unite from those that divide these two responses, we obviously remain far from an understanding of "lonesomeness"; and we shall get no closer before we have looked in greater detail at Huck's position in the natural and human worlds.

The "lonesomeness" of the Widow Douglas's and the Phelps farm, associated as it is with sadness, death, and ghosts, bespeaks a kind of malevolence in Nature; and malevolent indeed, very often, is the natural world of *Huckleberry Finn*. It is tempting to believe that Huck and Jim, so close to Nature, are at one with it. But proximity need not imply harmony. Jim's intimacy with Nature has given him a knowledge of its signs, yet as Huck complains and Jim concedes, the signs almost always signify bad luck. Worse, they prove true with ominous consistency, because in *Huckleberry Finn* superstition, however silly, acknowledges reality: bad luck is a sort of natural law, something you can count on; sooner or later the snakeskin is bound to "do its work." Leo Marx has discussed this threatening aspect of Clemens's Nature in "The Pilot and The Passenger: Landscape Conventions and the Style of *Huckleberry Finn*."[5] Between "Old Times on the Mississippi" and *Huckleberry Finn*, Clemens made various attempts to portray the terrors of Nature alongside its beauties. In "Old Times," Marx points out, the conflict between two visions—romantic and realistic—of the river, resulted in the conquest of the former by the latter: in a famous passage Clemens laments that when one really knows a river—as a steamboat pilot must—one no longer sees its surface beauties, only the dangers beneath. However, in *Huckleberry Finn*, argues Marx, the two

[5] *American Literature*, 28, No. 2 (May 1956), 129–45.

visions came at last into accord. Even as Huck details the river's glories he remarks, without anxiety, a monitory "streak on the water which you know by the look of the streak that there's a snag there in a swift current which breaks on it and makes that streak look that way" (p. 96). "Now at last," Marx writes, "through the consciousness of the boy, the two rivers are one"; and consequently *Huckleberry Finn* is "a book, rare in our literature, which manages to suggest the lovely possibilities of life in America without neglecting its terrors." I have related Marx's argument at some length because I intend to propose for it, presently, a slight but significant modification; for now, though, what matters is the presence of terror, of malevolence, in Clemens's Nature. In Marx's words, "To him the landscape, no matter how lovely, concealed a dangerous antagonist. He knew that nature had to be watched, resisted and—when possible—subdued."[6]

Odd as this will sound, in its frequent malevolence the natural world of *Huckleberry Finn* has much in common with that of *King Lear*. Jim, of course, appears costumed as Lear at the very beginning of Chapter 24, after he has shown Huck, at the very end of the previous chapter, the remorse he felt and still feels at having once mistreated his daughter in a rage. The storm on Jackson's Island and the cave in which Huck and Jim take shelter also evoke *Lear,* and are for our purposes even more significant parallels. Kent, on the heath in *Lear,* declares: "Since I was man,/Such sheets of fire, such bursts of horrid thunder,/Such groans of roaring wind and rain, I never/Remember to have heard" (III, ii, 45–48). Huck's idiom is hardly the same, but his meaning is similar:

Directly it begun to rain, and it rained like all fury, too, and I never see the wind blow so. It was one of these regular summer storms. It would get so dark that it looked all blue-black outside, and lovely . . . and next, when it was just about the bluest and blackest—*fst!* It was as bright as glory . . . dark as sin again in a second, and now you'd hear the thunder let go with an awful crash and then go rumbling, grumbling, tumbling down the sky towards the under side of the world. . . .

(p. 43)

Admittedly, what horrifies Kent makes Huck's blood rush; but just now the stimulus—for both, the extreme violence of Nature—means more than any difference in response. We must remember, moreover,

6 Marx, pp. 140, 143, 142.

that on Jackson's Island Huck has just begun his education, so when
he reaches for some more fish and hot corn-pone, turns to Jim, and
says contentedly, "I wouldn't want to be nowhere else but here,"
Jim properly admonishes him: "Well, you wouldn't a ben here, 'f it
hadn't a ben for Jim. You'd a ben down dah in de woods widout
any dinner, en gittn' mos' drownded, too, dat you would, honey"
(p. 43). In large measure, then, Huck owes his aesthetic enjoyment
of the storm to the warmth and dryness of the cave. In *Huckleberry
Finn* as in *King Lear,* "unaccommodated man" is but a "poor, bare,
fork'd animal" (III, iv, 106–8), and much more vulnerable than
accommodated man generally wishes to acknowledge.

I do not suggest that Clemens patterned any part of *Huckleberry
Finn* rigidly or consistently after *King Lear;* but the play may well
have influenced that part of his imagination which was working
out an attitude to Nature, a conception of "lonesomeness," and the
implications of these things for the novel's central human relationship. We do not know that Clemens read *King Lear,* though we
know that he saw it—around 1878, in a German production—and
that during three hours of unintelligible language he "never understood anything but the thunder and lightning . . ."[7] His book *Is
Shakespeare Dead?* (1909) defends the view that Bacon, rather
than the Stratford Shakespeare, probably wrote the Plays; but
whoever did write them was, according to Clemens, "equipped
beyond every other man of his time with wisdom, erudition, imagination, capaciousness of mind, grace and majesty of expression";
and his works, we are assured, "will endure until the last sun goes
down."[8] Robert Gale maintains that Clemens undoubtedly read
"numerous Elizabethan and Jacobean playwrights, including Shakespeare," during his extensive preparations for *The Prince and the
Pauper;* from this and other compelling evidence Gale argues the
influence of *Lear* on that book.[9] Edward Mendelsohn has aptly
remarked the similarity between *Romeo and Juliet* and the Granger-

---

[7] Clemens, *A Tramp Abroad,* ed. Charles Neider (New York: Harper and Row,
1977), p. 50 (Chap. 9). Even the thunder and lightning, Clemens adds, were "reversed
to suit German ideas, for the thunder came first and the lightning after."

[8] Clemens, *Is Shakespeare Dead?*, reprinted in *What Is Man? And Other Essays* (New
York: Harper and Bros., 1917), pp. 358, 373.

[9] *"The Prince and the Pauper* and *King Lear,"* *Mark Twain Journal,* 12, No. 1
(Spring 1963), 14.

ford episode in *Huckleberry Finn*.[10] And Chapter 21 of the novel gives us the Duke's brilliantly garbled soliloquy, composed of fragments from *Hamlet, Macbeth,* and *Richard III.* So it cannot be unreasonable to treat *King Lear* as one impetus to, or a loose referent of, Huck's and Jim's relation to each other and to Nature.

In *King Lear* the words "unaccommodated man" deepen in meaning to suggest not only homeless and robeless, but friendless man—as if human company were the most important form of protection demanded by a hostile natural world. In a setting whose "lonesomeness" outdoes anything else of the sort in literature, isolation becomes the worst form of exposure: Lear errs tragically in banishing Cordelia precisely because her love, as he discovers too late, was essential to his survival. Indeed it might have sheltered him from all, he learns, might even have removed the need for clothing and a roof. Having at last recognized the necessity and power of love, Lear pleads with Cordelia:

> Come let's away to prison:
> We two alone will sing like birds i' th' cage;
> ... So we'll live,
> And pray, and sing, and tell old tales, and laugh
> At gilded butterflies, and hear poor rogues
> Talk of court news; and we'll talk with them too—
> Who loses and who wins; who's in, who's out—
> And take upon 's the mystery of things
> As if we were God's spies; and we'll wear out,
> In a wall'd prison, packs and sects of great ones,
> That ebb and flow by th' moon.
>   (V, iii, 8–18)

The idyllic life Lear envisions is, ironically, one of absolute freedom in imprisonment; and in its outline it closely resembles Huck's and Jim's life on the raft between Huck's flight from the Grangerfords and the invasion of the Duke and King—the short but exquisite stretch of their journey which Huck will later remember in words that recall Lear's: "and we a floating along, talking, and singing, and laughing" (p. 167). In fact, too little attention has been paid to the sense in which Huck and Jim, practically speaking, are *imprisoned*

---

[10] "Mark Twain Confronts the Shakespeareans," *Mark Twain Journal,* 17, No. 1 (Winter 1973–74), 20.

on the river: two birds, as it were, in a cage. They do not take to it by choice, they cannot leave it in safety, and neither of them returns to it at the story's end.[11] Yet as they "lazy along" downstream, farther and farther from any chance at the freedom Jim set out after, surrendering themselves to the current, abandoning all obligation or purpose, they achieve, against the background of the river's "lonesomeness," that unity in love—that more authentic kind of freedom—which Lear longs for with Cordelia.[12] Liberated, as it seems, from time and space, for a moment they inhabit eternity. The great world ebbs and flows while Huck and Jim pause to take upon them, in Lear's words, "the mystery of things": "We had the sky, up there, all speckled with stars, and we used to lay on our backs and look up at them, and discuss about whether they was made, or only just happened—Jim he allowed they was made, but I allowed they happened . . ." (p. 97).

In *Huckleberry Finn* as in *Lear,* then, life needs, above all, other life. Therein, surely, lies the pathos of Huck's character: he is a fugitive from society who cannot be alone. When he is, the "lonesomeness" of Nature goes malevolently to work on him. Outside his room at the Widow's (see the first passage above), Nature speaks of death and the dead speak through Nature—and Huck would rather die himself than have to listen. The depressing concert of leaves and owl and whippowill and dog and wind makes him "so down-hearted and scared, I did wish I had some company." As if in answer to this wish, company and comfort arrive in the form of Tom Sawyer; but as soon as Huck leaves town for Jackson's Island and independence, he runs into his old problem: "When it was dark I set by my camp fire smoking, and feeling pretty satisfied; but by-and-by it got sort of lonesome . . ." (p. 35). (As in the Phelps farm passage, Huck's use of the impersonal form—"it got . . . lonesome"—allows his adjective to describe at once his surroundings

---

[11] Huck originally plans to take to the woods (pp. 25–26); and once he finds a canoe, he does not plan to stay on the river any longer than he has to (p. 29).

[12] Soon after they have passed Cairo, Huck and Jim decide that when a chance arises, they will "buy a canoe" in which to paddle back upstream (p. 77); but when later Huck actually happens on a canoe, he simply paddles off "to see if I couldn't get some berries" (p. 97), making no mention of the earlier plan. There is no better evidence that at this point Huck and Jim either do not remember or do not care that they are floating farther all the time from the free states.

and his state of mind.) To cheer himself Huck now sits on the bank, listens to the wash of the current, watches the sky and river: "there ain't no better way to put in time when you are lonesome," he asserts with momentary faith in Nature's curative power; "you can't stay so, you soon get over it" (p. 36). His faith here is the Romantic one typified in William Cullen Bryant's "Thanatopsis" (1821), which declared that Nature "glides/Into [man's] darker musings, with a mild/And healing sympathy, that steals away/Their sharpness ere he is aware." But we have already seen that Clemens's romanticism was always met, if not overpowered, by his inescapable sense of the real. In *Huckleberry Finn*, Nature's mild and healing sympathy proves finally a poor substitute for human companionship. After three days alone, Huck rejoices to find Jim on the island: "I was ever so glad to see Jim. I warn't lonesome, now" (pp. 37-38).

Huck's next attack of "lonesomeness" comes with his first separation from Jim on their trip downriver—a separation for which they have Nature, in the forms of a fog and a swift current, to thank. "If you think it ain't dismal and lonesome out in a fog that way, by yourself, in the night," Huck advises us, "you try it once—you'll see" (p. 68). His last attack (that recounted in the third passage above) follows Jim's betrayal by the Duke and King, at a moment when separation seems finally irrevocable, and Huck, for the first time since Jackson's Island, finds himself utterly alone. The resemblance between the Widow Douglas and Phelps farm passages has often been noted; but no one seems to have remarked that the two passages bracket Huck's close friendship with Jim—the one preceding it, the other following what appears to Huck, for the present, to be its end. The positioning of these passages indicates the importance of Jim's presence or absence to Huck's experience of "lonesomeness."

What Jim gives Huck is shelter from that something in Nature which speaks mournfully of, even urges Huck towards, death—that isolating quality of the landscape which is to Huck, we said, the primary referent of the word "lonesomeness." Jim has no power to alter Nature: its "lonesomeness" remains palpable on the river and seems to maintain even there—in the water's perfect stillness, in the sense of languor and sleepiness, in effects like those which Clemens, in his own sunrise account, calls "enchanting" and "haunting"—its connection with death and spirits. But Jim's company does transform Huck's *experience* of Nature, just as the cave on Jackson's Island does when it makes a storm seem "lovely"—seem not benevolent, but gorgeous in its malevolence, exciting in its power to do harm to anything but Huck himself. In the cave and on the river, what is terrifying in Nature becomes beautiful because it has ceased to be really dangerous; or, to put it more accurately, freedom from immediate danger allows Huck to see a beauty in natural malevolence that has been there all along. The river evokes in Huck the same sense of isolation he felt at the Widow's and on the Phelps farm—like the tourists in *Life on the Mississippi* he seems affected by the "deep, brooding loneliness and desolation of the vast river"— but now, precisely because Huck is not isolated; because, in Jim's company, he cannot *be* lonely, the sense has become delicious to him, and "lonesomeness" has become an object of aesthetic contemplation. (One might indeed suggest—without urging it—that death itself has been disarmed, if not made hazily attractive, by the sense of safety Jim's loving companionship provides.) If it is a paradox for Huck to be "lonesome" but not lonely, it is not a paradox beyond the reach of common experience. At one time or another, most of us have openly embraced an hour of melancholy solitude that would certainly have held no charm had we been threatened with absolute and inevitable solitariness; and like Huck, many of us have made this paradoxical gesture most readily in the paradoxical situation of a shared aloneness. Certainly Huck's century acknowledged a paradox like his own in the mingled awe, terror, and pleasure it relished— from positions of safety—as "sublime." So we may at last qualify Leo Marx: in *Huckleberry Finn,* Clemens managed to depict not only the beauty *and* terrors of Nature, but the beauty *of* its terrors to those who, freed of them, are able to view them with aesthetic detachment.

The critics with whose views our examination began treat Huck's lonesomeness as a response to the human world, or as a psychological phenomenon independent of Nature or humanity. But however alienated Huck may be from the society that rejects him and that he rejects in turn, the mood he calls "lonesomeness" is in fact—as I have tried to show—a reaction to the natural world, perhaps at bottom to the fact of death as it manifests itself in Nature. This mood and its cause link the river passage to the other "lonesomeness" passages; Jim, we have just seen, sets it apart from them. With Jim, Huck can bask in the very mood that makes him, when alone, almost wish for death. Tom Sawyer, Aunt Sally, the Widow—almost any one of Huck's companions can cause the mood to vanish; Jim alone, however, can make it a thing of beauty, perhaps because Jim alone makes no attempt to restrict or regulate Huck, but demands of him only what he can himself offer: love.

For in the generally bleak world of *Huckleberry Finn,* love is as necessary and as powerful as it is in *King Lear.* At moments in both works, it would seem proof not only against "lonesomeness" but against far more violent natural assaults. When Huck and Jim first board the raft, they bring their cave along in the form of a "snug wigwam to get under in blazing weather and rainy" (pp. 54-55); but they no longer need it by the time the Duke and King arrive, because they now have the superior shelter of their bond. Their new companions usurp the wigwam; a fierce storm blows up; yet Nature is once again as beautiful, in its hostility, as it was on Jackson's Island. And though Huck teases us by making us momentarily fear that a "regular ripper" of a wave will do him harm, the only real danger, as he spills overboard, is that Jim will die laughing at him, or he at us (p. 104). Their safety has become, for the present, as inviolable as their love.

Unfortunately love, however powerful, cannot overcome Huck's antipathy to the "sivilized" world. When Jim finally accepts a place in that world, as surely he must, Huck—as he must—refuses to follow. All we have said, however, makes Huck's decision to "light out for the Territory" the saddest moment of the book. In lighting out Huck preserves his independence but also commits himself once more to isolation; he renews his vulnerability to Nature's malevolence, and to "lonesomeness" especially. If he is independent, he is not quite free. The need for freedom, Leo Marx has suggested, is the central theme of *Huckleberry Finn,* so we must not ignore anything that our discussion of "lonesomeness" might reveal about it.[13] Marx himself believes that "freedom in this book specifically means freedom from society and its imperatives," and without entirely

[13] "Mr. Eliot, Mr. Trilling, and *Huckleberry Finn,*" *The American Scholar,* 22, No. 4 (Autumn 1953), 425–26.

refuting this definition, we can now refine it considerably.[14] For
Huckleberry Finn presents us with at least three different kinds
of freedom. Huck leaves for Jackson's Island on a quest for his kind
of freedom: freedom from restriction on the one hand and cruelty on
the other—from the ways of Miss Watson and those of pap. There
he meets Jim, who is seeking a different, if related kind of freedom,
freedom from the legal institution of slavery. When men come from
town to search the island, Huck's freedom is as much jeopardized
as Jim's, since discovery would no doubt force Huck back into the
custody of either the Widow or pap. "They're after us!" Huck
shouts (p. 53), and from mutual sympathy, not an identity of ends,
he and Jim join forces and begin their journey downriver. Their
quests, similar as they will at times appear, are not the same, and the
final chapters will make this point twice. As the two hit the raft
after the mixed-up and splendid rescue from the Phelps farm, Huck
sings out, *"Now,* old Jim, you're a free man *again,* and I bet you
won't ever be a slave no more" (p. 212). But in his excitement Huck
has here confused Jim's kind of freedom with his own, for Jim,
who has never yet been a free man in the legal sense, is deeper in
slave territory and farther from legal freedom than ever. The irony is
soon inverted, and the difference in quests underscored once more,
when a piece of paper gives Jim his freedom at last, and Aunt Sally
threatens to re-enslave Huck. At this hour of celebration we must
suddenly make terms with a deflating truth, that Huck's quest for
a life permanently free from cruelty and restriction has not, like
Jim's quest, ended. Indeed, it may well have no end, since as Roy
Harvey Pearce has pointed out, "even in the Territory, he will be only
one step ahead of the rest . . . dukes and dauphins, Aunt Sallies,
Colonel Sherburns, and Wilkses—civilizers all."[15]

Still, if Huck and Jim begin and end their voyage with their eyes
on two different freedoms, they discover, en route, a third and
common one. "You feel mighty free and easy and comfortable on a
raft," says Huck the moment he and Jim shove off from the
Grangerfords' (p. 95); and later, when the two seem for an instant
to have shaken the Duke and King, Huck has just enough time,
before their hopes die, to tell us that "it *did* seem so good to be free

14 Marx, p. 436.
15 " 'The End. Yours Truly, Huck Finn': Postscript," *Modern Language Quarterly,* 24,
No. 3 (Sept. 1963), 256.

again and all by ourselves on the big river and nobody to bother us"
(p. 161). The freedom of those two or three days between the
Grangerfords and the first arrival of the Duke and King, the freedom
we barely have a chance to remember before their second arrival, is
a freedom neither Huck nor Jim sets out to find; but it is the only
freedom they ever share. It is a freedom achieved in imprisonment,
the freedom of solitude in loving company. In the odd way that has
been described, it is also a freedom from Nature—which is only to
say, really, the freedom to see beauty in Nature's entire aspect, even
in its terrors, even in "lonesomeness." Though it might not, in
itself, make the journey a success; though it cannot last; and though
Huck is wise enough not to try to recapture it by returning to the
river alone, that freedom marks the very highest point in the novel.

The Reprobate Elect in
The Innocents Abroad
Robert Regan

I

SOMETIME in October, 1867, aboard the steamship *Quaker City,* Mark Twain made a surprising discovery: he discovered what the book he had been writing since June was about. The book was (or, more properly, was to be) *The Innocents Abroad, or The New Pilgrims' Progress*.[1] The version he had been engaged in writing for about four months took the form of travel letters to the *Alta California* of San Francisco and the New York *Tribune*.

Perhaps as much as a month before, in the second week of September, he and seven other men had left their cruise ship at Beirut. Guided by a dragoman named Abraham, attended by nineteen servingmen, followed by twenty-six pack mules bearing every conceivable camping accouterment, the eight had made their way through Lebanon, Syria, and Palestine on horseback. During the first week on the trail, Mark Twain wrote (and may well have posted) three letters to the *Alta*. They bear these datelines: "In Camp, Mountains of Lebanon, Syria, September 11th, 1867;" "In Camp near Temnin el Foka, Valley of Lebanon, Sept. 12th;" "In Camp, Eight Hours Beyond Damascus, September 17th."[2] These were the last *Alta* letters from abroad to bear precise dates. His dating the next twenty simply "September, 1867" supports the surmise that they were written later—most of them after he and his companions of the trail had returned to the *Quaker City* and the ship had set her bows toward America.[3]

---

[1] Hartford: American Publishing Company, 1869; hereafter cited in the text parenthetically as *IA*.

[2] *Traveling with the Innocents Abroad: Mark Twain's Original Reports from Europe and the Holy Land,* ed. Daniel Morley McKeithan (Norman: Univ. of Oklahoma Press, 1958), pp. 178, 183, 188; hereafter cited in the text parenthetically as *TIA*.

[3] Dewey Ganzel contends that the letter of 12 Sept. was the last to be written "in Palestine" (*Mark Twain Abroad: The Cruise of the "Quaker City"* [Chicago: Univ. of

It was in the seventh of these imprecisely dated letters—the eighth
if we count one to the *Tribune*—that the theme that was to constitute the bedrock of *The Innocents Abroad* showed its first out-
croppings:

> During luncheon, the pilgrim enthusiasts of our party . . . could
> scarcely eat, so anxious were they to "take shipping" and sail in very
> person upon the waters that had borne the vessels of the Apostles and
> upheld the sacred feet of the Saviour. I thought they cherished a sort of
> vague notion that a fervor such as theirs might peradventure earn for them
> a little private miracle of some kind or other to talk about when they got
> home. Their anxiety grew and their excitement augmented with every
> fleeting moment, until my fears were aroused and I began to have mis-
> givings that in their present condition they might break recklessly loose
> from all considerations of prudence and buy a whole fleet of ships to sail
> in instead of hiring a single one for an hour, as quiet folk are wont to do.
> I trembled to think of the ruined purses this day's performances might
> result in. Never before had I known them to lose their self-possession when
> a question of expenses was before the tribe, and now I could not help
> reflecting bodingly upon the intemperate zeal with which middle-aged
> men are apt to surfeit themselves upon a seductive folly which they have
> tasted for the first time.   (*TIA*, pp. 229–30)

Mark Twain's feigned anxiety was, every reader of *The Innocents
Abroad* will recall, unnecessary: the "pilgrim enthusiasts" prove to
be penny-pinchers, not prodigals. When the skipper of the only boat
in sight asks "two Napoleons—eight dollars" to take the party for
a day's sail, the pilgrims offer him half his price. Not deigning to
dicker, he simply shoves off, and the Americans are left standing on
the shore without a hope of sailing upon the sacred waters.

How the pilgrims abused each other! Each said it was the other's fault,
and each in turn denied it. No word was spoken by the sinners—even the
mildest sarcasm might have been dangerous at such a time. Sinners that
have been kept down and had examples held up to them, and suffered

---

Chicago Press, 1968], p. 230), but the precise and plausible dateline of the following letter
suggests that it too was written "In Camp." Strictures upon the "Vandalism" of "the boys"
in the letter datelined "Banias, September, 1868" (*TIA*, pp. 204–08) and the absence of any
criticism targeted at "pilgrims" lead me, for reasons that will become clear, to conclude
that all the letters before the one from Tiberias (*TIA*, pp. 229–36), which contains Mark
Twain's initial criticism of "pilgrims," were written before he decided to distinguish "boys"
from "pilgrims"—probably before the ship's sailing from Palestine. The composition of the
"Holy Land" letters may be divided into three phases, corresponding to *TIA*, pp. 178–93,
pp. 193–229, and pp. 229–306.

frequent lectures, and been so put upon in a moral way and in the matter of going slow and being serious and bottling up slang, and so crowded in regard to the matter of being proper and always and forever behaving, that their lives have become a burden to them, would not lag behind pilgrims at such a time as this, and wink furtively, and be joyful, and commit other such crimes, because it wouldn't occur to them to do it. Otherwise they would. (*TIA,* p. 232)

Here, in the thirty-seventh letter about the excursion he had written for the *Alta,* Mark Twain for the first time winnows chaff from wheat, separates "pilgrims" from "sinners." Without fanfare, without a hint to prepare readers for this remarkable development, he injects two hostile groups into his serial narrative. When he had used the word "pilgrims" in earlier letters, he had patently meant all the excursionists; the singular "pilgrim" he had even applied to himself (*TIA,* pp. 98, 182). Wouldn't *Alta* readers—attentive *Alta* readers— have blinked their eyes to see the word "pilgrims," which their favorite humorist had previously treated as jocularly eulogistic, used dyslogistically, divisively? Wouldn't such readers have been surprised—even puzzled—to detect that Abraham's tents sheltered two groups of tourists, one labeled "pilgrims," the other "sinners," and that communications between the two were bad? Without foreshadowing, a dramatic antagonism had made its appearance. Mark Twain had found the theme of his first great work, a theme he would rework in book after book, story after story.

It was the oldest and most persistent of American themes: the fraction of Election and Reprobation—Saints over Sinners, the Bornagain over the Unregenerated, those who are to be "held up" as good examples over those who must be "kept down" because they are bad. The oldest American theme, but inverted: like the other two radically American writers who produced great works in the 1860s, Whitman and Dickinson, Mark Twain accepted the Puritan paradigm but turned it upside down: the sheep are really goats, the goats sheep; the wheat is really chaff, the chaff wheat. He inverted the fraction.

Although his writings had never placed this contumacious conviction so conspicuously on display before, it was hardly new for him. Even before the *Quaker City* sailed, he had registered such a sentiment in a letter to his mother, who had apparently admonished her

wayward son to look for spiritual guidance to a St. Louis clergyman
who was to be a fellow-passenger:

> I am resigned to Rev. Mr. Hutchinson's or anybody else's supervision.
> I don't mind it. I am fixed. I have got a splendid, immoral, tobacco-
> smoking, wine-drinking, godless room-mate who is as good and true and
> right-minded a man as ever lived—a man whose blameless conduct and
> example will always be an eloquent sermon to all who come within their
> influence. But send on the professional preachers—there are none I like
> better to converse with. If they're not narrow minded and bigoted they
> make good companions.[4]

Here the "godless" becomes the "blameless"; the man whose "conduct" is an "eloquent sermon" makes the "professional preachers"
seem odds-on favorites to be "narrow minded and bigoted."

The "pilgrims" with whom the "sinners" rode through the Levant
were no more than semi-professional preachers, yet they did assuredly
preach to the "tobacco-smoking, wine-drinking godless." Mark
Twain takes them to task, however, not for the contents of their
sermons but for their lacking a call to preach. He represents them
as deficient in the qualities of true religion. The language in which
he describes the "pilgrim enthusiasts" intimates that their religion is
not just unreasoning but sensual (a "seductive folly" upon which
they would "surfeit themselves," an "intemperate zeal") and self-
seeking (they believed that their "fervor" would be rewarded with
a "private miracle" they could "talk about when they got home").
By contrast, the sober sinners, who resist the temptation to utter even
"the mildest sarcasm," seem meek enough to inherit the earth.

I have asserted that Mark Twain discovered his theme by the Sea
of Galilee; perhaps I should have said that the theme discovered
itself. The bedrock of meaning cropped out there, but whether Mark
Twain recognized it is open to question. He did not, in any event,
recognize it as a "lead" to be "followed." Readers of the letters from
the Middle East were to hear not one more word about the winning
"sinners," and the "pilgrims"—the targeted pilgrims—would come
under fire only six more times. Nevertheless, the caliber of ammuni-
tion Mark Twain uses against them is worth remarking.

Three times he chides the pilgrims for their lack of spontaneity

---

[4] *Mark Twain's Letters,* ed. Albert Bigelow Paine (New York: Harper & Brothers, 1917),
I, 126.

and independence: they see and even feel only what their guidebooks direct them to see and feel; their responses are prepared, platitudinous, predictable. "Our pilgrims"—that "our" effectively separates *them* from *us*—"taking the cue from the books . . . make it a point to be much affected when they behold" anything the guidebook authors "dwell with moving pathos upon . . ." (*TIA*, p. 237). Further on it is "your pilgrim," with the same effect: "your pilgrim that has marked his guide book all up with marks that signify 'Here be astonished,' is going to be astonished just at every one of those places, if it kills him" (*TIA*, p. 290). And once the pilgrims are almost— but not quite—spared: in spite of all their reading in lachrymose books about the Bible Lands, when the party first glimpsed Jerusalem, "not even our pilgrims wept. . . . If ever a party were peculiarly liable to tears, under such circumstances, it is our pilgrims. They are the very boys to go into sentimental convulsions at the merest shadow of a provocation. Yet they wept not over Jerusalem" (*TIA*, p. 265).

Equally numerous and more lethal are Mark Twain's fusillades at pilgrim vandalism. At Mary Magdalene's house "The pilgrims took down portions of the front wall for specimens as is their honored custom . . ." (*TIA*, p. 234). At Beth-el "The pilgrims took what was left of the hallowed ruin" of Jacob's pillows (*TIA*, p. 264). From the Plain of the Shepherds near Bethlehem "the pilgrims took some of the stone wall and hurried on" (*TIA*, p. 300). And in Christianity's *sanctum sanctorum*, the Church of the Holy Sepulchre, "Our pilgrims" find themselves "out of luck," "disappointed," because they are prevented from making "any collections worth having" (*TIA*, pp. 268, 270). Severe charges; but those two charges, an unbecoming dependence on guidebooks and a lust for souvenirs which drives them to demolish holy places, are the only complaints against the "pilgrims" Mark Twain was to include in the letters he wrote during the *Quaker City's* cruise.

After the ship's docking in New York, however, he sent one last letter to the *Alta*. It opens with a broadside aimed at all the pilgrims, not just at the sanctimonious men he had camped with. This is his first unfriendly reference to "pilgrims" which suggests that the group so designated exceeded three in number. He ventures that the *Quaker City's* "menagerie of pilgrims" would be talking of their adventures "from now till January—most of them are too old to last longer."

They can tell how they . . . cabbaged mosaics from the Baths of Caracalla
. . . how they "went through" the holy places of Palestine, and left their
private mark on every one of them . . . . Good-bye to the well-meaning
old gentlemen and ladies . . . . They thought they could have saved
Sodom and Gomorrah, and I thought it would have been unwise to risk
money on it. . . . Every night, in calm or storm, I always turned up in
their synagogue, in the after cabin, at seven bells, but they never came
near my stateroom. They called it a den of iniquity. But I cared not; there
were others who knew it as the home of modest merit.

The *Quaker City* party was said to be "mixed" but it was

not mixed enough—there were not blackguards enough on board in proportion to saints—there was not genuine piety enough to offset the
hypocrisy. Genuine piety! Do you know what constitutes a legal quorum
for prayer? It is in the Bible: "When two or three are gathered together,"
etc. You observe the number. It means two (or more) honest, sincere
Christians, of course. Well, we held one hundred and sixty-five prayer
meetings in the *Quaker City,* and one hundred and eighteen of them were
scandalous and illegal, because four out of the five real Christians on board
were too sea sick to be present at them, and so there wasn't a quorum.
I know. I kept a record . . . . They never could have stood a call of the
house, and they resented every attempt of mine to get one. (*TIA*,
pp. 309–11)

For "hypocrisy" look to the "saints," for "genuine piety" to "blackguards." Three years before, Emily Dickinson had published a little
poem beginning "Some keep the Sabbath going to Church—/ I keep
it, staying at Home—"; Mark Twain's situation is the same. For
"Church," read "their synagogue"; for "Home," read "my stateroom
. . . the home of modest merit." The true Elect had been in Mark
Twain's stateroom all along, while Reprobate "old gentlemen and
ladies," shrine-desecrators all, had "infested" the "synagogue," where
they congratulated each other on being the righteous few for whose
sake God would have spared the Cities of the Plain. But they were
wrong.

Yet the attack was wrong also, not ethically but aesthetically and
rhetorically. In taking the self-righteous, the self-congratulatory to
task, it is inadvisable to appear self-righteous, self-congratulatory.
Wisely Mark Twain discarded the final *Alta* letter when he made
the book. He discarded the letter, but its sentiments, more acceptably
expressed, were to be distributed through virtually every chapter of

The Innocents Abroad. If that delightfully digressive narrative has one thread which runs through all its great length, it is the identity of the "saints" and the "sinners"—although those words appear infrequently in the text.[5]

II

The word "sinners" does occur in *The Innocents Abroad* (Ch. 47, p. 498; Ch. 48, p. 512) as do two other terms denoting the group that made Mark Twain's stateroom its smoking-room, "the unregenerated" (Ch. 4, pp. 39, 45) and "the boys" (Ch. 5, p. 52; Ch. 7, p. 75; Ch. 23, p. 243; Ch. 28, p. 302; Ch. 30, p. 325; Ch. 32, p. 338), but the word which most frequently designates the Reprobate Elect is "we." The least conspicuous of Mark Twain's tinkerings with the *Quaker City* letters is also the most frequent and the most telling, the substitution of "we" for "I." On one single page of the part of the book treating the tour through France and Italy I count a dozen such changes (Ch. 17, p. 165).

The Innocents Abroad opens with four chapters in which first person pronouns are more often singular than plural. These treat Mark Twain's plans and arrangements before the sailing and his initial experiences aboard. Appropriately, he speaks here of and for himself alone: "I." When "we" appears in these four chapters and the two following chapters about the Azores it denotes Mark Twain and Party, but the party is not particularized. Five days after the ship left the Azores he was to make an entry in his notebook which foreshadowed the appearance in the book—not, it should be noted, in the letters—of a community of shared experience and common values, the reprobate elect. "Friday June [28]—Sat up all night playing dominoes in the smoking room with the purser & saw the sun rise— woke up Dan & the Dr. & called everybody else to see it."[6] We may disregard the purser and "everybody"; Dan, the Doctor, and the

---

[5] The division of pilgrims and sinners receives perceptive treatment from Henry Nash Smith in *Mark Twain: The Development of a Writer* (Cambridge: Harvard Univ. Press, 1962), pp. 42–51. See also his note on "pilgrim," p. 196, n. 43.5, which clarifies the use of the word in *TIA*, p. 196; *IA*, Ch. 22, p. 218, and perhaps in the subtitle of the book.

[6] *Mark Twain's Notebooks and Journals*, ed. Frederick Anderson, Michael B. Frank, and Kenneth Sanderson (Berkeley: Univ. of California Press, 1974), I, 348; hereafter cited in the text parenthetically as *MTN&J*.

author were to answer to the pronoun "we" through twenty-six chapters of *The Innocents Abroad*.

Daniel Slote of New York we have already encountered: he is the "godless" and "blameless" roommate. "The guide-persecuting Doctor of the *Innocents Abroad*," as Mark Twain later called him, was A. Reeves Jackson of Stroudsburg, Pennsylvania, ship's surgeon of the *Quaker City* and travel correspondent for a hometown paper, the Monroe County *Democrat*.[7] These two, hardly mentioned in the newspaper letters (*TIA*, pp. 58, 93, 101, 107–08, 303–04) become, after Mark Twain himself, the most fully realized characters in the book. The reason is apparent: they are essential to the book's theme. They were drawn from life, and accurately enough for Dr. Jackson to recognize himself in the book's doctor and to want others to recognize him.[8] Yet their depiction does not individualize the three reprobates. Their very real differences of appearance, background, and language are neglected in a way which is by no means typical of Mark Twain.[9] Whatever quality he ascribes to one seems to attach itself to all three. The doctor may, for example, initiate the richly symbolic gambits of one-upmanship they employ with European guides, but the other two share equally in his antiauthoritarian play.

Their solidarity and their separation from the pilgrims were matters of such importance as to demand dramatic treatment in the book. This Mark Twain provided by adding two memorable episodes, the one based on a real experience, the other a "stretcher" in a book that

[7] Jackson reported on the Azores in the Philadelphia *Press*, 22 July 1867. His letter suggested that others from Constantinople and beyond were to follow but none was published there. He did, however, report regularly to the Monroe County (Pa.) *Democrat* of Stroudsburg. The files of that paper were destroyed by fire, but in 1965 Leon T. Dickinson discovered an apparently complete set of clippings comprising eighteen letters in the possession of a family member. These he deposited in The Mark Twain Papers, Bancroft Library, University of California, Berkeley. Dates of publication have been cut away. The *Democrat* letters were not available to Dewey Ganzel: several matters of fact on which I shall (silently) correct his account are clarified by those letters. Mark Twain's identification of the "guide-persecuting Doctor" appears on the back of an envelope which contained a letter from Jackson dated 27 March 1872 (Mark Twain Papers).

[8] After his first wife's death in 1869, Jackson moved to Chicago, where he established a national reputation in gynecology and medical education. Virtually every biographical directory of the period mentions his role in *The Innocents Abroad*. He himself may be assumed the authority for the *DAB* assertion that "the jokes attributed to the Doctor were the verbatim report of Jackson's utterances."

[9] Compare "Mr. Brown," the conspicuously less fastidious fictitious traveling companion of Mark Twain's earlier journalism. Samples of Brown's contrastive role may be found in *TIA*, pp. 56–58, 136, and 155.

"told the truth, mainly." The factual scene takes place in a shop in Gibraltar.[10] Mark Twain finds himself "sold"—sold a pair of worthless gloves by a handsome saleswoman. He implores the boys not to "tell any of those old gossips in the ship" about his humiliation; then the other two discover that they all have been sold worthless gloves (*IA,* Ch. 7, pp. 73–75). Two dozen pages further along comes a scene in which the "boys" visit Marseilles' Zoological Gardens. There they see "a sort of tall, long-legged bird with a beak like a powder-horn, and close-fitting wings like the tails of a dress coat. . . . Such tranquil stupidity, such supernatural gravity, such self-righteousness, and such ineffable self-complacency as were in the countenance and attitude of that . . . preposterously uncomely bird" prompt them to name him "The Pilgrim." "He only seemed to say, 'Defile not Heaven's anointed with unsanctified hands.'" And Dan adds, "All he wants now is a Plymouth Collection"—the excursion's official hymnal (*IA,* Ch. 11, pp. 101–02). Although this scene sounds every bit as "real" as the incident in the glove-shop, it is highly unlikely that the "boys" visited a zoo in Marseilles.

The *Alta California's* correspondent did not publish a letter about that city, but the Monroe County *Democrat's* did. From Dr. Jackson's letter we learn that the "unsanctified" three went ashore late on the evening of 4 July and checked into a room—one room for the three of them—at the Grand Hotel du Louvre et de la Paix—an excellent establishment, the guidebooks say, but not an economical one. The next morning they toured the city by carriage. One can easily trace their path on a map: although Jackson misspells or misnames five of the nine places he mentions their visiting, all are identifiable. Such a tour would have consumed at least three hours, even if, as I suspect, they did not enter the two churches he speaks of: in comparison with Mark Twain's, Jackson's letters go heavy on churches, light on bars, cancan dancers, and *grisettes*—not surprising considering that his small-town audience included his wife, children, patients, and fellow leaders of Stroudsburg's Presbyterian congregation. After the morning tour, they made an excursion by boat to Chateau d'If—another three hours. Never did their path come within a mile of Marseilles' small zoo. They departed for Paris on the evening express at eight.

[10] The accounts of the episode in Jackson's *Democrat* letter and Mark Twain's notebook (*MTN&J,* I, 351) match precisely.

On the morning of 12 July they completed the twenty-hour return trip to Marseilles. They checked back into the same hotel. There Mark Twain must have written his *Alta* letter dated "Paris, July 12th, 1867," and there Jackson probably finished his long letter to the *Democrat* dated "Paris, July 11, 1867." Would these two, having just returned from Paris, where they packed ten days' sightseeing into five—including, Mark Twain says, the *Jardin des Plantes* with its famous *ménagerie* (*IA*, Ch. 15, p. 150)—heavy with fatigue from a day and night in the cramped French cars and faced with journalistic deadlines of sorts, have scurried off with Dan, a man with tastes quite as worldly as their own, to Marseilles' dinky little zoo? And would they have spent an hour there, stirring up an old stork, "pimply about the head . . . scaly about the legs," simply to discharge some of their animosity against the pilgrims? Unlikely on all scores, and most of all because these three men had apparently not at that point developed any special animosity toward the people Mark Twain would after the fact style pilgrims. "The Pilgrim" bird seems, then, to come from a fabulous bestiary. This intrusion of fiction into a work of almost journalistic reliability should assure us that the author knew what he was about—that he perceived the need for early treatment of the pilgrims as the boys' antagonists and as their foils.

A very slight adaptation of the *Alta* letter from Gibraltar had, four chapters earlier, addressed the same need. The letter had observed that "a crowd like ours . . . found enough to stare at" in Gibraltar (*TIA*, p. 22). The word "crowd" becomes "tribe" in *The Innocents Abroad* and is followed by this parenthetical gloss: "(somehow our pilgrims suggest that expression, because they march in a straggling procession through these foreign places with such an Indian-like air of complacency and independence about them)" (*IA*, Ch. 7, p. 69). Mark Twain then returned to his *Alta* letter for caricatures of three passengers who "are sometimes an annoyance": the "Oracle," "an innocent old ass," who gets all his information from guidebooks, gets it all wrong, and spews it out in a torrent of malapropisms; the "Lauriat of the Ship," or "Poet Lariat," as the Oracle calls him, inflictor of "barbarous rhymes" on the officials of every port; and the "Interrogation Point," the "young and green" source of foolish questions and "braggadocio about America." Most of this comes straight out of the *Alta* letter, but not the phrase that introduces the three.

That phrase is "Speaking of our pilgrims" (*IA,* Ch. 7, pp. 69–71; Ch. 10, p. 91). These three and the large "tribe" to which they adhere are, like the Holy Land three, "complacent," but they are not "sancti-monious"; they bear little resemblance to the image of the pious pilgrims Mark Twain had developed in the late *Alta* letters and to which he would return when he revised those letters for the book. But they not only expand the number of pilgrims from the Holy Land three; they also expand the meaning of "pilgrim" without blurring it. Either too old or too young to be reliable, they represent beclouded perception, distorted understanding, and grotesquely in-appropriate expression. "They" represent the opposite of all that "we" connotes in the book: "their" failures of comprehension and in-adequacies of language serve to remind the reader of "our" accuracy of vision, honesty of speech. Mark Twain and the boys, it should be noted, speak neither the artificially elevated language of the poet nor the bathetic vernacular of the Oracle. Theirs is the middle style, familiar but not vulgar. The slang in their speech is conspicuously labeled; it is introduced for comic effect; it does not suggest the normal level of their diction. Throughout the book Mark Twain takes pains to distinguish his style and the boys' from pilgrim style, both high pilgrim and low, both genteel pilgrim and vernacular.

The boys' solidarity is established and reinforced by their having to endure the "old gossips," "Heaven's anointed," and endure them together. Subsequently they would also have to endure such minor annoyances of travel as the dull razors of Continental barbers, the declivitous terrain of Continental billiard-tables: these fraternal rites are also additions made for the book. Through the long stretch of the book which concentrates upon the boys and their solidarity, however, they are not compelled to endure the pilgrims: neither in Paris nor in the cities of Italy do their paths cross. Yet if the boys are parted from the pilgrims, they encounter other American tourists like them—tourists whose preposterous behavior provides further con-trasts to the boys' "modest merit": pompous "Old Travelers," ig-norant art enthusiasts who fall into delirium before "smoke-dried old fire-screens" attributed to Old Masters, Europeanized Americans who have forgot their own language (*IA,* Ch. 12, pp. 110–11; Ch. 19, p. 192; Ch. 23, pp. 233–34; Ch. 25, p. 265).

Mark Twain does not allow the reader to lose sight of the *Quaker*

City Pilgrims entirely (*IA*, Ch. 25, p. 256) but the boys are not
reunited with them until Chapter 29. Dr. Jackson's letters confirm
enough details to assure us that *The Innocents Abroad* gives a generally accurate account of the end of the tour of Italy: the three
friends did not return from Rome to the ship because they anticipated—correctly—that the ship would be quarantined in Naples;
they took a train to that city instead and put up in a hotel at least
until the quarantine was lifted. On 3 August the Naples *Observer*
published a letter from Mark Twain. The letter pleads with the
authorities to "let us out" of the prison the ship had become for all
(*TIA*, p. 76), although the letter-writer was, clearly enough, not *in*.
Whether he was at that date *in* in spirit—whether he felt himself
a full member of the *Quaker City* family—remains an unresolved
question. The letter to the *Observer*, which he seems to have clipped
and sent to the *Alta*, where it appeared as part of his correspondence,
represents him as a member in good standing of the pilgrim crew.
But the letter was not to survive the revision process. For once the
book is closer to the actualities.

   Chapter 29 opens with the ship quarantined in Naples harbor. For
several days she has been "a prison" for the passengers aboard; but
"We that came by rail from Rome have escaped this misfortune."

> We go out every day in a boat and request them to come ashore. It soothes
> them. We lie ten steps from the ship and tell them how splendid the city
> is; and how much better the hotel fare is here than any where else in
> Europe; and how cool it is; and what frozen continents of ice cream there
> are; and what a time we are having cavorting about the country and sail-
> ing to the islands in the Bay. This tranquilizes them.   (p. 308)

Not a word about pilgrims; not a word about boys. But in the illustration on the facing page (Mark Twain took so active a hand in the
selection and design of the illustrations as to justify accounting them
a substantive element of the text)[11] four gentlemen and an oarsman
approach the stern of the ship in a dinghy. They look up at seven
forlorn figures on the fantail. The picture is captioned "SOOTHING
THE PILGRIMS."

---

[11] For a convincing argument on this point and on the authority of the first edition text,
see Robert H. Hirst's forthcoming *The Making of "The Innocents Abroad"* (Lincoln: Univ.
of Nebraska Press).

III

He always hated expanding, compressing, revising; he always hated being his own editor. He avoided the work when he could; when he could not, he did a slipshod job of it. *The Innocents Abroad* is not the most damaging evidence against him on that count, but it is damaging. By the departure from Naples, the halfway point in the book, he had used up only a third of his newspaper letters. More previously written material being ready to hand, more is used in the second half. Nothing in his letters from Athens, Constantinople, and the Black Sea ports, and probably nothing in his actual experiences during that part of the trip, would serve to dramatize the conflict between pilgrims and boys. In a stretch of fifty-five pages Mark Twain reminds the reader of the annoying pilgrims only once (*IA,* Ch. 32, p. 353) and of the boys he says not a word. In point of fact, the boys—the boys as the book had sketched them—had gone their separate ways. Dr. Jackson had joined Mark Twain and two other intrepid tourists for a midnight visit to the Acropolis in defiance of another quarantine, but their two companions were members of the elect—though not so labeled. The facts were playing Mark Twain false, but he failed to alter them. When the ship left Constantinople for the Black Sea, Dan remained behind. The book does not even register his absence. And the doctor, although aboard for the excursion into Russian waters, had in a sense also defected. There is good reason to believe that the philandering physician was trading the boys for a *female* attachment, Miss Julia Newell, another amateur travel-journalist, who would in time become his second wife. And Mark Twain himself was for a space all but absorbed in the synagogue crowd. When the passengers were received with flattering condescension by the Czar, he headed the committee of five gentlemen who drafted an Address "To His Imperial Majesty, Alexander II, Emperor of Russia." The first name subscribed to the address is Sam L. Clemens (*TIA,* pp. 145, 156). He reported the Imperial reception at embarrassing length in letters to both his newspapers. In *The Innocents Abroad* that material is much condensed but there remains almost more of it than the book can stand. He should have discarded it; instead, he provides a corrective, which works: Chapter 38 opens with a much-needed scene of self humiliation. A sailor on the forecastle delivers a parody of the address to the "third cook, crowned with a resplendent tin basin"; the performance is repeated on each watch; and the whole topic grows "tiresome" to the author of the Address (*IA*, Ch. 38, pp. 404–06).

That encounter brings Mark Twain back to himself and back to his theme. It is followed quickly by an attack on "PILGRIM PROPHECY-SAVANS" (that is the running-head on pages 408 and 409): "Pilgrims, always prone to find prophecies in the Bible, and often where none exist . . ." (*IA*, Ch. 38, p. 407). That comment originated in an *Alta* letter, but it began "Christian pilgrims" (*TIA*, p. 164). Thus the pilgrims are deprived of their protective Christian designation; they seem to become "our" pilgrims. One cannot, however, be quite sure: here and in four succeeding chapters the word "pilgrims" calls attention to the ridiculous appearance and behavior of the party, but it is probably the whole party, elect and reprobate, it denotes. A little more revision of small details would have been in order. By the opening of Chapter 42, however, the lines are being drawn more clearly: the "boys" appear again, this time to "simplify the spelling of Temnin el Foka—"They call it Jacksonville" (p. 438). That is new material—new in the sense that it does not come from a newspaper letter—but it is not altogether new. It continues a pattern of pointed humor: unlike the Oracle, unlike "Old Travelers" who pretend to encyclopedic knowledge of the geography, history, and language of every country they visit, the boys willingly reveal, and revel in revealing, the limitations of their competence. This little joke deserves our attention. Like every good joke, it *gets* our attention. But it need not detain us, for in the next chapter Mark Twain commences his large-scale, tendentious revisions. The pilgrims are the target; the aim is precise.

IV

At the outset of the tenting excursion through the Levant, Mark Twain entrusted to his notebook a scrap of information which he was never to share with his newspaper readers and which he would mention so casually, and only once, in *The Innocents Abroad* (Ch. 47, p. 490) that most readers overlook it: the pilgrims enjoyed separate and unequal accommodations: "Col. Denny, Church, & Dr. Birch in one large tent. Jack Van Nostrand, Davis & Moulton in the other. Dan Slote & I in the small one" (MTN&J, I, 417). Yet that note is the only hint of division—and it hardly suggests divisiveness—in all of his notebook record of the excursion: not once does that record set Denny, Church, and Birch apart from the other campers; not once does it call them pilgrims. The entries for the four-day trip from Beirut to Damascus are unusually brief; those for the third and fourth days are astonishingly short, considering how much Mark Twain was to make of those days in his book. "Sep. 13 . . . . Broke camp at 6.30 AM . . . & at 11 reached the magnificent ruins of Baalbec, marched about the ruined temples . . . 3 or 4 hours . . . . Rode 7 hours . . . & camped at 10.30 . . . ." And for the following day, Saturday: "Sept 14—Broke camp at 7 A.M. & make a fearful trip through the Zeb Dana valley . . . & nooned an hour at 1 PM at the celebrated fountain of Figia . . . the coldest water in the world.— Bathed in it. . . . Beautiful place . . . ." And he adds this bit of fancy, apparently for later humorous exploitation: "Where Baalam's ass lived—holy ground." The day's entries end with

Damascus.

Left the fountain at 1 P.M. (that infernal fountain took us at least 2 hours out of our way,) & reached Mahomet's look-out place over the wonderful garden & plain of Damascus & the beautiful city, in time to get a good long look & descend into the city before the gates were closed. (MTN&J, I, 418-19)

Nothing here, except perhaps the word "infernal," hints at the treatment he would eventually give those two days. The entry for Sunday could hardly be shorter: "Sept. 15.—Taken very sick at 4 AM." It's little wonder that the ailing traveler failed to give his newspaper readers an account of the ride from Ba'albek to Damascus. In *The Innocents Abroad,* however, those two days in the saddle were to provide the occasion for Mark Twain's most extended and penetrating assault on the pious tribe he calls "our pilgrims."

"Properly, with the sorry relics we bestrode, it was a three days' journey to Damascus. It was necessary that we should do it in less than two. It was necessary because our three pilgrims would not travel on the Sabbath day. We were all perfectly willing to keep the Sabbath day, but there are times when to keep the *letter* of a sacred law whose spirit is righteous, becomes a sin, and this was a case in point." Resonantly echoing II Corinthians iii.3, Mark Twain at last

broaches the moral theology of his gargantuan tract: serving the
letter, forgetful of the spirit, the pilgrims become sinners. "We
pleaded for the tired, ill-treated horses . . . . But when did ever self-
righteousness know the sentiment of pity? . . . We said that the
Saviour who pitied dumb beasts and taught that the ox must be
rescued from the mire even on the Sabbath day, would not have
counseled a forced march like this." After unsuccessfully urging the
imitation of Christ upon the Sabbatarians at some length, he observes,
in ironic exasperation: "We have given the pilgrims a good many
examples that might benefit them, but it is virtue thrown away" (*IA,*
Ch. 43, pp. 451–52). With stores of virtue to throw away, the sinners
become saints. The fraction is inverted: a curse falls upon those
thought blessed, a blessing upon those thought cursed.

Balaam's ass is quite unconnected with the geography of this episode but perhaps not with its theme. The ass helped his master dis-
cern whom he should curse, whom bless, taught him to choose the
true chosen people (Numbers xxii). Whether or not that was Mark
Twain's motive for pressing Balaam's ass into literary service, the
beast serves well in the anti-pilgrim rhetoric: "Not content with
doubling the legitimate stages, they switched off the main road and
went away out of the way to visit an absurd fountain called Figia,
because Baalam's ass had drank there once" (p. 453). And in the next
chapter, Mark Twain presents an excerpt from what he claims is
"the terse language of my note-book": "nooned an hour at the celebrated Baalam's Ass Fountain of Figia . . . guide-books do not say
Baalam's ass ever drank there—somebody been imposing on the pilgrims, may be" (*IA,* Ch. 44, p. 454). Even as Bible-scholars, the
pilgrims prove frauds.

Once again we may learn something about Mark Twain's intention
by asking how much of this new material is based on fact. It is
impossible to determine whether the horses were really "sorry relics"
or what pains they suffered, but this much can be ventured: the pace
their riders set on that Friday afternoon and Saturday was reasonably
but not heroically fast. The *Quaker City* eight did not devote as much
time to seeing Figia, or any other attraction, as their Cook's or
Murray's guidebooks urged upon them, but on the trail they set no
records. Mark Twain might easily have assured himself of that by
glancing at a travel book by a California acquaintance, J. Ross

Browne. Fifteen years earlier Browne's party had "left the ruins of Baalbek" at "about noon" and had reached Damascus the following afternoon.[12] Add two hours for the Fountain of Figia—Browne had made other detours but had neglected Figia—and the two accounts tally closely in time on the trail.

Tracing the daily itineraries Mark Twain recorded in his notebook reveals that in other comparable time-spans the party covered more ground: on the twenty-second and the forenoon of the twenty-third, for example, they trekked from El Genin (Ginae, Jennin) through Samaria and Shechem, where they lunched, to Lubia (Lebonah), where, having outdistanced their tents, they slept on the ground; then on to Shiloh, Bethel, and "All the way to Jerusalem, rocks—rocks—rocks. Roads infernal. Thought we never *would* get there." Their zigzag track for that period is at least half again as long as the Ba'albek to Figia to Damascus stages, and much more of it was up hill. Furthermore, here in *real* Bible-land, the party paused frequently for unhurried visits to places which do indeed have scriptural associations. They had to start early, of course, to keep to their taxing schedule: on the twenty-second, "Left Genin at 1 AM."; and the next morning, "Broke camp at 2.30 AM . . ." (MTN&J, I, 429–32). About this Mark Twain complained neither to his notebook nor, later, to his readers.

The twenty-second of September was a Sunday.

The pilgrims—at any rate *these* pilgrims—were not so strict about Sabbath observance as Mark Twain would have us believe. Lacking access to Colonel Denny's journal, the only record against which Mark Twain's can be systematically checked, Dewey Ganzel made the reasonable but wrong inference that our "sinners" and a back-sliding Birch risked Hell by faring forward on the Sabbath, leaving the "pilgrims"—he apparently means Church, Denny, and Davis—behind to keep a prayerful, restful Lord's Day in the tents. Not so: Denny's account of places visited that Sunday matches Mark Twain's; and he too testifies that, having failed to rendezvous with their tents, they were compelled to sleep on the ground.[13] Mark

12 *Yusef or The Journey of the Frangi. A Crusade in the East* (New York: Harper & Brothers, 1853), pp. 244–55. Other travel books and guidebooks of the period confirm that the party's pace was unexceptional.

13 Ganzel, pp. 228, 341. The journal of William R. Denny is in the Alderman Library, University of Virginia. Copy, Mark Twain Papers.

Twain again mentions that "the horses were cruelly tired" (*TIA*, p. 263; *IA*, Ch. 52, p. 554), but this time he does not blame their fatigue on Sabbatarian excesses. About the Sabbath he and Denny are equally silent. Nor in point of fact had either man's notebook mentioned the Sabbath the weekend before. It seems at least possible that the issue of Sabbath travel, always a favorite for Mark Twain, is a pure fiction—a serviceable fiction for dramatizing the differences, which were real enough, between the born-again and the unregenerated and for characterizing the pilgrims, the boys, and Mark Twain himself.

In the process of revising and expanding his travel letters to produce *The Innocents Abroad,* Mark Twain roughly doubled the number of attacks on the pilgrims and trebled their aggregate length. How many of the additions were inventions, departures from fact, it is impossible to say precisely, but their increase in number, length, and force leaves little doubt that he was aware of his theme and of the necessity of rendering it salient throughout the book. Having completed and delivered his manuscript, he had some trouble settling on a title.[14] His apparent favorite, "The New Pilgrims' Progress," was wisely relegated to subtitle status: its allusion to Bunyan is not really to the point. It is to be regretted that he and his audience had not read Edward Taylor, for that divine might have suggested a more apt title: "Mark Twain's Determinations Touching His Elect."

[14] *Mark Twain's Letters to his Publishers, 1867–1894,* ed. Hamlin Hill (Berkeley: Univ. of California Press, 1967), pp. 18–20.

Mark Twain: The Victorian of Southwestern Humor
Leland Krauth

W HEN Mark Twain moved into the New England culture, first in
1870 to its edge at Buffalo, and then in 1871 to one of its centers
at Hartford's Nook Farm, he came doubly disguised. Truly from the
South, he came to New England as a man from the West, and even
his Western identity was itself partially concealed by his fame as the
all-American traveler of *The Innocents Abroad*. While it is hyper-
bolic to say, as Van Wyck Brooks once did, that the New England
Twain entered was "emasculated by the Civil War," the war, together
with Westward migration, had reduced the male population of the
region, changing somewhat its cultural tone.[1] Many of the remaining writers and public figures were unwittingly participating in the
process of Victorianization that Ann Douglas has recently called the
"feminization of American culture."[2] In this context, as the deeper
layers of Mark Twain's personality expressed themselves, his presence
was notably—to use an old-fashioned term in a conventional way—
masculine. To genteel society he brought free drinking and smoking,
to morality he added humor, to sentiment, burlesque, to seriousness,
play. (Only Mark Twain's *study* had a billiards table.) He was in
part, as James M. Cox has observed, "an invader" of the dominant
culture of New England.[3]

While occupying New England, a secret Southerner in the North,
a man in a feminized world, Mark Twain extended himself imaginatively back into the world of his true origin, the Old Southwest. And
in this context, his presence was quite different. Twain's absorption of
and contributions to the traditions of Southwestern humor have been
extensively studied, but certain important aspects of his performance

[1] *The Ordeal of Mark Twain*, rev. ed. (1933; rpt. New York: Dutton, 1970), p. 91.
[2] *The Feminization of American Culture* (New York: Knopf, 1977).
[3] "Humor and America: The Southwest Bear Hunt," *Sewanee Review*, 83 (1975), 596.

as a Southwestern humorist in *Adventures of Huckleberry Finn* have not, I think, been fully perceived. For as he entered the territory of his past to create his finest fiction Twain brought to bear upon it a refinement more characteristic of New England than of the Old Southwest.

That Twain was steeped in the humorous traditions of the Old Southwest goes without saying these days. He owned personal copies of works by Augustus Baldwin Longstreet, Joseph M. Field, William Tappan Thompson, George Washington Harris, Johnson Jones Hooper, and Joseph G. Baldwin, and he planned to include most of these writers in *Mark Twain's Library of Humor*.[4] His knowledge of the tradition goes well beyond this, however, for as various critics have shown, the comic tradition of the Old Southwest was, in Bernard De Voto's words, the "matrix of Mark Twain's humor."[5] The scholarly investigation of his relationship to this tradition has thus established specific sources as well as the general influence of milieu, and the result is the widespread recognition that in Mark Twain "Southwestern humor reached its climax."[6] What kind of a climax was it?

The tensions that inform his masterpiece of Southwestern humor, *Huckleberry Finn*, were defined by Twain himself as he moved between his frontier days in the West and South and his genteel days to come in New England. Writing from New York in May 1867 as the Traveling Correspondent for the *Alta California*, Twain posted a now well-known notice of George Washington Harris' work. He praised a collection of Sut Lovingood's yarns, saying that the book "abounds in humor," and then he speculated that while it would "sell well in the West," the "Eastern people" would "call it coarse and possibly taboo it."[7] At the time of his report Twain was clearly in sympathy with Harris' humor, free from genteel taboos, but by the time he came to write *Huckleberry Finn* he was more firmly gov-

[4] For a listing of Twain's personal copies of Southwestern humorists, see Alan Gribben, *Mark Twain's Library: A Reconstruction*, 2 vols. (Boston: G. K. Hall, 1980); for the plans for *Mark Twain's Library of Humor*, see *Mark Twain's Notebooks & Journals*, II, ed. Frederick Anderson, Lin Salamo, and Bernard L. Stein (Berkeley: Univ. of California Press, 1975), 361–65.

[5] "The Matrix of Mark Twain's Humor," *Bookman*, 74 (1931), 172–78.

[6] M. Thomas Inge, "Introduction," *The Frontier Humorists: Critical Views* (Hamden, Conn.: Archon, 1975), p. 8.

[7] "Sut Lovingood," *Mark Twain's Travels With Mr. Brown*, ed. Franklin Walker and G. Ezra Dane (New York: Knopf, 1940), p. 221.

erned by a strong innate sense of propriety. And this is, I think, the key to understanding what he accomplishes within the tradition he employed. Twain reshapes the tradition of Southwestern humor by writing within it as a Victorian.[8]

To describe him as the Victorian of Southwestern humor is unfortunately to raise the specter of the long regional war waged so brilliantly by Brooks and De Voto (and often so dully by their followers) over Twain's "ordeal."[9] But I am not suggesting that the Wild Humorist of the Pacific Slope sold out to New England gentility at the cost of his artistry or that his art was fully nourished by the frontier he left behind him. On the contrary, I am emphasizing an *innate* propriety that was always a part of Mark Twain, a propriety that, if anything, marked him off from frontier life in the first place and finally led him to settle in New England. It was after all, to summon a single representative example, Twain himself, not those "sensitive & loyal subjects of the kingdom of heaven," Howells, Livy, and Livy's mother, who cleaned up the perceived impropriety of Huck's saying "they comb me all to hell."[10]

Twain's propriety, what I am calling his Victorianism, expressed itself in *Huckleberry Finn* in several ways. First, it led him to reshape some of the stock situations and characters common to the tradition of Southwestern humor. Second, it caused him to select from the raw materials of that tradition only certain subjects and, more important, to discard others. And third, it governed his creation of character, leading to the formation of a hero whose nature not only transcends the tradition but still challenges us today. Writing as a Victorian, Twain reformed Southwestern humor.

Four elements of *Huckleberry Finn* have repeatedly been singled out as particularly common to the tradition of Southwestern humor: the con-men (the Duke and the King), the camp meeting, the circus, and the Royal Nonesuch. But Twain's presentation of these tradi-

---

[8] Used casually in Twain scholarship for years, the term "Victorian" is general but apt. Many of his attitudes and values correspond remarkably with the ethos defined in such standard studies as Walter E. Houghton's *The Victorian Frame of Mind, 1830–1870* (New Haven: Yale Univ. Press, 1957) and Jerome H. Buckley's *The Victorian Temper: A Study in Literary Culture* (Cambridge: Harvard Univ. Press, 1951).

[9] See Brooks, *The Ordeal* and Bernard De Voto, *Mark Twain's America* (Boston: Little, Brown, 1932).

[10] *Mark Twain-Howells Letters*, ed. Henry Nash Smith and William M. Gibson, 2 vols. (Cambridge: Harvard Univ. Press, 1960), I, 122.

tional motifs is significantly different from the way they are treated by other Southwestern humorists. His greater complexity and seriousness have often been suggested, and in one of the most extended commentaries on his relation to Southwestern humor, Pascal Covici, Jr., has pointed out—as a distinguishing difference—a "preoccupation" in Twain "with revealing a discrepancy between seeming and reality."[11] This is certainly true, but what has been overlooked is the fact that Twain transforms the reality of such situations and characters even as he exposes their seeming. The camp meeting is a case in point.

Camp meetings were of course both realities of backwoods life and stock episodes in the humorous fiction that fastened onto that life. The differences between Twain's camp meeting and that of Johnson Jones Hooper in *Some Adventures of Captain Simon Suggs*, the literary work most often cited as a source, illustrate how Twain Victorianizes the tradition of Southwestern humor.[12] Hooper's camp meeting is at once an orgy, a fleecing, a thrill-filled happening, and a staged melodrama. The religious longings presumably informing the meeting are transparently bogus; the impulses that actually animate the gathering are sexual, monetary, sensational, and theatrical. Hooper is insistent upon the sensual aspect of the action. "Men and women," he writes, "rolled about on the ground, or lay sobbing or shouting in promiscuous heaps."[13] He exposes the sexual urgencies underlying the crowd's frenzy in a highly suggestive language:

"Keep the thing warm!" roared a sensual seeming man, of stout mould and florid countenance, who was exhorting among a bevy of young women, upon whom he was lavishing caresses. "Keep the thing warm, breethring!—come to the Lord, honey!" he added, as he vigorously hugged one of the damsels he sought to save.

[11] *Mark Twain's Humor: The Image of a World* (Dallas: Southern Methodist Univ. Press, 1962), p. 15.

[12] Hooper is cited as a source in *The Art of "Huckleberry Finn,"* ed. Hamlin Hill and Walter Blair (San Francisco: Chandler, 1962), p. 453, and in *Adventures of Huckleberry Finn,* ed. Sculley Bradley et al., 2nd ed. (New York: Norton, 1977), p. 253. For conflicting assessments of how successfully Twain uses Hooper, see De Voto, *Mark Twain's America*, p. 225, and Walter Blair, *Mark Twain & "Huck Finn"* (Berkeley: Univ. of California Press, 1960), pp. 279–81.

[13] *Some Adventures of Captain Simon Suggs* (Philadelphia: Carey and Hart, 1845), p. 119. Subsequent references to this edition are given parenthetically in my text. The camp meetings of both Hooper and Twain should be read in the light of such accounts of the "real thing" as those given in the *Autobiography of Peter Cartwright, The Backwoods Preacher,* ed. W. P. Strickland (Cincinnati: Cranston and Stowe, 1856).

. . . .

"Gl-o-*ree*!" yelled a huge . . . woman, as in a fit of the jerks, she threw herself convulsively from her feet, and fell "like a thousand of brick," across a diminutive old man in a little round hat, who was squeaking consolation to one of the mourners.

"Good Lord, have mercy!" ejaculated the little man. (pp. 120–21)

In his punning Hooper is daring as well as amusing. He writes here very much in the so-called strong masculine vein of Southwestern humor.

In his camp meeting Twain preserves the sense of the meeting's monetary, sensational, and theatrical impulses, but he all but eliminates the sexual. Huck gives us this description:

The women had on sun-bonnets; and some had linsey-woolsey frocks, some gingham ones, and a few of the young ones had on calico. Some of the young men was barefooted, and some of the children didn't have on any clothes but just a tow-linen shirt. Some of the old women was knitting, and some of the young folks was courting on the sly.[14]

This is far from the sexual antics of Hooper's fanatics, and it is far indeed from his ribald language. In fact, Huck's acknowledgment of covert play between the sexes is phrased in such a way as to suggest its essential innocence: "the young folks was courting on the sly." Twain does come somewhat closer to the sensual when he has Huck describe the crowd's response to the King's outlandish tale of conversion from piracy to missionary work, but again a transformation of the raw material of Southwestern humor is apparent:

So the king went all through the crowd with his hat, swabbing his eyes, and blessing the people and praising them and thanking them for being so good to the poor pirates away off there; and every little while the prettiest kind of girls, with the tears running down their cheeks, would up and ask him would he let them kiss him, for to remember him by; and he always done it; and some of them he hugged and kissed as many as five or six times—(p. 112)

The King is a bit of a lecher, though finally more interested in cash than kissing, and the young girls could be said to be sublimating their sexual urges, but what Twain invites us to laugh at them for is not their sublimated desires but their misplaced sentimentality.

14 *Adventures of Huckleberry Finn*, ed. Henry Nash Smith (Boston: Houghton Mifflin, 1958), p. 110. Subsequent references to this edition are given parenthetically in my text.

Twain's expurgation of the traditional camp meeting is representative of the way he Victorianizes the material of Southwestern humor. He effects similar changes in presenting his con men, the circus, and the Royal Nonesuch—his version of Gyascutus, that favorite exhibition of Southwestern lewdness. (Huck says the performance was enough to make "a cow laugh" [p. 127], but he characteristically declines to describe it.) In discussing Twain's ties to George Washington Harris (Harris of course creates a camp meeting that is almost as lascivious as Hooper's), one critic has suggested that they share a sense of "man's predisposition to dehumanize himself."[15] But more often than not in *Huckleberry Finn* Twain refuses to let his characters debase themselves by being the fully carnal, somewhat bestial creatures of their tradition.

Even more important than his virtual bowdlerizing of specific episodes common to Southwestern humor is Twain's selection of material from that body of writing. The traditional subjects of Southwestern humor have often been defined and even itemized. In the introduction to their fine collection, Hennig Cohen and William B. Dillingham offer this set of categories:

(1) The hunt

(2) Fights, mock fights, and animal fights

(3) Courtings, weddings, and honeymoons

(4) Frolics and dances

(5) Games, horse races, and other contests

(6) Militia drills

(7) Elections and electioneering

(8) The legislature and the courtroom

(9) Sermons, camp meetings, and religious experiences

(10) The visitor in a humble home

(11) The country boy in the city

(12) The riverboat

(13) Adventures of the rogue

(14) Pranks and tricks of the practical joker

(15) Gambling

(16) Trades and swindles

(17) Cures, sickness and bodily discomfort, medical treatments

(18) Drunks and drinking

(19) Dandies, foreigners, and city slickers

(20) Oddities and local eccentrics[16]

---

[15] Hennig Cohen, "Mark Twain's Sut Lovingood," in *The Lovingood Papers,* ed. Ben Harris McClary (Knoxville: Univ. of Tennessee Press, 1962), p. 21.

[16] *Humor of the Old Southwest,* 2nd. ed. (Athens: Univ. of Georgia Press, 1975), p. xvii.

While no single work of Southwestern humor contains all these, some come close. *Huckleberry Finn* does not. What is revealing, however, is not the number of these conventional topics absent from *Huckleberry Finn* but the particular kinds that are absent. It ignores, first of all, those subjects, like courtings, frolics, dances, weddings, and honeymoons, that naturally involve adult sexuality. And secondly, it omits entirely or else skims over those activities, like hunting, fighting, gambling, gaming, horse racing, heavy drinking, and military maneuvering, that are the traditional pastimes of manly backwoods living. (Whenever such activities do appear briefly they are targets of ridicule.) In short, Twain purges from the Southwestern tradition its exuberant celebration of rough-and-tumble masculinity.

D. H. Lawrence's famous dogmatic summary of the essential American "soul" may not do justice to the heroes of classic American fiction, but the summary is a fitting description of the recurrent hero of Southwestern humor: "hard, isolate, stoic, and a killer."[17] When Twain appropriates the type he disparages it far more than his predecessors do, and, unlike his forerunners in Southwestern humor, he reveals the pernicious traits in gentleman and commoner alike. The adult white males in *Huckleberry Finn* are indeed hard, isolate, stoic, and lethal. From the new Judge who threatens to reform the drunken Pap "with a shot-gun" to Colonel Sherburn, who does reform the drunken Boggs with a "pistol," the men in the novel are aggressive and destructive (pp. 21, 121). The book is surcharged with an atmosphere of imminent violence whose source is simply the nature of white males. The ferocity they embody erupts in the antics of Pap, in the search of the slave hunters, in the feud between the Grangerfords and Shepherdsons, in the relationship of the Duke to the King, in the mob that rides them out of town on a rail, and in the acts of the *Walter Scott* gang, as well as in the gunning down of Boggs. The terror of this masculine violence is intensified by its arbitrariness. When Huck is seeking information about Cairo the day after he has fooled the pair of slave hunters, he meets a nameless man setting a trotline from his skiff. Their encounter is emblematic of the male world of the novel:

[17] *Studies in Classic American Literature* (1922; rpt. Garden City, New York: Doubleday, 1951), p. 73.

"Mister, is that Cairo?"

"Cairo? no. You must be a blame' fool."

"What town is it, mister?"

"If you want to know, go and find out. If you stay here botherin' around me for about a half a minute longer, you'll get something you won't want."[18]   (p. 79)

Twain's imagination seems haunted by the memory of a gratuitous hostility in men that borders on violence. The memory is partly of literature, of the rough men who people Southwestern humor, but it is also a recollection of life, of his life in Hannibal, on the river, and in the West. And no doubt this image of man has something to do with the father, John Marshall Clemens, the Judge and Southern gentleman of whom Mark Twain once secretly recorded: "Silent, austere, of perfect probity and high principle; ungentle of manner toward his children, but always a gentleman in his phrasing—and never punished them—a look was enough, and more than enough."[19] Although Twain is sixty-two when he makes this notation, the remembrance of fear is still strong—"a look was enough, and more than enough." Hamlin Hill has recently suggested that "fear" was in fact "the controlling emotion" of Mark Twain's life.[20] Certainly fear is the dominant emotion in Huck Finn's experience, and it is most often a fear engendered by the men of his world (Huck is never afraid of women).

In their verbal and physical aggressions the men in *Huckleberry Finn* express their pride, uphold their honor, and assert their manhood—all of which seem for them somehow in question. Pap's raging complaint is that "*a man* can't get his rights" (p. 24, my italics), and Colonel Sherburn's phillipic turns precisely upon the question of what makes "a *man*" (p. 124, Twain's italics). The issue for Twain is far-reaching. Oddly, although it is central to his life, cropping up as a question of courage in his youth, his river piloting,

[18] In "The Raft Episode in *Huckleberry Finn,*" *Modern Fiction Studies*, 14 (1968), 11–20, Peter G. Beidler suggests that some of the meaning of Huck's encounter with the fisherman has been lost by the deletion of the raftsmen's passage. If, as Beidler believes, the omitted passage makes it clear that Huck and Jim have already passed Cairo, then its inclusion would explain why the fisherman thinks Huck is a "blame' fool." But there is still no explanation for his hostility and gratuitous threat of violence.

[19] Mark Twain, "Villagers of 1840–3," *Hannibal, Huck & Tom,* ed. Walter Blair (Berkeley: Univ. of California Press, 1969), p. 39.

[20] *Mark Twain: God's Fool* (New York: Harper & Row, 1973), p. 269.

his brief Civil War experience, his days in the West, and in particular in his abortive duel, Twain's sense of manliness has never been fully explored.[21] Yet from his Western sketches, on through *Huckleberry Finn* and *Simon Wheeler, Detective*, to the late essay "The United States of Lyncherdom," to mention only a few obvious examples, he was preoccupied with the idea of manliness. Significantly, it was bound up for him with two issues that are central to *Huckleberry Finn*: the sense of freedom and the concept of the gentleman. In an 1866 letter to his boyhood friend Will Bowen (a part of which was later to emerge in "Old Times on the Mississippi") Twain conflated manliness, independence, and gentlemanliness (all the italics are his):

> I am sorry to hear *any* harm of any pilot—for I hold those old river friends above all others, & I know that in genuine *manliness* they assay away above the common multitude. You know, yourself, Bill—or you *ought* to know it—that *all* men—kings & serfs alike—are *slaves* to other men & to circumstances—save, alone, the pilot—who comes at no man's beck or call, obeys no man's orders & scorns all men's suggestions. . . . It is a strange study,—a singular phenomenon, if you please, that the only real, independent & genuine *gentlemen* in the world go quietly up & down the Mississippi river, asking no homage of any one, seeking no popularity, no notoriety, & not caring a damn whether school keeps or not.[22]

Huck goes quietly down the Mississippi, asking "no homage of any one, seeking no popularity, no notoriety, & not caring a damn whether school keeps or not." It is no accident that when Huck struggles with his conscience, trying to bring himself to turn Jim in, Twain specifically has Huck denounce himself for his failure to do the "right" thing in the language of manhood. "I warn't," Huck says, "man enough—hadn't the spunk of a rabbit" (p. 76). On the contrary, of course. In resisting the pressures of his society, the norms that dictate Jim's return to slavery, Huck demonstrates not only his freedom but also his true manhood. Like the pilot of Twain's vision, Huck assays above the multitude in genuine manliness. His

[21] The sexual dimension of the issue is raised provocatively by G. Legman, *Mark Twain: The Mammoth Cod* (Milwaukee: Maledicta, 1976), pp. 1–17; but see also my very different "Mark Twain Fights Sam Clemens' Duel," *Mississippi Quarterly*, 33 (1980), 141–53.

[22] *Mark Twain's Letters to Will Bowen*, ed. Theodore Hornberger (Austin: Univ. of Texas Press, 1941), pp. 13–14.

fortitude in determining to free Jim at whatever cost to himself stands in stark contrast to the self-vaunting courage of the other white males of the novel—and of their prototypes in previous Southwestern humor. Twain recreates the hero of that tradition in Huck, replacing the aggressive, violent male with a passive, loving one. Further, through Jim, Twain ascribes to Huck an additional status. As a recent critic has pointed out, a number of "labels" are imposed on Huck, none of which fits the reality of his character.[23] Thus to the Widow Douglas he is a "poor lost lamb," and to Pap he is "a good deal of a big-bug," while to Miss Watson he is simply a "fool" (pp. 3, 18, 11). Only Jim, who comes to know Huck intimately on the raft, really apprehends the essence of Huck's character. He articulates for us the significance of Huck. On the most intimate level, Huck is "de ole true Huck," Jim's "bes' fren'," but Huck is for Jim also something more: he is a "white genlman" (p. 76).

Huck is the true man and gentleman of the novel, Twain's most radical departure from the tradition that nurtured him. Before Twain the gentleman was trapped in the frame of the Southwestern tale, reduced to moralizing about the action in polite language, while the free and the manly were represented by the unfeeling, amoral, violent vulgarians of the story itself.[24] But in Huck the free, the manly, and the moral coalesce. In order to create Huck—to recreate the conventional hero of the tradition—Twain altered the formal tactics of Southwestern humor in two important ways. First, he changed the frame, that structural division between the conventional gentleman narrator and his vulgar heroes which created a separation between the author's world of order, reason, and morality, and the actor's life of disorder, violence, and amorality. Twain eliminated this division by fusing, in the words of Kenneth Lynn, "the Gentleman and the Clown" into a "single character," into Huck himself.[25] Second,

---

[23] Louise K. Barnett, "Huck Finn: Picaro as Linguistic Outsider," *College Literature,* 6 (1979), 225.

[24] The seminal discussion of the frame device, a hallmark of Southwestern humor, is Walter Blair, *Native American Humor* (New York: American Book Co., 1937), pp. 90–92. Two useful yet differing perspectives on the humor generated by the frame are provided by Louis J. Budd, "Gentlemanly Humorists of the Old South," *Southern Folklore Quarterly,* 17 (1953), 232–40, who emphasizes the elite outlook of these humorists, and James M. Cox, "Humor of the Old Southwest," *The Comic Imagination in America,* ed. Louis D. Rubin, Jr. (New Brunswick: Rutgers Univ. Press, 1973), pp. 101–12, who acknowledges their gentility but nonetheless stresses their "cooperation" with the vulgar heroes.

[25] *Mark Twain "and" Southwestern Humor* (Boston: Little, Brown, 1959), p. 148.

Twain profoundly changed the tradition of Southwestern humor by changing the language of its narrative; he transformed, as James M. Cox has put it, the traditional "dialect" into "vernacular."[26] These changes gave birth to Huck, but their implications have not been fully understood.

The union of gentleman and vulgarian suggests, on the face of it, a re-alignment of sympathies—away from the conventional and elite toward the radical and common. This is in fact how Twain's achievement is frequently described. But I would suggest that the effect of the formal fusion is just the reverse: instead of committing himself to the common person through his union of gentleman and vulgarian, Mark Twain *elevates the common* beyond itself. The second formal act operates even more clearly in the same way. For to transform dialect into vernacular is to raise the crude language of a restricted region to the broader plain of a more versatile and more nearly universal speech.

Huck has, as recent critics have emphasized, a dual role in his novel: he is, in Alan Trachtenberg's terms, both "the verbalizer of the narrative" and "a character within the narrative."[27] As verbalizer of the narrative, although his language is vernacular, Huck preserves a linguistic decorum—a decorum that would have puzzled the likes of, say, Sut Lovingood, but pleased almost any of the Southwestern *authors*. Huck reports that the speech of Pap "was all the hottest kind of language" (p. 25), and he tells us that, while he himself had "stopped cussing" living at the Widow Douglas' because "the widow didn't like it," he "took to it again" (p. 22) living in the woods with Pap. But of course Huck never *uses* the words, his or Pap's. Huck's propriety of language within the vernacular is one sign of the infusion of the gentleman into Huck—of his more Victorian character. Another is Huck's treatment of sexual material. Here the verbalizer and the character become identical, for not only does Huck as narrator shy away from sexual or sexually suggestive language but Huck as actor also shuns the erotic. The most striking example of Huck's

[26] *Mark Twain: The Fate of Humor* (Princeton: Princeton Univ. Press, 1966), p. 167. While describing Huck's language as dialect rather than vernacular, David Carkeet, "The Dialects in *Huckleberry Finn*," *American Literature*, 51 (1979), 315–32, points out that among the various dialects Huck's is the *least* like the speech employed by traditional Southwestern humorists.

[27] "The Form of Freedom in *Adventures of Huckleberry Finn*," *Southern Review*, NS, 6 (1970), 960.

modesty occurs when he and Jim enter the floating house that contains the dead Pap. To the reader it is clear that the house—with its "naked" dead man, "old whisky bottles," "bed," two old dirty calico dresses," and "some women's underclothes" (pp. 43-44)—is either a bawdy house or a house where bawdy activities have been pursued. Huck's narrative gives no sign of whether he has taken this in, but what it does reveal is his response to the graffiti on the walls. Huck says, "all over the walls was the ignorantest kind of words and pictures, made with charcoal" (p. 44). His condemnation of such writings as "ignorantest" is more than a joke; it is indicative of the delicacy in Huck that leads him to keep his own narrative language free from crudity. Further, incorrect as it is, Huck's use of "ignorantest" draws some of its force from the recent conflict in his life between the widow Douglas, who would educate him in the ways of civilization, and Pap, who would keep him as ignorant as he is in order to insure that he is not "better'n" his father (p. 18). But Huck is clearly more civilized than Pap in speech as well as action (as verbalizer as well as character). Although Jim conceals the fact of Pap's death from Huck, Huck's rejection of the pornographic is tantamount to a rejection of the world of his father at its deepest core.[28]

Huck's avoidance of profanity and his disapproval of the pornographic point to his character as authentic gentleman, just as his courage in behalf of Jim points to his manliness. Transformed as he is from the crude, violent, and amoral hero of Southwestern humor, Huck can be seen as the unlikely representative of true civilization. Twain's novel thus presents more than a simple conflict between a debased society and a primitive goodness; it reveals in Huck the foundation of a genuine civilization. That foundation is nicely summed up in Ortega y Gasset's insistence that the human root of civilization is "the desire on the part of each individual to take others into consideration."[29] In these terms, Huck, the most considerate free person in the novel, is clearly the most civilized.

[28] If we take into account the distinction insisted upon by Watson Branch, "Hard-Hearted Huck: 'No Time to Be Sentimentering,' " *Studies in American Fiction*, 6 (1978), 212-18, between the past when the events of the narrative occurred and the present in which Huck writes of them, then Huck's description of the scene of Pap's death can be said to be informed by Huck's knowledge of the death.

[29] Jose Ortega y Gasset, *The Revolt of the Masses* (1932; rpt. New York: Norton, 1957), p. 76. For Ortega barbarism becomes the disposition "not" to "take others into account," a formulation that fits well the other free white men in the novel.'

Henry Nash Smith has called attention to the presence in the novel of "a residue of the eighteenth-century cult of sensibility,"[30] but no one to my knowledge has made the obvious connection between this cult of sensibility and Huck himself. The historical emphasis upon sensibility carried well beyond the eighteenth century of course, becoming a prominent feature of nineteenth-century Victorian life and art, especially the "feminized" American version of it. In attending to such emotionalism Twain was not only being true to his novel's setting in the 1830s or 1840s; he was also commenting on current postures in his own society. The sentimental was, in short, very much with Mark Twain. It was also *in* him. Twain's burlesque of the cult in *Huckleberry Finn* is in part, I believe, a check against his own susceptibility, and in part a diversion calculated to deflect our attention away from Huck's own overabundance of emotion. A further disguise of "de ole true Huck" is provided by Huck's role *as critic* of the sentimental. Huck memorably dismisses emotional outpourings as "tears and flapdoodle," "soul-butter and hogwash," "rot and slush" (p. 138). But Huck himself is governed by intense feeling, and at times he gives voice to his emotions in fairly sentimental ways. Unlike the various imposters in the novel who call themselves gentlemen, weeping soulful tears only to perpetrate violent acts, Huck is always a *gentle*-man. His tenderness is extraordinary. For he is, I suggest, Mark Twain's version of the eighteenth-century Man of Feeling.

The ideas that generated the Man of Feeling may be summarized as follows: first, the identification of virtue with acts of benevolence and with feelings of universal good will; second, the assumption that good affections, benevolent feelings, are the natural outgrowth of the heart of man; third, the conviction that tenderness is manly; and fourth, the belief that benevolent emotions, even anguished ones, result in pleasant, self-approving feelings.[31] The first three of these, I suggest, fit Huck's character perfectly. He is virtuous in his predisposition to aid virtually everyone he encounters, from the Widow Douglas to the *Walter Scott* gang, from the Grangerfords to the Shepherdsons, from Aunt Sally to Jim, from Mary Jane Wilks to

30 Henry Nash Smith, *Mark Twain: The Development of A Writer* (Cambridge: Harvard Univ. Press, 1962), p. 117.

31 I follow closely here R. S. Crane, "Suggestions Toward a Genealogy of the 'Man of Feeling'," *ELH*, 1 (1934), 205–30.

the con-men who would defraud her. This universal good will in Huck is indeed rooted in his heart, the one Twain praised as "sound."[32] And without question Huck's tenderness is manly; his tears are strong and genuine. Twain's departure from the archetype of the Man of Feeling lies in his rejection of the fourth engendering idea: the notion that pleasure can be derived from painful benevolent emotions. This is a crucial variation, one that saves Twain's character from absurd postures of self-approving joy, and more important, one that makes Huck a *comic* Man of Feeling. Huck never feels good about his goodness; his altruistic emotions—with the possible exception of his aid to Mary Jane—never give him egoistic satisfaction. For of course Huck always thinks that in following his fine feelings he is acting immorally. His confusion is the source of our laughter.

"I cried a little," Huck says, "when I was covering up Buck's face" (p. 98), and when he learns that Jim has been sold by the Duke and the King, he reports, "then I set down and cried; I couldn't help it" (p. 177). In his narrative Huck is recurrently tearful, but most often it is the refusal to set forth his feelings—"I ain't agoing to tell *all* that happened" (p. 97)—that persuades us of the depth and authenticity of his emotions. Huck's mode of narrating, in both its language and its flat, matter-of-fact style, conveys his tenderness without sentimental excess. Nothing is more persuasive in just this way than the moment when Huck, accompanied by Tom, who is for once silent and forgotten, first sees Jim in the privacy of the Phelps cabin after their forced separation: "We crept in under Jim's bed into the cabin, and pawed around and found the candle and lit it, and stood over Jim a while, and found him looking hearty and healthy, and then we woke him up gentle and gradual" (p. 207). At times, however, Huck's account, in style and language, flirts with the "rot and slush" of sentimental piety: "It was only a little thing to do, and no trouble; and it's the little things that smoothes people's roads the most, down here below" (p. 160). Only the fact that the "it" here is a *lie* (one that "wouldn't cost nothing" [p. 160]) saves Huck's utterance from emotional stickiness. What the remark reveals is how bound together in *Huckleberry Finn* humor and sentiment are.

Twain, who said surprisingly little about humor for a humorist, once insisted that "a man can never be a humorist, in thought or deed,

---

[32] Notebook #28a [I], TS, p. 35 (1895), Mark Twain Papers, as quoted in Smith, "Introduction," *Huckleberry Finn*, p. xvi.

until he can feel the springs of pathos."[33] It is often the pathos of
Huck's experience as gentle Man of Feeling that creates the humor
in the book. And this, too, is something new in the tradition of
Southwestern humor. What is generally thought to be Huck's finest
moment, his decision to steal Jim out of slavery and go to hell, is both
his greatest moment of pathos and one of the most humorous
moments in the entire book. The pathos emerges as Huck faces his
dilemma:

> I went to the raft, and set down in the wigwam to think. But I couldn't
> come to nothing. I thought till I wore my head sore, but I couldn't see
> no way out of the trouble. After all this long journey, and after all we'd
> done for them scoundrels, here was it all come to nothing, everything all
> busted up and ruined, because they could have the heart to serve Jim
> such a trick as that, and make him a slave again all his life, and amongst
> strangers, too, for forty dirty dollars. (pp. 177–78)

Huck's language remains steadfastly colloquial, and its earthy in-
correctness checks against sentimentality at the same time it provokes
amusement. But his style significantly veers away from its characteristic pattern. Huck most often writes run-on sentences that lack
subordination and so equalize the events he strings together.[34] Here,
however, emotion begins to build in the fourth sentence as Huck
registers in two subordinates the catastrophe of Jim's return to
slavery as a betrayal of a shared past: "After all this long journey,
and after all we'd done for them scoundrels, here was it all come to
nothing." The inversion, "here was it," is a further departure from
Huck's usually natural speech, one designed to focus and intensify
feeling. His emotion breaks into a moral indignation at the end that
is realized in the language of feeling hearts and in a syntax that
bespeaks compounding emotion: "because they could have the
heart to serve Jim such a trick as that, and make him a slave again all
his life, and amongst strangers, too, for forty dirty dollars."

The climax of Huck's feeling comes in the full recollection of his
time with Jim, one of the most admired passages in the novel:

---

[33] "Visit of Mark Twain/Wit and Humour," Sydney (Australia) *Morning Herald*, 17
September 1895, pp. 5–6, as reproduced in Louis J. Budd, "Mark Twain Talks Mostly
About Humor and Humorists," *Studies in American Humor*, 1 (1974), 11.

[34] For an extended examination of Huck's style and its implications, see Janet H.
McKay, " 'Tears and Flapdoodle': Point of View and Style in *The Adventures of Huckleberry
Finn*," *Style*, 10 (1976), 41–50.

I felt good and all washed clean of sin for the first time I had ever felt so in my life, and I knowed I could pray now. But I didn't do it straight off, but laid the paper down and set there thinking—thinking how good it was all this happened so, and how near I come to being lost and going to hell. And went on thinking. And got to thinking over our trip down the river; and I see Jim before me, all the time, in the day, and in the night-time, sometimes moonlight, sometimes storms, and we a floating along, talking, and singing, and laughing. But somehow I couldn't seem to strike no places to harden me against him, but only the other kind. I'd see him standing my watch on top of his'n, stead of calling me, so I could go on sleeping; and see him how glad he was when I come back out of the fog; and when I come to him again in the swamp, up there where the feud was; and such-like times; and would always call me honey, and pet me, and do everything he could think of for me, and how good he always was; and at last I struck the time I saved him by telling the men we had small-pox aboard, and he was so grateful, and said I was the best friend old Jim ever had in the world, and the *only* one he's got now; and then I happened to look around, and see that paper. (p. 179)

The pathos here is worthy of Dickens. Huck's style becomes rather conventionally poetic, as he employs repetition, alliteration, assonance, and artfully balanced rhythms. He is in fact writing in the cadences of gentility, evoking refined gentlemanly sentiment: "all the time, in the day, and in the night-time, sometimes moonlight, sometimes storms, and we floating along, talking, and singing, and laughing."[35] This is a touching, idealized image of the times on the raft, more lyric than any on-the-spot descriptions of them. This welling of pathetic emotion makes unbelievable, moving, and *comic* Huck's desperate resolution—"All right, then, I'll *go* to hell" (p. 180)—for of course we know that no one of such fine and tender feeling can be damned. Twain achieves here precisely what he once praised in William Dean Howells' fiction as the power to make the reader "cry inside" and "laugh all the time."[36]

[35] In *Democracy and the Novel* (New York: Oxford Univ. Press, 1978), pp. 109–14, Henry Nash Smith also calls attention to Huck's shift into a more conventional language and style. For Smith this betrays the moral contamination of Huck's consciousness by the dominant culture. I would add that it reveals as well the impress of the cult of sensibility. As he slides into a more or less conventionally poetic style, Huck voices the delicacy of feeling espoused, though seldom attained, by the dominant culture; writing for a moment in the cadences of gentility, he in effect authenticates the ideal of feeling so spuriously upheld by the culture.

[36] *Twain-Howells Letters*, II, 533.

Jesse Bier has explained one impetus behind Southwestern humor as a reaction against the "prettification" of American writing in the nineteenth century.[37] Twain was in turn reacting against the coarseness of the Southwestern tradition. While exerting to one degree or another his rowdy-side within the New England culture he invaded, Twain expressed his own propriety while writing within the tradition of Southwestern humor. (The impulse to run counter to the norm was always strong in this man who contained within himself so many contrary selves.) Far from being a simple bowdlerizing, Twain's Victorian reformation on the material and hero of Southwestern humor enacted a profound concept whose cultural implications are still challenging. In its tradition and beyond it to our time *Huckleberry Finn* is a radical novel.

Huckleberry Finn is still challenging today because of its portrayal of a Man of Feeling whose degree of tenderness defies not only the sexual stereotypes of Southwestern humor but also the still-prevailing values of our own times. Huck's delicacy and tenderness exceed, even today, the popular sense of what constitutes a man's feelings. Leslie Fiedler's now-famous perception of a secret "male love" at the center of *Huckleberry Finn* both points accurately to a core of feeling and misconstrues it into a "homoerotic" bond.[38] More recently, Harold H. Kolb, Jr., has reviewed Huck's "seemingly motiveless benignity" and ended by calling him a "seven dollar Friendship's Offering moral idealist."[39] Apparently, it is only by employing provocatively a skewed language of love, as Fiedler does, or by using ironically the sentimental language of nineteenth-century women's books, as Kolb does, that we can come to terms with Huck's fineness of feeling. His kind of manliness seems to elude our language for it, even today.

[37] *The Rise and Fall of American Humor* (New York: Holt Rinehart & Winston, 1968), p. 63.
[38] Leslie Fiedler, "Come Back to the Raft Ag'in, Huck Honey!", *Partisan Review*, 15 (1948), 666–67.
[39] Harold H. Kolb, Jr., "Mark Twain, Huck Finn, and Jacob Blivens: Gilt-Edged, Tree-Calf Morality in *The Adventures of Huckleberry Finn*," *Virginia Quarterly Review*, 55 (1979), 663.

How Mark Twain Survived
Sam Clemens' Reformation
Jeffrey Steinbrink

"**I**F I were settled I would quit all nonsense & swindle some ⟨poor⟩ girl into marrying me," Sam Clemens wrote Mary Mason Fairbanks. "But I wouldn't expect to be '*worthy*' of her. I wouldn't *have* a girl that *I* was worthy of. *She* wouldn't do. She wouldn't be respectable enough."[1] The letter was written on 12 December 1867, just fifteen days before he met Olivia Langdon, the girl he would in fact marry a little more than two years later. During those two years, at first with Mother Fairbanks' finger wagging at him in their correspondence, and then with his idealization of Olivia to encourage him, Clemens earnestly undertook a reformation of character that was intended to make him a conventionally "better" person—more religious, more regular in his habits, more refined, more comprehensively civilized. But if Sam Clemens grew up, got religion, and became respectable, what would become of Mark Twain? How does a man who believes—and hopes—that he has sown the last of his wild oats preserve the vitality of a character who has just risen to national prominence in large part by portraying himself as a heedless and irreverent vagabond?

My intention here is not to initiate a sweeping reassessment of the

---

[1] Quotations from letters by Mark Twain are drawn from the printer's copy of the first two volumes of *Mark Twain's Collected Letters*, prepared by the Mark Twain Project in the Bancroft Library for publication by the University of California Press. Dates of letters cited appear either in the text of the essay or in parentheses. All previously unpublished words by Mark Twain are © 1983 by Edward J. Willi and Manufacturers Hanover Trust Company as Trustees of the Mark Twain Foundation, which reserves all reproduction or dramatization rights in every medium. The symbol (*) appears in citations for these cases. Previously published letters by Mark Twain quoted from *Collected Letters* have been correctly established from the authoritative documents for the first time and are © 1983 by the Regents of the University of California. All quotations from Mark Twain are published here with the permission of the University of California Press and Robert H. Hirst, General Editor of the Mark Twain Project. The abbreviation MTP refers to the archive of the Mark Twain Papers, the Bancroft Library, University of California, Berkeley, California. The full text of letters cited may be found in the first two volumes of *Collected Letters* (Univ. of California Press, forthcoming 1984).

"repression" Clemens may have experienced at the hands of his wife
and other putative censors over the course of his career. It is, rather,
to examine a discrete, strategic moment in that career when he first
came seriously to test the prerogatives of "Mark Twain" as a literary
persona against what he took to be the demands and attractions of
Eastern propriety. I mean to confine my discussion to the years
1867–1869, when I think Clemens' reformist zeal was at its intensest
and when I believe the basic terms of accommodation between
writer and persona were at least provisionally established. During
this period he came East (for good, as it turned out), gained inter-
national renown and the beginnings of a considerable fortune with
the bestseller *Innocents Abroad*, won the hand of the very respectable
Miss Langdon, and settled down as a newspaper proprietor and
editor in Buffalo. Each of these accomplishments represented a profound change of circumstance and, potentially, of outlook in the
former Wild Humorist of the Pacific Slope; even in a life as charged
with fortuity and calamity as Clemens', this period is remarkable for
its compression of crucial choices and turns of fate. By the time it
drew to a close in the fall of 1869 with the move to Buffalo, the
most fundamental of Clemens' manifold lifelong reformations had
subsided, and Mark Twain, the persona, had survived, essentially
intact and somehow still intimately bound to his ostensibly more
"worthy" creator. Clemens' solution to the problem of gaining
respectability, that is to say, was not simply to divorce himself from
the persona; if anything, in fact, Sam Clemens and Mark Twain
grew closer together as the movement from Elmira to Buffalo to
Hartford progressed.

Clemens was determined to "improve," to become more conventionally respectable, *before* he met Olivia Langdon in December,
1867. During the *Quaker City* voyage that began in June of that year,
perhaps at the urging of Mary Fairbanks and others, he resolved that
the time had come to purge both his life and his writing of their
coarseness. This is not to say, as he himself sometimes implied, that
the early Clemens/Twain was an ignorant vulgarian, but rather that
the writer became increasingly self-conscious about what he considered his own limitations and those of the prevailing Western
humorists as he grew more successful. Dixon Wecter suggests that
Clemens was ready and even eager to come under the jurisdiction of
a good-hearted and domineering matron—a more formidable Widow

Douglas—by the time the *Quaker City* set sail.[2] With Mary Fairbanks just as eagerly playing the part of "Mother," a phase of Clemens' reformation which might be called comic, but not farcical, had begun.

Clemens spent most of this year-long comic phase on the road. In New York, probably on 27 December 1867, he met Olivia Langdon and passed a few days there with her and her family. While he may have been attracted to her at the time, he seems hardly to have been smitten, and he was not to see or even to correspond with her again until August of 1868, when the comic phase dramatically ended with his profession of love for her. Olivia may have been vaguely on his mind during this interim, but there is no evidence to show that he was consciously or deliberately "improving" for her sake. Instead, he was hustling up and down the east coast, returning to San Francisco and the Nevada lecture circuit, giving speeches, writing for newspapers and magazines, trying to complete the manuscript of *Innocents Abroad*, and periodically sending off dispatches to Mother Fairbanks regarding her cub's progress. "I *am* going to settle down some day," he assured her, "even if I have to do it in a cemetery" (17 June 1868).

Clemens' letters during this period are communiqués from an exhilaratingly *un*settled writer, one whose ethical/esthetic reformation is much less pressing than the day-to-day demands of editors and lecture sponsors. They indicate, however, that Clemens was mindful of his pledge to improve at a time when he was involved in revising the *Alta* letters and writing new material for *The Innocents Abroad*, whose manuscript would be virtually completed in June. Leon T. Dickinson has examined this work closely and observes that Clemens consistently pruned indelicacies, slang, and vulgarisms as he transformed his *Quaker City* correspondence into text for the book, changes that he seems to have been as pleased to make as Mother Fairbanks, for one, was to witness. Further, Dickinson argues that Clemens was able to effect these changes without robbing passages of their humor or vitality.[3] "Improving" as he was, Clemens seems also to have been determined to soften his attack on European culture in

---

[2] *Mark Twain to Mrs. Fairbanks* (San Marino, Cal.: Huntington Library, 1949), p. xxiii.

[3] "Mark Twain's Revisions in Writing *The Innocents Abroad*," *American Literature*, 19 (1947), 139–57. For a later consideration of these changes see Robert H. Hirst, "The Making of *The Innocents Abroad*: 1867–1872," Diss. Univ. of California, Berkeley, 1975.

the course of the *Innocents Abroad* revisions. A letter to Emeline Beach, another of his *Quaker City* companions, emphasizes the parallel he saw at the time between the literary and the personal reformations he was trying to accomplish: "I have joked about the old masters a good deal in my [*Alta California*] letters, but nearly all of that will have to come out. I cannot afford to expose my want of cultivation too much. Neither can I afford to remain so uncultivated—& shall not, if I am capable of rising above it" (10 February 1868*). The manuscript of *The Innocents Abroad*, then, was partially to bear witness to the writer's reformation.

Clemens' attitude toward the revision of both his book and his character reflected the mixture of play and seriousness which typified the comic phase of his reformation: He was able to regard himself, his work, and his persona with a bemused detachment that allowed him to maintain his balance as he anticipated and adjusted to his rising fortunes. The restraints under which he operated, most of them self-imposed, were mild, and his response to them ironic and tolerant. He seems at the time to have been neither threatened nor impaired by his ambition to become conventionally "better" because he himself was aware of its comic dimension and so remained in control of it. This ambition required no violent disjunction between his present and past selves, no repudiation of his earlier life or work for the sake of radical reform. There was no need to cut Samuel Clemens free of Mark Twain; the two could continue to stumble along together. Clemens was candid about his faults and shortcomings, but he was largely self-accepting, if not complacent, during the comic phase. "I am not as lazy as I was," he teased Mother Fairbanks, "—but I am lazy enough yet, for two people. But I am improving all the time" (12 December 1867). His stance was that of a meliorist and, at that, a meliorist whose attention to reform was easily distracted.

That posture was to change drastically in late August, 1868, when Clemens paid a long-postponed visit to Elmira and fell thoroughly in love with Olivia Langdon. By the time he departed from the Langdon household in early September he left behind a letter to his would-be sweetheart that reflected the changes in tone and attitude he had begun to undergo. "It is better to have loved & lost you," he wrote Olivia, who had of course turned aside his first advances, "than that my life should have remained forever the blank it was before. For once, at least, in the idle years that have drifted over me, I have seen the world all beautiful, & known what it was to hope. For once I have known what it was to feel my sluggish pulses stir with a living ambition" (7 September 1868). We look in vain for the wink or "snapper" that typically accompanies such a piece of florid writing from Mark Twain. But no wink is forthcoming; the letter continues for the most part in the same earnest, superheated fashion and then concludes with a revealing instance of revision: "Write me *something*," Clemens pleads. ". . . If it be a suggestion, I will entertain it; if it be an injunction, I will honor it; if it be a command I will obey it or ⟨break my royal neck⟩ exhaust my energies trying." The flippant "break my royal neck" has no place here and is virtually obliterated in the manuscript of the letter by a close-looped crossout.[4] The phrase is appropriate to Mark Twain, of course, as well as to the cub Sam Clemens, but it is clearly inappropriate in the discourse of a man who hopes to establish himself as a suitor worthy of Olivia Langdon. The gap had dramatically widened between what the writer of this letter had been and what he wished to become.

Clemens wanted to be taken seriously by Olivia and her parents—that is, to be taken as a serious *man*—and in the process he seems to have come to believe that he ought to take himself seriously as well. Thus began the melodramatic phase of his reformation, during which he sought more fervently than ever before to embrace conventional values and to "prove" himself according to conventional standards. It is reductive and unfair, as Max Eastman and Henry Nash Smith, among others, have cogently argued, to hold Olivia, the Langdons, or the East accountable for these accommodations on Clemens' part; his preconceived notions of respectability had more to do than they with the transformation of the ironist to the zealot.[5] His courtship of Olivia, however, lent urgency to his reformist intentions and encouraged him to believe that his change for the better could and should be radical rather than ameliorative. He seems, in fact, to have caught himself in the snare he set for her: The more emphatically he pledged himself to improve, the more feverishly he came to believe in the necessity and desirability of a sweeping reformation.

In his early letters he petitioned Olivia—as he had Mary Fair-

[4] Holograph letter in MTP.

[5] Smith, *Mark Twain: The Development of a Writer* (Cambridge: Harvard Univ. Press, 1962), p. 3; Eastman, "Mark Twain's Elmira," *Harper's Monthly Magazine*, 176 (1938), 629.

banks, whose name he freely invoked by way of precedent—to help him mend his heedless ways by assuming the "sisterly" role of ministering angel. "Give me a little room in that great heart of yours," he wrote, ". . . & if I fail to deserve it may I remain forever the homeless vagabond I am! If you & mother Fairbanks will only scold me & upbraid me now & then, I shall fight my way through the world, never fear" (7 September 1868). While Olivia seems to have been susceptible to his appeals, it was Clemens himself who ultimately took their message most to heart. What was needed, he came to believe, was a thorough overhaul of his character and at least a tacit repudiation of his earlier, unregenerate self.

That conclusion, however resolute, was not reached without a good deal of wrenching and ambivalence on Clemens' part. During the fall of 1868, while trying to convince Olivia, the Langdons, and himself that he would be settled, serious, and responsible, he seems instinctively and perhaps unconsciously to have sought release from the very respectability he was rushing to embrace. While visiting the Fairbanks during the fall lecture tour he wrote a piece entitled "A Mystery," which appeared in Abel Fairbanks' Cleveland *Herald* on 16 November.[6] In "A Mystery" Mark Twain complains that "one of those enigmas which we call a Double" has been marauding around the country, using his name "to borrow money, get rum for nothing, and procure credit at hotels." The Double abuses whatever privileges it can wring from the unwary, gives but a single lecture ("in Satan's Delight, Idaho"), and then lapses into fullscale dissipation: "It advertised Itself to lecture and didn't; It got supernaturally drunk at other people's expense; It continued Its relentless war upon helpless and unoffending boarding-houses. . . . And," complains the long-suffering writer, "It was leaving Its bills unsettled, and thereby ruining Its own good name and mine too." The Double is last seen riding a stolen horse north from Cleveland, itself a mysterious undertaking.

Clemens has fun on several levels in "A Mystery" and may be revealing a mix of personal feelings as well. Most obviously there is

---

[6] Cleveland *Herald*, 16 Nov. 1868, p. 2; clipping in MTP. The text of "A Mystery" will appear in "The Works of Mark Twain," *Early Tales & Sketches, Vol. 3*, ed. Edgar Marquess Branch and Robert H. Hirst, with the assistance of Harriet Eleanor Smith, forthcoming from the University of California Press. I thank Robert H. Hirst for bringing "A Mystery" to my attention.

the fun of Mark Twain's trying to pass himself off as a teetotaling pillar of virtue, protesting that his reputation will be devastated by the outrages of the Double: "It gets intoxicated—I do not. It steals horses—I do not. It imposes on theatre managers—I never do. It lies—I never do. It swindles landlords—I never get a chance." The reader chuckles along even before he gets to the snapper about swindling landlords because of what he knows of Mark Twain's self-confessed and well established history as a drinker and liar of Western proportions. So the snapper serves more importantly to direct the reader's attention back through the long paragraph which it concludes, a paragraph of Mark Twain's deadpan assertions about the unsuitability of this particular Double:

> Now to my mind there is something exceedingly strange about this Double of mine. No double was ever like it before, that I have heard of. Doubles usually have the same instincts, and act the same way as their originals—but this one don't. This one has struck out on an entirely new plan. It does according to its own notions entirely, without stopping to consider whether they are likely to be consistent with mine or not. It is an independent Double. It is a careless, free-and-easy Double. It is a Double which don't care whether school keeps or not, if I may use such an expression. If it would only do as I do. But it don't, and there is the mystery of it. . . .

Superficially the paragraph extends (and even belabors) Mark Twain's lament that the Double misrepresents him, the joke again arising from the reader's recognition that the traits the writer regards as "new" and "inconsistent" in the Double are among those which (the reader has long since come to believe) typify the Original. That is, he knows Mark Twain himself to be "independent . . . , careless, free-and-easy," just as he knows him to be a tippler and a truth-stretcher. The language of the paragraph reinforces the joke by reminding the reader of Mark Twain's rough edges even as he proclaims his respectability.

But on another level the contrast between Double and Original, between carelessness and responsibility, could not have been entirely a laughing matter for Clemens in November of 1868. His courtship of Olivia, which reinforced and in part depended upon his determination to reform, was driving him more and more sincerely to espouse the very respectability that Mark Twain fraudulently assumes in

"A Mystery." Ten days after the piece appeared in the Cleveland *Herald* he and Olivia would become provisionally engaged, a circumstance which bears witness to his own and the Langdons' faith in his potential to develop settled and responsible habits. However eager he may have been to enter into such a commitment, "A Mystery" imaginatively suggests his ambivalences about the prospect, ambivalences that he was probably unable to express in any other way. The Double, most notably, is "careless" not only of Mark Twain's alleged good example, but also of social proprieties generally. He is "independent" and "free-and-easy" in ways that the earlier Clemens/ Twain had been—that is, in ways that respectable people are not. Through this early and rather rudimentary use of the Other Self that was to figure so importantly in his work, Clemens betrayed confusion about the relationship between respectability and unregeneracy in his own makeup. Because the humor of the piece depends upon the implication that, despite his complaints, Mark Twain shares many of the Double's lamentable habits, "A Mystery" serves ultimately to reaffirm his bad-boy reputation. Moreover, it does so virtually on the eve of Clemens' engagement, at a time when he was consciously doing all he could to put such a reputation behind him. Unless Mark Twain, too, were to undergo a reformation, it would seem that the distinction between him and his creator, a distinction which had become increasingly blurred since Clemens introduced the pseudonym in 1863, would inevitably sharpen and the distance between them dramatically widen.

This process of dissociation may in fact have been at the back of Clemens' mind as he wrote "A Mystery." The piece closes with Mark Twain's discovery that his Double is no double after all, but "only a very ordinary flesh and blood young man, given to idleness, dissipation and villainy, and entirely unknown to me or any of my friends." One can almost hear erstwhile suitor Clemens, at this moment wishing that his own character were so genuinely undivided, enthusiastically disowning his earlier, unregenerate self and hoping that "his friends" the Langdons would be willing to overlook the resemblances between the two. The disfranchised *doppelgänger*, who in his penchant for idleness, dissipation and villainy bears a likeness to the "other," or disreputable, Clemens/Twain, is roundly denounced as "a rascal by nature, instinct, and education, and a very poor sort of rascal at that." But at the last moment, his righteous indignation spent, the writer admits a grudging sympathy for the imposter: "I ought to hate him, and yet the fact that he has been able to borrow money and get board on credit by representing himself to be me, is so comfortably flattering that I own to a sort of sneaking fondness for the outcast for demonstrating that such a thing was possible." The joke, serviceable in its own right, allows Mark Twain to soften his denunciation of the heedless young charlatan just as "A Mystery" ends, adding a final wrinkle of complexity to a piece already noteworthy for its overlapping layers of conscious and semiconscious irony. As we work through these layers we find writer, persona, and Double caught in tangles of imperfectly understood feeling, sometimes attracting, sometimes repelling or rejecting one another. Whatever else it may suggest, "A Mystery" demonstrates that just ten days before his provisional engagement, and probably while he was a guest in Mother Fairbanks' home, Clemens traded upon Mark Twain's reputation as a rough-and-tumble man of the world even as he insinuated a mild protest against the respectability to which he had pledged himself.

That pledge assumed the weight of a holy vow when he and Olivia became conditionally engaged on Thanksgiving, 1868. The conditions, he wrote to Mother Fairbanks, had principally to do with his convincing all involved that his reformation was genuine and consequential. "She must have time to *prove* her heart & make *sure* that her love is permanent," he said of Olivia. "And I must have time to *settle*, & create a new & better character, & prove myself in it & *I* desire these things, too" (26–27 November 1868). Earlier in the letter, in somber and stately language, he spoke of his intentions: "I touch no spiritous liquors after this day (although I have made no promises)—I shall do no act which you or Livy might be pained to hear of—I shall seek the society of the good—I shall be a *Christian*. I shall climb—climb—climb—toward this bright sun that is shining in the heaven of my happiness until all that is gross & unworthy is hidden in the mists & the darkness of that lower earth whence *you* first lifted my aspiring feet." There is no intentional humor here, none of the irony of "A Mystery," nor any of the teasing that characterized the cub's earlier correspondence with his mother. Clemens writes as the Rake Reformed, his grandiloquence and almost palpable earnestness emphasizing his melodramatic self-regard. In his fiction he had ridiculed and would continue to ridicule the self-proclaimed born-again sinner, but for a while, at least, in the fall of 1868, he seems with all sincerity to have wanted to play the part. His anxiety to improve, first substantially stirred by his own ambition and the proddings of Mary Fairbanks, threatened now to alienate him from his past and in so doing to open a chasm between writer and persona that not even Clemens' invention could bridge.

Reform had become a serious matter, and the past a source of embarrassment and chagrin. By way of promoting a good example for her family to follow, Clemens ingenuously quoted his new friend Reverend Joe Twichell to Olivia in a letter of 4 December*. Twichell had said, "I don't know anything about your past. . . . I don't care very much about your past, but I do care very much about your future." Over the next two months Clemens wrote frequently in this vein as his probation continued, summarizing his case to Olivia in a letter of 24 January 1869: "I have been, in times past, that which would be hateful in your eyes. . . . I say that what I have been I am not now; that I am striving & shall still strive to reach the highest altitude of worth, the highest Christian excellence. . . ." The best testimony of the Langdons' faith in this renunciation of a misspent youth is their approval of the couple's formal engagement on 4 February 1869. In order to gain that faith, and for the sake of a newly defined self-esteem, Clemens believed that he had to ransom his past to his future. What was he now to do with Mark Twain?

His circumstances at the time dictated at least a partial answer to the question. During the fall and winter of 1868–69 Clemens was under obligation to two contracts which would further Mark Twain's national reputation and keep him in the public eye through the following year. The first was his continuing obligation to his publisher, Elisha Bliss, to see *The Innocents Abroad* through the final stages of editing and revision, a process which was to last well into the summer of 1869. The second was his agreement to lecture during the 1868–69 season. One effect of these obligations was to make it impossible for Clemens entirely to set his persona aside during his courtship of Olivia, even had he wanted to. In fact, almost all of the letters which make up the early, idealizing phase of their relationship, when his intention to reform was most fervid, were written while he was on the lecture circuit, taking Mark Twain and "The American Vandal Abroad" before the public several nights a week.

This strikes me as a remarkable and a lucky coincidence, one of those biographical circumstances that force apparently irreconcilable aspects of a personality into an accommodation. Had such a circumstance *not* prevailed at the time, it is much more likely that the chasm between Samuel Clemens and Mark Twain would have widened irreparably, the latter becoming merely a caricature or mascot of the former. This had, after all, been the fate, virtually from the outset, of most other Western humorists, "phunny phellows" who had allowed tricks of dialect and spelling to become their stocks-in-trade. That Clemens may have wanted to repudiate Mark Twain as an avatar of his earlier, unregenerate self is suggested from time to time in his love letters, especially when he stresses the distinction between person and persona. On 4 December 1868*, for example, he wrote Olivia, ". . . your father & mother wanted to see whether I was going to prove that I have a private (& improving) character as well as a public one." By the end of the month he was vilifying his early work and, by implication, the earlier self responsible for it: *"Don't* read a word of that Jumping Frog book, Livy—*don't*. I hate to hear that infamous volume mentioned. I would be glad to know that every copy of it was burned, & gone forever. I'll never write another like it" (31 December 1868*). But the fact of the matter is that between 17 November 1868 and 3 March 1869 Mark Twain was obligated to give more than 40 lectures in cities in the Northeast and Midwest, and that Clemens had no choice but to come to terms with his persona at the very time when he was most deeply in the throes of reformation, writing Olivia almost nightly of his progress.

The result was an accommodation on both sides: Mark Twain saved Sam Clemens from himself, and the lover saw to it that the lecturer revealed a fuller measure than before of his humanity. The first of these claims has the ring of overstatement about it, I realize, but I believe it bears the ring of truth as well. The grueling winter lecture season provided an antidote for Clemens' melodramatic self-absorption by keeping him constantly in touch with qualities in his personality upon which Mark Twain thrived—detachment, irony, self-deprecation, and of course humor. Such an environment tempered the reformer's zeal and helped him to recognize the complex interdependence of both "halves" of the Clemens/Twain identity. At times he bemoaned the consequences of this interconnection, as when he complained to Mrs. Langdon, "I am in some sense a *public* man, . . . but my private character is hacked, ⟨& scorched⟩ & dissected,

& mixed up with my public one, & both suffer the more in consequence" (13 February 1869). However, this intermingling of private
and public character seems to have served Clemens well during his
probationary period, for if the lecturer helped the lover to keep his
feet on the ground, the lover was particularly determined that the
lecturer would come across as more than a bumpkin or a buffoon.

The lecture performances of 1868–69 offered at least a partial
solution to the problems that Clemens faced generally at the time in
presenting Mark Twain to "proper" Eastern audiences without evis-
cerating him. They were instrumental in allowing him to enlarge
and redefine the humorist's prerogatives. Those who attended these
performances saw the lecturer shamble across the stage, assume a
careless attitude at the lectern, and begin drawling out an anecdote,
apparently in the most laconic and indifferent way. Perhaps their
worst suspicions about Mark Twain were confirmed: Here was an
irreverent idler with little to recommend him but his cheek. As he
talked, however, a strange upheaval took place—first in isolated spots
in the hall, then in waves, then in sweeping explosions of laughter,
surprise, and recognition. The uninitiated realized that they had
been taken in: The indolence and indifference were part of a *pose*.
Mark Twain proved to be a very funny man, but not simply funny
in a broad or oafish way. His humor depended upon drollery, flashes
of wit, and bright ironies that challenged an audience and kept it
awake. The lecture platform allowed Clemens to *show* that Mark
Twain's unrefinement was superficial, that it juxtaposed and so only
rendered more powerful the operation of a complex and penetrating
intelligence. At a time when being taken seriously was of crucial
importance to Clemens, the 1868–69 lectures provided him the
opportunity to experiment with the vital tension between humor and
seriousness that was to characterize his best work. "Mere" humorists,
he felt, were content simply to make the public laugh; especially
when the impulse to reform was strong upon him, he was determined
to make it think and feel as well.

However sincere this determination, the fact is that manifestations
of reform in Mark Twain were much more modest, subtle, and
ameliorative than those which Clemens himself undertook; Mark
Twain remained the conservative partner in the complex equation of
identity, while Clemens was, for a time at least, the radical. Both
person and persona underwent change that carried them in the

direction of increasing moral responsibility, respectability, and even piety, but the persona stayed relatively stable while the person swung through dramatic arcs of regret, resolution, and reformation. Mark Twain's relative stability must have been a source of both comfort and consternation for Clemens as he strove to redefine his own "proper" identity during the year that followed his first declarations of love to Olivia in September of 1868. There was a kind of solidity and consistency about Mark Twain—qualities which were reinforced by his audience's expectations—that contrasted sharply with the radical mutability which Clemens and others wished to attribute to his own character at the time. Mark Twain had to remain essentially Mark Twain, after all, notwithstanding the broadening and deepening he was undergoing, but Clemens believed that he himself was to become something quite different from what he had been. Never before had there been such cause for isolating person from persona; never again would the two stand so clearly apart from one another.

It is hardly surprising, given this tension, that Clemens wrote comparatively little during this year of courtship and contrition. In a letter to his family of 4 June 1869 he acknowledged this drought and offered a partial explanation: "In twelve months (or rather I believe it is fourteen) I have earned just *eighty dollars* by my pen—⟨three⟩ two little magazine squibs & one newspaper letter—altogether the idlest, laziest 14 months I ever spent in my life. . . . I feel ashamed of my idleness, & yet I have had really *no* inclination to anything but court Livy. I haven't any other inclination *yet*." While there is some exaggeration of his inactivity here, perhaps because Clemens was late in sending money home to his mother, it is true that his productivity as a writer fell off sharply between September, 1868, and the following August, when he became an editor of the Buffalo *Express*. And while other circumstances undoubtedly contributed to this falling off—among them the winter lecture tour and the burden of reading proof for *The Innocents Abroad* in the spring—I believe that the primary cause of Clemens' unproductivity during this year of reform was his alienation from the imaginative resources embodied in Mark Twain. Person and persona had to be reconciled before these resources could again be successfully tapped.

That reconciliation came gradually as Clemens grew confident of Olivia's love and the fever of his passion to reform inevitably cooled. Eventually a new personal equilibrium was to evolve which would

integrate the Clemens/Twain identity once again and comfortably
blur distinctions between man and writer. Evidence of this evolution
emerges intermittently from Clemens' correspondence and from his
rare newspaper and magazine pieces of early 1869, among them an
article entitled "Personal Habits of the Siamese Twins," which was
written on 14 May and appeared in the August issue of *Packard's
Monthly*. Significantly, Clemens' treatment of the famous twins
Chang and Eng was "the first full expression of his recurring
interest in the puzzle of two individuals co-existing within a single
body."[7] Like "A Mystery," "Personal Habits" is a product of the
reformation year with obvious and inviting psychological overtones.
Writing about the sketch to Olivia on 14 May*, Clemens said, "I
put a lot of obscure jokes in it on purpose to tangle my little sweetheart," a teasing reference to her literalmindedness in trying to
fathom plays of wit or words. But the more provocative tangle in
"Personal Habits" is that involving the identities of Chang and Eng,
a tangle which Clemens must have seen, if only imperfectly, as a
grotesque and literal embodiment of a "double nature" not unlike
his own. "As men," he says in the piece, "the Twins have not always
lived in perfect accord; but, still, there has always been a bond
between them which made them unwilling to go away from each
other and dwell apart."[8] By May of 1869 Clemens may well have felt a
similar unwillingness—or recognized a similar inability—in the
matter of divorcing himself from his past and from those elements of
his character which were most recognizable in Mark Twain. "Personal Habits" obliquely implies such a recognition while it rather
clumsily explores the tension between sharply conflicting impulses
trapped within a single identity. Together with "A Mystery" it
demonstrates that Clemens' lifelong fascination with doubleness,
twinning, and paired consciences came first into focus as the disin-
tegrative fervor of self-reformation gradually gave way to the reconciliation of apparent polarities in his personality.

Even by the beginning of 1869 some of Clemens' zeal to reform was
exhausted and his more characteristic realism had begun to reassert
itself. Melodramatic self-recrimination deferred to intervals of candor

---

[7] Headnote to sketch #237, "The Works of Mark Twain," *Early Tales & Sketches*,
Vol. 4, ed. Edgar Marquess Branch and Robert H. Hirst, with the assistance of Harriet
Eleanor Smith, forthcoming from the University of California Press.

[8] "Personal Habits of the Siamese Twins," *Packard's Monthly*, NS 1 (1869), 249.

and whimsy, and to clear-headed reckonings of his chances to get ahead in Cleveland or Hartford or Buffalo. Evidence of this realistic or restorative phase of his reformation appears in a comparatively early courtship letter, where, in language reminiscent of his correspondence with Mrs. Fairbanks just a year earlier, he acknowledges his fiancée's imperfections and his own incipient worthiness. "I am grateful to God that you are *not* perfect," he tells Olivia. "God forbid that you should be an angel. I am not fit to mate with an angel— I could not *make* myself fit. But I can reach your altitude, in time, & I *will*" (5–7 December 1868*). As his confidence in her feelings matured, his declarations of intention grew less shrill. On 20 January 1869* he wrote, "I know that you are satisfied that whatever honest endeavor can do to make my character what it ought to be, I will faithfully do." Clemens is still the reformer in these representations, but no longer the desperate, sentimental acolyte come to worship at the shrine. Self-condemnation has begun to give way to self-understanding and self-acceptance; the petitioner is still penitent, but no longer abject. By May he could write Olivia, "I think we know each other well enough . . . to bear with the weaknesses & foolishnesses, & even wickednesses (of mine)" (letter dated 19–20 May 1869).

With the formal announcement of his engagement to Olivia Langdon on 4 February 1869 Clemens arrived at a psychological watershed. The strain of attainment was substantially behind him; the security of his hard-won position allowed him in exultant moments to relax and enjoy his prospects. "I don't sigh, & groan & howl so much, now, as I used to," he wrote the Twichells, "—no, I feel serene, & arrogant, & stuck-up—& I feel such pity for the world & every body in it but just us two" (letter dated 14 February 1869*). These spells of complacency were fleeting, and intermixed with them were periods of doubt and chagrin; but ease was gradually displacing urgency in the tone of Clemens' correspondence, and playfulness now vied with piety in his appeals to Olivia. "To tell the truth," he told her, "I love you so well that I *am* capable of misbehaving, just for the pleasure of hearing you scold" (12 January 1869*). Through the spring and summer of 1869 Clemens wondered at his good fortune and learned to trust it. On 4 June he confessed to Mother Fairbanks, "I had a dreadful time making this conquest, but that is all over, you know, & now I have to set up nights trying to think what I'll do next." The melodrama had ended happily.

By June of 1869 "what I'll do next" had come to be a professional as well as a personal question for Clemens. He was in the last stages of proofreading *The Innocents Abroad*, was obligated to prepare a lecture for the coming season, and had been relatively inactive as a writer of anything but love letters since his declarations to Olivia nearly a year earlier. But the restoration of his equilibrium was readying him to return to work. As Olivia and her family came to accept him, and as he concomitantly came to understand that a radical reformation of his character was unlooked for and unnecessary, he regained access to the sources of his vitality as a writer— his past, his skepticism, even his irreverence. The Langdons themselves stimulated and helped to sustain this restoration by rather remarkably and, it would seem, wholeheartedly accepting their would-be son-in-law in the few months that passed before the engagement was formally announced. It was of this confiding acceptance that Olivia wrote to her fiancé later in the year: "I am so happy, so perfectly at rest in you, so proud of the true nobility of your nature—it makes the whole world look so bright to me. . . ."[9] Clemens had proved "worthy," after all, and he may have come to understand that in many respects he had been essentially worthy all along.

These acts of trust and reinforcement shortened the psychological distance Clemens had to travel before returning to the equilibrium that allowed him once again to function as a professional writer. By the time he deliberately resumed that function in late August, 1869, by becoming an editor of the Buffalo *Express*, the strenuous and distortive melodramatic phase of his reformation had subsided, and he was in a position to consolidate the gains and losses it had brought on: Mark Twain and Samuel Clemens met just about where they had parted, although both had become more consciously "serious" and a bit more responsive to the conventions of the Eastern middle class; the Clemens/Twain identity was returning to the condition of careless integration which rendered its "halves" only imperfectly differentiable; and, most important, the bridge between Clemens' past and his future could remain intact, bearing the rich cargo of recollection and reminiscence that was to sustain his major work.

By the time Clemens assumed his responsibilities on the *Express*

[9] Holograph letter in MTP; letter dated 13 November 1869*.

he was sufficiently at peace with himself to turn in a characteristic Mark Twain performance at the very outset of his editorship. In his "Salutatory" of 21 August 1869 he wrote, "to the unoffending patrons of the paper, who are about to be exposed to constant attacks of my wisdom and learning": "I am simply going to do my plain, unpretending duty, when I cannot get out of it; I shall work diligently and honestly and faithfully at all times and upon all occasions, when privation and want shall compel me to do it; in writing, I shall always confine myself strictly to the truth, except when it is attended with inconvenience; I shall witheringly rebuke all forms of crime and misconduct, except when committed by the party inhabiting my own vest. . . ."[10] Much of Clemens' daily writing for the *Express* followed in this vein and no doubt served to satisfy his readers' expectations concerning Mark Twain's drollery and notoriety. But on 16 October he began a series of "Around the World" letters which, taken together, amounted to a substantial tapping of his Western experiences for the purposes of his art. Through them he was put back in contact with the material which would lead to the composition of *Roughing It* in 1870–71; in fact, the first "Around the World" letter, an account of California's Mono Lake, went on to become chapter 38 of the book. Clemens could not have made imaginative use of this material while he was melodramatically declaring his unworthiness and repudiating his past during the last months of 1868. It was only after passing through that phase of his reformation and regaining his balance as a man and a writer that he was able to draw with increasing confidence upon the resources which that past contained. His reformation was to continue, much more subtly, especially through the early years of his marriage. But the crisis had passed, and the most telling effect of its passing was the greater stability and even maturity which had evolved in the Clemens/Twain identity. Having survived intact the more desperate throes of his reformation, he came to benefit from the confidence which that survival inspired as he plunged ahead, into the important work of the 1870s.

[10] Buffalo *Express*, 21 Aug. 1869, p. 1; clipping in MTP.

Mark Twain and the Endangered Family
James Grove

L IKE Huckleberry Finn, Mark Twain often employed images of
endangered families when he told a story. His canon is filled
with people trying to cope with disrupted familial relations: mother
figures waiting for lost children to return; anguished relatives
searching for missing loved ones; children suddenly vulnerable
because they have lost parents; and families trying to survive
internecine conflicts. These images are often emotionally grounded in the tragedies haunting Twain's own life, and they help form
the nightmare world which broods within the web of his humor.

Yet, surprisingly, this preoccupation with the endangered family
has received little, extended critical attention.[1] Such neglect is
unfortunate, especially since this topic rests at the heart of Twain's
pessimism. It also helps define his abiding ambivalence toward the
family. My discussion, then, will examine how these images of
dislocation affect the literary strategies in some of his works; how
they occasionally undermine his satirical and philosophical stances;
how they work against his completing some risky fictional ideas;
and how they objectify and intensify the dilemmas facing the
protagonists in *The Adventures of Tom Sawyer* (1876) and *Adventures
of Huckleberry Finn* (1884).[2]

I

In *The Innocents Abroad* (1869), the narrator "Mark Twain"
encounters a tear-jug at Pisa, and it momentarily tempers his

[1] Many studies deal in some way with the theme of the family in Twain's works. But most
of them only suggest the importance of the endangered family to his artistic vision. Of these
studies, I am most indebted to Paul Baender, "Mark Twain's Transcendent Figure," Diss.
University of California, 1956; and Leland Krauth, "Mark Twain: At Home in the Gilded
Age," *Georgia Review*, 28 (1974), 105–13.
[2] In my allusions to the Twain biography, I have most relied on the following studies:
Hamlin Hill, *Mark Twain: God's Fool* (New York: Harper & Row, 1973); Justin Kaplan, *Mr.
Clemens and Mark Twain: A Biography* (New York: Simon and Schuster, 1966); Edith
Colgate Salsbury, *Susy and Mark Twain: Family Dialogues* (New York: Harper & Row,
1965); and Dixon Wecter, *Sam Clemens of Hannibal* (Boston: Houghton Mifflin, 1952).

habitual irreverence: "It spoke to us in a language of its own; and
with a pathos more tender than any words might bring, its mute
eloquence swept down the long roll of the centuries with its tale of
a vacant chair, a familiar footstep missed from a threshold, a
pleasant voice gone from a chorus, a vanished form!—a tale which
is always so new to us, so startling, so terrible, so benumbing to the
senses."[3] Here, as his persona dwells on the inevitability of grief,
Twain speaks as a fellow victim to an audience devoted to the ideal
of family life yet intensely aware that death finally hovered over all
homes—no matter how secure they seemed.[4] He touches the
strings of sentiment as he would in many later works employing
more concrete images of loss. In fact, his fiction, despite its humor,
frequently reminds one of this tear-jug. In its own complex
language, it speaks subtly, sentimentally, and angrily about a world
shadowed by "poverty and pain, hunger and cold and heartbreak,
bereavement, tears and shame, strife, malice and dishonor, age,
weariness, remorse."[5] And in depicting this world, Twain continually attempts to generate sympathy for his fictional families.

Yet this sympathy sometimes works against the overall moral
tone of his art. We especially see this subversive effect in *The
Gilded Age* (1874), *A Connecticut Yankee in King Arthur's Court*
(1889), *Pudd'nhead Wilson* (1894), and *The Mysterious Stranger*
manuscripts (1897–1908). For Twain, while attacking human
frailty in these works, also creates portraits of domesticity which
place the reader between somewhat contradictory points of view.
One is that of the satirist who angrily, unpityingly, and sometimes
misanthropically ridicules the human race. The other is that of the
family man who sympathizes with his vulnerable, foolish characters
when various forces threaten or destroy their happiness.

In *The Gilded Age*, sympathy for the endangered Hawkins and
Sellers families upsets Twain's and C. D. Warner's apparent

---

[3] "Author's National Edition" (New York: Harper, 1899–1900), I, 321.

[4] This awareness also helped account for the popularity of the era's graveyard literature
which often revolved around domestic death scenes. For discussions of this preoccupation,
see William E. Bridges, "Warm Hearth, Cold World: Social Perspectives on the Household
Poets," *American Quarterly*, 21 (1969), 764–69; Herbert Ross Brown, *The Sentimental Novel
in America 1789–1860* (Durham, N.C.: Duke Univ. Press, 1940); and Ann Douglas, *The
Feminization of American Culture* (New York: Knopf, 1977).

[5] "That Day in Eden," *The Writings of Mark Twain*, ed. Albert Bigelow Paine (New York:
Gabriel Wells, 1922–25), XXIX, 345.

intention to make this novel an attack on fraudulent legislative practices, among other things. Because we come to like these families, we want them to prosper, despite the fact that their success will eventually depend on the passage of the scandalous Tennessee land bill.[6] Twain most effectively nurtures this sympathy in the opening (and most interesting) section of *The Gilded Age* by creating a number of scenes highlighting the desolation and danger arising from familial loss. For instance, we see the orphaned Clay mourning over his dead mother, and Laura calling for her lost parents amid the wreckage of a steamboat accident. Suddenly vulnerable to the harsh realities surrounding them, the two children need protection, guidance, and love; and Twain wants his audience to be relieved when Silas and Nancy Hawkins give them a home. The Hawkinses become admirable because they so readily uphold the ideal of domestic life.

The steamboat accident in which Laura loses her parents also contains images revolving around the memory of Henry Clemens' death aboard the *Pennsylvania* in 1858. In describing the accident, Twain stresses its effect on the victims' relatives. He has one victim named Henry Worley (representing an idyllic portrait of brother Henry) selflessly worry about his mother (living in St. Louis just as Jane Clemens did at the time of her son's death). "Tell her a lie," Worley begs, "for a poor devil's sake, please. Say I was killed in an instant and never knew what hurt me. . . . It's hard to burn up in a coop like this. . . ."[7] Then Twain describes how a dying, gruesomely burned engineer blames a brother for the accident. This accusation centers on the imminent grief of the engineer's wife. He tells the brother: "You were on watch. You were the boss. . . . Take that! [his ring]—take it to my wife and tell her it comes from me by the hand of my murderer! Take it— and take my curse with it to blister your heart a hundred years . . ." (X, 54). Considering Twain's persistent and irrational guilt concerning his brother's death, this curse probably stems from the

---

[6] See Krauth's discussion of *The Gilded Age* (pp. 107–08). He makes this point, too, but he does not concentrate on how the image of the endangered family helps stimulate this sympathetic response toward the characters.

[7] "Author's National Edition" (New York: Harper, 1899–1900), X, 52. Subsequent reference to this work will be made in the text.

author's sense that he was once "the boss" who failed a loved one, therefore exposing the Clemens family to bereavement.[8]

These scenes, along with Silas Hawkins' decision to sell the family's beloved slaves and the pathetic deathbed scene, create an atmosphere in which the family is constantly endangered. It is an atmosphere owing much to the deaths which disrupted Twain's early family life and to the misguided financial decisions of John Marshall Clemens. Because we feel so much for the victims and their survivors, we begin to support, against our better judgment, any scheme that will save these families from more pain. The situation is similar to those found in many crime stories where we become so interested in the criminals' personal lives that we hope they escape detection. We forget that many of the problems besetting the novel's characters stem from their inability to escape the materialistic values fostered in the Hawkins' and Sellers' households. We also begin to hope that Laura will succeed in her scheme and that Colonel Sellers and Washington Hawkins will find some miraculous way to realize their scatterbrained dreams. Of course, Twain and Warner ultimately frustrate all these dishonest designs. But this moralistic ending does not destroy our sense that it would have been better for the schemes to succeed than for Laura to die.

In *Pudd'nhead Wilson*, Twain's sympathy for Roxy, in her struggle to save her son from being sold down the river, undermines his attempt to align the authorial voice with Wilson's ironic perspective (as evidenced in the maxims). As Philip Cohen has explained, Twain wrote this novel in three stages; and in the second stage (which includes the selling of Roxy down the river and her subsequent return to Dawson's Landing), he began to develop the quadroon as the proud, passionate force who wins our compassion and respect, regardless of her faults.[9] This development continued into the third stage of composition (chapters 1 through 4, 8 through 10, and part of 14)—the demands of Roxy's characterization finally working against Twain's efforts to create a

[8] Bryant Morey French in *Mark Twain and The Gilded Age* (Dallas: Southern Methodist Univ. Press, 1965) notes the relationship between the factual and fictional steamboat accidents (pp. 154, 313–14).

[9] "Aesthetic Anomalies in *Pudd'nhead Wilson*," *Studies in American Fiction*, 10 (1982), 55–69.

transcendent narrative voice truly distanced from the story's disrupted families.

Such detachment does rule the opening pages as Twain dissects the society of Dawson's Landing to display its corruption. This stance enables him to use truncated and disintegrating domestic relations symbolically as a means of suggesting the town's moral sterility. Judge and Mrs. Driscoll are childless although they have always desired a child. Mrs. Rachel Pratt is a widow who laments being childless. Pembroke Howard is a bachelor. Roxy's child does not know his father. Percy Driscoll neglects his parental responsibilities to speculate. Taken together, these fragmented families point to Twain's insinuation that sinister forces are eating away at the fertility and vitality of Dawson's Landing—these evils being the town's materialism and its enervating dependence on slavery.

Yet Twain soon returns to his emerging conception of Roxy, and this leads to the portrayal of her desperate actions to make Tom "white" and then, chapters later, to make him once more her son. Our attention is drawn to Roxy's maternal devotion as she fights for her child. She is a life-force countering all the sterility and irony surrounding her. At the same time, we lose interest in Wilson, who is not committed to any other person. Thus, narrative distance again succumbs to the pathos and terror of familial suffering, so that upon leaving the novel, we do not linger over Wilson's final courtroom machinations and vindication. Rather, we remember Twain's picture of Roxy in the courtroom. Having attempted to save what family she has, the woman hears Wilson accuse her son and realizes she has lost everything: "Roxy flung herself upon her knees, covered her face with her hands, and out through her sobs the words struggled: 'De Lord have mercy on me, po' misable sinner dat I is!' "[10]

Similarly, in *A Connecticut Yankee* and *The Mysterious Stranger* manuscripts, Twain's sympathetic and often sentimental portrayals of endangered families upset his strategy of pitting the wisdom of a transcendent figure against the unenlightened, degenerate behavior of the masses. Paul Baender, in studying the stylistic problems of these works, stresses this disruption in the proposed thematic

[10] "Author's National Edition" (New York: Harper, 1899–1900), p. 222.

intent. He writes that it occurs because the novels have "areas of sympathy not incorporated in Twain's figure-group scheme. For instance, there are images of families destroyed by tyrants, mothers deprived of their children, and other domestic violations which recur throughout *A Connecticut Yankee* and *The Mysterious Stranger*."[11] These images become most significant when they show the family as an object worthy of devotion notwithstanding every contrast between one transcendent figure and an inferior domestic group. Then the family becomes a force which raises our esteem for human beings.

Such images occur especially in *A Connecticut Yankee*. Wanting to debunk the myth of Camelot's glory while establishing Hank Morgan's nineteenth-century loyalty to the family as a "good," Twain portrays the Yankee's horror over the many ways in which poverty, injustice, and slavery disrupt the family in Arthur's kingdom. With Arthur, Hank endures the smallpox episode, with its dying mother who hopes her family will perish rather than live longer in this harsh kingdom. With Marco, he sees "the persons of shunned and tearful and houseless remnants of families whose homes had been taken from them and their parents butchered and hanged."[12] At Morgan Le Fay's the Yankee witnesses various horrors—all centered on Le Fay's perverse disregard for family relations. In addition, he hears stories about husbands and fathers committing suicide because of the tyranny of church and state, sees mothers and daughters burned, and watches the royal forces cruelly separate a married couple. The wife "struggled and fought and shrieked like one gone mad till a turn in the road hid her from sight" (p. 246).

Hank's compassion for these people prepares us for his devotion to his own family and his final despair over being irrevocably separated from Sandy and Hello-Central. It also links the Yankee to the very sixth-century people he often abhors. Although Hank eventually calls them "human muck" (p. 473), this epithet cannot make the audience forget that this "muck" includes the suffering

[11] Baender, p. 165.

[12] *A Connecticut Yankee in King Arthur's Court*, ed. Bernard L. Stein (Berkeley: Univ. of California Press, 1979), p. 353. Subsequent references to this work will be made in the text.

people who have so often played upon the Yankee's feelings. It cannot erase the suspicion that Hank's misanthropic view would soften if he saw another afflicted family. As a result, the Yankee's final pessimistic vision of the human condition is difficult to accept as the novel's only truth. Having too often seen the intrinsic worth of these people through portraits of their domestic sufferings, we see the Yankee's denunciation as an explosion which fails to represent the complexity of human existence as evidenced within this uncertain novel.

The same complication undermines, or at least qualifies, Satan's views in *The Mysterious Stranger* manuscripts. Again Twain dots the landscape with images of domestic desolation: Marget loses her beloved Father Peter when Father Adolf imprisons him; Frau Brandt becomes a blasphemer after her son drowns; Katrina fears that she has lost her "son," Satan; Satan crushes the little human families he has created; a girl, unjustly accused of witchcraft, burns at the stake as her mother cries out; and an old woman explains why she wants Satan and Theodor to burn her: "How long it is that I have wandered homeless—Oh, many years, many! . . . Once I had a home—I do not know where it was; and four sweet girls and a son. . . . All dead, now, poor things, these many years. . . . If you could have seen my son."[13]

As Theodor sees all this destruction and grieves over it, we frequently identify with his human response and once more feel a tenderness at odds with the transcendent figure's derisive attitude. Such suffering speaks to us, and it points to Twain's inability to accept completely his pessimistic view of human beings as worthless, animalistic, irredeemable creatures. We only need to look at his valuation of the family in this and other late works to realize his persistent belief—despite his philosophy—that human beings could find meaning, could even redeem themselves, through loving relations.

Thus, a part of Twain would have agreed with Alexis de Tocqueville's observation that in the shifting American culture a strong family existed to save the individual from being thrown

---

[13] *The Mysterious Stranger Manuscripts*, ed. William M. Gibson (Berkeley: Univ. of California Press, 1969), p. 325.

"back forever upon himself alone . . . within the solitude of his own heart."[14] Yet Twain also could never escape his sense that family happiness was always tenuous and that redemption often arose only after incidents of intense loss. Such is the tragic nature of his fictional world, and Satan stresses this fragility in "No. 44" when he warns Theodor about not braving the love of marriage because it inevitably ends in grief. Here, Satan mirrors Twain's own doubts about the wisdom of becoming committed to a potentially heartbreaking relationship—doubt emphasized within "In My Bitterness" (1897), a private lament for Susy Clemens and a diatribe against a God who seems to enjoy trapping human beings in a treacherous world. As Twain wrote, "He gives you a wife and children whom you adore only that through the spectacle of the wanton shames and miseries which He will inflict upon them He may tear the palpitating heart out of your breast."[15]

II

In objectifying his bittersweet vision of the family, Twain frequently created characters searching for lost loved ones. From *The Gilded Age* where Laura Hawkins fruitlessly looks for her father to *Captain Stormfield's Visit to Heaven* (1907) where a father and mother try to find their lost children in heaven, Twain used the image of the search to reveal both the fragility of domestic happiness and the tenacity of love. Usually, his interest in this image did not control his narratives. Instead it only surfaced momentarily to create a tragic ripple. But in two of his more interesting fragments, "Huck Finn and Tom Sawyer Among the Indians" (1884) and "The Great Dark" (1897–1908), this interest was going to provide the primary means for structuring them. Such a structure, however, in the end probably worked against his completing these stories, for it promised to bring him face to face with too many painful considerations about his own domestic life.

In the first fragment, he creates one of his most positive families, the Millses. They have an ideal relationship and through Huck's

---

[14] Alexis de Tocqueville, *Democracy in America*, ed. Phillips Bradley (New York: Knopf, 1960), II, 99.

[15] In *Fables of Man*, ed. John S. Tuckey (Berkeley: Univ. of California Press, 1972), p. 131.

reactions to them, Twain indicates his attraction to the intimate family circle. Often kissing and lovingly calling to one another, they initially make Huck uncomfortable, for the boy is not used to such open displays of affection. But Huck finally sees this family in an attractive light and calls them "the splendidist people in the world."[16] He especially praises their treatment of the daughter Peggy: "all the tribe doted on her. Why they took as much care of her as if she was made out of sugar or gold or something" (p. 99). Such love, with its great pride and concern for the daughter, embodies the beauty which the author desired in his own relationship with his girls—and which he best achieved in the golden years of the mid 1870s-early 1880s with the radiant, talented Susy.

However, with this strong family occupying the center of the narrative, the work lacks any strong sense of conflict. It is static, despite Huck's sometimes interesting comments about the Millses. Therefore, early in the story, Twain destroys this family as Indians kill the parents and sons while kidnapping Peggy and her sister. With this disaster, the work turns into a search narrative as Brace Johnson, Peggy's fiancé, doggedly trails the Indians (Huck, Tom, and Jim tag along). Yet this search also causes Twain to write himself into a deadend since Huck indicates that the Indians probably raped Peggy. Considering that this woman had been cast as a model of youthful, "unblemished" femininity and that she might have even reminded him of his own daughters—especially Susy—it is not surprising that Twain, diffident about sexual matters in most of his work, refused to pursue the search and have Brace find her. For such an end would have led this writer to a nightmarish vision of the destroyed heiress of all ages. Furthermore, it would have made him confront, for an extended period of time, the terrible fact that no matter how much he protected his girls they would never be immune from all dangers. There was always something waiting to hurt or destroy them, something he could not control—like the epilepsy and the spinal meningitis that eventually struck down Jean and Susy Clemens.[17]

[16] In *Mark Twain's Hannibal, Huck & Tom*, ed. Walter Blair (Berkeley: Univ. of California Press, 1969), p. 99. Subsequent reference to this work will be made in the text.

[17] About Twain's difficulties in finishing this story, Blair notes that besides the problem of the rape, the work was doomed by "weak characterization, plotting, thematic development,

In the "The Great Dark," Twain's notes for the unfinished sections of this dream narrative indicate that members of a phantom ship would eventually kidnap the children of the tale's primary family, the Edwardses. The anguished parents would then chase the ship for fifteen years attempting to rescue their offspring. Twain foreshadows the terrors of this search in the completed part of the fragment by describing a momentary disappearance of the children. Mrs. Edwards, thinking they are gone forever, becomes hysterical: "She tore loose from us and was gone in a moment, flying along the dark decks and shrieking the children's names with a despairing pathos that broke one's heart to hear it. . . . For she was a mother and her children were lost. That says it all. She would hunt for them as long as she had strength to move. And that is what she did, hour after hour, wailing and moaning . . . until she was exhausted and fell in a swoon."[18]

Finally the children are found and this early episode ends happily. But Twain's plans for the later, longer search show that he wanted the narrative to end in catastrophe.[19] First, the Edwardses' captain, who has also lost his children to the phantom ship, would experience the deaths of his son and daughter. Their deaths would cause him to become a blasphemer remindful of the narrator in "In My Bitterness." Then one of the Edwardses' children would be stabbed to death just as her parents reached her. And, after a long overland journey, Mr. Edwards would discover the mummified bodies of his other children. In every sense, then, this dream narrative was to become a vehicle for embodying Twain's most pessimistic view of human fate.

One can argue that as his initial enthusiasm for this work waned Twain realized that he faced the hard prospect of continuing a narrative which would feed off his own domestic tragedies—

---

and handling of fictional point of view" (*Hannibal, Huck & Tom*, p. 91). Everett Emerson in *The Authentic Mark Twain* (Philadelphia: Univ. of Pennsylvania Press, 1984) suggests that Twain's "inability to continue the story was not, apparently, simply that his tank had run dry; rather, he seems to have been unable to continue the story as a result of Huck's loss of innocence" caused by the boy's facing Peggy's probable fate (p. 149).

[18] *Mark Twain's "Which Was the Dream?" and Other Symbolic Writings of the Later Years*, ed. John S. Tuckey (Berkeley: Univ. of California Press, 1967), pp. 143–44.

[19] For discussions about the conclusion to "The Great Dark," see Bernard DeVoto, *Mark Twain at Work* (Cambridge: Harvard Univ. Press, 1942), pp. 122–23; and Tuckey in his introduction to "*Dream*," pp. 100–01.

especially the death of daughter Susy. It would be a torturous task, and the knowledge of this probably helped him decide not to finish "The Great Dark." He knew that this tale, with its culminating disaster, would be like another story he had once intended to write. As he indicated to William Dean Howells, this other story would end with the death of the protagonist's daughter. She would be carried "to him when he had been through all other possible misfortune—& I said it couldn't be done as it ought to be done except by a man who had lived it—it must be written with the blood out of a man's heart."[20] Certainly Twain had lived it, and something in him wanted to write it as a means of coping with his grief and guilt over Susy's death. It would objectify his feeling that he was the victim of a cruel world, a victim who had tried but was unable to protect his beloved child.[21] But in the end, this work would have cost him too much.

III

So far, this discussion has centered on how the image of the endangered family sometimes subverted Twain's artistic intentions. But such subversions are not the rule. For in his two great "Boy's Books," *Tom Sawyer* and *Huckleberry Finn*, his image of the family in danger often reinforces and deepens Twain's desire to convey his ambivalence about domestic life. Specifically, as Huck and Tom struggle to reconcile their attraction toward stable home environments with their need for personal independence, tension arises. Twain counterpoints images of aborted family reunions with images of joyous returns—the uneasy relationships between these images reflecting the conflicts within the boys. Besides upsetting the nostalgic and comic surfaces of these novels, this counterpointing enables Twain to confront the possibility that the breakup of the family, despite all the pain it causes, might sometimes have a positive outcome. It might force people to see the world for themselves, away from the restrictions of domesticity.

In *Tom Sawyer*, Twain creates a protagonist with a fragmented

---

[20] *Mark Twain-Howells Letters: The Correspondence of Samuel L. Clemens and William Dean Howells, 1872–1910*, ed. Henry Nash Smith and William M. Gibson (Cambridge: Harvard Univ. Press, 1960), II, 669–70.
[21] See *Twain at Work*, pp. 118–20.

family background, for Tom's mother and father have died. The boy thus lives in Aunt Polly's respectable home, which he frequently finds confining. Occasionally, his frustrations cause him to fantasize about destroying the security of this shelter. For example, after Polly unjustly blames him for breaking a sugar bowl, Tom lapses into a vengeful, melodramatic daydream in which he punishes her by being "brought home from the river, dead, with his curls all wet. . . his sore heart at rest. How she would throw herself upon him, and how her tears would fall like rain."[22] This passage plays upon and mocks the language of the sentimental domestic literature of the nineteenth century. Yet Tom, luxuriating over the dream of being an outcast and a victim, also vividly imagines the sorts of grief and loss which were real to Twain and his audience.

Death in the family, which domestic literature often confronted and exploited in bathetic yet terrifying portraits of grief, gives Tom's adolescent vision a sting, a mixed tone which is heard again in the boy's parallel daydream stemming from a quarrel with Becky Thatcher. He now imagines becoming a wanderer divorced from family and love: "Thus he would die—out in the cold world, with no shelter over his homeless head, no friendly hand to wipe the death-damps from his brow, no loving face to bend pityingly over him when the great agony came" (p. 55). In this saccharine lament, Tom enjoys the feeling of being deliciously wronged. But his "death" also enables him to sense the cost of being too alone. It pictures one of the great fears of his culture: that a loved one might die "in the wilderness" away from the emotional and spiritual comforts of the family.[23]

---

[22] *The Adventures of Tom Sawyer* ; *Tom Sawyer Abroad*; *Tom Sawyer, Detective*, ed. John C. Gerber, Paul Baender, and Terry Firkins (Berkeley: Univ. of California Press, 1980), p. 40. Subsequent reference to this work will be made in the text.

[23] For a study of this fear, see Lewis O. Saum, "Death in the Popular Mind of Pre-Civil War America," in *Death in America*, ed. David E. Stannard (Philadelphia: Univ. of Pennsylvania Press, 1974), pp. 30–48. After moving to the Far West in 1861, Twain expressed this apprehension in a letter to Horatio Phillips. Writing about a mutual friend who was near death, he noted that "the fact of his dying here among comparative strangers, with no relative within thousands of miles of him and no woman to lay the blessing of her hand upon his aching head; and soothe his weary heart to its last sleep with the music of her woman's voice will shed a gloom over us all, when the sad event is consummated. May you die at home . . ."—29 October 1861, Mark Twain Papers. These previously unpublished

Such ambivalence persists even in Tom's happier fantasy about
becoming a pirate who rejects the ordinary, including the conventional family. In one way, he vicariously realizes this dream
through his friendship with Huck, for the latter's enviable freedom
largely arises out of an irrevocably lost homelife. Therefore, Tom
uses this friendship to make his own life seem more rebellious and
less domestic. This same urge for freedom also leads to the
Jackson's Island adventure where Tom appears—for the first
time—to be physically breaking away from his aunt's world. But in
this novel, whose structure often revolves around Tom's leaving
and returning to the family circle, the island's attractions are not
powerful enough to withstand his longings for security. So Tom
sneaks home, secretly watches Polly's grief, and considers ending
the charade. But he decides against such a reunion, cruelly and
selfishly delaying his return to make it more grand. In addition,
this decision is connected to the boy's daydream of making Polly
suffer for unjustly accusing him. His island adventure has placed
her in the bereaved state which he had earlier imagined. She is now
the victim, he is now in control; and Tom's willingness to let her
suffer throws a shadow over his comically triumphant return at the
church.

The glorious return is also a bit muted because Huck, the
outsider, has no family to welcome him back. He stands outside
the happiness until the Widow Douglas decides to be his family.
Her decision, though, does not erase the contrast between the
boys' feelings about domesticity, for Huck, unlike Tom, never fits
comfortably into the family. We especially see this near the end of
the novel when Huck after he is safe from Injun Joe goes back to
his hogshead home alone. Only in response to Tom's coercion will
Huck agree to return to the Widow's.

Tom's rebellions, then, are usually playful, dream-like acts of a
conventional boy's imagination. Through them, he wants to make
an impression on the grown-ups but not disrupt forever his stable
domestic life. Huck, however, feels no such dependence, although

words are copyrighted 1985 by the Mark Twain Foundation, which reserves all reproduction
or dramatization rights in every medium. They are published with permission of the
University of California Press and Robert H. Hirst, General Editor of the Mark Twain
Project.

he is sometimes lonely; and through Huck's discomfort at the Widow's (a respectable family circle fragmented by its lack of a father figure), Twain establishes a deeper sense of ambivalence which will become more dynamic in *Huckleberry Finn* where we may directly view Huck's inner turmoil.[24]

Huck's uncertainty is strikingly revealed in the lies he tells to protect Jim and himself. As critics have noted, Huck in conversations with Judith Loftus, the slave-catchers, the Grangerfords, and the Duke and King creates families for himself and then imagines them disrupted or destroyed.[25] These lies, so filled with sickness and grief and orphans, point to Huck's ability to play upon the sentiments and fears of the people he meets. Like them, he waxes sentimental over graveyard poetry such as Emmeline Grangerford's; and this link enables Huck to understand and exploit his listeners' emotions to make them pity or avoid him. Thus, he escapes or defuses certain treacherous situations.

Yet, at a deeper level, Huck's lies, as Henry Nash Smith notes, are "improvisations on the themes of [Huck's] own life"; as "projections of Huck's unconscious, they reveal the gloomy substratum of his personality."[26] By imagining himself part of these families, the orphan perhaps realizes vicariously his longings for a background complete with loved ones who care for him. Yet, in subsequently destroying these families, Huck also seems to objectify his dark knowledge of the family's fragility: his knowledge that dangers forever threaten even the most secure homes. Finally, these stories also perhaps betray his latent hostility toward all the domestic worlds which might entrap him. For in disrupting his ties with one imaginary family after another, Huck is undermining his own longings for security; he is unconsciously destroying those settings before they can envelop and control his imagination. Therefore, these lies reflect Huck's repeated desire to escape families which attract, confuse, and endanger him.

---

[24] Huck's and Tom's different views toward the family finally reflect the playful and irreverent sides of Twain's humor which Louis J. Budd discusses in *Our Mark Twain* (Philadelphia; Univ. of Pennsylvania Press, 1983), pp. 25–26.

[25] See, for example, Henry Nash Smith, Introd., *Adventures of Huckleberry Finn* (Boston: Houghton Mifflin, 1958), pp. v–xxix; and Eric Solomon, "*Huckleberry Finn* Once More," *College English*, 22 (1960), 172–78.

[26] Smith, Introd., *Huckleberry Finn*, pp. xix–xx.

To create a context for these stories, Twain fills the novel with problematical, disrupted family relations. In the opening pages, we see Huck struggling over his comfortable but restricted life with his surrogate mothers, the Widow and Miss Watson; enduring a dreadful reunion with Pap; and deciding to escape all such associations by orchestrating his own "murder." As Huck "kills" himself, Twain creates a situation mindful of the Jackson's Island episode in *Tom Sawyer*, for the community again searches for a lost "son." But in contrast to the earlier incident, this rebellion is finally no romantic lark. Rather, it is a thorough rejection of all previous domestic ties.

For the rest of the novel, Huck encounters and often runs away from one dangerous family environment after another. At the same time, he must attempt to preserve his always threatened relationship with Jim—their repeated separations and reunions becoming subtle signs of the boy's increasing emotional dependence upon the black man. For example, we see their joyous reunions after the Grangerford-Shepherdson episode, where two strong families feud to the death, and after the Sherburn-Boggs shooting, where the murdered man's daughter "throws herself on her father, crying and saying, 'Oh, he's killed him, he's killed him!' "[27] After these scenes of destruction, the renewal of the raft's homelife represents for Huck a return to peace, freedom, beauty, and love.

The basis for Huck's growing respect for Jim becomes salient when Twain juxtaposes the Duke and King's lack of familial feeling with Jim's persistent devotion to his lost wife and children. While Jim thinks about freeing his disrupted family, regardless of the dangers, the Duke and King act out the sham reunion at the Wilkses'. The scoundrels' plans, which include the breaking up of slave families and the undermining of the returning brothers' role as responsible relatives, threaten the Wilks girls' hopes for future security. And Huck, who adores the girls and who is always drawn to the ideal of the strong, loving family—although he usually feels restricted within the everyday realization of this ideal—finally refuses to go along with the Duke and King's scheme.

[27] *The Art of Huckleberry Finn*, 2nd ed., ed. Hamlin Hill and Walter Blair (San Francisco: Chandler, 1969), p. 206. Subsequent reference to this work will be made in the text.

Huck's love and loyalty toward Jim obviously motivate his shock when the Duke and King sell the black man to Silas Phelps. Expecting to return to him, Huck suddenly finds Jim gone—their hopes shattered. This realization forces him to make the climactic decision to free Jim; and in this novel of many separations and reunions, Huck's search leads to his joyous "reunion" with the Phelps family, to his coming into contact with Jim again (although this meeting is muted by the black man's imprisonment), and to his renewed relations with Tom Sawyer.

All these returns in part account for the final pages' comic tone. Nevertheless, there is a bittersweet quality to this section, and it is tied to Twain's interest in juxtaposing images of separation and reunion. This serious side is apparent when Huck stays in his room on the night of Jim's attempted escape: he remains in bed and fears that he will not see his endangered friends again. We also see it while Sally waits for her lost nephew "Sid Sawyer," although her anxiety is allayed when she sees the wounded but saved boy. Even more significantly, this other side is revealed in Huck's resistance to the idea that his life with the Phelpses may become permanent. Having been part of this family, Huck recognizes that such a life would be a mixed blessing. While he knows that their home promises security (and no more reunions with Pap will undermine it), he reacts against it because he realizes that such safety will restrict his freedom. Moreover, he seems just as reluctant to return to the Widow's equally safe home. Thus, the novel ends with Huck thinking about lighting "out for the territory" and separating from the family again.[28]

IV

All these images of separation, death, and bereavement represent an important side of Twain's art, especially since they often control his vision of the family. This becomes even clearer when one thinks of his other works, both fiction and non-fiction, which employ these images. In an 1864 *San Francisco Call* article ("Sad

[28] Jose Barchilon and Joel S. Kovel attempt to explain Huck's final resistance to the family in "*Huckleberry Finn*: A Psychoanalytic Study," *Journal of the American Psychoanalytic Association*, 14 (1966), 775–814. They see much of the narrative revolving around Huck's "unconscious conflicts" arising out of the death of his mother and subsequent "absence of a nurturing object." They argue that these conflicts, in forming the unhappy side of Huck's personality, cannot be resolved: Huck wants such a mother, but his rage against losing his own makes him reject the various maternal figures he encounters.

Accident—Death of Jerome Rice"), a seaman's wife expects to be soon reunited with her long absent husband; but he has died at sea and she will soon face his corpse. A mother in "The Brummell-Arabella Fragment" (1870s?) travels to see her daughter; but as a telegraph message indicates: "Mary-died-8-30-P.-M.-Mother-arrived-five minutes-too late-to-see-her."[29] Another mother, Aunt Rachel of "A True Story" (1874), has lost all her children, except one, to the slave-traders. Miles Hendon in *The Prince and the Pauper* (1881) prepares the Prince for their glorious reception at the Hendon home; but they arrive to find treachery and death. There is also the bizarre "The Californian's Tale" (1893) about a man demented by his wife's sudden, permanent disappearance; and in *Following the Equator* (1897), Twain is drawn to the story of the *Duncan Dunbar*'s wreck. In carrying many daughters and wives back to their native Australia, the ship sinks just before it gets home, in sight of relatives anxiously waiting to see loved ones again.

Such images point to Twain's recognition of life's harshness: of the risks in being separated from family, of the relentlessness of time, and of the griefs waiting to darken the domestic circle. These are the truths he stressed in a letter to Howells about Susy's death. Feeling caught in a world which tortured human beings with calculating malice, he wrote: "What a ghastly tragedy it was; how cruel it was; how exactly & precisely it was planned; & how remorsefully every detail of the dispensation was carried out."[30] These are also the truths which, thirty years before, he had sentimentally written about in his farewell column for the *Alta California*. About to go back to his boyhood home, he was prepared to "share the fate of many another longing exile who wanders back . . . to find . . . graves where he looked for firesides, grief where he had pictured joy . . . everywhere change!"[31]

[29] *Mark Twain's Satires & Burlesques*, ed. Franklin R. Rogers (Berkeley: Univ. of California Press, 1967), p. 215.

[30] *Twain-Howells Letters*, II, 663.

[31] "Mark Twain's Farewell," in *Mark Twain's Western Years* by Ivan Benson (Stanford University: Stanford Univ. Press, 1938), p. 212. Phillipe Ariès in *Western Attitudes Toward Death: From the Middle Ages to the Present*, trans. Patricia M. Ranum (Baltimore: John Hopkins Univ. Press, 1974), sees some of Twain's works as reflecting the "exaggeration of mourning in the nineteenth century" when in both Europe and America "survivors accepted the death of another person with greater difficulty than in the past. . . . The death which is feared is no longer so much the death of the self as the death of another . . ." (pp. 67–68).

Finally, these images suggest some of Twain's deepest longings, specifically his desires to destroy the family which always had the potential to restrict and hurt him. In fact, there seems to be a morbid pleasure resting behind his persistent use of these images, as if he is fascinated and awed by his power to play the cruel God with his fictional families. For, as God, he is no longer the victim; rather his imagination allows him to transcend the family and be removed from its responsibilities and grief—at least temporarily. Thus, as with Huck's "stories," Twain's are multi-layered attempts to cope with, understand, and perhaps escape the always alluring domestic world which both soothed and wounded him.

Notes on Contributors

Paul Baender (1926-). University of Chicago, 1956-1960; University of Iowa, 1960-. Edited Mark Twain's *What Is Man? and Other Philosophical Writings* (1973); Textual Editor for *Roughing It* (1972) and *The Adventures of Tom Sawyer; Tom Sawyer Abroad; Tom Sawyer, Detective* (1980).

Gladys Carmen Bellamy (1904-1973). North Texas State College, 1943-1944; University of Oklahoma, 1944-1949; Southwestern State College (later Southwestern Oklahoma State University), 1949-1967. *Mark Twain as Literary Artist* (1950).

Stanley Brodwin (1930-). Hofstra University, 1958-. *Mark Twain in the Pulpit: Theology in the Major Works* (forthcoming).

Clinton S. Burhans, Jr. (1924-). University of Maryland, 1952-1953; University of British Columbia, 1955-1959; Michigan State University, 1959-.

Everett Carter (1919-). Claremont College, 1947-1949; University of California, Berkeley, 1949-1957; University of California, Davis, 1957-. *Howells and the Age of Realism* (1954); *The American Idea: The Literary Response to American Optimism* (1977); edited *The Damnation of Theron Ware* (1960).

James Grove (1949-). Mount Mercy College, 1980-.

Hamlin Hill (1931-). University of New Mexico, 1959-1961, 1963-1968, 1975-1986; University of Wyoming, 1961-1963; University of Chicago, 1968-1975; Ralph L. Thomas Professor of Liberal Arts, Texas A&M University 1986-. *Mark Twain and Elisha Bliss* (1964); *Mark Twain: God's Fool* (1973); (with Walter Blair) *America's Humor: From Poor Richard to Doonesbury* (1978); edited *Mark Twain's Letters to His Publishers, 1867-1894* (1967).

Leland Krauth (1941-). University of Colorado, 1967-; University of Kent, 1974-1975.

Fred W. Lorch (1893-1967). Iowa State University, 1921-1959. *The Trouble Begins at Eight: Mark Twain's Lecture Tours* (1968).

Leo Marx (1919-). University of Minnesota, 1949-1958; Amherst College, 1958-1977; William R. Kenan, Jr., Professor of American Cultural History, Massachusetts Institute of Technology, 1977-. *The Machine in the Garden: Technology and the Pastoral Ideal in America* (1964); edited *The Americanness of Walt Whitman* (1960).

Bruce Michelson (1948-). University of Illinois, 1976-.

Robert Regan (1930-). Centenary College of Louisiana, 1955-1956; University of Virginia, 1963-1967; University of Pennsylvania, 1968-. *Unpromising Heroes:*

Mark Twain and His Characters (1966); edited *Poe: A Collection of Critical Essays* (1967).

Paul Schacht (1955-). New York State University College, Geneseo, 1985-.

George M. Spangler (1937-). California State University, Fullerton, 1966-.

Jeffrey Steinbrink (1945-). Behrend Campus, Pennsylvania State University, 1968-1971; University of North Carolina, 1974-1975; Franklin and Marshall College, 1975-.

Albert E. Stone, Jr. (1924-). Casaday School, 1949-1952; Yale University, 1955-1962; Emory University, 1962-1977; University of Iowa, 1977-. *The Innocent Eye: Childhood in Mark Twain's Imagination* (1961); *Autobiographical Occasions and Original Acts* (1982); edited *Twentieth Century Interpretations of "The Ambassadors"* (1969).

John S. Tuckey (1921-). Purdue University, Calumet Campus, 1953-. (Frederick L. Hovde Distinguished Professor of English, 1981-). *Mark Twain & Little Satan: The Writing of "The Mysterious Stranger"* (1963); edited *Mark Twain's Which Was the Dream? and Other Symbolic Writings of the Later Years* (1967); *Mark Twain's "The Mysterious Stranger" and the Critics* (1968); *Mark Twain's Fables of Man* (1972); *The Devil's Race-Track: Mark Twain's Great Dark Writings* (1980); *No. 44, The Mysterious Stranger* (1982).

Hyatt Howe Waggoner (1913-). University of Omaha, 1939-1942; University of Kansas City, 1942-1956; Brown University, 1956-1979. *The Heel of Elohim: Science and Values in Modern American Poetry* (1950); *Hawthorne: A Critical Study* (1955); *William Faulkner: From Jefferson to the World* (1959); *American Poets: From the Puritans to the Present* (1968; 1984); *Emerson as Poet* (1974); *The Presence of Hawthorne* (1979); *American Visionary Poetry* (1982).

Dixon Wecter (1906-1950). University of Texas, 1930-1931; University of Denver, 1933-1934; University of Colorado, 1934-1939; University of California, Los Angeles, 1939-1950. Literary Editor of the Mark Twain Estate, 1946-1950. *The Saga of American Society* (1937); *The Hero in America* (1941); *When Johnny Comes Marching Home* (1944); *The Age of the Great Depression, 1929-1941* (1948); *Sam Clemens of Hannibal* (1952); edited *The Love Letters of Mark Twain* (1949); *Mark Twain to Mrs. Fairbanks* (1949).

Index

This index is centered on Mark Twain. The titles of his writings appear as main entries, and an unqualified entry such as "burlesque" or "determinism" refers directly to the content of those writings. The names of his fictional characters (such as Colonel Sherburn or Tom Sawyer) are not inverted for alphabetical ordering.

Library of Congress Cataloging-in-Publication Data
On Mark Twain.
(The Best from American literature)
Includes index.
    1. Twain, Mark, 1835–1910—Criticism and interpreta-
tion. I. Budd, Louis J. II. Cady, Edwin Harrison.
III. Series.
PS1338.05 1987 818'.409 87–9020
ISBN 0–8223–0759–6